WHITE HEAT

A NOVEL BY

C. C. Risenhoover

BASKERVILLE
PUBLISHERS, LTD
DALLAS · NEW YORK · DUBLIN

BASKERVILLE Publishers, Ltd.
7540 LBJ/Suite 125, Dallas, TX 75251-1008

Library of Congress Catalog Card Number: 91-077072
ISBN: 0-9627509-3-X

Manufactured in the United States of America
First Printing

To my parents,
who always wanted more
for their children
than they wanted for themselves

By C. C. Risenhoover

Dead Even

Blood Bath

Matt McCall

Child Stalker

Wine, Murder & Blueberry Sundaes

Murder at the final Four

Satan's Mark

Happy Birthday Jesus

Larry Hagman

Once Upon a Texas Train

Reluctant Killer

ONE

Randy Joe Keegan stood on the pitching rubber, his entire body a study in concentration. His eyes were fixed on the catcher, waiting for the sign.

It was hot.

The sun poured down on him and sweat had turned his uniform two shades of gray.

Fastball.

Only after receiving and accepting the sign did his attention turn to the man standing at the plate menacingly swinging a bat.

Strong looking. Muscular upper body and a semi-crouching stance.

He didn't have a book on the guy, didn't know what he could and couldn't hit. It was a matter of judging the man's stance, the way his feet were positioned, the way he was swinging the bat.

Hell, he decided with irrational bravado, the sonofabitch can't hit my stuff, no matter where I throw it. None of them can.

The batter, a couple of day's growth of beard shaded by the bill of his cap, glared at Randy Joe.

He glared back. He was the youngest player on the field, but no one could intimidate Randy Joe Keegan.

The signal from the catcher, the pitcher and hitter sizing each other up, all of it took place in a matter of seconds. But it seemed longer, as if the slightest motion on the field, even the movement of eyes, was frozen in time. And in spite of the unbearable

Kansas heat that scorched this baseball diamond in Wichita, in spite of Randy Joe's soggy uniform, the knowledgeable baseball crowd sensed the coolness of the young pitcher. His aura, his presence, intimidated them like the first chill of winter.

Just watching him warm up, guys in the crowd who had played the game experienced chill bumps. They didn't understand why, but watching the young man throw made them nervous. With a baseball in his hand, he was a person to be feared.

The crowd was big, loud and boisterous, more than fifteen thousand, the largest single gathering Randy Joe had ever played before. And he figured only a smattering of people in the big crowd was for his team.

He loved it that way.

He loved the fact that the pitcher opposing him on this day had great stuff, that in the first half of the first inning his pitching adversary had gotten the Jason Longhorns out in one, two, three fashion, that from early indications this game was going to be a nail-biter.

He loved battling another team and he loved battling their fans, sending everyone who was against him home in defeat. Just the thought of it got his adrenalin gushing.

But the big crowd, the noise, the boos and catcalls, none of it mattered now. The crowd became hazy and indistinguishable, as in a dream. All his concentration, all his energy, was centered on the man with the bat.

It was showtime.

Randy Joe swung into his windup.

First, the high leg kick.

Then his entire body catapulted off the mound and toward the catcher. There was the blur of arm movement. The baseball exploded out of his hand.

With unbelievable speed the white sphere instantly covered the distance from pitcher's hand to batter.

When Randy Joe let loose the ball he immediately sensed it was going off course, high and inside. He instinctively yelled a warning, but knew the ball would reach the batter before he heard it.

The speed of the pitch paralyzed the hitter, caused him to freeze at the plate. Randy Joe could see the fear swell up in the man's eyes. He wanted to do something to help the guy, but there was nothing he could do.

Luckily, the ball hit the bill of the batter's cap and sent it spinning off his head. The baseball then careened off the backstop. In a delayed reaction the hitter fell backward to the ground, stirring up the dust.

The crowd noise had died to a hush by the time Randy Joe reached the fallen man. It picked up again, somewhat uneasily, when Wichita fans realized their guy was okay. Dugouts of both teams had emptied, but the umpires had things under control. No one seemed anxious to start anything.

Concerned, Randy Joe asked the man on the ground, "You okay?"

"Yeah, I'm okay," the guy snarled. "But you do that again, you little sonofabitch, and I'll take your head off."

In spite of his competitive nature, Randy Joe, for the most part, seemed mild-mannered. But he had a violent, sometimes uncontrollable, temper that was easy to ignite. His face flushed red and he challenged, "What's wrong with now, asshole?"

He started toward his adversary, who was a good thirty pounds heavier, but his catcher stepped between them and said, "Now you don't wanna go get yo'self throwed outta dis game, Randy Joe."

"Play ball!" the umpire commanded.

The guy who had been hit by the pitch went to first base and Randy Joe went to the mound. The crowd had turned up its volume and boos were exploding off a wall of hot summer air that hung over the playing field. The opposing team's players began some serious bench jockeying that left little to the imagination concerning Randy Joe's lineage.

He grinned and looked in for the sign. This was more like it. Now that his initial nervousness was over he was feeling good. Strong.

The number two hitter for the Wichita Tornadoes looked like a carbon copy of the first, solidly built and in his late twenties. Randy Joe surmised that he, like the first man, probably had spent a lot of days loading bales of hay in the hot Kansas sun.

Randy Joe took his stretch, checked the runner at first, then fired another fastball. It didn't get anywhere close to the plate. It slipped off his fingers and sailed into the stands, causing a loud rumble from the fans.

The runner at first trotted on down to second and the umpire threw Randy Joe a new ball. He rubbed it up, stepped back up on the pitching rubber and peered in for the sign. After getting the catcher's signal he looked into the hitter's eyes and saw the fear there.

Can't say as I blame him, he thought. I'm wilder than a March hare today.

He knew he'd eventually settle down, but right now he felt strong enough to throw a baseball through a brick wall. Who the hell needed rest between games? It was the importance of the game that mattered. He was so pumped up his chest was about to explode.

Going into his stretch, checking the runner at second, he again unloaded a fastball toward home plate. This one traveled a little truer, but it was still high and inside and forced the batter to hit the dirt.

The hitter glared and Randy Joe shrugged his shoulders, as if to say, "Hey, I'm trying to get it over the plate. What's happening isn't intentional."

The batter knew that. It was too big a game to risk base on balls or hit batsmen to prove a point. There was too much at stake.

Randy Joe threw two more inside to the guy and walked him. Then he walked the next batter on four high, tight pitches, causing catcher Buck Frazier to come out to the mound for a visit. He was joined by Muddy Tate, the shortstop and manager, who said, "If you hurtin', Randy Joe, we kin bring Gar in to pitch."

"Hell, I'm not hurtin'," Randy Joe said. "I just feel too strong."

Buck nodded agreement. The team was used to Randy Joe's occasional wild streaks. Teams hadn't been able to take advantage of his wildness to score many runs, but there was a lot on the table this day. The money they'd get from this game would make their season. Muddy didn't want to blow it.

"Jest take a little off de ball," Muddy suggested. "Den maybe you kin git it over."

Randy Joe shook his head in disagreement. "You know I don't give in to a hitter."

Muddy said, "Well..."

"Look, Muddy, if I don't get the next hitter you can take me out. But you and the rest of the guys can sit down. Buck and me...we're gonna play some catch."

Buck grinned. He'd seen the fire in Randy Joe's eyes before. He knew what the young pitcher was capable of doing when he had his control.

The home plate umpire moved toward them, demanding that they get the game underway again. Muddy sighed, "Jest git'em out."

Wichita's cleanup hitter was a muscled-up guy who measured at least six-feet, two inches and weighed in at around two hundred and forty pounds. The first three in the Tornadoes lineup had batted from the left side, but this brute of a man was a righthanded hitter. His appearance at the plate caused a ripple of increased noise among the already excited crowd. They were expecting the big slugger either to walk or nail a fastball and drive it over the fence. The partisan crowd didn't like the young pitcher. Not only was he wild and arrogant, but he was pitching for a colored team. They wanted to see him driven off the mound, his head hanging in shame.

Must be Casey, Randy Joe thought, amused that he would remember the old baseball poem at such a tense moment. But the truth was, he wasn't tense at all. He had every confidence that this Casey would fare no better than the one in the poem.

The batter was leftfielder Greg Braddock, who would be a senior at the University of Oklahoma in September. He had led the Big Seven Conference in home runs and runs batted in while posting a batting average of .325. He had been given a summer job in Wichita so he could play for the semi-pro Tornadoes.

Braddock had not been a disappointment. He led the Wichita

team in the same categories in which he had led Oklahoma. He had major league scouts drooling. And there were no fewer than sixteen of them in the stands, watching Randy Joe, too.

Randy Joe liked to pitch to the big sticks on any team. He'd never been hit hard by the muscled-up guys. Any problems he experienced were usually from little spray hitters. He started Braddock off with a fastball just under his chin, one that had the big man gulping air and falling backward. But Braddock didn't spend a lot of time in the dirt. He was up quickly and digging in, showing no emotion regarding the close pitch. Randy Joe saw there was no fear in his eyes.

This guy's a hitter, he thought, appreciatively. He admired an opponent who understood the game, who didn't get his nose out of joint because of a close pitch, one whose eyes didn't flinch when he stepped back to the plate.

Randy Joe had forsaken the stretch for the full windup. He didn't give a rat's ass how far the runners got off base because he wasn't going to let them go anywhere. A glint came into his eyes as if to say, "Enough."

Then he did something to further incite the crowd. He motioned to Braddock that he was going to throw him a curveball. That's when Braddock did a doubletake, and doubt set in regarding the crazy kid on the mound. He had to be crazy, a white kid pitching for an all-Negro team.

Randy Joe had thrown ten pitches, all balls. He'd hit a batter, walked two and then come inside on the cleanup hitter. Now he was telling his adversary what pitch he was going to throw.

Braddock didn't believe him.

Randy Joe wound up, launched himself toward the plate and let the ball fly from his fingers. The big slugger saw it coming right at him. He fell backward to get away from the baseball.

It broke right over the plate.

"Striiiike!"

Braddock whistled under his breath. He'd never seen such a curveball. He stepped back to the plate without showing any emotion.

Again Randy Joe motioned that he was going to throw a

curve, causing the crowd to go into a real tizzy.

This kid is bonkers, Braddock thought. Maybe he's telling me the truth. He was determined to hang in this time, to follow the curveball, if necessary, all the way into the catcher's mitt. He wasn't afraid of a curveball. He'd hit a lot of them out of ball yards. The worst that could happen was that he'd be hit by the pitch. But then, he'd taken some off his body for the team before. It was no big deal. This kid on the mound, though, he wasn't just crazy. He threw heat like no one he'd ever faced before. His teammates kept calling him White Heat.

For all his good intentions, when Braddock saw the ball coming at him he reacted instinctively. He bailed out.

Swoosh, the ball broke over the plate.

"Striiike!" the umpire said.

Braddock stepped back to the plate. This time he nervously pawed the ground with his spikes, digging in. He didn't plan to be fooled again.

To the sound of intensified boos, Randy Joe once more signaled Braddock as to what he was going to throw.

Fastball.

The big slugger was rapidly becoming a believer.

Randy Joe lurched off the mound toward home plate. The ball exploded out of his grip and was a white blur speeding toward the catcher, about waist-high and right down the center of the plate, right in Braddock's power zone.

The big man's eyes were fixed on the ball, the barrel of his bat moving toward it with deadly accuracy. Then the ball tailed in, dropped, and left him awkwardly swinging at nothing but air.

At first the crowd sat in stunned silence. Then Randy Joe incited them further, grinning and tipping his cap to the stands. The chorus of boos shook the stadium.

But that wasn't enough for him. When the next hitter, catcher Joe Bartosh, stepped up to the plate, Randy Joe held up three fingers and gave an unmistakable signal that he was going to throw him nothing but fastballs. Bartosh and the crowd had no trouble interpreting the young pitcher's hand signals. He was also indicating that he was going to mow the catcher down with just three pitches.

Like Braddock, Bartosh was a righthanded hitter and no slouch in the slugging department. He was second to Braddock in home runs and runs batted in and was hitting slightly above three hundred. Twenty-five years old, he was five feet, eleven inches tall and weighed in at two hundred pounds. He was known for his bad temper. Randy Joe's hotdogging didn't set well with him.

Bartosh angrily pounded his bat on the plate and got ready, swinging his bat over the plate several times before cocking it. Randy Joe came with the express, a pitch so fast that no one in the crowd could even see the blur of the ball in its flight. The ball had already popped in the catcher's mitt before Bartosh weakly swung at it.

The next pitch to Bartosh was another heater that he couldn't get around on. Randy Joe had only to look into the man's eyes to see the frustration. With the two pitches he knew he now owned the Wichita catcher.

Bartosh hated what was happening in his mind, the fear of failure that was going through it. But he'd never faced baseballs traveling as fast as the two the young pitcher had thrown him. And given the looks of his adversary, it was hard to understand. The kid wasn't big and he was so young that his face couldn't grow anything but peach fuzz. His appearance couldn't intimidate anyone.

Bartosh didn't want to admit it, but it was with some reluctance that he stepped back to the plate. He did his best to get a grip on himself, to fight the fear in his mind. He was determined to protect the plate, to shorten up on his swing and to get at least a piece of the ball.

Then the ball was coming toward the plate again and Bartosh swung at it, but much too early. Randy Joe had fooled him, thown him a slow curveball. All his baseball senses had been geared for a fastball, which the pitcher had indicated he was going to throw.

He glared angrily at the young man on the mound, highly pissed off by the deception. Randy Joe grinned and shrugged his shoulders as if to say, "Hey, so I lied."

It had not been a quality trip to the plate for the Wichita

catcher and it had been closely observed by the on-deck hitter, third baseman Lewis Murphy. He was another power hitter the scouts were interested in, a sophomore at Kansas State University.

Murphy, six feet and a hundred and eighty-five pounds, was not one to be intimidated by any pitcher. At least, he'd never been intimidated before. But there was something about the one on the mound that worried him. The kid was just a tad too wild and too damned fast for comfort. Braddock and Bartosh were two guys who generally always made contact and they'd been made to look silly. He determined not to take the big cut, to shorten his swing and make sure he got a piece of the ball. He wanted the scouts in the stands to know that he wasn't just a power hitter but also a smart one, that he could adjust.

What now?

The crowd was going into a frenzy.

The pitcher was asking his infielders and outfielders to sit.

Muddy Tate trotted to the mound from his shortstop position and asked, "What you tryin' to do, Randy Joe, git us all killed?"

"I'm gonna strike the shithead out."

"Dat don't matter none," Muddy said. "You done agitated dese folks enough."

"Dizzy Dean had his infielders and outfielders sit while he struck some guys out once," Randy Joe argued.

"His infielders and outfielders wasn't coloreds wid nothin' but white faces in de stands. We ain't sittin'."

Randy Joe shrugged his shoulders. "Figured somethin' like that would destroy the other team's confidence. Besides, a few black faces are in the stands."

Muddy grinned. "Yo' eyes is better dan mine. But we ain't 'xactly in de majority."

"You're right...we ain't. Anyway, I'm gonna strike this guy out 'cause I'm thirsty and need a drink of water."

"Dat's what I want you to do."

Randy Joe's energy was boiling, so Lewis Murphy didn't have a chance. A dandy curveball, a blazing fastball, a hard slider and he was history. The fans booed and Randy Joe tipped his cap as he walked toward the dugout. It was the least he could do to acknowledge their appreciation for his performance.

Man, this is wonderful, he thought. It's so much better than cutting cypress trees in the swamp, which was what he'd been doing in May.

TWO

Three Months Earlier

The five-foot cottonmouth moccasin was coiled on top of the stump, its nasty tongue darting and its fangs drooling venom, acting as though it was pissed off by the intrusion. The thing was as big around as one of Randy Joe Keegan's arms. He could have avoided it, just changed his direction. Instead he did what any red-blooded boy would do. He cut the snake in two with his axe.

It was an early Saturday morning in May. Randy Joe's shirt was soggy with sweat. The perspiration wasn't the result of seeing the snake, though, admittedly, seeing the things often caused him to have chills and the sweats. He suspected, under certain circumstances, that one of the really big ones could make him shit in his pants. It had never happened, but he didn't discount the possibility.

Before the day was over he would see fifty more snakes or maybe a hundred. But it was the ones he wouldn't see that really worried him, those that might slither up behind him. Or those that might play chameleon, camouflaging themselves near cypress knees where they could bury their fangs in him when he least expected it.

His shirt was soggy from the damned humidity. Even when it was decently cool on the surrounding hillsides the swamp was an oven. And that's where he was, in the swamp cutting cypress trees with a logging crew.

It was 1954. Randy Joe was more than a month short of seventeen. The logging job paid ten dollars a day for ten hours work. That didn't include the hour ride to the swamp and the ride home. Or the lunch break, which was the only break he got during the day.

He wasn't, of course, the only one making just ten dollars a day for the backbreaking work. But he was the youngest.

And the whitest.

The foreman was white, too, only it was hard to tell. And he didn't exactly work, just told the logging crew what to do and when to do it. His name was J.B. Smith, and days in the sun had burned his skin brown. His face was like wrinkled leather.

J.B. was a tall man with stooped shoulders that subtracted a couple of inches from his actual height. His hair was graying and slicked back. His sideburns were trimmed even with the bottoms of his rather large ears.

For six days a week J.B. Smith was a logging foreman. On Sundays he was a preacher. He was tough on the job, expected a day's work for a day's pay, but he was fair. And in spite of looking like he'd been carved right out of the swamp, he had kind blue eyes.

Randy Joe didn't call him J.B. back then. He called him Mr. Smith.

J.B. had a prominent nose, which seemed appropriate to Randy Joe because he was damn hard-nosed about sin, or what he thought was sin. Randy Joe's and J.B.'s interpretation of sin didn't jibe.

Regardless, J.B. had given Randy Joe the Saturday job cutting logs, and the promise of a job doing the same for the summer. In August the swamp would be like the fires of hell.

He figured J.B. had given him the job because of his father, who worked for the same lumber company. Randy Joe guessed his dad and J.B. had about the same status. His dad worked at the sawmill where the logs were cut into lumber. J.B. was ramrod over most of the crews that fed logs to the mill.

J.B. and his wife Sarah lived next door to the Keegans, in a gray company-owned house. The rows of houses for the white workers all looked the same.

That May morning when Randy Joe was sopping wet with sweat, J.B. Smith looked like he had just gotten up off an ironing board. He always looked that way. He wore khaki pants and a shirt to match, both starched and ironed.

He wore a freshly washed and ironed set of khakis every day, which seemed a little ridiculous in the swamp. J.B. never got dirty. He didn't even sweat, no matter how hot it got. He would just hang around his pickup, where the big water cooler was, and occasionally tell the workers what to do.

J.B.'s pickup was a GMC. All the log trucks were GMCs. If it wasn't a GMC, J.B. didn't think it was a truck.

J.B. wore a tan cowboy hat that came close to matching his khaki outfit, and brown cowboy boots. Even his pickup was khaki and brown. And his boots always looked like they'd just been shined. Randy Joe suspected that when he and the other men were not looking J.B. was shining his boots.

Randy Joe's logging partner was Iron Man Davis, a colored man with a muscular upper body and arms that looked as though they had been forged from steel. He was so black that he glistened, especially when he was sweating, which was practically all the time.

Iron Man just knew one way to work, which was all out.

His head was almost square and he didn't have much of a neck. His eyes were rounded, very dark brown, and there was an abundance of white surrounding the pupils. He had a big flattened nose that spread across his face, heavy pursed lips, and two missing front teeth.

Iron Man dipped snuff and spit through the two missing teeth. He generally sang gospel songs while he worked. When he wasn't singing he was smiling or laughing.

From spring through the fall Iron Man didn't wear a shirt, just overalls and brogans with no socks. He didn't wear a hat and Randy Joe doubted that he'd ever owned a pair of gloves. But when he was working one end of a crosscut saw and Randy Joe the other, he made his co-worker find muscles he didn't even know he had.

When they were in rhythm chopping on a tree, Randy Joe didn't dare get out of sync for fear that Iron Man might cut the handle of his axe in two.

Iron Man was probably sixty years old. He had been doing the same thing six days a week for more than forty years. Watching him work, seeing the joy on his face, depressed the hell out of Randy Joe. As far as he was concerned, Iron Man was in prison, and his only way out was death. Randy Joe had a small, gnawing fear that the log woods or sawmill would become his prison, too.

He did have one ace in the hole. Most people would have considered it a longshot, but Randy Joe was arrogant enough to believe he could beat the odds. Maybe it was just bravado, not arrogance. He didn't even consider the odds. He figured all he needed was for just one major league baseball scout to see him pitch. That would get him out of the slime of the swamp and the drudgery of the sawmill.

That's what occupied Randy Joe's mind while he and Iron Man were felling big cypress trees. Randy Joe dreamed of playing baseball in pinstripes, pitching before a capacity crowd at Yankee Stadium.

In the interim, though, he was not dressed in pinstripes. He was wearing a long-sleeved heavy cotton flannel shirt, jeans, lace-up hunting boots, a kerchief around his neck and a baseball cap on his head. He was also wearing work gloves and his face was covered with mosquito repellant. He kept a bottle of the stuff in his pocket.

No matter how much of the mosquito repellant Randy Joe used, the insects never left him alone. He didn't understand how Iron Man could take it. Mosquitoes would cover him and he paid no attention to them.

Snakes were a different story. He didn't even like for Randy Joe to talk about snakes. Randy Joe didn't like to talk about snakes himself, but he did. He did it because he had a bit of a mean streak in him, and enjoyed wiping the smile off Iron Man's face. What surprised the hell out of him was the fact that as long as Iron Man had worked in the log woods, which included the swamp, he'd never been bitten by one of the sonofabitches.

While they were preparing a big cypress, getting it ready to be cut, Randy Joe asked, "Iron Man, did you see the size of that big fucker I cut in two? He was a couple of feet longer than my dick. Not any bigger around, of course."

Iron Man tried to smile, but couldn't. He just let fly with a stream of snuff juice between his missing teeth. The brown spit hit the swamp water and disappeared. It was clearer and cleaner than the swamp water.

"Hell," Randy Joe continued, "I'll bet that old snake was a peewee compared to some of the ones out here in the swamp. You ever see any alligators out here?"

"Noooo, sir," Iron Man drawled. "I don't believes dey's no alligators in dis swamp."

"Got to be some alligators in here," Randy Joe said. "Hell, this is alligator country."

"Noooo, sir," Iron Man argued. "Mr. J.B., he'd tell us if dey was any alligators 'round here."

"Hell, he doesn't know," Randy Joe said. "He'd tell us if he knew, but he just doesn't. People don't see alligators anyway...not until they've stepped on 'em, or 'til an old gator sneaks up and bites a chunk outta their leg."

Iron Man's eyes took on a worried look. "Mr. Randy, you likes to bullshit better dan any white boy I ever knowed."

Randy Joe chuckled, then said, "Hey, believe what you want, Iron Man, but I'm tellin' you...I'm gonna be watching for alligators. And I hope they're a bunch of alligators in here. They eat snakes, you know."

"Dey does?"

"You bet your sweet ass they do," Randy Joe replied. "But you never did tell me if you've seen a bigger cottonmouth than the one I killed."

"He was a big'un," Iron Man said. "I can't say I ever seed a bigger one."

"You ever eaten any snake, Iron Man?"

"'Course I ain't eat no snake," he replied, indignantly.

Randy Joe shrugged his shoulders. "Don't get your nose

outta joint. Orientals eat'em. And people out in West Texas eat rattlesnakes like we eat chicken."

"I don't know nothin' 'bout no Ori...whatever you says dey is. And I ain't believin' no folks in West Texas eats no rattlesnakes, either."

"Suit yourself. But you can find that information in just about any book."

Of course, Iron Man couldn't read. He'd been deprived of the opportunity of going to school. That was one of the many benefits of being born black in East Texas.

For the rest of the morning the logging crews went about the task of felling big cypress trees and chasing snakes away from cypress knees around the trunks, and from stumps and fallen logs. For a change the snakes seemed anxious to avoid the human invaders, so Randy Joe didn't get another shot at one with his axe.

Though the sun was shining brightly on the hillsides it seemed like a gray day in the swampy terrain. The cypress trees were gray. The Spanish moss hanging from them was gray. Even the swamp water was gray.

The morning was one of sawing and chopping, of bringing the big trees down in the wet and muck of the swamp. Iron Man had no formal education, but could make a tree fall exactly where he wanted. He was, Randy Joe acknowledged, a pro.

He knew that's why J.B. Smith had wanted Iron Man to be his partner. As a logger he was the best. He worked like the devil was after him, but he was careful and knew exactly what he was doing. He worked hard because he was scared of losing a job that paid ten dollars a day, afraid he couldn't find anything better. He probably couldn't have, not in East Texas. But Iron Man loved the work, too. He was as proud of his profession as he'd have been of being a doctor or lawyer.

Iron Man's regular partner during the week didn't work on Saturdays. Randy Joe felt a little guilty about that, figuring J.B. had bumped the guy in order to give him a job. But maybe that wasn't the case. J.B. had told him that Iron Man would be his regular partner during the summer, too, which would be six grueling days a week.

"What about the guy who usually works with you?" Randy Joe asked. "Isn't he pissed about me bein' your partner?"

"He don't care who he works wid," Iron Man replied. "He jest wants to work."

Iron Man and Randy Joe would bring a tree crashing down in the swamp, then trim it. It would be snaked out of the wet and muck to dry land with a team of mules. The logs would then be loaded on a GMC truck and hauled to the sawmill. Supervising the loading of the logs seemed to be the most important aspect of the operation to J.B., more than all that was required to get a log to dry land where a truck was waiting.

The mule skinner was Hank Jones, a wiry little black man with a small head that seemed to disappear into a grease-stained straw hat that had seen better days. While Iron Man was a couple of inches short of six-feet and weighed one-eighty, Hank was no taller than five-feet, seven inches and would have been hard pressed to push the scales to a hundred and thirty.

Despite his fragile appearance, Hank was as strong as one of his mules. His arms were minuscule in comparison to Iron Man's, but he had tremendous upper body strength and powerful legs.

Hank was fifty-five, his hair already snow white. He had a white beard, dark eyes, a small nose and ears, and a slight limp. Iron Man told Randy Joe that Hank limped because a mule had stepped on his foot when he was just a kid.

Hank was better paid than those who were mere common laborers. He got two dollars more a day because of his skill handling a team. And because the mules, Jake and Jack, belonged to him.

At first Randy Joe envied Hank the extra money because he didn't think handling a team of mules was as hard as the work he and Iron Man did. But he finally realized that Hank was really worse off. He had to feed and take care of his mules.

When noon came that May day Randy Joe sloshed out of the swamp and onto dry land to gorge himself on whatever delights his mother had put in his lunch pail. It had been a long time since breakfast and he was hungry. But just as important as eating was the opportunity to bullshit with the other loggers.

Randy Joe could have gone over to J.B.'s khaki and brown GMC pickup, eaten lunch there and talked to him. But he thought it was more fun, and more interesting, to talk to the colored guys. Back then they were called Negroes or coloreds if a person wanted to be respectful, *niggers* if he didn't.

Anyway, Randy Joe liked it because J.B. never came around close to where he was eating and talking to the coloreds. He figured it was because J.B. was afraid he might hear one of them say something profane. Then he'd feel compelled to witness to them.

To me, at least, Randy Joe thought.

He figured J.B. didn't feel any compulsion to try to save the soul of a black man. There was considerable doubt in the white religious community whether coloreds even had souls, no matter how revved up they got singing gospel songs. Any chance of salvation they had was in the hands of Negro preachers. And the prevailing opinion was that if God did choose to save any of them, He would bleach them out and make them white.

Iron Man had brought his lunch in an old syrup bucket, which was the type container used by all the Negroes. Randy Joe's mother had bought him one of those regular black lunch pails that even had a thermos inside. He would have preferred to carry his lunch in a syrup bucket. He thought it added to the aura he ascribed to loggers.

A couple of the colored loggers raised sugar cane and made syrup, so Randy Joe figured they had an abundance of buckets on hand. And he figured they ate a lot of syrup because every one of them brought syrup biscuits for lunch. He was the only one with sandwiches made with store-bought bread.

"What you got there, Iron Man?" Randy Joe asked.

They were both sitting, backs against a tree, and Iron Man was rummaging through his syrup bucket. A colony of ants scurried about near their feet, anxious for leftovers.

"Salt pork sandwich," Iron Man grunted.

"How many you got?"

"Three."

"I'll trade you a baloney sandwich for one."

"Why you wanna do dat?"

"'Cause I like salt pork."

Iron Man handed him a biscuit sandwich that had just been lying loose in his syrup bucket and he handed his partner a baloney sandwich wrapped in wax paper. Between the two slices of bread of Randy Joe's sandwich were three thick pieces of baloney, lettuce, pickles and mayonnaise. Inside Iron Man's biscuit was a piece of fried salt pork and mustard.

Randy Joe didn't figure he was doing Iron Man a favor. He really did like salt pork, if it was cooked right. And he was sure Iron Man's wife knew how to cook it. He was not disappointed.

Randy Joe thought there was one right way to cook salt pork for a sandwich, which was the way his mother did it. First, she boiled it to get some of the salt out. Then she fried it. When she used it to season dried beans she didn't boil the salt out. She just tossed a chunk in the beans while they were boiling, which seasoned them just right. Or as close to right as was possible with dried beans.

Randy Joe figured he was something of an expert on dried navy or pinto beans. His mother cooked the damned things three or four times a week. He also knew the baloney sandwich was a delicacy to Iron Man. The colored guys never had store-bought bread or lunchmeat in their buckets. They always had biscuits or cornbread, usually with salt pork or syrup.

It was easy enough to trade the baloney sandwich for Iron Man's biscuit and salt pork because he had another baloney sandwich in his lunch pail. Besides, even if he hadn't had another baloney sandwich in the pail the trade would have been worth it just to see the enjoyment Iron Man got out of eating the sandwich.

"Damn it, Iron Man," Randy Joe said, "didn't you even spit out your snuff before eatin' that sandwich?"

Iron Man grinned, showing where the two missing teeth had been, along with his snuff-stained ones. "No need to. I always swallows my snuff. No need lettin' it go to waste."

Randy Joe knew his partner was a connoisseur of Garrett Snuff, but figured he was putting him on. Iron Man never used any other brand and didn't like the other men *borrowing* snuff from him. The story was that when one man asked Iron Man too often for a dip of his snuff the old man laid a trap for the moocher. He started carrying around a snuff box that had ground-up worms in it, which he offered right away the next time he was asked.

Before Randy Joe could comment further on Iron Man's love affair with snuff Hank Jones brought his bucket over and sat across from them. He dug in the bucket, found a syrup biscuit, and chomped on it with relish.

With his mouth full he said, "I seed dat game you pitched de other night, Mr. Randy."

"Why don't you just call me Randy? I keep tellin' you and Iron Man that."

Hank grinned. "Old ways is hard to break. And I ain't sho' I wants to break 'em anyway."

Randy Joe sighed. "What did you think of the game?"

"I think you sho' can throw dat tater. How many dem boys you strike out?"

"Seventeen," Randy Joe answered. "I'm still pissed about that skinny-assed third baseman gettin' a hit."

The reference was to a Tuesday night game against Nederland High School. Randy Joe had thrown a three to nothing shutout. But even with all the strikeouts in the seven-inning game he had been lucky that Nederland hadn't scored. Not only did the skinny-assed third baseman get a hit, the only one he allowed, but he'd walked him twice. He'd also walked three other batters and hit four.

"Dem boys from Nederland, dey sho' was scared o' you," Hank said. "Can't say dat I blame 'em. You is wild as a unbroke mule."

"Don't start in on me, Hank. My dad's always sayin' if the strike zone was high and inside I might become the greatest pitcher in baseball."

Hank laughed, then asked, "Did you go to de game, Iron Man?" Of course, he already knew the answer.

"I ain't payin' no dollar to go to no baseball game."

"It ain't gonna cost you no dollar," Hank said. "Dey lets coloreds in free. I done told you dat no tellin' how many times."

Iron Man grunted, "Maybe I go de next time."

"Well, you oughta go to support your old partner," Randy Joe quipped. "It doesn't look right, you not bein' there."

Hank grinned. "It sho' don't."

Randy Joe started drinking milk from his thermos and was complaining about his wet socks and boots when Sleepy Jones and Yank Johnson showed up. Sleepy, as far as Randy Joe knew, was not related to Hank, even though they shared the same last name. About twenty percent of the coloreds in Jason County shared it, which still put it in second place behind Davis.

Sleepy didn't look anything like Hank, but he dressed like him. All four Negro men wore standard blue overalls that were faded from harsh washing, just as they all wore scuffed-up brogans. Iron Man was the only one who didn't wear a shirt. The others wore cotton shirts bought on credit at the lumber company store, like just about everything else they bought.

The store wasn't risking anything when they gave an employee credit. An employee could charge no more than he had coming from the company. And all charges were deducted from his pay. Employees even paid a premium for the credit. Cash would have bought more at other stores in town.

The company store owned Randy Joe's folks, too, along with everyone else, black or white, who worked for the lumber company. People who didn't work for the company didn't shop there.

Sleepy was younger than the other loggers. He was just a shade over thirty and was an imposing sight sloshing around in the swamp. He was six-feet, four inches tall, but probably weighed no more than Iron Man. Randy Joe thought he looked like an ebony Ichabod Crane.

Sleepy's overalls were a little short, showing a few inches of skin between his brogans and the bottoms of the pant legs. His feet were so huge that the company store had to special-order his brogans.

Sleepy was a graduate of the all-Negro high school on the east side of town. He'd been something of a basketball star and decent student there, but there was no scholarship for him. He'd hoped for an offer from an all-Negro school, but it never came. And there weren't any colleges from up north recruiting in Jason

County.

He'd spent a couple of years in the Army as a cook's helper, then returned to work in the log woods. He had taken his daddy's place. His daddy had died on the job.

Randy Joe didn't know Sleepy's given name. He doubted that many other people did. He just knew Sleepy had eyes that made him look like he was almost asleep, and that he could doze off at the drop of a hat. He was especially prone to slumber after drinking a little wine. And anytime he got a few coins in his pocket he went searching for a bootlegger.

Jason was a dry county, a place where it was illegal to sell drinking alcohol of any kind. A person either made his own brew or drove for an hour to Silsbee to buy it at a package store.

Bootleggers saved the drive. The important thing to remember was to buy liquor from a Sheriff-approved bootlegger. If caught with booze from an unauthorized bootlegger, especially a colored one, you could end up in the slammer. The best that could happen was that the sheriff would simply take all the money the company store had missed.

Skinny as he was, Sleepy was a fairly handsome young man when he dressed up. For special occasions he got rid of the short-legged overalls and the shirt with sleeves that were too short. He had some decent threads, which, Randy Joe guessed, he'd bought in Beaumont. He dressed up for ball games and to go to colored nightclubs that were not supposed to exist in Jason County, but did because the sheriff owned a piece of them.

When Jason County was dry everyone wanted to be sheriff because of the money that could be made bootlegging. Years later, when it became wet, and the sheriff had to live on a county salary, no one wanted the job.

Yank Johnson was muscular, but no taller than five-nine. He weighed close to two hundred without an ounce of fat. He'd gotten his name from yanking boards and timbers off the sawmill's green chain, so called because it was the conveyor system that carried freshly cut and treated green lumber to where it could be stacked on bunks. It was then hauled to the kiln or lumber yard for drying.

Randy Joe had worked on the green chain the previous

summer, which he considered three months of hell on earth. He knew it was a dirty job because he was the only white doing it.

After being cut, the green boards and timbers — twelve, fourteen and sixteen footers — went through vats of chemicals, were marked for grade by an inspector, and came roaring down the chain. The speed of the chain could be controlled, but that chore went to a foreman who didn't want the laborers to have time to think what was happening.

Randy Joe had gone through a pair of work gloves a week. They'd stay wet from the chemicals and come apart in five or six days. He considered himself strong, but at the end of the day he'd just go home, take a bath, gulp down some supper and hit the mattress.

After a summer on the green chain Randy Joe was actually anxious for school to start, anxious to go back to class and work only on Saturdays. He had been able to quit the green chain before the end of August because football practice started before school began. Football practice in the heat of August wasn't pleasant either, but it was easier than the green chain. Anything was.

Anyway, Yank had worked on the green chain for years. Finally, though, his back had given out on him and he had gotten the logging job. Randy Joe could see the pain on Yank's face anytime he was working a crosscut saw or swinging his axe.

But Yank knew he had to work. He wasn't about to lay up and complain, let somebody else take care of him. He was just forty-five. He needed to work twenty to twenty-five more years.

Randy Joe was well-versed in bigotry. It was as common as dirt, something a white man felt was his duty. But some of the attitudes around him made Randy Joe uneasy. He worked with Negro men, watched them sweat under the same sun beating down on him, knew their muscles ached as his did.

"You bring yo' glove and de catcher's mitt?" Sleepy asked.

"Yeah," Randy Joe replied, "but you sure you wanna do this?"

Sleepy laughed. "Show me what you got, Randy."

Unlike Iron Man and Hank, neither Sleepy nor Yank called him Mr. Randy. He liked that.

"He got mo' dan you wants to handle," Yank said. "I seed him pitch last Tuesday night. You don't want any of 'em."

"What you talkin' 'bout?" Sleepy responded. "I seed him pitch, too. You know I played a little hardball, Yank."

"You ain't played catcher fo' no pitcher like Randy here," Yank argued.

"Hey, don't worry 'bout it," Randy Joe said. "We're just gonna play a little catch. Nobody's gonna get hurt."

On the previous Saturday Sleepy had suggested that Randy Joe bring the catcher's mitt, his glove and a ball. Lunch took about fifteen minutes. After eating they usually just talked bullshit. Playing a little catch wouldn't change that. Baseball was always an integral part of the conversation.

Hank, Sleepy and Yank were avid fans. They rarely missed a local game, whether it was played by the white high school, black high school, or the semi-pro Negro Jason Longhorns.

Randy Joe measured off sixty-feet, six inches, or as close to it as he could get. Then he and Sleepy started playing catch.

Tall as he was, squatting and holding the catcher's mitt up as a target, Sleepy made a comical sight in his short overalls and boat-like brogans.

Randy Joe tossed the ball easily for a good ten minutes, making adjustments for his wet and heavy boots. He liked to think he had a fluid motion, and he did. But it was restricted by his clothing, especially the soggy boots.

"Ain't you warm yet?" Sleepy asked.

"Pretty warm. Why?"

"Well, show me somethin'."

"What you want me to throw?"

"It don't matter none."

"Don't you wanna know what I'm gonna throw?"

"You jest throws it and I'll catch it."

Randy Joe started off with a fastball, but not his best one. He was just six-feet tall and a hundred-sixty. But when the adrenalin was flowing he could really bring it, at speeds of ninety-five miles-an-hour and better.

What he threw Sleepy was about eighty-five miles an hour, but any fastball he threw tended to sink. He had a natural sinker.

When the baseball left his hand it was going straight enough, but when it got to what was the imaginary home plate it fell off the table. This one whacked the toe of Sleepy's left brogan.

"Damn!" Sleepy hollered in pain. Hank, Iron Man and Yank hooted. Randy Joe wanted to laugh, too, but knew it wasn't funny. He'd fouled a lot of baseballs off his feet.

"You okay?"

Sleepy managed a grin, though Randy Joe figured one or more of his toes were hurting like hell. His brogans were pretty well worn out, the soles in front separated from the leather to where there wasn't all that much protection.

"I'm all right," Sleepy said. "Dat ball...it jest surprised me...droppin' down like dat."

"Most every fastball I throw is gonna drop like that," Randy Joe said. "If I hold the seams different I can make it rise, but daddy says a low sinker is harder to hit. Now, don't you want me to tell you what I'm gonna throw?"

"No need," Sleepy replied. "You jest throws it. I'll catch it."

"You is crazy as Mr. Randy," Iron Man said.

For the next few minutes Randy Joe fed Sleepy a steady diet of fastballs. Though some were in the ninety-plus miles-per-hour range, Sleepy either knocked them down or caught them.

The pitch and catch game attracted the attention of J.B. and a couple of the white guys who drove log trucks.

"Okay, do you think you can handle a curveball?" Randy Joe asked.

While he had that good sinking fastball the curveball was really Randy Joe's bread and butter pitch. He'd been told by umpires that a lot of big league pitchers would give their left nut, or whichever was most important, for his curveball. It didn't break until it got right to the plate, then dropped as if it were made of steel. High school batters just couldn't hit it.

"Jest go ahead and brings it," Sleepy said.

Randy Joe wasn't sure he'd ever thrown a better curveball than the one Sleepy saw. It had that good tight spin on it, then when it reached the imaginary homeplate it scooted left, dipped, and took a bite out of the ground right in front of the awkwardly crouching Sleepy, who tried to get the mitt in front of it, but stopped it instead with his balls. He fell over clutching his groin while Hank, Iron Man and Yank howled in derision.

The two truck drivers were laughing, too, and J.B. even had a smile on his normally somber face. Randy Joe didn't want to laugh, but with everyone else breaking up he couldn't control himself.

Finally, when Sleepy stopped rolling around on the ground and groaning, Randy Joe asked, "You okay?"

Sleepy gave a sheepish grin and replied, "Dat was one fine curveball."

"I think we'd better call it a day," Randy Joe said.

"Naw, naw...no need to do dat," Sleepy said. "I know what dat curveball do now."

"So does we," Yank said, laughing. "It hits you right in de balls."

They continued playing catch and Randy Joe took it easy. After all, the poor guy had been hit on the toes and the balls. But just before it was time to go back to work Randy Joe decided to try his knuckleball. It was a pitch he'd been working on, but not too seriously. He'd never even thrown it in a game.

"Knuckleball," he called out. Sleepy nodded that he was ready, though he probably had no idea what Randy Joe was talking about.

Randy Joe's motion was just as if he was throwing a fastball, but when the baseball left his hand it fluttered and sailed like it was supposed to do. He saw the confused look in Sleepy's eyes, then watched him lunge at the ball with the mitt extended forward.

The ball hit him right between the eyes.

Sleepy was suddenly falling backward. Randy Joe could hear the sound of laughter from their audience as he rushed forward to Sleepy's aid. The erstwhile catcher was lying on his back, his arms and legs in spread eagle fashion.

Randy Joe was afraid he was really hurt, but Sleepy looked up, grinned and said, "As hard as you is to catch, Randy, I don't know how anybody ever gets a hit."

When the day's work finally ended, when the last tree was felled, the loggers all got in the back of J.B.'s GMC pickup and he drove them back to what most people referred to as *Milltown*. Randy Joe could have ridden up front with J.B., but chose to ride in the back with the other loggers. They were the people he worked with and he liked their bullshit better than J.B.'s.

He did get in the cab of the pickup after Iron Man, Sleepy and Yank got out of the truck. Hank, because of his mules, had his own transportation.

When J.B. drove up to his house, which was right next door to where the Keegans lived, Randy Joe immediately noticed something wasn't right at his folks' house. There was a new Cadillac parked in front.

THREE

Most of the people in Jason, in Jason County for that matter, thought of Simmy Weatherspoon as an *uppity nigger*. It wasn't because Simmy was arrogant. The truth was, he went overboard to be respectful.

The problem was that Simmy had achieved a financial status that put him among the top ten percent in Jason County. Most white people figured that was improper. And how he got his money was subject to considerable speculation. He was a pulp-wood contractor who had twenty trucks hauling pulpwood to the paper mills at Lufkin and Evadale. There were all kinds of questions as to where he got the money to buy that many trucks.

Most of the coloreds in Jason lived in what was called *Nigger Quarters*, which were lumber company-owned shotgun houses with no indoor toilets. Simmy, on the other hand, lived a few miles out of town in what was considered a mansion. Hell, it was a mansion.

In 1954 Simmy was fifty years old. He had been born in the Quarters, but unlike his father, never worked for the sawmill. He went as far as he could in school, which was the eighth grade, no minor accomplishment for the times. Then he started working with a pulpwood crew. He saved his money, bought a truck; saved more money and bought another truck. That, at least, was one story.

Other stories were that he had won some money gambling to get his start; that he had run a string of colored hookers; that he had been, and was, a sheriff-authorized bootlegger; that he was being financed by a bunch of colored criminals from Chicago; that Eleanor Roosevelt had bankrolled him; and that he was the evil force behind all the outlaw Negro nightclubs in the county.

Simmy never talked about what he had or where he got it. He just had it, which, he figured, was all anyone needed to know.

When Randy Joe went in the front door Simmy was the first person he saw in what passed for a living room. He was sitting in a straight-backed wooden chair, across the small room from his parents, who were sitting on a dilapidated couch.

Nobody bothered to stand. His dad simply said, "Randy Joe, you know Simmy, don't you?"

He nodded. Simmy did the same. The truth was that Randy Joe didn't really know him. He'd seen the Negro pulpwood contractor at ball games, knew who he was, and maybe had even exchanged greetings with him on such occasions. But he really didn't know the man. It's just that saying you know somebody in a small town is different than saying you know somebody in a big city. In a small town everybody is supposed to know everybody else. It's just the nature of things.

"Simmy...he wants to ask you somethin'," Randy Joe's father said.

Randy Joe pulled up another straight hardbacked wooden chair and sat facing Simmy. The visitor didn't seem to be in any hurry to say what was on his mind, or maybe he was just nervous. Randy Joe figured he wasn't accustomed to such poverty.

Finally Simmy said, "I was jest wonderin' if you'd like to

pitch a game fo' de Jason Longhorns?"

Randy Joe's face registered considerable surprise. In 1954 any white boy in East Texas would have been a little shocked if it was suggested that he pitch a game for an all-Negro team.

Simmy owned the Jason Longhorns. Randy Joe had seen them play. They were good. Damn good. When Jackie Robinson brought a team of barnstorming Negro pros to Jason to play the Longhorns during the Major League off-season, Simmy's team had come out on top.

The Longhorns were called a semi-pro team, but the truth was that none of the players worked during baseball season. Simmy had recruited them from all over the country. They were pros. A couple of Longhorns had even made it to the majors.

"'Course I'll pay you to pitch de game," Simmy continued. "I'll pay you fifty dollars."

For fifty dollars Randy Joe would have pitched a double-header against the Yankees. Actually, he would have pitched against the Yankees for nothing but the opportunity to show his stuff. Money wasn't the reason he played baseball. But it took him five days of logging in the swamp to make fifty dollars. Simmy was offering him that much to do something he loved,

"The game you want me to pitch...when is it?"

"Next Sunday," Simmy said. "Not tomorrow, but de Sunday after dat. And you gonna be pitchin' 'gainst an all-white team."

Randy Joe looked at his father. R.M. Keegan shrugged his shoulders and said, "I don't guess there's any harm in you pitchin' the game. Your high school season will be over."

Simmy smiled real big and Randy Joe asked, "What time you want me at the ball park?"

"De game starts at two. If you there at one, dat'll be plenty early. I'll bring a uniform by fo' you next week."

It hadn't dawned on Randy Joe that he'd be wearing a Longhorns uniform. He didn't have any objection. The Longhorns uniforms were a helluva lot sharper than those worn by his high school team.

"This team I'll be pitchin' against...what can you tell me about 'em?"

Simmy smiled. "Dey's out o' Lake Charles, Louisiana.

Dey's in the Gulf Coast League. It's an exhibition game fo' dem."

Randy Joe couldn't believe it. The team he'd be pitching against was a minor league club, affiliated with one of the big teams, maybe even the New York Yankees. But even if Lake Charles wasn't a Yankees farm team, it was a chance to show his stuff to the pros. Simmy could have withdrawn his offer of fifty dollars and Randy Joe would have figured out a way to pay him to pitch the game.

Simmy was nothing like the Negroes Randy Joe worked with. He was heavy and soft, with the beginnings of a Santa Claus belly.

Simmy's cheeks were, obviously, swollen by the good life, lots of fine food, including plenty of sweets. He usually had a cigar stuck in his mouth and he wore nice clothes. If he'd ever worn overalls and brogans it had been quite a while back.

Randy Joe had heard Simmy had a wife and several kids, though his live-in wife was not the mother of all of them. Simmy liked young women, eighteen to twenty-two years old. Randy Joe couldn't blame him for that. Everything was relative. Randy Joe had the hots for a twenty-two year old teacher at his high school. He figured when he was fifty he might still have the hots for twenty-two year olds.

The conversation was strained. Simmy was anxious to leave and Randy Joe's folks were just as anxious for him to go. Having a Negro visit your house set the neighbors to talking.

Randy Joe walked Simmy out to his car and felt compelled to ask, "Why do you want me to pitch this game? You got some good pitchers."

"Dat's right...I has some good pitchers, but I ain't got no pitchers like you. You de best I ever seed. You reminds me of me when I was young."

Randy Joe was flattered. "You pitched?"

"All 'round dese parts," Simmy replied. "I pitched fo' everybody who'd let me pitch fo'em. Hardly ever lost a game, neither. And you like me. You ain't gonna lose many games, not wid what you has."

"Well, I appreciate your confidence."

"You don't need my confidence," Simmy said, "you has enough of yo' own. Dat fastball and curveball is all de confidence you needs."

When Simmy drove off Randy Joe noticed Mrs. Smith was standing at a window, watching. He waved, but she didn't wave back. He guessed she was embarrassed to be caught spying.

When he went back inside his brother and sisters had come out of the woodwork. He figured his folks had sent them out of the room while Simmy was there.

There were six Keegan kids, two boys and four girls. Randy Joe was the oldest. Some people thought Randolph McKinley and Bernice Keegan were Catholics, which would also have accounted for the fact that they didn't attend a church. There wasn't a Catholic church in Jason. Randy Joe's explanation for his brother and all his sisters was that his folks were just passionate Protestants.

R.M. Keegan, in truth, didn't have much truck with religion. It would have messed up his weekends, which were for fishing and hunting. Bernice, on the other hand, had been raised a footwashing Pentecostal but backslid and became a Baptist, which, because of her religious upbringing, was about as liberal as she dared get. Bernice didn't go to church because her workload increased on the weekends.

The house the Keegan family lived in had only three bedrooms, all small, and one bathroom. Randy Joe's parents had one of the bedrooms, four girls shared another, and he and his brother had the other.

After Simmy's departure Bernice Keegan started putting supper on the table and everyone jockeyed for a place. Randy Joe took the same chair every time, but the girls could never make up their minds. Randy Joe wasn't sure if their indecision was just the nature of his sisters or a malady shared by all females.

While the house and the furniture weren't much, the food Bernice Keegan put on the table was always outstanding. If anyone left the table hungry it was their own fault. Cooking for eight, she was given to excesses. She didn't have any little bowls.

The menu that Saturday night was chicken-fried steak, green

beans, mashed potatoes, gravy and biscuits. It was a typical Saturday supper, washed down with iced tea.

Randy Joe had four big pieces of chicken-fried steak.

"You gonna be pitchin' for them niggers?" his brother Tommy Frank asked. He already knew the answer. The walls were so thin, the house so small, that anything said could be heard throughout.

"What's the difference between playin' with 'em in a real game and playin' with 'em at the ballfield in the Quarters?" Randy Joe asked.

"Nobody pays no attention when we play with 'em over here," Tommy Frank replied.

The kid had a point. In Jason's social pecking order the whites who worked for the sawmill weren't ranked all that much higher than the Negroes, but they did have a bit more status. The white Milltown kids were tolerated because the all-white high school would have been hard put to field competitive athletic teams without them. The sawmill kids were stereotyped as tougher than those who lived in the spic-and-span houses with fences and nice furniture.

Randy Joe knew deep down that the only reason towns-people accepted him was because he could pass and run with a football, shoot a basketball, and pitch and hit a baseball. But their tolerance of a Milltown kid might be put to a test if he openly played baseball for a Negro team. What he did in Milltown was one thing, but what he did to upset the status quo in Jason was something else.

The only thing that separated the Keegan house from the Quarters was a railroad spur. The company house that they occupied was, of course, nicer than those rented to colored sawmill workers. For one thing the house had a regular roof, not a tin one like the shotgun houses in the Quarters. It had six rooms and an indoor bathroom. The shotgun houses owned by the lumber company had only three rooms and an outdoor john. The outhouses were the same red color as the houses. The lumber company believed in uniformity.

If anyone living in one of the lumber company's shotgun houses wanted to take a bath they had to do it in a washtub, one of those shiny tin ones from the company store that was also used for washing clothes. They had to heat the water on a woodstove. None of the houses had natural gas, or even butane.

The lumber company had seen to it that the Negroes had electricity and water, which they paid for at the company store at the same time they paid their house rent and grocery bill. By the time a colored man making a dollar an hour paid the company store for his groceries, clothes, house rent, electricity and water, there was very little, if anything, left.

It wasn't much better for a white man. He paid more rent for a gray house than a colored man paid for one of the little red ones. The white men in supervisory positions at the sawmill made a little more than the Negro common laborers, but not enough to brag about. That's why Bernice Keegan also did parttime cooking for a restaurant, and why Randy Joe had parttime and summer jobs from the time he was a little kid.

There was always parttime work for an aggressive white kid, but a colored kid could expect nothing more than a slap in the face. If he wanted to work he could quit school and get a job at the sawmill.

Randy Joe knew the folks in the neat, white houses didn't consider his family all that much better off than the coloreds. He tended to agree. There was a bitterness that came from being poor. It was a bitterness that could choke dreams and stifle ingenuity. He was determined to keep it from doing that to him.

Randy Joe figured that neither the whites nor blacks who worked for the sawmill really knew how bad off they were, that if they ever found out they'd just lie down and die because of the hopelessness of the situation. Or start a rebellion. That's what he would do if the only thing in his future was the sawmill.

But he had the dream to sustain him, temporarily. The dream would enable him to take his mother and father, his brother and sisters, out of the trap. If that meant playing baseball with a bunch of Negroes, so be it. All he knew was that when he wanted to play a little baseball or softball there were a lot of Negroes around who were eager to accommodate. That couldn't be said for the kids who lived in those spic-and-span white houses. Maybe they didn't need dreams.

The lumber company had built what passed for a softball diamond on some land adjacent to its colored rent houses, even put up some dim lights. On summer evenings coloreds and whites who worked for the sawmill got together and played ball. It was kind of strange because white men who normally wouldn't even associate with Negroes, except for having to work with them, had no qualms about playing ball with them.

The white people Randy Joe knew were opposed to integrating the schools, even more opposed to going to church with Negroes. Except for softball a Negro was a second-class citizen, and that's all there was to it.

This all flashed through Randy Joe's mind in a split-second, triggered by his brother's question about pitching for the "niggers." The question didn't surprise him, either, because Tommy Frank had been racially conditioned like everyone else in Milltown. He played with colored kids, too, but that was on his own turf. Taking that association out of Milltown was something else.

Randy Joe said, "I don't give a damn what anyone around this town thinks."

Randy Joe figured his mother wanted to say something to the contrary but couldn't. She and his father didn't care much for the townspeople and had said so often enough around the house. They felt as much like outsiders in Jason as he did.

"Well, I'll bet you some of those town girls you go with ain't gonna like it," Jo Beth said, "especially Anna Louise Lake."

Jo Beth was fourteen, tall for her age, and had a head full of common sense. The oldest of the girls, she was also the most practical. She accepted her station in life with more grace than Randy Joe did.

"I don't go with Anna Louise...at least not on a regular basis."

Jo Beth was pretty, with soft brown hair and dark brown eyes, but Randy Joe thought she had a mean mouth. "It's not 'cause you ain't tried," she said. "Mr. Lake...I'll bet he panics every time you walk up to their door."

His mother laughed, his dad smiled, and Randy Joe countered, "I get along fine with Mr. Lake."

"Sure you do," Jo Beth said, sarcastically. "But I'll bet he doesn't want you for a son-in-law."

"You'd better stick to talkin' about something you know somethin' about," said Randy Joe.

"I know a lot more than you think," she said. "Kids at school...they talk."

"I want you kids to quit your fussin'," her father said.

Jo Beth countered, "We ain't fussin'." She was the only one of his children who could talk back to him, even correct him, and get away with it. "Randy Joe...he's the one with all the town friends. But they wouldn't be such good friends if he didn't play football and baseball."

Randy Joe knew she was right, but wanted to think that Anna Louise and a lot of the other town girls liked him for himself, that it was their parents who were prejudiced against him. "Maybe you oughta play," he said, sarcastically, "and somebody would like you."

"That's enough," their father said. They knew he meant it.

While Randy Joe played football, and was good at it, he wasn't in love with the sport. He played because of peer pressure. And he always worried about injuring his throwing hand or arm. He feared an injury might take away the dream.

There was a lot of conversation at supper that night, about a lot of different things. But the thing that was on Randy Joe's mind was Simmy Weatherspoon's visit, what he was going to do for the Jason Longhorns. He couldn't help but believe it was a pivotal period in his life, that maybe, just maybe, it was the real beginning of his dream.

The only thing Randy Joe loved more than his dream was his mother. After having six kids Bernice Keegan was still a strikingly beautiful woman. She had kind brown eyes, a soft smile, and sunshine-kissed auburn hair. Randy Joe saw in her everything he ever hoped to have in a wife. And she was part of his dream. With the money he was going to earn playing ball, he planned to buy her the kind of home and life he thought she deserved.

He loved his father, too, but might have had more respect for him than love. R.M. Keegan looked a lot like J.B. Smith. He had a leathery face, stooped shoulders and a lean body. But Keegan's slender build was because he was hyperactive. He never relaxed.

As supper was ending that Saturday evening Jo Beth piped up again. "You have a date tonight?"

"Not that it's any of your business, but yeah," Randy Joe replied, "I have a date tonight."

"Who with?"

He could have ignored the question, but saw no reason to allow her curiosity to boil over. "Patti Sue."

From the look on her face he could tell she approved, which made him think he'd made a mistake in asking Patti Sue out. Of course, he figured Jo Beth approved because Patti Sue's daddy drove a butane truck or something like that. And she lived out in the country, wasn't a town girl. Jo Beth reveled in her Milltown roots, and resented the snobbish town girls.

"I like Patti Sue," Jo Beth said, "but I can't say much for her taste in boys...goin' out with you."

Randy Joe noticed that his daddy smiled, which figured because he'd always been partial to smartasses like Jo Beth. Randy Joe wanted to say, "Who gives a rat's ass what you like?" but knew that wouldn't fly with his mother or father. They didn't go to church, but they didn't truck with profanity. His dad would let some curse words spew from his mouth on occasion, but he wouldn't tolerate it from his kids.

Randy Joe's mother and daddy, mostly his mother, had decided that at fourteen Jo Beth was too young to date. But they let her go out with girlfriends on Friday and Saturday nights. Randy Joe knew that was almost the same as dating. She always ended up with some boy. The only difference was, the little hard dick Jo Beth ended up with didn't have to undergo the scrutiny of his parents.

Randy Joe sometimes thought his parents were more concerned about who he was with than who was with Jo Beth. It was as if they didn't trust him, which he suspected was the result of his daddy's running around when he was younger. He didn't think either of his parents were aware that he knew they'd gone through some troubled times, primarily because R.M. Keegan had not been one to turn a woman down.

Sex, of course, was a taboo subject. His parents never talked to him about it. He figured they assumed that when someone reached a certain age sexual knowledge was revealed to them from on high.

It had been revealed to Randy Joe, quite wonderfully, a year earlier in Mr. and Mrs. Max Turner's garage. Their daughter Gretchen, a hot-blooded young thing with better than average tits, had allowed him to sample her wares. It was his first time. Gretchen's, too.

The only frightful thing about the first experience was that it was done without a condom, and both Gretchen and Randy Joe worried that her belly might balloon. For subsequent sexual encounters with Gretchen he'd been prepared.

He liked Gretchen. A lot. But he could never get that romantic feeling for her that he had for Anna Louise Lake, the banker's daughter. In truth, Gretchen had a better figure, tits and wheels. She was a better overall package. But, for some reason, he was enamored with Anna Louise.

Maybe it was because Anna Louise was more sophisticated. She dressed better and knew how to carry herself, whereas Gretchen was a Milltown brat who had a mouth like a stopped up toilet when she was riled.

Still, he liked her as a friend. And she did provide him with considerable relief. Most of his friends had to resort to hand jobs to clean their pipes, but he had Gretchen.

Gretchen had red shoulder length hair and freckles that danced like stars across the bridge of her nose. Her eyes were green. Sometimes she wore polka dot panties, which reminded him of her freckles. As to whether or not she was pretty, he'd have to admit she ranked in the top ten in his high school, maybe even the top five. That wasn't too shabby, because his high school had some outstanding girls.

After supper Randy Joe filled the bathtub with hot water and spent a few minutes soaking his weary bones. It gave him a chance to think about Patti Sue and to get a hard-on, which, he knew, was about all he would get from her. Patti Sue definitely ranked in the top five in his high school, but she didn't put out. They had done some heavy necking, of course, but anytime his

hands wandered into forbidden territory Patti Sue turned as cold
as a Texas blue norther.

Knowing he could have his way with Gretchen, some of his
friends wondered why he bothered with Patti Sue at all. Frankly,
he didn't know. Maybe Patti Sue's virginity was a challenge to
him, though deep in his heart he knew she would retain her virtue
until she crawled between the sheets with her husband. In bizarre
moments, he'd even entertained the idea of going as far as
matrimony to get what he wanted from Patti Sue.

The real truth is, he thought, I really don't know why I let
Patti Sue jerk me around. Maybe it's because I'm almost
seventeen years old and my brain is connected to my cock.

Soaking there in the tub he also had time to think about Anna
Louise Lake. Her beauty didn't rank with Patti Sue's or
Gretchen's. But he wanted her, too. Again he thought, maybe it
was part of youthfulness to want to monopolize every pretty
piece of tail he came in contact with. But maybe Anna Louise
was part of the dream.

Randy Joe thought Patti Sue's soft brown hair looked as
though it had been spun by a fairy's wand, one of those real
make-believe fairies created by Walt Disney, not a limp-wristed
guy with a lisp. Her hair was like his mother's when she was
younger. And her eyes were dark brown pools of liquid that
engulfed him. She had a beautiful body, especially the tits and
legs, plus an angelic face. It was easy to go overboard picturing
Patti Sue in his mind.

Anna Louise was a hand-painted China doll, overly white,
She seemed almost mystical, possibly because she came from
such a sterile environment. Randy Joe figured if Anna Louise
ever visited a house in Milltown, which he was pretty sure she
would never do, she might overcome being as pure as a cake of
Ivory soap. He did like the way she carried herself, with the high
degree of respectability expected by her family. She worked
very hard at being the perfect daughter.

Anna Louise had a decent body, but it was nothing like Patti
Sue's or Gretchen's. Her eyes were a pale cold blue, which
seemed a match for thin lips that seldom smiled. Randy Joe had
never seen her laugh for the sheer joy of it. Anna Louise never

lost control. She had a prominent nose and the page-boy cut of her sandy hair added to her stoic aura. She was five-feet, six inches tall, which gave her a couple of inches on both Patti Sue and Gretchen.

As to why he thought he could successfully romance Anna Louise, as to why he would want to, Randy Joe didn't know. Maybe it was because she came from a world he did not know, but one he thought he wanted to know. The dream, again.

He knew at an early age that he did not want to spend his life working at the sawmill. Given a choice of that or death, he thought his preference would be dying for his country in some foreign land as a result of some heroic action. Dying for something special, not wasting away at a deadend job—that was important to him.

Sitting there that evening in a tub of hot water he contemplated that pitching a game for a colored team might well be pushing him toward the heroic action and death scenario. If he didn't make it to the big leagues. However, at the time he thought the possibility of failure to make it to the big show was slight.

But what would Anna Louise think? What would her parents think? What would the townspeople of Jason think? In pitching the game, in identifying himself with the Jason Longhorns, was he forever destroying the possibility of acceptance by Jason society? Would he be labeled a nigger lover?

He laughed and thought, To hell with'em if they can't take a joke.

FOUR

"You want some popcorn, hotdog, Coke, hamburger?" Randy Joe asked Patti Sue.

"Just a Coke," she replied.

"How about you guys?" he asked Weaver Severage and Jolene Claxton, both of whom were in the back seat of the car sucking on each other's faces, panting like a couple of dogs in heat.

Weave, Randy Joe's best friend, and Jolene were double dating with them, which didn't set all that well with Patti Sue. She didn't have anything against Jolene, but she'd never warmed up to Weave, couldn't understand why he and Randy Joe were such good friends.

She had told Randy Joe, "You've got nothing in common. He's a goofoff, goin' nowhere. All he'll do is drag you down."

He didn't particularly appreciate Patti Sue's evaluation of Weave, but knew she didn't give a damn whether he did or not. He certainly hadn't been all that excited when Weave had insisted on double-dating with them. With Weave and Jolene making out in the back seat, Patti Sue was keeping him at bay in the front. He figured Patti Sue would be more amorous if Weave and Jolene weren't around. She'd been more fun in the past, when they'd been by themselves.

They were at the drive-in movie theater, which was about the only place to take a girl in Jason. Well, there was a downtown theater, but you couldn't make out with all the adults there and the balcony was reserved for coloreds.

That was something else Randy Joe couldn't understand. The balcony had the best seats in the house. If the white business community wanted to penalize Negroes for being black, why did they give them the best seats?

Weave's reason for double-dating was simple. His folks didn't have a car. So when he had suggested to Jolene that they go to the drive-in movie it was conditional on Randy Joe providing the wheels. The Keegans had a fifty-one Plymouth sedan, which had perfect seats for serious dating. The car was green, which had earned it the nickname the *Green Hornet.*

In response to Randy Joe's question about what they wanted from the snack bar, Weave said, "I'll have a couple of hamburgers all the way, an order of fries, a big Coke and a large popcorn. What do you want Jolene?"

"That sounds good to me," she replied.

Patti Sue got an incredulous look on her face and it wasn't from watching the movie screen.

En route to the concession stand Randy Joe stopped by the little boys room to drain his lizard and improve his literary knowledge. The latest graffiti were disappointing, mostly the usual crude drawings of body parts.

Waiting for the healthy food orders placed by Weave and Jolene, he pondered Patti Sue's analysis of his best friend. She was right in saying they were different. For one thing, Weave didn't worry about escaping Milltown. He accepted his lot in life, and seemed content to go along with the expectations people had of Milltown kids. And while making good grades in school was important to Randy Joe, Weave was content to get by.

His arms loaded down, Randy Joe arrived back at the Plymouth and dispensed the goodies. He'd gotten a Coke and popcorn for himself. If Patti Sue was averse to doing even a little smooching, he figured he might as well do a little eating. Popcorn was a favorite food.

After saying she didn't want anything but a Coke, Patti Sue ate half his popcorn. Then the most she would do was let him hold her hand. For a change he even watched the movie, *High Noon*, starring Gary Cooper. Cooper had won an Academy Award for it in 1952, but things didn't get to Jason that fast.

The movie was over at ten-thirty and he figured they could get in an hour of parking before taking the girls home. Curfew for both of them was midnight. But Patti Sue wasn't buying his parking plan. She claimed she had a headache and that it would be best for all concerned if she went home.

Randy Joe said that was dandy with him. During the evening she'd been about as much fun as the green chain.

After parking the Plymouth at her house he walked her to the front door, which put them out of sight of the car. Hidden from Weave's and Jolene's eyes, her mood softened a bit and she got ready for a goodnight kiss. But he just thanked her for going out with him and walked away. He knew how to out-bitch a bitch. In fact, going back to the car he felt pretty good about his "I don't give a damn" attitude. He was young, inexperienced, but he knew how to drive women crazy.

"Patti Sue on the rag or somethin'?" Jolene asked when he got back in the car. She had a mouth the equal of Gretchen's, and she didn't have to be mad to use it.

He shrugged his shoulders. "Who knows? Who cares?"

"Maybe she's pissed 'cause you're gonna pitch a game for them niggers," Weave said. He'd told them about Simmy's offer and his acceptance on the way to the drive-in.

"Naw, I don't think that's it," he said, not wanting to tell Weave the real reason for her foul mood.

He got the car going and Jolene piped up, "Well...serves you right, Randy Joe. If you'd brought Gretchen we coulda had some fun."

"I can't see where Patti Sue bein' along slowed down your fun any," he quipped.

Jolene giggled. "What I meant was, you coulda had some fun."

"Hell, I had fun," he said. "I wanted to see the movie."

"Sure...and I want two inches cut off the end of my dick," Weave said.

"You can be crass, Weave, real crass," Randy Joe said. "Long as you brought it up, though, two inches off the end of your dick would leave you with nothin'."

Weave laughed. Jolene joined in, but said, "You must notta

seen what I been feelin'."

Randy Joe laughed. "You usin' that green banana trick again, Weave?"

Weave was six-four and a solid two hundred. In athletics, though, he lacked something. The head football coach, who was an asshole anyway, thought Randy Joe, had labeled Weave a coward because he refused to play.

In Jason, if a boy didn't play football he wasn't anybody. It didn't matter that Weave was the school's top scorer in basketball and that he'd garnered all sorts of track honors. He didn't play football, so he was perceived to be yellow.

Weave was passive. He wasn't just slow to anger, he never angered. Randy Joe would get so pissed at the football coach he'd try to tear someone else's head off. But Weave wasn't that way.

So Patti Sue was right about the way Weave and Randy Joe differed in personality. Randy Joe couldn't stand to lose and wouldn't back down to anyone. But win, lose or draw, Weave didn't give a damn.

"Where we going?" Weave asked.

"Nowhere in particular," Randy Joe replied. "I'll just drive around and let you and Jolene make out."

"That don't seem fair," he said.

"One of these days you're gonna realize life's not fair," Randy Joe said.

"Don't argue with Randy Joe," Jolene said.

So he drove them around and let them feel each other up in the back seat. It gave him a chance to think about pitching the game for Simmy's team the following Sunday. He had one more game to pitch for Jason High School on Tuesday, which, if victorious, would give Jason a bi-district championship. There was no state baseball championship in Jason's classification.

Randy Joe wasn't worried about beating another high-school team. He had already won seventeen, lost none, and the Tuesday night game would cap off a perfect year for him.

His thoughts rambled. He wondered why Weave was so hung up on Jolene Claxton. Weave was probably the best-looking guy in high school, whereas Jolene didn't even rank in Randy Joe's top twenty-five. She was around five-feet, two inches tall, with unruly blonde hair, blue eyes and a little turned up nose. She was thin, didn't have much of a shape—in fact, she was flat-chested.

Yet Weave, with dark hair, dark eyes and a movie star face, was crazy about her. Most guys were envious of Weave's looks and build. Randy Joe would have taken the looks and build in a New York minute, as long as he wasn't required to take Weave's mind with them. He didn't want a mind that would pick Jolene from all the available women. It was another case of Weave settling for less than he could have had.

He parked the car in front of Jolene's house at eleven-fifty, which gave Weave a chance to hunch on her some more on her darkened front porch. When Weave came back to the car and opened the door and the interior light came on. Randy Joe laughed. There was a big wet spot on the crotch of Weave's slacks.

"If you're gonna go out with Jolene," he suggested, "you oughta wear dark slacks. Or you'd better hang a rubber on your dick."

Weave grinned. "She's somethin', ain't she?"

"She's somethin', all right," Randy Joe agreed, his thoughts not coinciding all that well with Weave's.

He headed down to Big Bill's Cafe which was the only place open in Jason after midnight. As restaurants went it wasn't much on looks or food quality, but did a booming business.

The cafe's owner was Bill Perkins, a tall, rotund man with thinning sandy hair and the jowls of a bulldog. Before opening the restaurant he'd owned a service station. His fingernails indicated that he still liked to tinker with car engines.

Randy Joe and Weave grabbed a booth by one of the windows that needed to be washed. There were a number of cuts in the burgundy vinyl seats that had been patched with tape and the window's open drapes were stained at the bottom, as though the roof had leaked and water had run down them.

The waitress was Lola, a frumpy old gal in her fifties, with gray hair in a bun and a pooched out peter-belly covered by a small apron. She had more wrinkles than a dried frog.

Both Weave and Randy Joe ordered Cokes. Weave also

asked for a double order of french fries.

"So, you're really gonna pitch for them niggers," Weave said.

"Any reason I shouldn't?"

"I don't have any. Some other people might."

"Then screw'em," Randy Joe said. "Hell, I just wanna play ball."

"I know. But you know what's gonna happen, don't you?"

"What?"

"We're gonna graduate next year and get drafted, that's what."

"So...what's that got to do with me playin' baseball?"

"Well, I think you're plannin' on gettin' outta high school and goin' right into the pros."

"That's my plan," Randy Joe admitted, "but if I get drafted I get drafted. It's just for two years."

"I'm thinkin' about maybe making a career out of it," Weave said. "But I'd rather be in the Air Force than the Army. I was hopin' we could go in together."

"You mean enlist?"

"Yeah."

"That's sure not in my plans. And this is the first I've heard about you goin' into the Air Force. When did all this come about?"

"I don't see I've got much choice."

"Weave, we all have choices."

"You do," he said. "Hell, Randy Joe, you could go to college if you wanted to...get a football scholarship. You got the grades."

"Hell, Weave, so could you...get a basketball or track scholarship."

Weave shook his head. "No, I couldn't make it in college. I'm just barely gettin' by in high school."

The waitress brought their Cokes and the fries. Weave used an entire bottle of catsup. The place was pretty quiet, a couple of truck-driver types eating at the counter. Most customers were just drinking coffee.

"You know, Weave, I just can't believe this Air Force crap you've come up with."

"Why not?"

"Well, you never said anything about it before."

"I hadn't thought about it before."

"Well, what made you think of it now?"

"Jolene and me...it's gettin' pretty serious."

"Oh, damn."

"What does that mean?"

"It means you oughta get your brains off the end of your pecker, that's what it means. You wanna be a seventeen- or eighteen-year-old daddy?"

"I ain't gonna get her pregnant."

"Not intentionally, you're not. Man, you haven't been anywhere...you haven't done anything. And now you're thinkin' about goin' in the Air Force and settlin' down with Jolene. You're not being fair to yourself."

Weave's face flushed and he looked like he might want to argue the point, but about that time Big Bill Perkins gave up his stool by the cash register and sauntered over to their booth. A toothpick dangled from a corner of his big lips.

"Randy Joe...Weave...how you boys doin'?"

They acknowledged that they were doing just fine.

"Heard somethin' in the back tonight, didn't know whether to believe it or not," Big Bill said.

"What did you hear?" Randy Joe asked, knowing that he really didn't have to ask for Big Bill to provide the information.

"Heared you was gonna pitch a game for the Jason Long-horns next Sunday."

Randy Joe grinned. "News travels fast. I didn't know I was gonna pitch the game until a little after six this evenin'."

"It's Sunday morning," Weave reminded.

"Yesterday evenin', then," Randy Joe said. "What do you think about me pitchin' the game, Big Bill?"

His brow furrowed and he replied, "It ain't one of your better moves."

"You're gonna be there, aren't you?"

"Oh, yeah, I'll be there," he promised. "I 'spect a lot of white folks are gonna be there. But this ain't the best thing you could be doin', Randy Joe. I don't know what folks are gonna think about you playin' ball with a bunch of niggers."

"You feed colored people here at the restaurant, don't you?" Randy Joe said, the tone of his voice argumentative.

"That's different, Randy Joe. I feed 'em in the back, not out here with the white folks."

There was a back entry to the cafe, with a sign over the door that read *Colored Only*. What Big Bill had for Negroes was just a counter and some stools in the back part of the kitchen.

"It wouldn't bother me if they ate out here with us," Randy Joe said.

Big Bill frowned. "You don't wanna be sayin' stuff like that. Things are fine just like they are."

"What you're sayin' is the green of their money is fine. It's just the black of their faces you don't like."

Randy Joe didn't know if there was a Ku Klux Klan chapter in Jason or not. If there was, it sure wasn't active. But if anything like the Klan existed in his hometown, he'd have bet Weave's balls that Big Bill was its honcho. Bill looked like a man who would be very much at home in a sheet.

Randy Joe enjoyed bugging the cafe owner, so he continued, "Your cook back there, she's colored, isn't she?"

"Well, yeah, she's..."

"There you go then," he said. "I'd just as soon eat with a colored as have one prepare my food."

Big Bill chuckled. "I see what you're up to, Randy Joe, and it ain't gonna work. You just love agitatin' me, don't you?"

"He loves agitatin' anybody," Weave said.

"Well, he's ain't gonna get me worked up," Big Bill said. "If he wants to play ball with a bunch of coons, fine and dandy. And if he wants to eat in the back with the niggers, that's fine, too."

"I might just take you up on that Big Bill," Randy Joe said. "I've always suspected the coloreds were getting better food back there than we're getting out here. It's bound to be better."

Big Bill laughed, sighed, shook his head in resignation and sauntered back toward his stool behind the cash register. A customer was waiting to pay.

"You shouldn't give Big Bill such a hard time," Weave said. "He likes you."

"So he likes me. He's still an asshole."

Big Bill Perkins was an avid high school football fan, provided the team with some financial support, and was a general pain in the butt. He liked to hang around the coaches and do favors for them.

"I don't guess there's any chance you'll go in the Air Force with me on the buddy system," Weave said.

Randy Joe gave him a look of dismay. "It's not likely."

Weave laughed, but he looked a little sad, too. "The Army's gonna get you."

"The Army's gonna get me for two years, not four. And they might not get me."

Weave changed the subject. "You excited about pitchin' the game for the niggers?"

Randy Joe shrugged his shoulders. "Yeah. The high school teams we've been playing aren't much competition. This will be a good test."

"You'll do okay. You always do."

Randy Joe smiled. "I appreciate your confidence, but this time I'm gonna be throwin' against pros."

"You'll still do all right. And you know it."

"Yeah...I guess I do."

They paid Big Bill and Randy Joe drove Weave home. They lived only a couple of blocks apart. The Keegans had a slightly nicer house. Randy Joe's dad was more like a foreman than Weave's.

"You gonna be around in the morning?" Weave asked after Randy Joe parked the car in front of his house.

"You kiddin'? You know dad's gonna wanta go fishin'. Anytime I'm off school or work he wants to go fishin'."

That was not exactly true. During the hunting season his father always wanted to go hunting. And he wasn't really complaining, because he enjoyed fishing and hunting. When it came down to a choice, he preferred fishing.

No more than ten minutes after dropping Weave at his house, Randy Joe crawled into the double bed he shared with Tommy Frank, who was snoring. Randy Joe started thinking about his debut with the Jason Longhorns. It was going to be interesting, very interesting. The problem was that his thinking was keeping him from sleeping. And in a very short time his dad was going to be up, rarin' to go fishing.

His bedroom was located on a corner of the house, with sets of windows on two walls. There were no curtains on the windows, just shades, and the windows had been raised to let in the cool spring breeze blowing softly from the south.

At first the voice outside the window was like something hazy in a dream, whispering carried by the wind. But then he recognized it.

He checked Tommy Frank, saw that nothing short of a hurricane was going to wake him, then went to the window and said in a whisper, "Gretchen, what in the hell are you doing here?"

"I couldn't sleep," she answered. "Can you come outside?"

Gretchen lived just a couple of houses down.

He slipped into his pants and shoes, didn't bother with a shirt, and went outside to join Gretchen. They got in the back seat of the Plymouth.

About thirty minutes later he went back in his house. This time he fell asleep almost immediately.

FIVE

Randy Joe could make it on two hours sleep a night. It was a good thing, too. Otherwise he wouldn't have had a night life. His dad was an early riser, day in and day out. Weekends were no exception. And R.M. Keegan was most impatient for daylight when he was going hunting or fishing.

That Sunday morning in May he was up at four a.m., ready to head for the creek. Randy Joe could hear him rummaging around in the kitchen, making coffee. Randy Joe was up and dressed by four-fifteen. Thirty minutes later they had polished off a breakfast of biscuits, sausage, gravy and coffee prepared by his mother.

As his father headed the car westward toward Trout Creek, Randy Joe wondered about the name of the stream. There weren't any trout in East Texas. He guessed it might be because some of the locals called bass green trout, which pissed his father off. When it came to fish and game his dad was a stickler for proper identification.

It was still dark when they arrived at a little stream that emptied into Trout Creek. It was where they seined minnows. Randy Joe got in the water with his end of the seine. His dad operated his end from the bank. It gave Randy Joe no peace to think that a cottonmouth moccasin might be in the creek with him, or that they might seine one up with the minnows.

They had seined a big snake up once. They beat it to death and killed all the minnows.

It took them only a few minutes to seine up a bucket full of minnows, which R.M. Keegan preferred to call shiners. They drove a little further to a dirt road that led down toward Trout Creek.

When the road petered out they left the car and walked about a half-mile to the creek. Randy Joe let his dad lead the way down the overgrown trail. He always marveled how the man shuffled along and never seemed to be worried about snakes. His dad joked that snakes got the second person, not the first. Randy Joe suspected that was a lot of bullshit, so was content to walk behind him.

He was always amazed by his dad's good eyes. R.M. Keegan could take an ordinary match, set it up and retreat twenty-five or thirty yards, then light it with a bullet from a twenty-two caliber rifle. Randy Joe didn't think there was anyone better with a rifle.

His dad was known for steady nerves and control. Teaching Randy Joe to pitch, he demonstrated control by using a popsicle stick for a home plate. He would point the stick directly at the pitching mound, then could throw twenty straight fastballs right over it and in the strike zone. He had a good curveball, too, and he could normally break at least eighteen of twenty pitches right over the popsicle stick.

Randy Joe also thought his dad could throw an axe better than anyone. More than one snake had been cut in half with a toss from R.M. Keegan's spinning hatchet.

Daylight was just creeping through and above the big trees that occupied the banks along Trout Creek when they arrived at one of their favorite fishing holes. It was in a swampy area less than an hour's drive from the Louisiana line.

Randy Joe's father knew a lot about the outdoors and survival and he had taught him simple but effective ways to catch fish. Neither of them had a rod and reel, just a cane pole with a line, hook, sinker and bobber. The barb of the hook went through the back of a minnow, then the bait was dropped into a likely spot. When the bobber disappeared under the surface, an upward jerk on the pole usually hung a fish.

They normally caught black bass and crappie, though they would occasionally catch a goggleye or catfish. Sometimes they even hooked a bowfin, which, if any size, could tear up their rig.

The hole they started fishing that Sunday was within sight of where Trout Creek emptied into the Angelina River. They often hunted squirrels in the big timber along the river.

A large tree had fallen across the creek. They used it like a bridge to the other bank. There was considerable brush in the hole, which provided good cover for both forage and gamefish.

They sat on the gently sloping banks, watching the bobbers being gently tugged around on the surface by the wounded minnows. There was little conversation. There was just appreciation for the beauty of nature, the feeling of dawn waking up all their senses, the sight and sound of a gentle breeze rippling through the tops of the trees. Birds were chirping, squirrels were chattering. The peace here was right for the souls of men.

Randy Joe had been weaned on a creek bank. His mother and father had started taking him fishing when he was just a baby. When the time came for him to give up sucking his mother's breasts, his parents told him a hoot owl had stolen his mother's milk.

"You've got a bite," his dad said.

Randy Joe had been lost in thought. Sure enough, the bobber was being tugged ever so gently. Then the fish took it beneath the surface. He gave the fish a second or two to mouth the minnow, then arched his pole upward. The hook struck home and his hands felt the weight of the fish on the other end of the line.

Soon after a terribly unfair battle he had the two-pound bass on the bank. He grasped its lower lip between his thumb and forefinger, disconnected the hook, put the fish on a stringer and staked it out in the water. He then put another minnow on his hook, flipped it out in the water, lay back on the sloping bank and waited for another hungry fish.

"Looks like it's gonna be a good day," his dad said.

Looking at his father, talking to him, Randy Joe figured it would be hard for anyone to believe he'd been a war hero, honored with Silver and Bronze Stars, or that he'd been one of General George Patton's boys. Randy Joe could mentally picture him plodding along, doing his duty. without a lot of hoopla.

"Guess fishin' is out for next Sunday, huh?" his dad said.

"I guess so. I don't wanna to be too tired when I pitch."

"You'll do okay."

"I don't know. I've never pitched against pros before."

R.M. Keegan smiled. "They've probably never hit against anybody like you before, either."

His confidence made Randy Joe feel good. He wasn't lacking in the stuff himself, but considered his father the most knowledgeable person in the world when it came to pitching. He believed his father could have been a major league pitcher if he hadn't been wounded during the war.

"Dad, I don't think Big Bill was too happy to learn I was gonna pitch the game."

His father laughed. "Big Bill...he's an asshole. If you feel okay about it, that's what counts."

"I wanna do it, but...well, people might say a lot of stuff. I don't wanna cause you and mom any problems."

"Hell, you're not gonna cause us any problems. You oughta know by now that I don't give a shit what some of the people in town say. I'd a whole lot rather trust niggers than some of the people who run Jason."

R.M. Keegan wasn't colorblind. He was a man who was a product of his environment. But he had great respect for hardworking colored people. He used the word nigger because it was so commonplace in everyday language that he considered it benign. What he couldn't tolerate was a man, black or white, who didn't take care of his family, or didn't work hard.

Randy Joe knew the Negroes who worked for his dad seemed to like him, though most thought he worked them harder than was necessary. However, he demanded just as much work of himself, so they also thought he was fair. He would bullshit with the Negro laborers, do damn near anything to help a colored person who worked hard. But there were lines between the races that had been drawn long ago and for the most part he respected them.

"Before you start thinkin' about next Sunday's game," his dad warned, "You'd better take care of business Tuesday night. You've got to beat Bridge City."

Randy Joe agreed, but it was hard for him to worry about a high school team. The season had gone so well that he had yet to face a high school hitter who worried him. Oh, there were always skinny kids like the one from Nederland who could work him for a base on balls. But he had no trouble with the guys who fancied themselves hitters. R.M. Keegan's bobber dived beneath the surface and he landed a bass about the same size as Randy Joe's.

They caught a few more fish out of the hole, then headed up the creek fishing various holes above and below ripples. By eleven o'clock they had a full stringer. R.M. Keegan suggested they call it a day.

That was fine with Randy Joe. He was getting hungry for what he knew his mother was fixing for Sunday dinner — beef roast, mashed potatoes, gravy, green beans and biscuits. His only regret was that his father would insist they clean the fish. It was the worst part about going fishing, that and eating the damn things.

SIX

On Monday Randy Joe started taking some real heat. By then word of his decision to pitch for the Longhorns had spread like wildfire throughout the school. It might have been worse if the students and faculty hadn't been preoccupied with thoughts about the championship game the following night.

"What's this bullshit about you pitchin' for that nigger team?" Vic Marshall asked. Marshall was the head football coach and attempted to teach algebra.

"Yeah, coach, I'm gonna pitch for'em."

"That's a dumbshit thing to do."

Randy Joe shrugged his shoulders. "Maybe."

"Son," the coach said, "you're jeopardizing everything you've worked for."

"That depends on what you think I'm workin' for."

"I'll tell you this...I can get you a football scholarship to just about any Southwest Conference school."

"If I go to college it won't be to play football."

Marshall's face reddened. Randy Joe Keegan frustrated the hell out of him. He figured the kid could be a great football player if he wanted. He was the best high school quarterback he'd ever coached.

"Damn it, Randy Joe, don't you go screwin' up now. I'm countin' on you this fall."

Randy Joe heaved a weary sigh. "Hell, coach, I'll be out there on the field in August...sweatin' my balls off with the rest of the assholes."

"You'd better be," Marshall warned. "And watch your fuckin' language, too."

Marshall didn't want his players using profanity. He was also a Sunday School teacher at Jason's First Baptist Church.

"You ready for tomorrow night?" the coach asked.

"Yeah, I'm ready."

"Game means a lot to the school."

"Means a lot to me, too," Randy Joe said.

"Well, I don't want you thinkin' about that nigger game on Sunday when you oughta be thinkin' about Bridge City tomorrow night."

"I wasn't thinkin' about Sunday until you brought it up."

Randy Joe knew the coach didn't give a damn about baseball, and if he had his way the school wouldn't field a baseball team.

Marshall had cornered Randy Joe after an algebra class, asked him to stay so he could talk to him. Randy Joe had sensed what was coming. He knew the coach had a hard-on for anyone of a different color.

"Randy Joe, where you workin' this summer?" Marshall asked.

"I'm gonna be loggin', cuttin' cypress trees down in the swamp."

The coach nodded approval. "Good, good...that's good hard work...oughta keep you in shape. When you come out for football in August I want you mean and ready."

"Oh, I'll be ready," Randy Joe said. "Your practices aren't as tough as what I'll be doin'."

Marshall grinned. "You sayin' my practices aren't tough? Some of the other boys wouldn't like hearin' you say that."

The coach prided himself on the way he trained his boys. He treated them the way he had been treated in Marine Corps boot camp. He was brutal, even sadistic, in his approach to the game. He liked the fact he could make every player cry uncle, except for Randy Joe Keegan. No matter how much he ran the kid, how tough the tackling and blocking, how long practice lasted, Randy Joe stayed cool. While his attitude infuriated him, the coach admired his toughness.

"I guess they're tough enough," Randy Joe admitted, "for guys who haven't worked on the green chain or done any loggin', like the town guys who are gonna lie around on their asses all summer and get fat."

Marshall laughed uneasily. "You don't have much respect for the boys who don't live in Milltown, do you?"

"Not much."

There was something about this kid that bothered Marshall, something a little frightening. The coach was a solid two hundred and thirty pounder, thirty-three years old, and he'd been through the college football wars. But for some reason he shied away from being too confrontational with Randy Joe Keegan.

"You might consider bein' on a little better terms with your teammates," Marshall said. "After all, they'll be blockin' for you."

Randy Joe shrugged his shoulders. "That's their job. Besides, I'm on pretty good terms with everybody. I just don't like lardasses and they know it."

"Wish you'd reconsider playin' for those niggers," the coach said. "Nothing good can come out of it. Word gets out and it might affect your eligibility."

"How's that?"

"They play for money, don't they?"

"I guess."

Randy Joe wasn't about to tell the coach about the fifty dollars Simmy had promised him. What the asshole didn't know wouldn't hurt him.

"Think about it," Marshall said. "Think about it long and hard. Maybe then you'll do the right thing."

Randy Joe laughed. "I thought you wanted me thinkin' about the game with Bridge City."

The coach managed a grin, though it was tough. "Yeah, I did say that, didn't I?"

Randy Joe had expected some guff from Marshall, who enjoyed interfering in the lives of his players. The only thing he liked about the man was his wife. Sheila Marshall, five years younger than her husband, was a keeper.

Patti Sue approached him just before his final morning class and asked, "Do you have lunch plans?"

"No...guess I'll just eat the slop in the cafeteria like always."

"Can we eat together? I wanna talk to you."

"Sure...don't see why not."

"Well, I know Weave usually eats with you."

"Hey...I'll tell him we have some private things to discuss." She smiled. "Thanks."

After class Weave routinely intercepted him on the way to the lunch room, but he said, "Sorry, pal...Patti Sue has some serious stuff to lay on me at lunch."

"Yeah...what kinda stuff?"

"Don't ask me. She just said she wanted to talk to me."

"Without me around, you mean," Weave said.

"Don't take it personal. There's a lotta stuff I don't tell you myself."

Weave laughed. "Yeah, but I usually find out."

Randy Joe met Patti Sue at the lunch room entrance and they went through the line together. The school cafeteria made Randy Joe even more grateful for his mother's meals. They found a table where no one was sitting, but knew they couldn't count on it staying that way. The table next to them was occupied by several freshmen girls who were giggling and talking. Some of their chatter was about him.

"So, Patti Sue, what do you wanna talk about?"

"Mainly, I just want to apologize."

"For what?"

"For Saturday night."

Randy Joe shrugged his shoulders. "You don't owe me an apology."

"Maybe not, but I'm givin' you one anyway. I was upset that Weave and Jolene went to the movie with us."

He grinned. "Upset, hell...you were mad."

She laughed. "Okay...mad. But that still doesn't excuse the way I acted."

"Does this mean you're gonna go out with me again?" he asked, amused.

"You already knew that, silly."

"That's not a very good way to talk to someone you're apologizing to."

She sighed. "I guess not, but if the shoe fits..."

"Look, Patti Sue, I wasn't all that happy about Weave and Jolene taggin' along with us. You know how Weave is...he just kinda invites himself."

"That's your fault."

"I guess so. But he's my friend...my best friend."

"We're not gonna get into this discussion," she said. "I know you two are close and you don't see him the way everyone else does."

Her statement agitated him. "Just how does everyone else see him?"

"You don't wanna know," she said.

"Yeah...I do. Are you gonna tell me, or not?"

"He's a loser."

"Why, because he doesn't play football?"

"Randy Joe, you play football for the same reason Weave doesn't play. You're a winner and he's a loser."

"You know, Patti Sue, for a discussion that started off with an apology, you're gettin' real close to pissin' me off."

"I'm sorry," she said. "But I do hope the next time we go out...if you ever invite me again...there'll just be the two of us."

He asked, "This is all you wanted to talk to me

about...apologize and tell me Weave is a loser?"

"Well...not exactly."

"What else?"

"I don't want you to pitch for that nigger team."

The request surprised him and made him suspicious. He hadn't expected something like this from Patti Sue. She had never indicated prejudice toward anyone.

"Who put you up to this, Patti Sue?"

"No one."

"I don't believe that."

"A lotta people are concerned."

"What's a lot?"

"A lotta the kids here in school don't think it's a good idea."

"Really," Randy Joe said after taking a sip of his milk. "I didn't think the kids in this school gave a damn what I did. Tell me more."

"You're makin' fun."

"Yeah...I guess I am. The students here don't give a damn about doodley squat. And I don't think any of them, except for maybe Weave, gives a damn about what happens to me. So why don't you tell me the truth, Patti Sue...about who put you up to this."

"I'm tellin' the truth. Some of the parents have talked to some of the kids about it and they're hopin' you won't do it."

Randy Joe laughed. "So it's some of the parents tellin' their kids what I should do. You know what's amazing to me? I didn't even agree to pitch until Saturday night. Now the whole town knows about it. Simmy's not gonna have to advertise the game."

She pouted. "So you're goin' ahead with it."

"Yeah, I am. I don't know why you were the one chosen to talk to me, but I'm really sorry it was you."

"I guess everyone thinks we're close."

He paused before answering, then said, "I'd like to think we are. I'd like to think we're gonna be even closer. But I'm gonna pitch the game. I've given my word to a man and I don't go back on my word."

"You're talkin' about Simmy Weatherspoon," she said.

"Yeah...he's a man, isn't he? From what I know of him, I'd

come a whole lot closer to trustin' him than some of the white folks in Jason."

"Coach Marshall..."

"Coach Marshall? Why's his name comin' up in this conversation?"

"He came by the house yesterday and visited with my folks."

"Oh, yeah. Does he do that often?"

"Well...no."

"Let me guess...Coach Marshall talked to your folks about how I was gonna pitch for the Longhorns?"

"Yes, but I could have told them. You told me the night before."

"But you didn't. Why's that?"

"I just didn't think about it."

"When I told you about it Saturday night you didn't act like it was a big deal. At least, you didn't say anything about it. My guess is that it didn't bother you until Coach Marshall came to your house and talked to your folks."

She said, "The reason I didn't talk to you about it Saturday night was because Weave and Jolene were in the car. I didn't like it then any more than I do now."

"Did Coach Marshall say where he learned about my impendin' sin?"

"It's not funny, Randy Joe."

"So it's not funny. Are you gonna answer my question or not?"

She replied, "Coach Marshall said Big Bill told him about it."

Randy Joe shook his head in mock dismay, smiled and asked, "Can I assume, Patti Sue, that Coach Marshall wanted you to talk to me?"

She fidgeted. "He might have said something. But a lot of the kids asked me to say somethin', too."

It was easy enough for Randy Joe to figure. Coach Marshall had been out rallying the troops, most likely with the help of Big Bill. He was certain the coach hadn't gone only to Patti Sue's home. He'd probably gone to the homes of a number of his supporters.

"You'd better finish your lunch," Randy Joe told Patti Sue, chuckling. "When this stuff gets cold it turns to glue."

She knew the conversation about the game was over.

"I thought the movie was good Saturday night," she said.

"It coulda been better," he said, "if you'd been friendlier."

SEVEN

While Randy Joe Keegan was catching flak at the high school, Simmy Weatherspoon was basking in the glory of having talked the young man into pitching for the Longhorns.

"You done went and done it now, Simmy," said Zeke Lott. "Dat boy's de finest pitcher I ever seed."

Zeke was a baker for the town's only bakery. It was just one of his many jobs. He, along with his wife and kids, also had a cleaning service for local stores. And when Zeke wasn't baking or running a vacuum cleaner he might be mowing or weeding someone's yard. There was only one thing that would make Zeke quit working for a few hours. A baseball game. The man loved the game with all his heart and soul. He had watched every game that Randy Joe Keegan had ever pitched.

"I done told you now," Zeke continued, "dat boy's a natural. I done seed a lot of pitchers, but I ain't never seed one dat kin do what he can wid a baseball."

They were standing outside the bakery and Simmy was grinning from ear to ear. "You don't has to sell me on Randy Joe Keegan. I been watchin' dat boy pitch, too. And you right, Zeke, he's a natural born pitcher."

"Wid him throwin' fo' de Longhorns, dey ain't no tellin' how many folks gonna show up next Sunday," Zeke said. "How in de world did you git him to pitch fo' you? I know Randy Joe ain't got no quarrel with colored folks, but I done figured his folks wouldn't let him pitch fo' de Longhorns."

"Dey didn't seem to mind," Simmy said. "Dey's nice folks."

"Oh, I know dey's nice, but dey's some folks in dis town ain't gonna like Randy Joe pitchin' fo' no coloreds. What you gonna do 'bout dat, Simmy? You has to live wid dese folks."

Simmy shrugged his shoulders. "I ain't gonna say nothin' if dey don't say nothin'."

"You know some of 'em gonna say somethin', though."

"Maybe. We jest has to wait and see."

Simmy knew what he was doing. He'd watched Randy Joe Keegan perform on the football field and baseball diamond. He knew there was a special quality in the boy, a toughness hard to find in a grown man. And Simmy wasn't worried about catching flak from the white high school's administration. After all, they were using his baseball field free of charge for the school's baseball games.

He had two years earlier bought a baseball park from a defunct professional franchise in Louisiana. He'd brought the fences, the stands and the lights to Jason. And about two miles east of town, on land he owned, he'd built the finest baseball park within a seventy-five mile radius of Jason. The only baseball park better was the park used by the Beaumont club of the Texas League.

After his baseball stadium was built Simmy had invited the white high school to use it free of charge. His offer was quickly accepted because the school had been using a terrible facility near a rodeo arena. It had limited seating and no lighting. Simmy's park, on the other hand, seated five thousand, almost as many as the high school football stadium. And Jason's population was only seven thousand or so.

Simmy had never offered it to the black school. The black school played its baseball games on its football field where the shortest distance to the rightfield fence was no more than two hundred feet. Leftfield was forever.

When the white school played its games at Simmy's park there was segregated seating. The whites occupied the covered stands behind home plate and curving back along the first and third base lines. Further down the third base line were some uncovered stands where the coloreds sat. The situation was reversed when the Longhorns played, though as a rule white fans arrogantly sat anywhere they chose.

Simmy didn't mind. He wanted as many baseball fans as possible to attend Longhorns games. He didn't care where they sat. He didn't have a hard-on for whites because of segregation. He knew change was coming, that it was inevitable.

After his conversation with Zeke, Simmy drove his Cadillac over to Big Bill's Cafe, parked it in the back and went in the back door marked *Colored Only*. He ordered a cup of coffee from the cook, who also served as a waitress for the colored patrons.

While the serving area for whites in the front of the cafe couldn't be termed lavish, it was several steps up from the area Big Bill provided for Negroes. The counter for the latter was set amidst pots, pans and garbage cans. There was an open view of the grill and stove where the cook worked and the sinks where the dishes were washed.

Two other Negroes shared the counter with Simmy at eight-thirty a.m. Both were eating what he considered a late breakfast. He'd been up since four-thirty. He met with his pulpwood crews every weekday morning at five-thirty to give them instructions for the day.

"What's dis I hear 'bout you gettin' dat white boy...Mr. Randy Joe...to pitch fo' de Longhorns?" Nate Oliver asked between bites of biscuit and runny egg yolk.

Simmy put a generous helping of sugar in his coffee, stirred, sipped, then said, "You done heard right, Nate. Randy Joe...he gonna be pitchin' fo' de Longhorns next Sunday."

"Worst thing I ever heard," Nate grunted. "How de Longhorns gonna be an all-colored team if you has a white boy pitchin' fo' 'em."

Nate was in his seventies, wrinkled and outspoken. His fear had died the day he was forced to retire from the sawmill. Nate's resentment at his lot in life seemed to permeate his small frame.

He felt he'd been put out to pasture with a lot of good years left. Now he was forced to find whatever day work he could to supplement his Social Security check. And odd jobs were hard to find.

"I never said nothin' 'bout de Longhorns bein' no all-colored team," Simmy said. "De team we gonna be playin'...it's all white."

"Don't seem right," Nate said, argumentatively. "Dey's jest too many changes in de air to suit me. Like when dat boy Jackie Robinson done went up and started playin' wid dem Dodgers, like he was too good to play fo' de coloreds."

"My god, Nate," Simmy said, "Jackie Robinson's been wid de Dodgers six...seven years now. Dey's a lot o' coloreds playin' in de major leagues."

Nate argued, "Dat don't make it right. What you think, Tate?"

The question was directed to Nate's eating partner, Tate Moore, who seemed more interested in a biscuit and his coffee than in the conversation. Tate was probably the same age as Nate. He, too, had been let go by the sawmill because of his age and, like his friend, now did odd jobs to supplement his monthly Social Security check. Tate was an inch or two taller than Nate, but just as wrinkled.

"Whatever you says is fine wid me, Nate," Tate said. Simmy figured chances were pretty good that Tate didn't really hear the question because he had a hearing problem.

"Damn it, Tate, you need to has opinions of yo' own," Nate said.

Simmy asked, "Nate, why you think Jackie Robinson oughta not to be playin' wid the Dodgers. And what's wrong wid Randy Joe pitchin' fo' de Longhorns?"

Nate gave Simmy what passed for an incredulous look. "You know de Bible says dey ought not to be no mixin' of de races."

"I can't see where coloreds and whites playin' ball together is mixin' de races," Simmy said.

"What you call it den?"

"I jest call it playin' baseball...gettin' along wid one 'nother."

Nate grunted. "Simmy, you done be a smart man...everybody

know dat. But you don't know de scriptures."

"Where in the scriptures do it say whites folks and coloreds ain't 'posed to play baseball together?" Simmy asked.

"It's in de Bible," Nate assured. "It sho' is."

Simmy shook his head in mock dismay and said, "You get yo' Bible and show me, Nate."

Nate got up off his stool and said, "I ain't got no time now, Simmy. C'mon, Tate, we got yard work to do."

Simmy watched the two old men go out the back door of the restaurant, then returned to the serious business of drinking his coffee. The cook, a big, black jovial woman named Bertha, brought the pot and refilled his cup.

"What you think about all dis, Bertha?" Simmy asked.

"I ain't got no opinion," she replied. "I don't think Mr. Big Bill wants me to have no opinions."

Knowing Big Bill Perkins as he did, Simmy could identify with what Bertha was saying. Bill Big was not the kindest employer in Jason. He worked people long and hard, and for as little money as he could possibly pay them.

No sooner had Bertha sauntered back to the stove on her heavy legs than the door between the kitchen and front of the restaurant opened. And in walked Big Bill, a toothpick dangling from the corner of his lips. He immediately spotted Simmy and made his way to the counter.

"How's tricks, Simmy?"

"Jest fine, Big Bill."

"Glad to know things are goin' good for ya."

"Business good for you?" Simmy questioned.

Big Bill laughed. "Must be. I gotta bunch o' old Ford and Chevrolet cars and pickups parked in front of the place and your Cadillac parked in the back."

Simmy could read the envy and innuendo in Big Bill's voice. He knew the cafe owner didn't like colored people, except in positions comparable to slavery. It was one of the reasons he frequented Big Bill's place. Simmy knew he could buy and sell Big Bill several times over.

"Hear you gotta big game comin' up next Sunday against an all- white team," Big Bill said.

"Dat's right. We playin' an exhibition game 'gainst a professional team."

"And the Keegan boy's pitchin' for you?"

"Dat's right."

"You think that's a good idea, Simmy?"

"What you mean?"

"I mean...we never had no trouble between the coloreds and whites here in Jason. Don't you think this might stir somethin' up?"

Simmy feigned ignorance. "I can't see why."

"When you start mixin' whites and coloreds you're just askin' for trouble. I don't even think it's a good idea for your team to be playin' some all white team."

"Whites and coloreds works together at the sawmill," Simmy said. "Dey even plays softball together over at Milltown."

Big Bill's face flushed. "That's different. Ain't the same thing."

Again, Simmy feigned ignorance. "I don't understand."

Big Bill grunted. "Never mind...just take my word for it. It ain't the same. Just remember this town's been good to you, Simmy."

"Oh, dat's fo' sure," the pulpwood contractor said, patronizingly. "I ain't forgettin'."

"Well, it sure seems like it."

"Why you wanna say dat, Big Bill?"

"Usin' Randy Joe the way you're doin'...it ain't a good idea. You might think about that before next Sunday."

"Oh, I'll do dat, Big Bill."

The cafe owner's fat face took on a pleased look, as if he'd just solved all the world's problems. He believed he'd made Simmy see the light. "Well, I'm glad we got an understandin', Simmy."

Simmy smiled. "We got dat sure enough."

When Simmy drove his big Cadillac away from the cafe, past all the old Ford and Chevrolet cars and pickups, he was still smiling. He made a mental note to give Big Bill a free ticket to Sunday's game.

EIGHT

At baseball practice on Monday afternoon Randy Joe was expecting Coach Leon Rice to say something to him about his planned pitching debut for the Longhorns.

He didn't.

Rice seemed more intent on readying his charges for Tuesday night's game against Bridge City. It was a season-making game. If they won, it would be Jason's first bi-district baseball championship.

The school had come close the previous year, but had lost the championship game. A lot of people blamed Rice because he had chosen to start a senior pitcher instead of Randy Joe. The Bulldogs bi-district foe, Nederland, had bombed the senior for five runs in the first inning. Randy Joe relieved and pitched shutout ball the rest of the way, but the team hadn't been able to overcome Nederland's lead.

Randy Joe, who had won fifteen and lost none the previous year, didn't blame the coach. He was confident he could have won the game, but appreciated the coach's loyalty to the senior.

Randy Joe also appreciated the fact that Coach Rice didn't consider his teaching as secondary to coaching. He was as demanding in the classroom as on the baseball field.

The coach had played outfield for the University of Texas, then spent three years in the Cleveland Indians farm system. He was thirty-five years old, and had been at Jason for seven years.

Randy Joe had learned a lot of baseball from Rice, though most of his knowledge about pitching came from his father.

Randy Joe's Monday workout consisted of running, shagging flies and batting practice. Lefthand pitcher Monte Roper and righthander Dusty Jackson would be his relief if Bridge City caused him any grief. He knew neither player expected to see any action.

Roper, a senior, and Jackson, a junior, were town boys with limited ability. Roper had won two, lost three. Jackson had one win and one loss.

"Understand you're pitchin' for the nigger team next Sunday," Monte said as they were jogging along in the outfield.

"You understand right."

Dusty chipped in, "It's all over school...all over town."

"Good, maybe there'll be a big crowd. You guys gonna be there?" He knew if Monte and Dusty came to the game it would be with the hope of seeing him lose.

"I'm gonna be there," Dusty said, "if you pitch the game."

"Well, you're gonna be there then."

Monte said, "I hear there's some people tryin' to stop you from pitchin' it."

Randy Joe laughed. "You mean Coach Marshall? Hell, he can't stop me from doin' anything. I don't know why he wants to." Monte and Dusty were also on the football team and would eat a yard of Marshall's shit.

"Ever think he might be tryin' to stop you for your own good?" Monte asked. He had been the backup quarterback.

"Not in a million years. Anything that asshole does is for his own good. He's like an old woman...can't stop meddling in other people's business."

"It's not just Coach Marshall who doesn't want you pitchin' for the niggers," Dusty said.

"No, that asshole Big Bill doesn't want me to either. How 'bout your dad, Dusty...he say anything? I know Coach Marshall called him."

Dusty didn't deny the accusation. Randy Joe wasn't sure who all the coach had called. "I can't say he likes it much," Dusty said.

"And I can't see where it's any of his business, can you?"

Dusty's face flushed. Even the shade from the bill of his cap couldn't hide it. After a previous confrontation with Randy Joe, Monte had had to have some stitches. Everyone knew Randy Joe enjoyed fighting, that he could be animal-wild.

Monte said, "Ever occur to you, Randy Joe, that some people are just concerned about you makin' a mistake?"

"A mistake for who? Them or me?"

"Well, it's not gonna do anybody a lotta good," Monte replied.

Roper's father owned an insurance agency and Jackson's father was a management person for the local electric utility. Both had been on the school board and were staunch supporters of the athletic program, especially football.

"Only person it can hurt is me," Randy Joe said.

Dusty said, "You know some people are callin' you a nigger lover."

Randy Joe laughed. "Not to my face. You haven't been callin' me that have you, Dusty?"

"I know better."

"You know better than what...to call me that or to call me that to my face?"

Dusty forced a smile. "I know you ain't a nigger lover."

"No you don't."

Both Dusty's and Monte's faces showed confusion. They always had trouble reading Randy Joe. And they sure as hell didn't want to read him wrong.

"Damn, I hate this runnin'," Monte said.

"You're lucky you won't have to be runnin' for Coach Marshall in August," Dusty said. "I hear college coaches are easier than he is."

"I hope so," Monte said. He was going to Stephen F. Austin College at Nacogdoches, Texas on a football scholarship.

"Marshall's a pussy," Randy Joe said. "He just thinks he's tough."

"He's tough enough for me," Monte said.

"What he does is much ado about nothin'," Randy Joe said. "There's no reason for the shit he does. It's like doin' busywork in class."

"You never have liked him," Dusty said, "and I don't know why."

"I don't like him 'cause he's an asshole."

Neither Monte nor Dusty responded. Randy Joe was always trying to stir up trouble. "We've done enough runnin'," Monte said. "Let's shag some flies."

"Go ahead," Randy Joe said. "I'll spin my wheels some more."

Dusty didn't have to be asked twice to quit running. He and Monte positioned themselves in rightfield where they could talk and chase batting practice balls. "Coach Marshall talk to your dad?" Monte asked Dusty.

"Yeah...did he talk to yours?"

"Yeah."

"What do you think?"

"About what...the shithead pitchin' for the niggers?"

"Yeah, among other things," Dusty replied.

"I don't give a fuck what he does, but dad says it's only gonna stir up trouble for the rest of us."

"Yeah...that's what my dad says. He says they're already wantin' to go to school and church with us."

"That's just the troublemakers," Monte said. "The good ones don't want that. But I believe that bastard Randy Joe is a nigger lover."

"Shit, Monte, what do you expect? All those Milltown people live like niggers."

"You're right, Dusty. Randy Joe's nothin' but white trash...close to a nigger as you can get without bein' black."

"Your dad say anything about what's gonna be done to keep Randy Joe from pitchin' the game?"

"I heard him talkin' about there was goin' to be a lot of pressure put on that black bastard Simmy Weatherspoon."

"That's something I can't understand," Dusty said, "a nigger like him with all that money."

"Some damn Yankees are financin' him, you can bet on that. Hell, you know that team Randy Joe's supposed to pitch against is a white team...some major league farm club outta Louisiana. Those bastards who own the major league teams won't be satisfied 'til the niggers take over...proved it when they brought that fuckin' Jackie Robinson up."

Dusty lamented, "My dad says major league baseball is goin' to hell in a handbasket because of the niggers. Boxin' is already there."

They stopped talking when Randy Joe jogged by. "You two solving all the world's problems?" he asked.

NINE

Bridge City's first hitter stepped to the plate at exactly seven thirty-two on Tuesday night. Second baseman George Wilder was a stockily-built kid, five-nine, one-sixty. He was an excellent hitter, very aggressive at the plate.

Seconds after digging in, the righthand hitter was unconscious, a victim of Randy Joe Keegan's first high and inside fastball. The ball had clobbered the top of Wilder's head, then rolled up the backstop screen until it hit the tin roof covering the stands. The crowd that had been whooping it up went quiet with fear.

Randy Joe rushed to the aid of the fallen player, but was pushed back by coaches for both teams and by Wilder's teammates. He could only stand helplessly in the background, a lump in his chest making him hyperventilate while others tended to the injured player.

Along the fence that stretched down the third base line Iron Man Davis asked, "What Mr. Randy done hit dat boy in de head fo'?"

"De pitch jest got 'way from 'em," Hank Jones explained.

Hank had talked Iron Man into going to the game, the first time the older logger had ever been to a game involving white teams. He was there because of Randy Joe.

"Man dat dig in 'gainst Randy ain't gotta lotta sense," opined Sleepy Jones. He and Yank Johnson were standing with Hank and Iron Man.

"You de one ain't got no sense," Yank said. "How dat boy gonna know Mr. Randy as wild as he is?"

Sleepy came back, "He oughta know jest watchin' him warm up. You seed how wild he was den."

"Sleepy got a point, Yank," Hank said. "You jest has to look out there and see dat boy throws a few and you know dat you don't wanna be diggin' in on' 'im."

Iron Man said, "It don't look like it matter none what dat boy do. Mr. Randy throw atta man...ain't no way he gonna move quick enough to get outta de way."

"You has a point, too," Hank agreed.

Iron Man was wearing a plaid cotton shirt with his overalls. The faded blue overalls were clean, but he hadn't changed his worn-out brogans, which he was wearing with no socks. Hank was wearing new overalls, a new shirt, new brogans and no hat. His snow-white hair and beard glistened in the bright lights. Yank had duplicated Hank in dress, but Sleepy was splendor itself in perfectly-fitted pegged lavender slacks, pointed-toe black patent leather shoes with a mirror finish, and a black silk longsleeve shirt with the top three buttons open.

Sleepy's dress prompted Iron Man to say, "You keep spendin' all yo' money on clothes, you never gonna have nothin'."

"What you got?" Sleepy asked.

Yank laughed. "Iron Man's so tight he still got fo' cents o' de first nickel he ever made."

"So what good de money if he ain't gonna spend it?" Sleepy asked. "De old man gonna die and somebody else gonna spend it fo' 'em."

The game didn't get back underway until seven forty-five, after George Wilder had been taken to the hospital, still unconscious. Thinking about Wilder gave Randy Joe a queasy feeling in his stomach.

The second hitter for Bridge City was a fidgety Elton Riggs, right fielder and lefthand hitter. Riggs was on his tiptoes in the batter's box, ready to bail out in any direction. Randy Joe's first pitch was a fastball away, but Riggs' right foot went toward the dugout on the first base side. He should have been easy prey, but Randy Joe walked him on four straight pitches.

He asked for a new baseball. He paced around the mound rubbing it up, then stepped on the rubber to face first baseman Charley Nelson, Bridge City's leading hitter. Nelson, also a lefthand hitter, was clubbing the baseball at almost a four hundred clip.

Randy Joe also walked him on four straight pitches.

Bases loaded. No one out.

Coach Leon Rice made a visit to the mound. Monte Roper and Dusty Jackson started working in the bullpen. "You okay, Randy Joe?" Rice asked. Catcher Freeman Ware and the entire Jason infield had joined the coach at the mound.

The young pitcher shrugged his shoulders. "I guess."

"The boy you hit...he's gonna be okay."

Randy Joe could still vividly recall the sickening sound of the baseball hitting Wilder's head. Rice continued, "What you've gotta do is concentrate. Concentrate on each hitter. Concentrate. I know you can get these guys."

Randy Joe knew he could get them, too. But he had to put Wilder out of his mind, let the dream take over. It was a matter of mind control.

Suddenly, he wasn't in Simmy's ballpark. He was wearing pinstripes, standing on the mound at Yankee Stadium. The crowd noise was deafening and the guy standing at the plate in the gray uniform was threatening his dream.

Frank Carrier, Bridge City's third baseman, had been a defensive end on the football team and was hitting over three hundred, with twenty home runs. Both Carrier and Nelson were attracting a lot of attention from major league scouts, two of whom were in the stands.

Carrier had no way of knowing the kind of mood changes Randy Joe could go through in the course of a game. He just saw the junior righthander as somewhat wild and erratic, not the kind of pitcher to dig in on. He also figured that Wilder being hit in the head might be to his team's advantage, because it seemed to have shaken Randy Joe Keegan.

A righthand hitter, Carrier saw Randy Joe's first pitch coming right at him. He fell backwards out of the batter's box and the ball broke over the plate. He'd never seen such a curveball, nor had he ever seen a curveball that moved so fast. In the dugout he and his teammates had talked bravely, but they were really in awe of the kind of speed Randy Joe had on his fastball. Now Carrier swore that the first curveball thrown to him was faster than any fastball he'd ever faced.

Carrier prided himself on his great eyesight, his ability to pick up the rotation of the ball and immediately analyze what it was going to do. But the guy on the mound was too quick for his great eyes. He wanted to hang tough, but another curveball had him bailing out again.

"Striiike two!"

After what happened to Wilder there was no way Carrier was going to dig in. But he had to give a good account of himself. There were scouts in the stands, not to mention his parents and girlfriend. He couldn't let this pitcher make a monkey out of him.

With great resolve Carrier swung his bat over the plate a few times, then cocked it. He was ready, figured Keegan was going to give him another fast curveball.

Sure enough the curveball came, but it was ever so slow.

A changeup.

Carrier did his best to control the bat, but couldn't. He was way out in front of the pitch. All he could do was glare at the pitcher, toss his bat down in disgust and return to the dugout.

The crowd had been silent when Randy Joe hit George Wilder and walked the next two batters. With each strike to Carrier the crowd noise had intensified. The predominantly Jason crowd was back in the game, including Iron Man, Hank, Sleepy and Yank. They were all excited, almost jumping with joy.

"My partner...he make dat other boy look silly," Iron Man said.

"You ever try to hit a baseball, ol' man?" Sleepy asked.

"No...but it don't look all dat hard to me."

"Den you oughta try it," Yank said, laughing. "Maybe you can bat 'gainst Randy."

"I ain't in no hurry to hit no baseball," Iron Man said.

The number five hitter in the Bridge City lineup was left fielder Pete Manley, swinging from the right side. He was a nuisance hitter who made good contact with the ball. He was hitting above three hundred, had sixteen doubles on the year and no home runs.

Randy Joe didn't waste any time with him.

One blazing fastball peeled the peach fuzz off Manley's chin. Two dandy curves that caught the inside corner of the plate had him bailing out of the batter's box. Randy Joe then polished him off with a fastball on the outside corner.

Righthand hitter and center fielder Bobby Stills didn't have a prayer. He was six-feet tall, a hundred and fifty-five pounds, had a two seventy-five batting average and no home runs. He was always a threat to bunt and had a lot of walks. Stills, a sophomore, hoped to work Randy Joe for a base on balls. But his plan backfired. Randy Joe threw him three blazing fastballs that tailed in and nipped the inside corner. Stills was a nervous wreck when he meekly handed his bat to the batboy.

Max and Lisa Turner, Gretchen's parents, were sitting in seats just in front of R.M. and Bernice Keegan. A grinning Max turned and said, "Typical innin' for Randy Joe. A hit batter, two walks and three strikeouts."

R.M. laughed. "He hasn't thrown one in the stands...yet." Then in a more somber tone he said, "I just hope the kid he hit is okay."

"I'm sure he will be," Max said.

Bridge City was throwing a big righthanded submariner named Toby Fullwood. He had won fifteen, lost none, and had a minuscule earned run average. It was not as low as Randy Joe's but it was under two. He was a senior, stood six-feet, three inches tall and weighed one hundred and ninety-five pounds. He had attracted the attention of a lot of major league scouts who liked his size, his unique delivery, and the speed with which he could throw the ball.

The Jason Bulldogs had not faced a submariner during the

year, but Randy Joe liked the possibilities. Though he pitched righthanded he was a switch hitter and would bat from the left side against Fullwood.

Over the big speakers that reverberated through the ballpark the announcer boomed, "Leading off...center fielder Russ Petry."

The crowd responded with an appreciative rumble. Russ was a tough Milltown kid, just five-feet, nine inches tall and one hundred and forty pounds. But he could fly. He was a contact hitter, had an average just above three hundred, and was not afraid to take one for the team. The problem was Fullwood threw almost as hard as Randy Joe. The Bulldogs hadn't faced his kind of speed during the season.

Russ, swinging from the right side, had difficulty picking up the ball from the underhand delivery used by the big righthander. The ball seemed to rise, then dropped over the inside corner.

"Striiike one!"

The tough little junior got set again, cocked his bat and waited. Fullwood's next pitch was almost a duplicate of the first, but this time Russ swung and hit a nubber to the mound. Fullwood tossed him out with a flick of the wrist.

Second baseman Jordan Summers then stepped to the plate to the appreciative applause of the partisan crowd. He was a preacher's kid, one who wasn't a disappointment to his dad. Jordan, a senior, was a serious student, also serious about life and baseball. He was a .270 hitter and a hard out who almost always made contact with the ball.

Fullwood struck him out on three straight pitches, all of which rose from his release point and seemed to fall hard at the plate. The submariner's pitches were close to the speed of some of the best pitchers in the major leagues.

"Now batting for the Bulldogs...Randy Joe Keegan."

The announcement brought a rumble of intensified excitement from the big crowd, which numbered close to five thousand. Randy Joe, batting number three in the order, was not what was considered a normal pitcher when it came to hitting. He was a hard out, too, hitting twelve points over four hundred with twenty doubles and seventeen home runs. When he wasn't pitching he played shortstop or outfield.

Randy Joe had watched Fullwood carefully when he was pitching to Russ and Jordan. Because he was hitting from the left side he figured he had a little advantage over the first two hitters. No doubt that Fullwood was tough, but he felt like he could hit him.

Fullwood's first pitch was a fastball that came right at Randy Joe's head. He went sprawling to the ground and dust kicked up around home plate. The crowd booed and Fullwood exhibited some false concern. It had been a message pitch, pure and simple. Fullwood was saying, "You throw at us, we'll throw at you."

While the pitch raised the ire of the partisan crowd, it didn't bother Randy Joe. He had halfway expected it. It's what he would have done if a member of his team had been hit by a pitch. It was the way the game was supposed to be played. But when Fullwood knocked him down with the next pitch, that was a different matter. Enough was enough. He'd gotten the message.

"Dat boy tryin' to hit Mr. Randy," Iron Man said.

"It sho' look dat way," Hank agreed.

"He tellin' Randy not to hit any mo' of dere players," Sleepy said.

Yank laughed. "I wouldn't wanna be dat pitcher when he have to bat 'gainst Randy."

Randy Joe's temperature was rising, his anger bouncing off the walls of his brain like a ping-pong ball. He dug in, made sure that Fullwood knew he couldn't be scared.

Fullwood's next pitch picked up the black on the outside of the plate. Randy Joe knew it was a strike, but he let it go. He wanted something he could turn on, something he could pull. The Bridge City pitcher then came in with his version of a curveball, which also nicked the outside corner. It was still not the pitch Randy Joe wanted. He crowded even closer to the plate, guessing Fullwood would again try to pitch him outside.

Bridge City's senior catcher, Sonny Case, noticed that Randy Joe had moved closer to the plate. That's when he figured it was time to have Fullwood bring one on the inside corner, to fist Randy Joe and tie him up.

Fullwood got Case's message and went into his windup, but

just before he delivered the ball Randy Joe backed away from the plate. Again, it was a matter of playing the guessing game.

The pitch was a blur of a fastball, a lot of movement on it. But Randy Joe's eyes were fixed on the ball with the kind of concentration few people found possible. At just the right moment the bat started forward, the swing vintage Ted Williams. The ball exploded off the barrel of the bat, a screaming line drive that passed inches over the glove of leaping second baseman Don Ward.

Right fielder Elton Riggs and center fielder Bobby Stills were both off at the crack of the bat, but there was no way they could cut this drive off. It caromed noisily off the the green tin fence in right center field, about three hundred and seventy feet from home plate. By the time Stills got it back to the infield Randy Joe was standing on third base.

The crowd noise was a roar, almost drowning out the announcer. "Ladies and gentlemen, batting cleanup...third baseman Eddie Rouse."

Rouse was a town boy but not a snob. He was a junior. He was solid, a running back on the football team. But more important at the moment, he was a bona fide righthand power hitter with a three thirty-three batting average. He was a couple of homers short of Randy Joe's total. They were tied for runs batted in.

Fullwood started Eddie off with two high and inside pitches that had him bailing out of the batter's box. He then struck him out on three straight pitches.

There was a lot of spirit in the Bridge City dugout, much of it attributable to Fullwood. "C'mon, we can hit this guy. Let's nail the bastard."

Bridge City coach Corky Maurstad might have disapproved of the terminology used to describe Randy Joe Keegan, but he didn't hear it. He'd already gone down to the third base coaching box. His assistant coach occupied the first base coaching box.

Maurstad's mind was on the game, but he was also distracted with worry about George Wilder. What if the kid didn't make it? What was he going to say to the parents? He was glad Wilder's parents hadn't made the trip to Jason.

Then he received a breath of fresh air from the otherwise stifling hot and humid evening. The public address announcer's voice boomed, "Ladies and gentlemen...good news. George Wilder, the young man hit by the pitch, is okay. It was a mild concussion. He'll be back at the ballpark before the game's over."

The crowd voiced its approval and the lump in Maurstad's throat melted. He saw Randy Joe Keegan heave a sigh of relief.

Bridge City's number seven hitter was Sonny Case, a senior catcher who was two hundred pounds of muscle. Case had some power, but didn't make contact all that often. He had a mediocre batting average that could be forgiven because of his defensive skills. He was adept at digging balls out of the dirt with his mitt, blocking the plate and throwing out runners.

As big and strong as he was, the righthand hitter became a lightweight when he had to face Randy Joe's fastball and curve. He went down on three pitches, bailing out on two curveballs.

Bridge City shortstop Scott Painter was called a Punch-and-Judy hitter. He, too, fanned on three pitches.

That brought pitcher Toby Fullwood to the plate. In spite of his size he was not that great with the bat. He was hitting only .220 with no extra base blows. And when he stepped in the batter's box he was nervous. Randy Joe flashed a sly grin.

Fullwood's feet didn't want to stay still. He was standing on eggs. He wanted to exhibit a brave front but his legs felt rubbery. He knew what was coming.

Fastball — right under his chin. The Bridge City pitcher fell awkwardly in the dirt. He knew it was a message pitch.

Sleepy hooted, then said to Iron Man, Hank and Yank, "I done told you dat boy make a bad mistake when he throw at Randy."

Fullwood had faced fast pitchers before, though none as fast as Randy Joe Keegan. But he was not going to be bullied.

Randy Joe unleashed another blazing fastball that came inside about chest high and sat Fullwood on his butt again. The message was getting clearer. He'd thrown two at Randy Joe and now the Jason pitcher had thrown two at him. It was old-fashioned baseball.

When the Bridge City pitcher stepped back in the batter's box it was so gingerly that his spikes barely penetrated the ground. He was ready to bail out. Randy Joe finished him off with three fastballs.

The crowd was now very much into the game. Big Bill Perkins turned to Coach Vic Marshall, sitting next to him, and said, "Can you believe with all the trouble he had with the first three hitters the little shit's struck out six in a row?"

His mouth full of popcorn, Marshall said, "Hell, Big Bill, we both know Randy Joe Keegan's somethin' special on the baseball...and the football field."

Big Bill, who had a bag of popcorn of his own, agreed. "Right. That's why we've gotta keep him from screwin' up with that bunch o' niggers."

"I thought you told me you had an understandin' with Simmy?"

"I do...but you know you can't trust no nigger."

Marshall laughed. "A nigger will lie and a nigger will steal. Heard that all my life."

Down behind the chain-link fence on the third base line, just beyond the dugout occupied by the Jason Bulldogs, Simmy was talking to Zeke Lott, unaware of any agreement with Big Bill Perkins. It was something Big Bill had read into their conversation at the cafe.

"What I tell you?" Zeke said. "I done told you Randy Joe would get hisself straightened out."

"You didn't have to tell me," Simmy responded. "I done seed de boy pitch befo'. But he sho' has a wild streak."

"Dat's what makes him good. Ain't no hitter gonna dig in on him."

Simmy said, "What makes him good is dat fastball and curve. Now, bein' a little wild don't hurt nothin' either."

Lewis Alexander, a tough Milltown kid led off the bottom of the second for Jason. Lewis was wiry and fragile-looking, weighing just a hundred and forty-five pounds. He was a lefthander, played right field.

Fullwood, still shaken by the close pitches from Randy Joe, had trouble finding the plate. He got one pitch over, but ended up walking Lewis. That got the crowd excited because Lewis could fly. He didn't hit with power, but when he got on base he was always a threat to steal. The problem was that Fullwood had a good move to first and Bridge City's catcher, Sonny Case, had a great arm.

Coach Rice gave Gary Steele the bunt sign. Gary, a town boy who played first base, didn't like the signal. He was a lefthander from Smart Aleck City and thought he could pull the ball on any pitcher, except for Randy Joe. He didn't even like to take batting practice when his teammate was throwing at half-speed.

Gary decided to ignore the sign. His dad was one of the wealthiest men in town, a big wheel on the school board, and could buy and sell Leon Rice several times over. Besides, he was a senior. This was his last game, and he would, by god, play it his way. So he moved his out-of-shape five-foot, ten-inch, two hundred pound body into the batter's box, got ready and cocked his bat.

Gary Steele was not a good hitter, except in his mind. If Fullwood had blazed away with his best stuff chances are that Gary wouldn't have touched the ball. But the Bridge City pitcher was still a little shaky and took something off. Gary hit a nice hopper to shortstop Scott Painter, who flipped to Don Ward at second, who relayed to Charley Nelson at first for a bang-bang doubleplay. Rice buried his face in his hands.

Sullen, Gary returned to the dugout. Randy Joe slammed him against the back wall. "Why in the hell didn't you bunt?"

A lot of people could scare the pudgy first baseman. Randy Joe was at the top of the list. Gary thought Randy Joe was an unwinnable fight waiting to happen. He saw him as volatile and crazy. "I...I didn't see the signal," he replied, fearfully.

"You lyin' sacka shit," Randy Joe said. "You saw it. You just think you're too smart to follow coach's directions. Miss another signal and I'll personally kick your ass."

Jason's six-foot, one-eighty catcher Freeman Ware stepped to the plate and promptly singled up the middle. His hit made Gary Steele's failure all the more glaring. If Lewis Alexander had been sacrificed to second he would have scored easily.

Freeman, who was also a tough cookie from Milltown, died at first when left fielder Charley Thurman went down on strikes.

In the third inning the top of Bridge City's order was up again, but this time there were no hit batsmen and no bases on balls. Randy Joe went through the trio like a knife through warm butter, striking all of them out.

"That's nine strikeouts in a row," Gretchen said to Weave and Jolene, who had ridden to the game with her parents.

"I imagine Randy Joe would trade a few of those strikeouts for a couple o' runs," Weave said. "That guy Fullwood looks pretty tough."

Angrily, Jolene said, "We would have a run if that pussy Gary Steele hadn't hit into a doubleplay."

Weave laughed. "Whoa now. We woulda had a run if he'd gotten Lewis to second. And what's with you callin' him a pussy."

"He is."

"I ain't denyin' that," Weave said, "but it kinda surprises me when somethin' like that comes outta your mouth."

Gretchen chuckled. "Don't be a weenie, Weave. I'll bet you've used the word often enough." Then she continued in a whisper, "Why isn't it okay for us girls to say 'fuck,' I wonder?"

Weave's face flushed red. He glanced around to make sure she hadn't been heard, then he whispered, "Damn it, Gretchen, it ain't ladylike."

"Do you think Randy Joe would like me more if I was more ladylike?"

"Hell, I don't know...probably."

"Then I'll give it a whirl," she said.

Lewis Foster led off the bottom of the first for the Bulldogs. He was a slightly-built Milltown boy who played shortstop when Randy Joe was pitching or wasn't playing the position. Though he was hitting in the ninth spot he was a pretty tough out. Fullwood, however, had now regained his composure and was throwing with the confidence he exhibited in the first inning. Lewis went down on strikes.

Russ Petry then came to the plate and hit a pop fly to right that was hauled in by Elton Riggs. Jordan Summers was again a strikeout victim.

In the dugout Fullwood again exhorted his rejuvenated teammates. Coach Maurstad had words of encouragement before taking his station in the third base coaching box. They were all finding it hard to believe that Randy Joe had struck out nine in a row.

"He ain't that good," Sonny Case said with false bravado. "We can hit this guy."

Frank Carrier, Pete Manley and Bobby Stills, the numbers four, five and six hitters, couldn't. They all went down on strikes.

Randy Joe was leading off the bottom of the fourth, causing Zeke to ponder with Simmy, "Wonder how dis boy Fullwood gonna throw to Randy Joe? He hit 'em hard de last time."

"He look like he throwin' pretty good," Simmy said. "You think he gonna throw at Randy Joe dis time?"

Zeke laughed. "He ain't no fool."

Randy Joe's stance at the plate exuded confidence. Fullwood wanted to throw at his adversary, to show him that he was in control, but realized he was going to be batting third in the top of the fifth.

It wasn't intentional. Maybe it was just his subconscious telling him what to do. Fullwood walked Randy Joe on four outside pitches. With every ball he threw the partisan crowd booed.

"Damn, talk about a downer," Max Turner said.

R.M. Keegan smiled. "What would you have done?"

Max grinned. "Probably the same thing Fullwood did."

Fullwood threw several times to first to keep Randy Joe close, but he primarily concentrated on hard-hitting third baseman Eddie Rouse. It was not Eddie's night. Fullwood got him on strikes.

Then little Lewis Alexander poked a single up the middle. Randy Joe would, ordinarily, have raced to third. But the center fielder was playing Lewis extremely shallow. He halted at second.

Gary Steele came to the plate again. And this time Fullwood, his confidence back in place, showed him no mercy. He struck him out on three pitches.

It was up to catcher Freeman Ware to knock the run home. He tried. He hit a long drive to the warning track in left, but Pete Manley made a spectacular catch.

Patti Sue said to her parents Arthur and Nancy Trainor, "Twelve straight strikeouts. Wonder if Randy Joe can keep it up."

Her dad laughed. "Well, I can see why those niggers want 'im pitchin' for 'em."

"Hush," Nancy said, looking furtively around them. "You're talkin' too loud, Arthur."

The Bridge City Cardinals sent the bottom third of their order to the plate in the top of the fifth. Their gray uniforms with red piping and letters were sodden evidence of the humid evening. But their tour at the plate was shortlived. Randy Joe sat them all down on strikes.

"My god, fifteen straight strikeouts," Vic Marshall said. Even though he didn't like baseball he could appreciate what was happening.

"They ain't got no hits either," Big Bill said.

Marshall said to J.D. and Dorothy Lake who were sitting nearby, "Ever see anything like this, Mr. Lake?"

Lake shook his head, affirming he hadn't.

In Jason's bottom of the fifth Charley Thurman bounced an easy grounder to second and was thrown out. Light-hitting Lewis Foster struck out, but Russ Petry flared a single to left. That brought up Jordan Summers who tapped a slow roller down the third base line. Frank Carrier couldn't get a handle on it so Jordan was safe at first.

Two on, two out and Randy Joe Keegan stepping to the plate. Coach Corky Maurstad decided it was time to visit the mound. "How you feelin'?" he asked.

"Fine, coach."

"You wanna pitch to this guy?"

"Yeah, I wanna pitch to him."

The infielders and catcher had joined the coach at the mound. "Okay," he said, "Keegan's dangerous. Remember, we just need one. You guys drop back as far as you can and just try to knock anything down in the holes. We still have a base open here, so don't let anything get through."

Fullwood knew his best pitch was a fastball. If he was going to be beaten he wanted it to be on his best pitch. He figured on throwing his counterpart nothing but fastballs, his very best fastballs.

He looked in at Randy Joe and hated him. The guy seemed so confident, so ready. He looked as though he could hit the best Bob Feller had to offer. That's when Fullwood lost his concentration, when he again couldn't find the plate. All his pitches sailed outside.

Randy Joe trotted to first and the other two runners moved up a notch. Bases loaded and Eddie Rouse at the plate. Fullwood knew Rouse was supposed to be almost as good a hitter as Keegan, but for some reason he didn't fear him. He'd already rung him up twice on strikeouts. He did it a third time.

There were two major league baseball scouts in the stands, both of whom had come to watch Bridge City's Toby Fullwood and Frank Carrier. They'd heard about Randy Joe Keegan, but the boy was only a junior. They'd never seen him play.

Yankees scout Tommy McGuire asked his counterpart, "What do you think about Keegan?"

"Little thin to be a starter, don't know if he could take the grind of a pro season," replied Pirates scout Slap Peterson.

McGuire knew Peterson was lying through his teeth, that he'd sign Randy Joe Keegan quicker than a frog could zap a fly. But he could play the game, too. "Yeah, Slap, you're probably right."

They looked at each other and both started laughing.

"You gonna be hangin' around Jason a lot next spring, are you? Peterson asked.

"You damn well better know it," McGuire said.

"I guess we'll see a lot of each other then."

In the top of the sixth Randy Joe again faced the top of the Cardinals order. Don Ward was an easy strikeout victim. So was Elton Riggs and Charley Nelson. But things fell apart with the strikeout of Nelson. Freeman Ware dropped the third strike.

That wasn't unusual with the kind of stuff Randy Joe had. It was just a matter of Freeman throwing out the speedy Nelson, who was off and running after swinging and noticing that the catcher had blocked, not caught the ball. Freeman had ample time to throw Nelson out. He threw Gary Steele a perfect strike, but the first baseman was hotdogging it and the ball caromed off his glove and into foul ground down the right field line. Nelson went all the way to third.

If looks could have killed, Gary Steele would have been dead. It wasn't just Randy Joe. Most of the team, with a few notable exceptions, wanted his hide. Monte Roper and Dusty Jackson were secretly glad about what happened. They were hoping Bridge City would score and Randy Joe Keegan would lose. A championship wasn't as important as their hatred.

Two down and Frank Carrier at the plate. Randy Joe had owned the third baseman, striking him out on his two previous at bats. This time he got two strikes on Carrier, but when he tried to get a third one by the big guy got wood on the ball.

It wasn't much, just a softly hit ball down the first base line.

But Gary Steele booted it.

There was a collective moan from the crowd, all of whom thought the grounder meant Bridge City's half of the inning was over. But now Charley Nelson had crossed home plate with the first run of the game and Carrier was on first. It seemed almost anti-climactic when Randy Joe whiffed Pete Manley to record his nineteenth strikeout in six innings.

Anna Louise Lake was sitting with her best friend, Doris Mason, trying to show the proper concern for what happened. "I feel so sorry for Gary," she said. "He always tries so hard."

Doris agreed and said, "Everybody's gonna blame Gary if we lose the game. But it's Freeman's fault. He should've caught the ball."

Anna Louise nodded. "I can guarantee you Randy Joe will be on Gary's case. He's such a perfectionist...in everything."

"Hard to understand," Doris said, "him bein' from Milltown."

"Daddy says he's the proudest poor boy he's ever met."

"You're not serious about him are you, Anna Louise?"

"Oh, no...we're just friends. Daddy says it's good to know people from all walks of life. But you don't have to get in bed with them."

"Do you realize what you said?" Doris asked, laughing. Anna Louise smiled. "That is kind of funny...isn't it?"

Doris said, "My daddy says Randy Joe wants to pitch for that nigger team 'cause he's hateful and wants to give the town a black eye."

"Mother and daddy talked about it. I think some people are gonna stop him from doin' it."

Lewis Alexander did his best to get something started for Jason. He worked Fullwood to a three-two count and then slapped a hard grounder to short. He was easily thrown out.

Gary Steele stepped to the plate to a very scattered ovation. Many in the crowd wanted to boo, but they didn't. There were some optimists in the crowd who believed in miracles, that Gary would redeem himself with a big hit, maybe even a home run. But Gary didn't rise to the occasion. He struck out, weakly.

Freeman Ware was a clutch player, one who had proved his mettle many times. When Fullwood got a pitch on the inside corner he slapped it between short and third for a base hit. The effort was wasted, however, because Charley Thurman grounded to short.

When Randy Joe stepped on the mound to begin the seventh and final inning he had a no-hitter and nineteen strikeouts in six innings. Yet he was trailing one to nothing and in danger of losing the game.

Cardinals center fielder Bobby Stills, twice a strikeout victim, was the first hitter. This time he faced Randy Joe with more confidence. The unearned run, the way Fullwood was pitching, it all contributed to a newfound winning spirit among the Bridge City players.

Randy Joe was aware of what was happening, the way momentum had slipped away from his team with Gary Steele's two errors. So he threw Stills a pitch high and tight, sending him sprawling.

Stills got back into the batter's box, but it was with less confidence. He'd been brought back to earth. The kid on the mound was one mean sonofabitch. So there really wasn't any contest. Randy Joe was still throwing his fastball at ninety-plus miles-per-hour and still had a curveball that made righthand hitters bail out of the batter's box. He seemed to be getting stronger.

Stills went down on strikes.

So did catcher Sonny Case.

When weak-hitting shortstop Scott Painter came to the plate, Randy Joe summoned his catcher. They met halfway between the mound and home plate and talked briefly, then went back to their positions. The crowd murmured its surprise. Randy Joe was giving Painter an intentional base on balls. It was so unexpected that Coach Rice couldn't get out of the dugout quickly enough to stop it. He buried his face in his hands.

Randy Joe Keegan could be exasperating and unpredictable. Some of the things he did were looney tunes. But then Rice realized what his young hurler had done this time. He'd walked the weak-hitting shortstop so he could pitch to Fullwood. That's when a real lump of fear welled up in the coach's throat. Was Randy Joe going to throw at Fullwood? What did he have in his mind?

Fullwood's mind was working overtime, too. He had hoped that he wouldn't have to face Jason's wild young pitcher again. He was hoping his team would go down one-two-three, and that he could then go out and do the same to the Jason team. He was confident that one run was enough. But Randy Joe's unnecessary action had now shaken him. It had also shaken the entire Bridge City team, including Coach Maurstad.

"Careful up there," Maurstad told Fullwood.

The warning was unnecessary. The Cardinals pitcher approached the plate cautiously. It didn't give him any peace of mind to look out on the mound and see Randy Joe smiling.

Fullwood took his stance, swung his bat tentatively, then cocked it. He was further surprised when Randy Joe signaled that he was going to throw a curveball. He didn't know what to think, didn't know whether or not to believe his adversary, didn't understand why the Jason pitcher would make such a gesture.

But Fullwood was determined to stand strong against anything thrown to him. What he saw was a pitch coming right at him. And fast. He had no choice but to bail out of the batter's box.

"Striiike!" the umpire hollered. The beautiful curveball

broke right over the inside corner.

Randy Joe signaled that his next pitch was going to be a fastball. It was, but it almost too fast for Fullwood to see. The ball ran in on his wrists and Fullwood found himself swinging at it anemically, reluctantly, like he was trying to fight off a bee that was too close.

It became painfully clear in Fullwood's mind why his adversary had intentionally walked Scott Painter. He wanted to humiliate him, to make him look weak and foolish in front of his parents, his girlfriend, his teammates and the big league scouts in the stands. Fullwood's anger boiled. He wanted to somehow humiliate Randy Joe Keegan in front of this big crowd, his friends and teammates.

There was no way he was going to do it with the bat. Randy Joe signaled that he was going to throw a curveball, did, and punched Fullwood out on strikes.

Randy Joe came into the dugout and Leon Rice asked, "What was that all about?" Randy Joe shrugged his shoulders. He didn't want to talk about it. And Rice had to take his place in the third base coaching box, which kept him from trying to get an answer.

Fullwood, after receiving instructions from his coach, went to the mount to face Jason's number nine hitter, shortstop Lewis Foster. Lewis had struck out in his previous two appearances and Fullwood didn't anticipate any trouble from him on his third trip. However, Fullwood was still simmering from humiliation at Randy Joe's hands and Lewis was determined to get on base. The young shortstop worked the count to two-two, then dropped a soft liner into right field for a base hit.

Coach Leon Rice played it by the book. When at home play to tie, when on the road play to win. So he gave Russ Petry the bunt sign. Fullwood knew what to expect so he threw the pitch high and tight, hoping the Jason hitter would pop up the bunt attempt. Russ laid off the pitch and took it for ball one.

Fullwood again delivered the pitch high and tight and the Bulldogs centerfielder didn't offer.

"Ball two!"

Fullwood knew he couldn't risk another ball. Russ knew it, too. When the submariner got his next pitch out over the plate and about waist high the Jason hitter laid down a perfect sacrifice bunt. It was fielded by third baseman Frank Carrier, who threw him out at first.

Now Lewis Foster was at second in scoring position. Any kind of hit through the infield and the fleet Lewis would score. The responsibility for getting that hit was in the hands of Jordan Summers, who had struck out twice and been on by an error. The Bulldogs second baseman again proved no match for Fullwood. The big righthander struck him out on three pitches.

The big crowd's stomping and noise shook the stands. Coming to the plate was Randy Joe Keegan, which prompted Coach Maurstad to visit the mound. It was a signal for the catcher and infielders to join him.

Toby Fullwood had pitched a heckuva game. No runs, six hits and eleven strikeouts. His effort paled only in comparison to Randy Joe's twenty-two strikeouts and no hits. But Bridge City had the lead and Maurstad wanted to keep it.

"Okay, okay," he said, "one more out and we've got'em. Now, Toby, we've got first base open...so do you wanna pitch to this guy? You've struck out the hitter after Keegan three straight times."

For Maurstad even to suggest the possibility of walking the Jason hitter went against all his baseball experience. The book said, never put the winning run on base. But something about Randy Joe Keegan made the Bridge City coach want to go against the book, against all his experience.

Maurstad was a good coach, though, a players coach, and thought the final decision ought to rest with Fullwood. After all, he'd been tough when it counted. It had been his mound work over the season that had brought them to this championship game.

"I wanna pitch to him," Fullwood said. Subconsciously, he might have felt it was the only way he could regain the respect of his teammates, which he thought Randy Joe had taken away from him in the top of the seventh.

"Okay," Maurstad agreed, "but don't give him anything good to hit. Remember, first base is open."

Still seething, Fullwood looked at the confident lefthand

swinger standing in the batter's box. He wasn't going to hotdog it, but he was going to make Randy Joe remember him. His first pitch was high and inside, causing Randy Joe to hit the dirt. The next pitch was a duplicate, causing the same result.

Fullwood wasn't worried. He had good control. He knew he could still strike out Randy Joe. But his adversary didn't look a bit worried. He just stood there in his white uniform with the maroon letters and piping, swinging his big bat nonchalantly. Fullwood wanted to knock him down again, but knew he had to get his third pitch over the plate.

He did.

Over the fat part of the plate.

He heard the sickening crack of the bat, then stood and watched the ball sail over the rightfield fence three hundred and sixty-feet from home.

TEN

On Wednesday Randy Joe basked in the glory of the school's first baseball championship. It did not, of course, bring the accolades of a football championship. Football was king at Texas high schools.

But there was excitement enough. It was, after all, the first no-hitter ever thrown by a Jason High School pitcher. And the most strikeouts ever recorded by a Bulldogs pitcher in a seven inning game.

Randy Joe held all the school records. He'd pitched several one- and two-hit games, but had always lost possible no-hitters to fluke or scratch hits. Now he'd pitched his first and it came at the best possible time, in a championship game.

The twenty-two strikeouts was a milestone. He had averaged fourteen strikeouts per game during his high school career.

Randy Joe was most excited about the two major league scouts he had met after the game. They'd asked him when he'd be pitching again and he'd said Sunday, for the Jason Long-horns. The revelation hadn't made them look at him as though he had a forked tail and pitchfork.

But in school he was feeling the cold wind of change toward him. Many of the town kids who'd been friendly in the past now ignored him. He figured it was an attitude passed on by their parents. And he believed some of the parental concern was orchestrated by Coach Marshall.

After class Marshall again confronted him about pitching for the Longhorns. "You given any thought to what we talked about on Monday?"

"Well, to tell you the truth, coach, I've been kinda busy...you know, thinkin' about the game against Bridge City. And next week we have finals and all."

Marshall shook his head and uttered a kind of disgusted grunt. "You can bullshit everybody else, but don't try to bullshit me, Randy Joe. That mind of yours is always spinnin', always plottin'."

Randy Joe laughed. "Damn, coach, I don't know what you're talkin' about. Is it algebra?"

Marshall scowled. He figured his student already knew more algebra than he did, as if that mattered. Teaching algebra was an ordeal he endured to coach high school football. "You better start thinkin' about what you're doin', Randy Joe. Remember, what you're plannin' to do affects a lotta people."

"I'll think about it," Randy Joe promised, though he'd already made up his mind. He just hoped Simmy wouldn't chicken out on the deal. He was pretty sure the Longhorns owner was being pressured, too.

He talked to Coach Rice after biology class. Rice hadn't said a word about him pitching for the black team. "I'm not gonna tell you to do it or not do it," Rice said. "That's a decision you have to make on your own."

"What I don't understand is why so many people are gettin'

so uptight about it," Randy Joe said. "You'd think I was plannin' to steal somethin' or kill somebody."

Rice laughed. "Some people probably think what you're doing is worse. You're making 'em think of what's coming...of what people know in their hearts is coming but don't want to admit or accept."

"What do you mean?"

"Ten...twenty years from now people right here in Jason won't think anything about a white boy playin' ball with Negroes. That's because Negro kids will be going to school right here, be involved in everything white students are involved in."

"You really think that's gonna happen?" Randy Joe asked.

"It's inevitable. The South can't hide its head in the sand forever. You know that, Randy Joe. So does every other intelligent person in this town. That's why you concern them...you're hurryin' the process. Stirring up the winds of change."

Randy Joe chuckled. "It's more like a storm with some people. But hey, coach, I wouldn't even have thought about pitchin' for the Longhorns if Simmy hadn't asked me."

Rice smiled. "Simmy...now there's a man who knows a lot more than most people around here think he knows. He comes on as the poor old uneducated colored man who got lucky, but he knew exactly what he was doin' when he asked you to pitch for his team."

"Are you sayin' he's using me?"

"The way I see it," Rice replied, "the two of you are usin' each other. You're gettin' a chance to do what you want...play baseball...and he's gettin' a helluva pitcher, plus a chance to make a little local history. Simmy's a smart man. He knows change is on the way and he wants to be one of the instigators."

"You'd better watch what you say, coach, or some people will be calling you nigger lover the way they're callin' me."

"I've been called worse," Rice said.

"You're not against it...the Negroes going to school with us?"

"Should I be?"

"I don't know. I've always been taught it wasn't right."

"You must not have believed it," Rice said, "or you wouldn't be playin' ball with them."

"That's different."

"Is it?" Rice questioned. "It takes more cooperation to play ball together than it does to sit in a classroom together. It takes more cooperation to work together than to go to school or church together."

Randy Joe knew he was right. He and catcher Freeman Ware depended a lot more on each other on the baseball field than in the classroom. That was true of his relationship with all the players. And in felling a big cypress tree he worked a lot closer with Iron Man than he ever worked in school with his classmates.

"I guess you're right, but I can't see it happenin' anytime soon."

"I said ten...twenty years. It might take a hundred. There'll be lots of resistance, lots of anger on both sides. People will be hurt...even killed. But change is inevitable. People in this town know it...maybe only subconsciously, but they know it. And they hate it and are gonna resist it as long as possible."

"I guess Big Bill will be a leader in resistin' it."

Rice smiled. "How Big Bill can think he's better than anyone else...well, I can't understand it."

Randy Joe knew Big Bill wasn't high on Rice's list. The baseball coach wasn't high on Big Bill's either.

"But enough about that," the coach said. "Do you wanna tell me why you walked the number eight hitter last night to get to Fullwood?"

Randy Joe shrugged his shoulders. "No particular reason. It just seemed like the thing to do at the time."

"Well, it worked out okay," Rice said, "but I can't say something like that's ever a good idea. Keep on pulling stunts like that and one of these days one of 'em will backfire on you."

"You're probably right," Randy Joe said.

The rest of the day passed slowly, the way days always did when the school year was winding down. Randy Joe felt an advanced case of laziness in his bones. Maybe it was what some people called spring fever. It disappeared when the bell rang ending his final class.

It was about two miles to school. He walked it morning and evening, except in bad weather, when his mother drove him and his sisters. The residents of Milltown had registered complaints with the school board about the lack of a school bus for the sawmill community, but their words fell on deaf ears.

Randy Joe had never minded the walk to and from school. It gave him time to think and, because his sojourn took him through what was known as downtown Jason, he'd met a lot of interesting people over the years. One of those was Zeke Lott.

The baker yelled a greeting and Randy Joe crossed the street to talk to him. "You sho' pitched a fine game last night," Zeke said.

"You were there?"

"You know I ain't never missed no game you ever pitched."

"I know...but I didn't see you."

"Dat was a big crowd...biggest I ever seed at de park. Finest game I ever seed, too."

"Yeah...I guess we were lucky."

Zeke feigned disbelief. "What you mean lucky? Dey ain't no luck to it. You jest one fine baseball player."

Randy Joe liked Zeke's compliment, but said, "Well, it never hurts to have a little luck, too."

"Dat wasn't luck you got dem twenty-two strikeouts, or when you hit dat ball over de fence. You fix it where dat pitcher got no choice but to pitch to you or be a coward. You ain't walked dat boy ahead of'im, ain't no way he gonna pitch to you."

"I don't guess we'll ever know," Randy Joe said. "But to tell you the truth, I don't know why I walked the guy to get to Fullwood...just somethin' in my mind told me to do it."

"You keep listenin' to yo' mind," Zeke said, "and you do okay. And you come by de bakery in the mornin'. I has a dozen donuts fo' you."

Zeke always gave him a dozen donuts when he pitched a good game. He'd collected a lot of donuts over the years. As for listening to his mind, Coach Rice had indicated that might not always be a good idea.

"You gonna be at the game Sunday?" Randy Joe asked.

Zeke again showed dismay. "You know I ain't gonna miss

dat game. I wanna see you play against de pros outta Lake Charles."

"Pros," Randy Joe mused. "They might rough me up. It won't be like pitchin' to high school kids." He didn't believe it, but it seemed the right thing to say.

"You throw like you did last night and dey ain't nobody gonna rough you up," Zeke assured.

Randy Joe exchanged a few more pleasantries with Zeke and then headed east until he came to Main Street. He figured it wasn't the kind of a street that people wrote poetry about, or even mentioned in letters to their relatives. It looked pretty much like the Main Street of any small town of Jason's size.

Randy Joe turned left on Main and walked past the First State Bank, past a gift shop, a drugstore, the movie theater, a five and dime and a furniture store. He crossed a street, then turned right and crossed Main to another drugstore. It was a hangout for high school kids because it had a bigger soda fountain than Jason's other drugstore.

He acknowledged greetings as he walked past the magazine and pulp novel racks, the racks filled with greeting cards and the counter and shelves lined with perfumes and cosmetic products. Like the other drugstore in town, non-prescription drugs occupied only a small space. And it was a gift shop, beauty supply house and book store besides being a soda fountain.

"Here, Randy Joe," said Anna Louise Lake. She'd already occupied a booth. Sitting across from her was Doris Mason. He preferred a snake's company to that of Doris Mason.

Seats at the booths were a sickly green vinyl. Randy Joe scooted in beside Anna Louise and ordered a cherry Coke. The girls had milkshakes.

"Crowded," Randy Joe said, observing that every booth and table was occupied. "You'd think some of these clowns would be home studyin'...gettin' ready for finals."

Anna Louise smiled, but Doris laughed and said, "Maybe they're smart enough they don't have to study. And come to think of it, why aren't you home studyin'?"

Randy Joe had hoped Doris wouldn't speak, just sit there like a manikin with her Orphan Annie hair, oversized mouth and eyes that gave the distinct impression that no one was home. "I've been studyin' all year," he said. "I'm ready. Besides, Doris, I was making conversation. I was hopin' there wouldn't be such a crowd here."

"You seemed to enjoy the crowd last night."

"Well...that was different."

"It was a wonderful game," Anna Louise said, hoping to change the direction of the conversation and curb the hostility that always existed between her friend and Randy Joe. "Daddy said there was a big writeup about it in the Beaumont paper."

"It was a nice writeup," Randy Joe agreed.

"My daddy said two big league scouts talked to you after the game," Doris said.

"Yeah...one from the Yankees and one from the Pirates."

"What did they say?" Anna Louise asked.

"They said they'd be watchin' me...Sunday and next year."

"Sunday," Doris said, making a face. "You're not gonna pitch for those niggers, are you? I heard some people in town were going to stop you from doin' it."

Randy Joe laughed. "How in the hell is anyone gonna stop me?"

"Randy Joe, do you think it's a good idea?" Anna Louise asked. "I mean...why stir up things unnecessarily?"

"Well, Anna Louise, to answer your questions...yeah, I think it's a helluva good idea. And I'm not doin' it to stir anything up. I just wanna play baseball ."

"What Anna Louise is tryin' to tell you," Doris said, "is that what you're plannin' to do can't do you any good in this town."

Randy Joe sucked some of his cherry Coke through a straw and said, "What can and can't do me any good in this town doesn't mean a rat's...well, this isn't where I'm plannin' to live the rest of my life. People oughta have better things to do than try to mind my business."

"Jason's a good town, Randy Joe," Anna Louise said. "There are a lot of good people here. Some of them just want what's best for you."

He laughed. "Sure they do."

"What Anna Louise is tellin' you," Doris said, "is that this town's been good to you and you oughta appreciate it."

"You know, Doris, if Anna Louise wants to tell me somethin' she's perfectly capable of doing it without your help. If you haven't noticed, I'm sittin' right here beside her."

"Doris is just tryin' to be helpful," Anna Louise said.

"Then let her be helpful to someone else," Randy Joe said, angrily. "It seems everybody knows what's best for me...Coach Marshall, everyone. I'm gonna make my own decisions, though. It's my life."

His outburst quieted Anna Louise and Doris. There was an awkward silence. "Okay, I'm sorry," he said. "I just don't need a lotta people tellin' me what to do. I don't care how well-meaning they are."

Anna Louise sighed, then said, "What are your plans this summer?"

He laughed. "Oh, for six days a week I'll be working in the swamp...cuttin' cypress trees ten hours a day."

"That sounds interesting," she said.

He laughed again. "It's interestin' if you like to wade around in the muck and heat and fight off water moccasins and mosquitoes. What are you gonna be doin'?"

"Mother and I are going to Europe. Doris and her mother are going with us."

He contemplated the great financial chasm between them. She was going to Europe. He was going to the swamp. She'd never know want and he wasn't sure he'd ever know anything else.

"That's great," he said. "I know you'll enjoy it."

"You ever been to Europe?" Doris asked, hatefully.

"No, but I've been to Oklahoma and I understand there's not that much difference," he joked.

The girls couldn't help but laugh, even Anna Louise, who often acted as though laughter was a weakness of some kind. Then Randy Joe proceeded to tell them what they should see in Europe. He was so knowledgeable about the geography of the world that even Doris was impressed.

"I can't believe you know so much about Europe," Anna Louise said.

He shrugged his shoulders. "I spend a lotta time in the library."

"Oh, look...there's Gary," Doris said. Gary Steele had just come in the door. She motioned for him to come sit next to her.

Anna Louise had suggested to Randy Joe that he meet her after school at the drugstore. He hadn't counted on Doris. Or Gary. He was still seething about Gary's errors in the Bridge City game. And he didn't like the tubby bastard anyway.

Gary slid his fat butt in beside Doris. "How y'all doing?"

Anna Louise and Doris said they were doing fine. Randy Joe said nothing. He just gave Gary a look of annoyance and a nod.

"Randy Joe, have you seen Gary's new car?" Doris asked, coyly.

"Yeah, I've seen it," he acknowledged.

The car was a brand new yellow Buick convertible, an early graduation present from Gary's folks. Both Doris and Anna Louise drove new cars to and from school, but the cars belonged to their parents. Doris, well-schooled in such things by her mother, liked to keep Milltown people in their place.

"I just love your new car, Gary," she said, beaming.

"Thanks...I really like it."

Randy Joe slid out of the booth, stood and said, "If you girls will excuse me...I have to go."

"So soon?" Anna Louise questioned.

"Afraid so."

"Too bad," Doris said. "If you could stay maybe we could talk Gary into takin' us for a ride in his new car."

Randy Joe wanted to say that he'd like to stick the Buick ragtop up her ass and Gary's, but instead said, "I'm sure he'll take you for another ride, Doris."

She dated Gary, had been in the car daily, or nightly. Randy Joe knew what she was trying to do and refused to let her ruffle him. He waved goodbye and headed home.

"He left because I came in," Gary said.

"I don't think so," Anna Louise responded.

"Gary's right," Doris said. "Randy Joe's mad about last night. He blames Gary for the other team scorin'. And it wasn't Gary's fault."

"That's not the way Randy Joe sees it," Gary said. "He thinks he's perfect...never makes a mistake. Well, he may have a straight A average, but he's still just poor white trash from Milltown."

Doris warned, "Now, Gary, be careful what you say about Randy Joe in front of Anna Louise. You know she goes out with him sometimes."

Anna Louise's face reddened. "I've just been out with him a few times...to special events and stuff."

"I've often wanted to ask you, Anna Louise, what does your daddy say about you seein' Randy Joe?" Gary asked.

The attack by people she considered friends made Anna Louise defensive. "He doesn't say much. Well, he told me I shouldn't go with him except to things where there were lots of people around."

"That's good advice," Gary said, "but the truth of the matter is you shouldn't go with him to anything. It can't help your reputation. He's not one of us...never will be."

Doris agreed. "If he plays for that nigger team...well, I hope you won't go with him at all. You go out with someone who's a nigger lover and it's not gonna set too well with decent people."

"I...I thought some people in town were gonna keep him from playin'," Anna Louise said.

Doris gave her friend an incredulous look. "Sometimes I don't understand you, Anna Louise. You heard Randy Joe say right here that it didn't matter what other people thought, that he was gonna do exactly what he wanted to do. And he wants to play for those niggers."

"Well now, what he wants and what he gets might be two different things," Gary said. "I heard pressure is bein' put on Simmy Weatherspoon to keep Randy Joe from pitchin'. I don't know whether I want him to do that or not. I'd kind of like to see Randy Joe pitch that game."

Doris looked puzzled. "Why's that?"

"He'll be pitchin' against a professional team. I'd like to see if he's as good as he thinks he is. And another thing...I don't care if he ruins himself in this town. I'm gonna be livin' here the rest of my life and I don't really wanta share my town with Randy Joe

Keegan. He's a little too uppity for someone from Milltown."

Anna Louise said, "In all the time I've known you, Gary, I never knew how you felt about Randy Joe. I mean...the two of you played on the same teams and all that."

Gary laughed. "You mean the old teamwork thing... pulling together, all that stuff. That's bullshit. I can say it now I'm graduatin'. I've never liked Randy Joe Keegan...never will."

Anna Louise didn't object to the dissecting of Randy Joe Keegan. He wasn't that important, though he had stirred her as no other boy had. If his parents only had the kind of money and prestige that her parents had, then maybe there could be something between them. Gary and Doris were right. She shouldn't be wasting her time on a boy whose only dream was to be a baseball player. Even if he succeeded there was still his family to consider. Randy Joe might fit in, but they couldn't.

"If Randy Joe pitches for the Negroes on Sunday, are you goin'?" Anna Louise asked Gary.

"Yeah...I'm goin'. I wouldn't miss it."

"And you, Doris?"

"If Gary asks me."

"Consider yourself asked," he said.

"Would you mind if I went with you?" Asked Anna Louise.

"Not at all," Gary said. "In fact, if you're agreeable, Monte's been wantin' to go out with you. We could double date, maybe get somethin' to eat after the game and take in a movie."

Anna Louise frowned. "Monte Roper...I don't know."

"Oh, c'mon, Anna Louise," Doris encouraged. "Monte's a nice guy."

Gary laughed. "I like him. He can't stand Randy Joe either."

"So he's hopin' to see Randy Joe lose, too?" Anna Louise said.

"He'd love it," Gary said. "If Randy Joe pitches the game there'll be a lot of people there wantin' to see him get his."

"I know I would," Doris said.

"But what if Randy Joe wins the game?" Anna Louise asked.

"Even if he wins he loses," Gary said, "because he's playin' for a buncha niggers."

ELEVEN

Walking home Randy Joe had time to ponder his drugstore conversation with Anna Louise and Doris, along with Gary Steele's arrival. He had left because he was afraid his anger might erupt, that he might beat the guy senseless.

But why did he hate Gary so much? Because the Steeles had so much? Financially, Gary's dad was on a par with Anna Louise's father. James Steele was an attorney, but his law practice didn't account for his wealth. Gary's grandfather had willed oil and gas holdings up around Kilgore and Longview.

Seeing people with so much, especially those who hadn't earned it by the sweat of their brow, often infuriated Randy Joe. His father and mother had worked hard all their lives, yet they had nothing. They didn't own a home, didn't really even own the used Plymouth they drove. Their monthly payments to a finance company allowed them to drive it.

It bothered him that people like J.D. Lake, James Steele and George Mason, Doris' father, spent their days in suits and ties with no real worries about money, thanks to inherited fortunes. George Mason was in real estate and insurance, a company passed on to him by his father. He owned half of downtown Jason.

It was unfair as hell. His dad had to sweat in the sun day after day to eke out a living and his mother had to stand on tired legs cooking in a restaurant. But his arm could change things for them. God had given it to him. It was up to him to use it.

Randy Joe refused to be depressed for long. The dream

wouldn't let him. The day would come when people wouldn't think of him as just another kid from Milltown, but as the greatest baseball player who ever lived. It was his destiny.

For the moment, though, things could have been better. He could do without the snide remarks and asshole ways of Gary and Doris.

He didn't really care if Anna Louise and Doris went to Europe. If the place was so damned great, why were people over there lined up trying to immigrate to America? What bothered him was Doris, flaunting her family's wealth, as if he didn't know all about it.

And sure, he'd like to have a brand new Buick convertible. But he'd like it even better if his parents had a new car. With it he wanted his mother to have a nice new home and decent furniture. He wanted a lot for his parents because he believed they had given him a lot.

They were responsible for his great arm, his good mind and body, and for his spirit. What they had given him was worth a lot. He would never be a lardass like Gary Steele, would never have to make a teacher fear his father's school board ties to make a grade.

Anna Louise, Doris, Gary, their fathers were all on the school board. Anna Louise was the decent one. She wasn't threatening to teachers, didn't need her father's power.

Randy Joe's regret was that he hadn't really had a chance to punish Gary on the football field. Gary stayed clear of punishment. Coach Marshall had taken good care of him. Gary wore a uniform, but he had never played in games except in situations where he could avoid real contact. He also hadn't really practiced, had always claimed to have some nagging knee injury. It cleared up when football season was over. He had been given three football letters, all unearned.

Randy Joe sighed and picked up his pace, crossing Crooked Creek, which separated Milltown from the rest of Jason. When it really came down to it, it didn't matter. Gary Steele would go off to college, then return to Jason and probably marry Doris. They'd have a couple of kids as rotten as they were and Gary would probably be mayor and on the school board.

It was enough to make a guy puke.

Randy Joe saw Simmy Weatherspoon's big Cadillac parked in front of his house. His immediate fear was that some of the townspeople had gotten to Simmy, that he'd come to tell him he couldn't pitch.

Simmy was sitting in his car. He got out, smiling, and held up a new Longhorns uniform. "Hope dis fits you okay. If it don't fit jest right, den yo' mama kin fix it."

The uniform looked beautiful to Randy Joe, the word Longhorns emblazoned across the front and a Longhorn emblem on the left sleeve. Big numbers, five and two, on the back.

"Dey ain't suppose to be no fifty-two," Simmy explained. "I done bought fifteen new uniforms dat suppose to be ten through twenty-five. But on de last uniform de lady what sewed on de numbers got mixed up, so you gets fifty-two instead of twenty-five. I hope you don't mind."

Randy Joe smiled. "Hell, fifty-two's always been my favorite number."

TWELVE

J.D. Lake felt uncomfortable about a clandestine meeting with James Steele, George Mason, Big Bill Perkins and Coach Vic Marshall. Marshall had suggested they meet after the bank closed on Wednesday.

"We got some good publicity from the game last night," Mason said.

"Yeah, I thought the article in the Beaumont paper was good," Marshall said.

"My concern about the article," Steele interjected, is the part that said in *spite of two errors by first baseman Gary Steele, Randy Joe Keegan* did this and that. It's like everything bad that happened was Gary's fault and everything good was because of Randy Joe."

"Well, that was unfortunate wording," Marshall lied. "Freeman Ware didn't make that good a throw to Gary on the missed third strike. And the ball that got by Gary took a real bad hop. It could have been called a hit just as well as an error."

Steele's face showed he appreciated Marshall's words, but Lake, Perkins and Mason knew there was nothing behind them.

The four visitors to the bank all had comfortable chairs pulled up close to Lake's big desk. "Well, you know why we're all here, J.D.," Big Bill said. "We got ourselves a situation that...if we don't take care of it...could get outta hand."

"You're talking about the Keegan boy pitching for Simmy Weatherspoon's team, of course?" Lake said.

"That's right," Marshall said. "Word about this gets out and it can't do the town any good."

Mason chimed in. "Way you avoid trouble is to nip it in the bud." Lake leaned back in his big chair. He didn't have his suit coat on and his guard stripe burgundy and navy tie lay at parade rest on his oversized stomach. "I don't know what we can do about it."

Mason, dressed in a grey chalk stripe suit, his tie a navy pindot on a red ground, leaned forward in his chair and said, "There's a helluva lot we can do about it, J.D. You, James and myself are the power in this town. You can start by tellin' us what Simmy Weatherspoon's position is here at the bank. What does he owe you? When a man owes you money, you can get him to do just about anything you want him to do."

Lake sighed. "Ethically, I can't discuss a customer's financial situation with the bank. None of you would want me discussin' your financial situation with someone else."

"Damn it, J.D., it's not the same thing," Steele said. "We're talking about a nigger here. And I don't have to remind you that George and I probably have more money in your bank than anyone in town."

Lake's face flushed. "Not as much as Simmy Weatherspoon."

"What?" The shock on Steele's face was palpable. There was a similar frozen disbelief on the faces of the others.

"Well, James, you brought it up," Lake said. "Simmy's got more money in my bank than you and George."

First State Bank was a privately owned family bank. Its board of directors consisted of Lake, his two brothers and a sister.

"Are you telling us that Simmy Weatherspoon doesn't owe the bank any money?" Mason questioned.

"That's exactly what I'm telling you," Lake replied. "In fact, this isn't the only bank Simmy does business with. It's my understandin' he has considerable money in a bank over at Lufkin and in another one in Beaumont. I think he owns stock in the Beaumont bank."

Big Bill shook his head in dismay and anger. "Damn it to hell, what's the world comin' to? You know we're in a heap of trouble when a nigger can own stock in a bank."

Steele, wearing a navy blazer and navy regimental silk tie, said, "This puts a whole new light on things. Hell, J.D., I figured Simmy owed you money...figured he was mortgaged up to his black ass."

"He may owe somebody, but it's not me," the banker said.

Big Bill looked at Steele, then Mason. "George...James, what are we gonna do? You figured J.D. here could put the squeeze on Simmy, but it don't look like that'll work."

"Sure as hell doesn't," Steele conceded.

Marshall said, "We gotta do somethin'."

Steele suggested, "Why don't you tell Randy Joe, if he plays for the niggers he can't play football this year?"

"Can't threaten him. He'll say fine and forget about football."

"You can do without him, can't you?" Steele asked.

"Yeah," Marshall replied, "if you don't mind a losin' season."

"Little bastard," Steele said. "Why is it someone like him has to be such a great athlete?"

"How 'bout scarin' the other niggers?" Big Bill suggested.

"Maybe J.D. here could threaten to foreclose on'em or somethin' and they'd put pressure on Simmy."

Mason laughed. "Foreclose on what? The way J.D. loans money, the kind of collateral he gets, I'm bettin' there's not a nigger in town who's got a loan with this bank."

Lake smiled. "The Negroes in town all borrow their money from a finance company down in Beaumont. They'll loan money on anything...old ragged furniture, broken down cars, anything. They send a man up here every week to collect."

Marshall asked, "Do the Keegans owe you any money?"

Steele grunted. "My guess is that J.D. doesn't loan money to anyone on the south side of Crooked Creek."

Again Lake smiled. "The people in Milltown borrow their money from finance companies in Beaumont, too."

"I don't really know Randy Joe's dad," Mason said, "but maybe we could talk to'im...explain things to'im."

Big Bill's brow furrowed. "The man's got a bad temper...bad as Randy Joe's. He was in the war, you know...shot up a bit. When you talk to'im you're talkin' to a lit stick of dynamite with a short fuse."

Steele laughed. "You're sayin' you don't want to talk to him?"

"It wouldn't do no good," Big Bill said.

Marshall agreed. "Big Bill's right. R.M. Keegan's a difficult man, not one to be intimidated."

"Damn it," Steele said, "we're not talkin' about intimidation. We're talkin' about reasonin' with the man, telling him the implications of what his boy's about to do."

"You kin talk to'im if you want to," Big Bill said, "but it won't do no good for me to do it."

"What if all of us went?" Steele suggested.

"I think it would piss him off good," Big Bill replied. "All of us goin' would look like we were tryin' to pressure him. And Keegan don't like me."

"J.D., your daughter dates him," Steele said.

Lake's face flushed red again. "Not really. But I wouldn't get her involved in this if she did."

"Sorry, J.D., maybe I worded it wrong," Steele said. "Gary

did tell me, though, that Randy Joe was sweet on Anna Louise. You get a boy that's sweet on a girl...he'll do damn near anything for her."

Lake said, angrily, "I'm not involvin' Anna Louise in this."

"Damn it, J.D.," Steele continued, "there's a lot involved here. Anna Louise might end up livin' in this town and your grandchildren might end up goin' to school with niggers."

"That's gonna happen whether we stop the Keegan boy from pitchin' for the Negro team or not," said Lake.

The banker wished he hadn't said it. There was a stunned silence. Integration was inevitable, but no one wanted to admit it.

Big Bill said, "Well, by god, it'll be over my dead body."

"We have to fight this thing," Marshall said. "We can't just lie down and let the government shove this shit down our throats."

"Amen to that," Mason said. He was a deacon at the First Baptist Church, used the word amen about as often as he used a conjunction or preposition. "I can't believe, J.D., that you're not willin' to use everything in your power to stop this godless threat."

"I'm willin' to do just about anything," Lake said, "except use my daughter. I'll go talk to R.M. Keegan, see what he says. He's never said anything crossways to me."

Big Bill grunted. "I'd get the sheriff to go with me."

"You know, that may not be a bad idea," Steele said. "It would let him know who's in charge in this town."

"If I'm gonna do it, it's not gonna be with the sheriff," the banker said. "I'll just go reason with him and we'll see what happens."

"And what if he's not reasonable?" Steele asked.

"I have an idea," Marshall said.

The men all turned an attentive ear to the coach, who cleared his throat and continued with, "If R.M. Keegan won't listen to reason, Aaron Berkley's one of us."

"Good idea," Mason said. "Aaron's a deacon up at the church, too."

"I don't get it," Big Bill said.

Steele said, "Aaron's the superintendent at the lumber company. He's Keegan's boss. If he puts the pressure on Keegan, well..."

Lake filled the silence. "I don't like it, James. What you're talkin' about is gettin' Aaron to threaten R.M. Keegan's job. What if Keegan just tells him to take the job and shove it?"

Steele replied, "Keegan's not exactly an asset to the community."

"Vic, I can't believe you suggested this," Lake said. "If Keegan loses his job, then the football team loses Randy Joe."

The look on Marshall's face indicated some shame that his mouth had outrun his brain. But he said with bravado, "Keegan won't give up his job to let Randy Joe pitch for a bunch of niggers."

"I hope you're right," Lake said.

"When you gonna talk to Keegan?" Steele asked Lake.

"Why put it off," he said. "I'll do it tonight."

THIRTEEN

When J.D. Lake arrived at the Keegan house Bernice and her girls were putting supper on the table. He was greeted by eight-year-old Nelda Jean, who had sparkling blue eyes and blonde hair that exploded in every direction. "I'd like to see your daddy."

"Daddy, there's a man here to see you."

R.M. Keegan appeared. "Mr. Lake...come on in."

The banker stepped inside and saw the table. "I've come at

a bad time," he said. "I can come back later."

"Who is it?" Bernice called out.

"It's Mr. Lake...from the bank."

"Well, tell him to come on in and have some supper."

"No...no thank you," Lake said.

"You eaten?" Keegan asked.

"No, but..." '

"It's settled then," Keegan said. "She'll think you're afraid of her cookin' if you don't eat."

Keegan's manner made Lake fearful of refusing. There was a kind of power to the man that he hadn't noticed before in their casual encounters. Maybe it was because he was in his home.

The house was humble, the furniture the kind found in a salvage store. Nothing matched, but everything was spotlessly clean. It said something about the woman of the house, about the entire family for that matter.

The children were introduced. They all looked freshly washed, as did their clothes.

"Randy Joe?" Lake inquired.

"Oh, he and Weave are doin' somethin'," Bernice Keegan explained. "Jo Beth...you take Mr. Lake's coat and put it on the bed."

"Why don't you come outta that tie and roll up your sleeves?" Keegan invited.

"No, I...yeah, that's a good idea."

Dinner, supper they called it, was going to be a lot different than normal Lake thought. He, his wife Dorothy and Anna Louise were usually waited on by the maid and cook. Tonight he was surrounded by the pleasant faces of seven strangers, yet he felt comfortable. He was made to feel as if he ate with the Keegans every evening.

He always had wine with dinner. Here there was a giant glass of iced tea. R.M. Keegan said, "Hope you like iced tea. We got sweetmilk or buttermilk if you don't."

"No, iced tea's fine, Mr. Keegan."

"You're gonna have to quit callin' me Mr. Keegan. Just call me R.M. and call the wife here Bernice."

"That's fine...if you'll call me J.D."

Keegan laughed. "J.D. it is then."

The meal was simple. Pinto beans, turnip greens, fried okra, cornbread and ham. But Lake swore it was the best he'd ever tasted. He said so.

"Oh, you're just bein' nice," Bernice said. "If I'd known you were comin' I'd have fixed somethin' special. Besides, you eat stuff I fix down at the cafe."

"Nothing like this, Bernice. This is about as special a meal as a man could want. Everything's delicious."

"Wait'll you taste the peach cobbler," Tommy Frank said.

"I'm looking forward to it," Lake said.

Over the next fifteen or twenty minutes the banker found himself embroiled in the family's typical supper conversation, most of which involved what the kids were doing at school. He thought about dinner conversations with Dorothy and Anna Louise. They worked at saying the right things. At the Keegans' table there was no pretense. There was laughter and a general camaraderie that he never experienced at home.

Then Bernice brought in the peach cobbler. "You want some milk with your cobbler, J.D.? Or coffee?"

"Milk sounds good," he said.

"Make mine buttermilk," Keegan said.

"Tell you what, Bernice, make mine buttermilk, too," Lake said. "I've never had buttermilk with peach cobbler."

Keegan laughed. "I see you need a little educatin'."

"You might be right," Lake agreed.

The peach cobbler was better than Lake could even imagine. The food had been wonderful, but the warmth of this family had made it even more so to the banker. He wished Dorothy and Anna Louise had been with him. Sadly, he decided they probably wouldn't have gotten as much from the meal and companionship. Dorothy would have been too concerned with the surroundings.

"You said you wanted to talk to me, J.D."

"Yes...I do. Privately...if possible."

Keegan laughed. "Well, we'd better go outside then...take a walk. My kids have the best ears in the county."

They walked out on the porch, then into the yard, close to

where Lake's Cadillac was parked. It was a clear night. The stars and moon looked close. The banker said, "What I need to talk to you about...well, I'm not all that comfortable doing it."

"Say whatever you have to say. I know you're here about Randy Joe pitchin' for Simmy's team."

"Well, I really apologize for..."

Keegan shrugged. "You don't have to apologize. Everyone's entitled to their own opinion. You ain't the only one thinks he shouldn't be pitchin' for Simmy's team. I've heard it all day at work...from whites and coloreds."

"Negroes don't want him playin'?" Lake asked, puzzled.

"That shouldn't surprise you. They know some of the towns-people can make things bad for'em if they don't act the way some people think they oughta act. They're just like white people. Some of them are afraid of change, too."

Lake wondered where the man was that Big Bill had talked about. Keegan was warm, open, friendly, intelligent. Standing out by his car on this warm spring evening, Lake felt he could talk to Keegan about any subject.

"You're right about bein' afraid of change," Lake said. "It's not that I have anything against Negroes, it's just..."

Keegan laughed. "You just want 'em to stay in their place."

"Yes...I suppose that's true."

"And you wanna define their place."

"I guess that's true, too," Lake chuckled, uneasily.

"No offense, J.D., but if I'd been born colored I'd be permanently pissed off because of people like you. For that matter, if I was a colored I'd be pissed off about people like me. I've got a bunch of'em workin' for me... and I work'em hard. I say I'm fair...and I am... relatively speaking. But the truth is there's nothin' fair about the whole situation."

It was Lake's turn to shrug his shoulders. "It's not my fault they were born colored."

"That's true, J.D., just like you had nothin' to do with me bein' born poor and you bein' born rich. But the fact you didn't have nothin' to do with my situation don't keep me from resentin' how you got rich. Hell, I've worked hard all my life, spent four years in the Army gettin' my ass shot off, and what have I got to show for it? I live in a rent house with furniture you'd throw in the trash, drive a used car that I owe more on than it's worth, and don't even have a bank account. But I got more than any colored man in town except Simmy."

Lake was surprised. "You've got a wonderful family."

Keegan smiled. "Yeah, J.D., that's somethin' you can have if you don't have nothin' else in this world. I'm proud of my kids...all of'em. I want'em to have a chance. They're the reason I didn't mind goin' to war...the reason I work my ass off every day. I want'em to have more outta life than I have."

"That's very noble, R.M. Very noble."

"I don't know nothin' about that. I just figure that's what every poor man wants for his kids...whether he's white or black. It's all relative. The coloreds look up here and see these houses we're livin' in, and their goal is to get what we got. They ain't thinkin' beyond us...not thinkin' about the pretty white houses the people in town live in, or the new cars they drive. They just want what we got."

Lake was puzzled. "I'm not sure what you're tellin' me."

"I'm tellin' you I know the people in town are worried about change...about the coloreds goin' to the white school and maybe even to their church houses. And the white sawmill workers think they have a lot to lose. Maybe I do, too."

"Does this mean you're not going to let Randy Joe pitch the game for Simmy's team?" Lake asked.

"No, it don't," Keegan replied. "Randy Joe will be seventeen this next month. The way I look at it, he's his own man. The boy works harder than just about any man I know and he's gotta right to make his own decisions."

"But you said yourself..."

"J.D., I'm a prejudiced sonofabitch. It's the way I was raised, which don't make it right. But why should I side with a bunch of people from town against the coloreds? Hell, I'm more like a colored than I am like one of you. You're a nice enough fella, but on the whole the coloreds treat me a helluva lot better than anyone from town's ever treated me. They treat Randy Joe a lot better, too."

Lake countered, "Until this evening, R.M., I really didn't

know you. As for Randy Joe, he's one of the best-liked young men in town. And now that I know you..."

"When you leave here this evenin', J.D., things will go back to bein' just like they've been between us. You're always welcome to come over here and have a meal with us. But your wife ain't gonna invite Bernice and me over to your house for supper. We wouldn't fit anyway. It's easier for a rich man to have supper at a poor man's house than it is for a poor man and his family to have supper at a rich man's house. It's easier to come down than it is to go up.

"As for Randy Joe," Keegan continued, "he's been accepted by a few people in town because he's an athlete. You take that away, though, and he's just another kid from Milltown. He's a good football player...which is the only reason Vic Marshall tolerates him. But he can be a great baseball player. He has more natural ability than anyone I've ever seen play the game. Simmy knows that, too. So if you want me to tell 'im not to pitch for Simmy's team...well, that's just not gonna happen."

Lake pondered what Keegan had said. "You've given me a lot to think about, R.M. You're right about us not wantin' change. I'm the first to admit it, though I know it's inevitable. I will tell you this, though. There are a lot of people on the other side of the creek who have it in their heads that if Randy Joe pitches this game it'll hurt the town. I'm not so sure myself. I'm just going to say that you'd better watch your back because there are some people who aren't going to take kindly to your position."

Keegan laughed. "I've had to watch my back all my life. I hope you ain't in the bunch that's after my ass."

"I won't be," the banker promised, "but I won't be tryin' to stop them either."

"Fair enough," Keegan said. "I appreciate it when a man's straight with me."

Lake sighed. "I wish I understood it. All I really want is a simple, uncomplicated life. You can tell Randy Joe that he's not making that kind of life very easy for me."

Keegan laughed again. "I won't tell you what he might say about that."

Lake smiled. "Please don't."

"You gonna be at the game Sunday? I mean...if we ain't run outta town by then?"

"I'll be there," the banker said, laughing. "That was quite a game last night. You must be awfully proud of your son."

"I am, but then...I'm proud of all my children."

Driving home Lake thought about the Keegans and his conversation with R.M. He liked the man and his family. They were hardy people, the kind it took to tame what had been a wild frontier. He hoped they hadn't outlived their usefulness.

FOURTEEN

Randy Joe ate supper at Weave's house on Wednesday evening. It was okay but Gloria Severage couldn't hold a candle to his mother when it came to cooking. It wasn't the food that disturbed him. It was part of the conversation initiated by Andrew Severage, Weave's father.

"What's this crap about you pitchin' for the nigger team?"

"Yessir, I'm gonna be pitchin' for'em on Sunday."

"Damn it, son, it's bad enough your daddy and I have to work with the bastards."

Andrew Severage was a big, foreboding man who looked like he always needed a shave. He was six-two and weighed well over two hundred pounds, but there wasn't an ounce of fat on him. He had dark recessed eyes and jowls that reminded Randy Joe of a bulldog.

There wasn't much Randy Joe could say, but he tried. "The team they're playin' is white."

The big man grunted. "Makes it even worse...you tryin' to help a bunch o' niggers beat a white team."

"Now Andy, it ain't none of our business," said Gloria.

She was a small woman, worn thin by the workload of taking care of a moody husband and four kids. In addition to Weave she had three girls, all younger, who were also sitting at the table busily eating.

"What's your dad say about all this?" Severage asked, paying absolutely no attention to his wife.

Randy Joe forked some corn, shrugged his shoulders and replied, "He didn't say I couldn't."

"Well, R.M.'s a lot more tolerant than I am. He'll give a nigger a lot more leeway."

"You ought not to say anything else," his wife warned.

"Damn it woman, you'll tell me be quiet when the niggers are rapin' and marryin' white women. You start lettin' them think they're as good as we are and they'll start takin' over."

No one responded to his outburst. Weave and his sisters, who were used to it, just kept their heads down.

In a more pleading tone Severage continued, "Randy Joe, don't you see what they're doin'? They ain't got no pitcher that can beat a white team so they're gettin' you to do it for them."

"I don't know...they got some pretty good pitchers."

"They're good when they're playin' another nigger team," Severage argued, "but they'll fall apart playin' a white team."

Randy Joe wanted to laugh, but didn't. Later, when they were outside the house, Weave said, "Sorry about that. You know my dad's got a hard-on for niggers. I don't like 'em myself."

"Well, you'd better start likin 'em," Randy Joe said.

"The niggers you mean?"

"In the Air Force one of 'em is liable to be givin' you orders."

"You're shittin' me."

"No I ain't. You better get used to the idea."

Weave said, "I don't know if I can."

On his way home Randy Joe was intercepted by Gretchen, looking very good in yellow shorts. "Did you know J.D. Lake had supper at your house?" she asked.

"You're kiddin'?"

Gretchen laughed. "No I'm not. What's goin' on, Randy Joe? Did you knock up Anna Louise?"

He shook his head. "You're unbelievable...you know that? I can't imagine J.D. Lake visitin' my house, let alone eatin' there." Then his thought processes started ginning. "It's the game. It has somethin' to do with the game."

"You're talkin' about Sunday...when you're supposed to pitch for the colored team?"

"I'm not just supposed to, I'm goin' to."

"Daddy says you shouldn't do it."

"Well, that seems to be the consensus, but I don't give a rat's ass. I'm gonna do what I wanna do."

"No matter what, huh?"

"Yeah, Gretch, no matter what."

"You wanna go for a walk?" she asked.

"Later...after I've found out why Mr. Lake was at my house. I'll see you in thirty minutes or so."

"Good," she said. "I'm curious, too."

Randy Joe went in the front door. His father was sitting in what passed for the easy chair, reading a pulp novel. Mary Lynne was playing with her doll. His other sisters and Tommy Frank were doing homework.

"Where's mom?" Randy Joe asked.

His dad looked up from the book. "She's in the kitchen."

"Mr. Lake ate supper with us," Jo Beth said.

Tommy Frank said, "Yeah, can you believe it?"

"I already heard."

His father laid the book on the floor. "You know, I think I'm ready for a little more cobbler."

They went into the dining room. Bernice, who'd heard them talking, came out of the kitchen carrying two bowls of dessert, a glass of buttermilk and two cups of coffee. "Okay, you gonna tell me why Mr. Lake was here or just make me guess?" Randy Joe asked.

R.M. smiled. "I imagine you know why he was here."

"It was about the game Sunday, wasn't it?"

"That's right," R.M. said. "Seems like he represents a group of people who don't want you to pitch the game."

"I'm surprised he'd come here and talk to you about it. In fact, it tees me off."

Bernice said, "Mr. Lake...J.D. seems like a nice man."

R.M. agreed. "I wouldn't get too upset with him, son. I think he felt kinda bad about comin' here to talk to me about it. I think he was pressured by some other people."

"It doesn't matter. He had no business..."

"When you stir up a hornet's nest you gotta expect some buzzing," his dad said. "The folks in town...they don't understand you playin' with coloreds. They take the money the coloreds bring to town, but they don't want to be bothered with'em. They sure don't want'em goin' to their schools and churches."

Randy Joe sighed with resignation. "The way I see it, pitchin' for Simmy's team ain't gonna open up the white school and churches to the colored people."

"Course it ain't," his father agreed, "but the people can see it comin'. You pitchin' for'em is kinda symbolic of it happenin'."

"That's sorta what Coach Rice told me."

"Well, he's right," R.M. said.

"I'll say this," Bernice interjected, "there's a lotta colored women I'd rather associate with than some of the ones in town."

Randy Joe wanted to say, "You really don't have much choice, mom." Instead, he said, "Good cobbler, mom."

She smiled. "Mr. Lake liked it, too."

"Mom, dad...I don't wanna cause y'all any grief. If you don't want me to pitch the game, I won't."

Randy Joe's parents looked at each other. Then his father said, "You told Simmy you'd do it. When you give somebody your word...don't matter if they're black or white...you keep it."

"But if it's gonna cause you and mom trouble..."

"Don't you worry 'bout that, son," Bernice said. "You just listen to what your father says."

R.M. laughed. "That's more than you ever do, Bernice. Far as this causing us trouble, Randy Joe...we were born to trouble. It's part of bein' poor...growing' up that way. Course there's advantages to bein' poor. Can't threaten to take somethin' away from you that you ain't got. All we got is you kids."

Then he laughed and jokingly continued, "And nobody wants any of you knotheads."

Randy Joe laughed, then soberly said, "I hear some men at the mill are givin' you a hard time...maybe even Weave's dad."

"Tell you what, son...if any of 'em gives me too hard a time, I'll whip their ass."

"So you want me to pitch?"

"Well, at first I wasn't all that sure," his father said, "but the more shit I hear about it the more...yeah, I want you to pitch the game. You told Simmy you'd do it and, by god, you oughta do it."

"It's settled then," Randy Joe said. "I didn't want y'all catchin' a lot of crap from the people here in Milltown."

Jo Beth appeared in the doorway. "Talk about someone catchin' crap, what about your brother and sisters? We're catchin' a lot of it."

Tommy Frank, standing behind her, said, "That's right. We're all being called nigger lovers because of you."

"So you're sayin' you don't want me to pitch because people are calling y'all nigger lovers?"

"Hell no," Jo Beth said. "Screw'em."

Bernice's face reddened. "Now you watch your mouth, young lady."

Randy Joe looked at his dad's face and saw that it was all he could do to keep from laughing.

When Randy Joe arrived at the Turners' house Gretchen was sitting in the porch swing. "Well?"

"Well, what?"

"You know. Why was Anna Louise's dad at your house?"

"Just why I told you earlier. There are some concerned citizens in town who don't want me to pitch Sunday."

"There are some people in Milltown who feel the same way."

"And some people in the Quarters," he continued.

She laughed. "I don't know about that. You're the one who hangs out with the colored kids."

"I play ball with a few of the guys...that's all."

She stretched her wonderful legs and said, "Seems daddy did

say somethin' at supper about some of the colored men at the mill not bein' all that pleased you were gonna pitch the game. Or maybe he said they felt like they had to act like they weren't pleased."

He laughed. "In order to please their white bosses, huh?"

"That's the way daddy read it," she replied, smiling.

"Do you think I'm makin' a mistake, Gretchen?"

She gave him a light kiss on the lips. "I don't know. I don't even care. Whether you pitch the game or not isn't gonna change the way I feel about you."

He could always count on Gretchen, rain or shine. She didn't have the polished ceramic exterior of Anna Louise. Or the moodiness of Patti Sue. She had a sharp tongue... But he always knew where he stood with her. She could be tough, but she could be tender. And he knew that she loved him, that he was her only love.

He returned her kiss, but with more passion. She said in a whisper, "You'd better not start somethin' we can't finish in a porch swing."

He laughed. "It might be a little uncomfortable...doin' it in the porch swing."

"If my parents weren't around we might try it.

Randy Joe believed her. "Are you goin' Sunday?"

"Have I ever missed one of your games?"

"No, but I never pitched one like this before."

"I'll be there...sittin' with Jolene and Weave. My parents will be there...sittin' with your parents, like always. I think everybody's gonna be there. All the people who don't want you to pitch will be there."

He thought for a few seconds, then said, "You know...this will be a nine inning game. I'm used to pitchin' seven innings. I wonder how that's gonna affect me?"

Gretchen laughed. "You're askin' the wrong person."

He smiled. "I'd better talk to dad...see what he says."

Her tone turned serious. "Randy Joe, I don't know why you're doin' this...but I hope it works out the way you want."

"You know what I want, Gretch."

"I know your dream...and I hope it comes true. But if it

doesn't, there's still a lot to life."

"Not for me."

"I don't know why you say stuff like that. Teachers say you've got the best mind in school."

He laughed. "Teachers in Jason don't have much to work with."

"Don't be such a smartass. You know good and well you can be anything you wanna be."

"I just wanna be a baseball player...the best baseball player who ever lived."

"You just wanna to be famous," she said.

"Yeah...I guess so. I wanna shove that fame up the noses of some of the clowns in town."

"You know that's pretty childish."

He laughed. "Maybe, but that doesn't keep me from wantin' to do it. I deserve a little childishness. I've never been a kid. I've been workin' since I was able to walk. Everything's been serious with me. What's fun for other people isn't fun for me. I just want to compete and win, compete and win."

"I know," she said. "Whether you like it or not, Randy Joe Keegan, I probably know you better than anybody. I know you wanna come back here in all your baseball glory just to rub people's noses in your fame. I can't blame you because you've been used...by people like Coach Marshall. And there are people like Gary Steele who won't face up to you, who do a lotta talkin' behind your back. But they aren't important. Bein' yourself...that's important."

"The only reason I'd come back to this town is because my folks live here...because you live here."

"You can show the people here even if you're in New York or some other place. As for comin' back to see me, I don't..." She became tearful.

"What's wrong?"

She pulled herself together. "I...I know we don't have much of a future together, Randy Joe. If we were together in the future I'd always remind you of Milltown. And that's somethin' you don't wanna be reminded of. That's why you're interested in Anna Louise Lake. She reminds you of where you wanna be, not where you are."

Randy Joe had known from the time he first met her that Gretchen was a smart young lady. The conversation reinforced his thinking. "Let's not get into a bunch of heavy stuff right now," he said. "I was hopin' we could go out after the game Sunday night."

"All you ever have to do is ask."

FIFTEEN

Early Thursday morning J.D. Lake met with Big Bill Perkins, Vic Marshall, James Steele and George Mason at Big Bill's Cafe. Lake had never been in the place before and hoped never to be there again. After he'd told the four about the meeting with R.M. Keegan, James Steele said, "I don't see where we gotta choice then. We need to talk to Aaron Berkley, get him to put the pressure on Keegan."

"I agree," Mason said.

Lake asked, "Isn't that dangerous, James? I mean, if you start threatening a man's job, doesn't he have a lawsuit?"

Steele laughed. "Let me worry about the law. The white trash in Milltown don't know any more about the law than the niggers do."

The banker said, "Yes, but I think..."

Steele interrupted. "It's settled then. George, since Aaron's one of your fellow deacons, ask him to meet us for lunch."

"Where you wanna meet?" Mason asked.

Big Bill volunteered, "Y'all can meet here."

Steele gave him a disdainful look. "Naw, we'll meet at Sanborn's Restaurant. It's quieter...be easier for us to talk."

"What time?" Big Bill asked.

"You and Vic don't need to be there," Steele said. "George, J.D. and I can handle this."

Big Bill didn't like it, but because of Steele's wealth and power he kept his mouth shut.

"Count me out," Lake said. "I don't feel good about this."

Angrily, Steele said, "Then you don't have to be there either, J.D. But you'd better decide whose side you're on."

There was an awkward silence, then Lake said, "I can be there, but I don't know what I can contribute."

"You don't have to contribute anything," Steele said. "It'll just be good for Aaron to see that the town's leaders are united."

Mason said, "I don't know if you thought about this, James, but Mrs. Keegan works at Sanborn's."

"So?"

"Just thought I'd mention it."

"She works in the kitchen," Steele said, disdainfully.

The fact Bernice Keegan worked at the restaurant was one reason Lake didn't want to be included. He didn't want Bernice to see him with Aaron Berkley, her husband's boss. She would hold him responsible when Berkley put pressure on her husband.

Lake arrived at Sanborn's Restaurant at eleven fifty-five. Steele and Mason were already there. They had occupied a table that would give them considerable privacy.

Sanborn's was the nicest restaurant in Jason. It was not elaborate by big city standards, but was four stars above Big Bill's Cafe. The place had good lunches, thanks to Bernice Keegan, and a cordial atmosphere.

"Aaron coming?" Lake asked.

"He's on his way," Mason replied.

Lake began to feel queasy. A serving window separated the kitchen from the dining area. There was no way to escape Bernice Keegan's eyes. The talk at the table was a hum in Lake's ears. Then Aaron Berkley arrived. He was a tall, well-built man in his late forties. His hair was greying at the temples, but he had a full head of it that might be described as an everyday brown. His eyes were hazel and he had a prominent nose, a wide mouth and strong chin.

"Aaron, glad you could make it," Steele said.

Berkley smiled. "My pleasure."

He meant it. The lumber company superintendent lived in town, but wasn't used to being asked to lunch by Jason's elite. He was probably the highest-salaried man in town, but there was still a stigma attached to working for the lumber company.

"We need to get together for lunch like this more often," Mason suggested. "I see you at church, Aaron, but that's about it."

"I'd like that," Berkley said. "It'd be a nice change from eatin' at my desk."

"They keep you hoppin' at the mill, do they?" Steele asked. "How many people you got workin' there now?"

Berkley pondered the question, then replied, "You start countin' the loggin' crews and all...and some of those are independents...the company employs about a thousand people."

Steele said, "Mostly niggers, right?"

"Yeah...the majority. But we have about two hundred whites who make their livin' at the mill. Or in some way connected to it."

They all ordered the plate lunch and Berkley said, "You know, R.M. Keegan's wife...Randy Joe's mother...cooks lunch here durin' the week. Ain't nobody makes better chicken-fried steak."

"You know Keegan pretty well, do you?" Mason asked.

Berkley sipped some tea from a cold, perspiring glass and replied, "I'm not sure anybody really knows R.M. But yeah...I know all the white men...and most of the niggers...workin' for the company. That boy of R.M.'s is some kinda pitcher, ain't he?"

"He's that," Steele agreed. "I guess you know he's plannin' to pitch a game for the nigger team on Sunday."

"Yeah, I heard...surprised me some, too."

"How's that?" Mason asked.

"Just surprised that R.M. would let'em do it. He's pretty tough on the niggers that work for him."

"He abuses them some way?" Steele questioned.

Berkley laughed. "He works'em hard...sometimes forgets to

let'em have their morning and afternoon break. R.M.'s one of those people who puts his head down and starts workin' when the morning whistle blows and don't let up 'til it blows again."

"How important is R.M. Keegan to the company?" Lake asked.

"There's only a few sawmill people in the country who can do what he does. We gotta couple of men he's trainin' right now."

The banker felt better. Maybe Berkley would be a little more difficult to manipulate than Steele and Mason had thought. Mason cleared his throat and said, "If what you say about Keegan is true...it makes what we have to ask you a whole lot harder."

"What's that?" Berkley asked.

"Aaron," Mason said, "I think I know you well enough to know how you believe. Correct me if I'm wrong...but I don't think you want niggers in our church, do you?"

"Well...no. Course not."

"That's what it's comin' to, Aaron," Mason said. "Personally, I think it's the result of a lotta godless Communists who've infiltrated our government. They're out to stir up the niggers and cause us a lotta trouble."

Berkley nodded agreement. "I've said for a long time, if we don't watch it the Communists are gonna take over."

Steele put his two cents in. "People tend to think the Communists are in the cities, not in town's like Jason. But they're everywhere."

"Amen to that," Mason said. "Now you take this ball game on Sunday...a nigger team playing a white team. Who arranged somethin' like that? What sense is there to it? It seems innocent enough, I guess, though I wouldn't wanna be one of the whites playin' in the game. What I'm sayin' is, every white boy who plays in that game is fallin' right into the Communist trap."

Lake couldn't believe what he was hearing, but saw Berkley was swallowing Mason's bait hook, line and sinker. Hell, maybe Mason and Steele even believed what they were saying. Maybe he should believe it. Maybe it was true. All he knew was, Mason and Steele would soon be reeling the lumber company superintendent in and it was sickening.

"You make a real good point, George," Steele said. "You sure make me think. I'm thinkin', what do we know about Simmy Weatherspoon? Where did the man's money come from? The Communists could really use someone like Simmy. I mean...the niggers all respect him. They'd follow him, do what he asked'em to do."

Mason responded to Steele, but his words were strictly for Berkley. "Niggers like Simmy Weatherspoon aren't gonna be satisfied until they have a free run of our churches and school. I don't know about you, Aaron, but I don't want that."

Berkley swallowed the lump that was in his throat and said, "I don't want it either, George."

"Well, whether you realize it or not, Aaron, you have somethin' to say about it," Mason said. "You read your Bible. You know that sometimes God chooses one man to stand in the gap...one man to do His Will. In this case, Aaron, I think you're that man."

Lake wanted to puke.

Berkley said, puzzled, "I know what you say is true, George...about God sometimes choosin' a man. But I don't know what I can do about all this stuff you been talkin' about."

Mason smiled. "God asked David to kill a giant, but he doesn't always ask somethin' that big from a person He chooses. In this case I think He just wants you to talk to R.M. Keegan, to tell him that Randy Joe ought not to be pitchin' a game for the niggers."

"Well, I..."

"Don't you see, Aaron, you'll be helpin' Randy Joe and his daddy. We know neither one of them is a Communist, but if Randy Joe pitches that game they'll be helpin' the Communists without even knowin' it."

"I...I don't think R.M. will listen to me."

Steele said, "You've gotta make him listen. You might even have to threaten him a little bit."

"Oh, I don't know about that. He's got a serious temper."

"When He called us, God never told us it would be easy," Mason said. "He said we'd be tried as if by fire."

"You don't want the niggers and Communists taking over, do you?" Steele asked, angrily. "George here tells me you're a good American, that you wanna do what's right."

"I do," Berkley said. "I didn't fight in the war like R.M. did, but I'm a good American. I was just needed here at home."

"You don't have to explain," Steele said. "Important duties at home kept everybody at this table from goin' to war, but we're all good Americans. Not fightin' in a war doesn't mean a man's not a good American."

"I think fightin' in the war mighta done somethin' to R.M., though," Berkley said. "It mighta made him a tad crazy. I'm just worried about what he'll do when I bring this up."

"Aaron, Aaron," Mason said in semi-scolding fashion, "the Lord promised to protect His children. You got nothin' to worry about. Just tell Keegan it's not a good idea for Randy Joe to pitch the game...that it might even cost him his job."

Berkley crawfished. "That's the part I don't know about. He's liable to go slapdab crazy when I say that."

Mason said, soothingly, "I keep telling you, Aaron, the Lord's in this. You know He's gonna be right there with you. I've prayed about this. I know it's the right thing to do."

"That's the gospel truth," Steele agreed. "You know the Lord wants us to stop this thing before it gets outta hand. You got kids...grandchildren growin' up here. You don't want'em goin' to school with niggers, do you?"

Berkley's resolve seemed to strengthen. "No...no, I don't. I'll talk to R.M."

"You gotta do more than talk, Aaron," Mason said. "You gotta make him realize the consequences."

"I will," Berkley said, his voice ringing with patriotic fervor.

When he got back to the bank Lake went about his tasks like a zombie. He couldn't get his mind off the luncheon conversation, or what might be happening at the lumber company.

Word came about three o'clock. Berkley had called R.M. Keegan into his office. He had told him what consequences he faced if Randy Joe pitched the game. Keegan had gone berserk, and had leaped over Berkley's desk after him. He had to be restrained by three other men. Berkley had to fire him.

Lake slumped back in his chair, frustration burning inside him. It wasn't right. He wanted to do something for the Keegans. But then all his strength and resolve dissipated.

He knew he wouldn't do anything.

SIXTEEN

Randy Joe stopped at the drugstore after school. He was having a cherry Coke when he got word about his dad. He ran all the way home. He slowed to a trot when he reached the steps of the porch. When he opened the screen door and walked into the house he saw his mother and father. They were sitting at the dining table, coffee cups in front of them. He joined them.

"You heard?" his dad said.

"Yeah...what happened?"

The older Keegan laughed. "I guess you could say I told'em to take their job and shove it."

"I heard you were fired."

Keegan laughed again. "When I went across Aaron Berkley's desk and slammed him against the wall, I'd say that was the same as quittin'."

"Why'd you do that?" Randy Joe asked, troubled.

"He pissed me off."

"He told your daddy, if you pitched the game on Sunday he'd lose his job," Bernice said.

"He what?"

Keegan shrugged his shoulders. "That's what he said, son."

Randy Joe was shaken. "Dad, no game's that important."

"It is now."

Bernice said, "It's hard to believe but J.D. Lake's behind

this. At least he's part of it. He had lunch at the restaurant today with Aaron Berkley, James Steele and George Mason."

"I think J.D.'s having to go along with it, but I don't think he's behind it," Keegan said.

"R.M.," Bernice said, angrily, "I don't see how you can sit there and be so calm about all this. That man sat here at our table, ate our food, then went and did somethin' like this."

Keegan chuckled. "We invited him. He didn't invite himself."

"That don't matter. I thought he was different, but he's just like the rest of'em."

"Bernice, what you think's your own business, but J.D. never told you he was any different from the other people in town. My guess is that James Steele is really the one pullin' all the strings."

"Gary's dad," Randy Joe said with disdain. "I been lookin' for an excuse to kick Gary in his fat ass."

"Well, you're not gonna do it," his dad said. "That's probably just what they want. I'm surprised they ain't sent the sheriff out to arrest me for attackin' Aaron. They got the law in their pocket, like everything else."

"The game's not important now," Randy Joe said.

Keegan's face flushed red. "That's where you're wrong, son. It's more important now than it ever was. I've taken a stand, by god, and Keegans don't back down."

"But what are you gonna do?"

"Hell, I was lookin' for a job when I found this one."

"I can't say I'll be sorry to leave this place," Bernice said.

Randy Joe had always said he wanted to leave, too. Now he was having second thoughts. It was like being run out of town. He would make somebody pay. He would give Gary Steele a major league ass kicking.

"Where you gonna look for a job?" Randy Joe asked.

"It's not gonna take much lookin', son. Couple of sawmills over in Louisiana been tryin' to hire me for years...one down in Mississippi, too. I just hate to mess up your final year of school."

"Don't worry about it, dad. It's the least of my worries."

"Randy Joe, Aaron Berkley said you couldn't have your job

either," Bernice said. "He doesn't want the mill's money goin' to a Keegan. He told your daddy we had to be outta this house in two weeks."

"That sonofabitch." He could see his mother had been crying.

"Hell, I'll have somethin' before two weeks is up," his father said with a touch of bravado in his voice. "Probably by Monday."

"What about your job, mom?"

"Oh, Mr. Sanborn hasn't said anything...yet. But if J.D. Lake, James Steele or George Mason want me fired, he'll fire me."

"They're gonna want it," R.M. said. "They've gone this far, so they'll go all the way. They want the Keegans bowing down to'em, kissing their asses. And that's not gonna happen."

"Your daddy could go back to work for the mill," Bernice said.

"Sure, if I wanna kiss Aaron Berkley's ass," R.M. replied. "I'd have to keep Randy Joe from pitchin' the game Sunday and I'd have to apologize. It'll be a cold day in hell before I do either one."

"Mom, do you think dad oughta apologize?"

Keegan grunted, "Don't make no difference what she thinks."

"I beg your pardon, R.M. It damn sure does make a difference what I think...and don't you forget it. But no, I don't think your dad oughta apologize. If he did Aaron Berkley would own'im. And we're not the kinda people to be owned."

Randy Joe knew she was right. There was no turning back.

His dad said, "You can set a broken bone, but what goes on in your head ain't so easy to fix. I thought Aaron Berkley was my friend."

Randy Joe talked to his parents for another thirty minutes, then decided he needed to get out of the house to think. He borrowed the car without knowing where he was going . He just planned to be alone and had the car started when Gretchen came up to the window.

"I heard," she said, sorrowfully.

"Yeah...helluva deal, ain't it? I screwed up everything."

"It's not your fault."

"The hell it ain't. If I wasn't so all-fired anxious to pitch a game for a bunch of...well, it wouldn't have happened."

"Your daddy wanted you to do it," she said.

"Maybe...or maybe he and mom just didn't want to tell me no again. Maybe I forced'em into sayin' they wanted me to pitch."

"Randy Joe, I don't think anyone can force your dad into anything, not you or anybody else."

She was right. R.M. Keegan had a soft spot for his kids, but he'd never let one of them do something that he thought might be harmful to them. To him it had just been a game, not the racial thing it had become for certain people.

Randy Joe sighed. "You're right. Wanna go for a ride?"

"I'll have to tell mom and dad something. When daddy came in a while ago he was really mad about what Mr. Berkley did to your dad. Now he says you gotta pitch the game, says you gotta show Berkley and the townspeople they can't push Milltown folks around."

"Tell him thanks," Randy Joe said. "Tell your folks we're goin' to get a Coke."

Gretchen disappeared for a few minutes, then reappeared and got in the car. She was wearing green shorts and a halter top that revealed plenty of her tanned legs and body. He was stirred by her closeness.

Randy Joe put the car in gear and a few minutes later was rolling over the west bridge on Crooked Creek. There were two bridges over the creek separating Jason proper from Milltown. As they approached downtown Randy Joe saw Zeke Lott sweeping off the sidewalk in front of a hardware store. The baker saw the green Plymouth coming and started waving his arms, motioning Randy Joe to pull over. He did and Zeke came up to the car and bent down at his window.

"I sho' sorry to hear 'bout what happen to yo' daddy," he said. "It ain't right. All de colored folks in town upset 'bout it."

"Well, I appreciate it, Zeke, but I don't guess there's much anybody can do."

"Now don't you go thinkin' dat way. I happen to know dat

somethin's bein' done right dis minute."

Curious, Randy Joe asked, "What you talkin' about, Zeke?"

"Ain't 'pose to say, but things gonna be different tomorrow."

"How they gonna be different?"

"Like I say, I ain't 'pose to say. But I will tell you dat Simmy done gone to see a man."

"What man?"

"Dat I can't say, but you tell yo' momma and daddy not to be worryin' none. Everythin's gonna be okay."

"Well, we appreciate you thinkin' about us, Zeke...Simmy, too. I just hope he's still gonna let me pitch the game."

"Oh, he countin' on it all right," Zeke said. "But jest you wait and see...everythin's gonna get fixed. Jest tell yo' daddy dat all de folks in de Quarters is behind 'im. Everythin' gonna be okay."

Driving away Gretchen asked, "Now what do you think Zeke meant?"

Randy Joe shrugged his shoulders. "I don't know. I think it was just talk. I'm curious, though...about who Simmy is goin' to see. Hell, that may just be talk, too."

"Are Simmy and Zeke good friends?"

"I think so. I see 'em together at all the ball games."

Randy Joe didn't want to go to a place where he'd run into a lot of kids from school, so he stopped at a service station and purchased a couple of Cokes. Then he drove west of town. For several miles they didn't talk, then he said matter-of-factly, "We're gonna have to move, you know."

"I know," she said, sadly.

"Dad's talkin' about Louisiana or Mississippi. He can get work there."

She was sitting close to him. She moved even closer. "You...you could stay here and finish your senior year."

He laughed. "Now how in the hell could I do that?"

"My folks...they'd let you stay with us."

His mood softened. "Yeah...I guess they would. But the way things are between us, Gretch, I don't think that's a good idea. I'd have a little trouble sleepin' by myself with you under the same roof. And I don't think your folks are ready for us to start sharin' a bed."

She laughed. "No, they're not...but we could control our-selves for a few months."

"Speak for yourself," he said, laughing. Then, soberly, he continued, "If I stayed I'd have to get a job. My folks couldn't afford to support me livin' in a different place. And you know them...they wouldn't let your folks feed and house me for nothin'."

"You could get a job," she said, wanting to believe he was actually considering staying.

"If I stayed here and played football for Jason some of the people in town would see to it that I had a job. But the day football season was over...that would be the end of it."

She knew he was telling the truth about the townspeople, especially about Coach Vic Marshall and some of the people connected with the school. So she sighed and said, "You're right, of course."

Randy Joe finally stopped the car, pulled her even closer and kissed her. He then headed the car back toward town and home.

Thinking about the events of the day, about the probability that Randy Joe was going to be leaving Jason and Milltown, a sudden chill enveloped Gretchen. She didn't like what was happening, the winds of change over which she had no control. She wasn't much at praying, but in her mind there was a prayer that Zeke Lott was right, that Simmy Weatherspoon was going to do something to repair what had happened to R.M. Keegan.

But what could a colored man do?

SEVENTEEN

James Steele felt good about Thursday's events and his part in them. He'd spent the afternoon at his office where he'd received the telephone call from George Mason telling him about Aaron Berkley's encounter with R.M. Keegan. It had gone the way he hoped it would.

Dinner with his family that evening was special because he was able to tell Gary how he'd orchestrated much of what had happened. Gary gave him hero status for his role in bringing the Keegans to their knees.

"What's gonna happen to Randy Joe and his family?" Marcie, Steele's fourteen-year-old daughter, asked.

Gary laughed. "Who cares?"

Steele smiled. "Gary makes a good point, Marcie. They'll be leavin' Jason, of course, which will be good riddance...just more white trash we won't have to mess with."

"I don't think you accomplished much," his wife Mary Ann said. "More people just like them will take their place."

Steele wished Mary Ann would keep her mouth shut. The cold wench tended to discount all his victories, make them seem insignificant.

"Well, maybe Keegan's replacement won't have as many in his family," he said. "Hopefully, he won't have a kid like Randy Joe."

"I've always liked Randy Joe," Marcie said. "I think he's nice. He sure is good-looking."

Gary shook his head in disgust. "I always thought you were

stupid, Marcie...now I know it."

Mary Ann warned, "Don't talk to your sister like that."

Gary whined, "Mom, the way Randy Joe's treated me, I think..."

"Randy Joe's treated you the way you oughta be treated," Marcie said. "You're nothin' but a crybaby."

"That's enough," Steele said, angrily. "I'll not have talk about the Keegans disrupting this family."

"Well, James, you brought them up," Mary Ann said, coldly. "You seem to be so proud of running them out of town."

"Anytime you can get some of the poor white trash and niggers outta your town, you oughta be proud."

She laughed. "Your town, huh?"

"Damned right, it's my town. It was my daddy's town and now it's mine. Anything wrong with that, Mary Ann?"

She knew she'd pushed it about as far as possible without things getting really nasty. She sighed. "No...nothin' at all. After all, I guess that makes it half mine."

It was her way of reminding him that Texas was a community property state. If he decided to split the blanket with her she got fifty percent of everything he owned. She enjoyed reminding him.

Mary Ann had grown up prim and proper in Jason. Her father had owned a grocery store and provided well for his family. She had never wanted for anything. She had gone to Stephen F. Austin College, where James Steele had discovered her. They'd known each other all their lives, but when she was a high school freshman he was a senior. The same scenario existed in college, but by then she had blossomed into a beautiful young woman.

Steele had gone to law school, but his journey through life had not been helpful to his fellow man. Mary Ann found him petty and mean-spirited, obsessed with arranging the downfall of those he considered his enemies.

Steele disliked and distrusted poor people. And to be both poor and colored was the worst of sins. He hated Negroes.

Mary Ann had lived with his greed, anger and propensity for revenge. The children were her excuse for being tolerant, but lately she was wavering in her commitment to them. Gary was becoming a mirror image of his father and she hated it. There were days when she wanted to take Marcie and flee.

Steele said, "I didn't know you wanted half the town."

"I don't."

"Well, I don't care what anyone says," Marcie interrupted, "I'm gonna miss Jo Beth Keegan. She's a neat girl and I like her."

Scornfully, Steele said, "I'm sure, Marcie, that you can find classier friends than the Keegan girl."

"Maybe...if I wanted to."

Steele had wanted it to be a victory dinner. Sullen, he ate in silence. Gary followed his father's lead.

Things were different at the Lake home, where J.D., over dinner, was having difficulty conversing with his wife and daughter. The cook had fixed all his favorites, but the lump in his throat made swallowing difficult.

"It's all over town," Anna Louise said, "about Randy Joe's father getting fired. I guess that means he's not going to finish school here. I'll bet Coach Marshall is sick."

Lake wanted to say "I hope so," but instead cleared his throat and said, "Maybe Randy Joe can stay with some of his friends...finish up here and play football." He knew the likelihood of that happening was one in a million, but felt compelled to say it.

"I just don't understand why it happened now," Dorothy said. "Do you think it had anything to do with Randy Joe planning to pitch for the colored team, J.D.?"

"Probably had somethin' to do with it," he replied. Lake hadn't told his wife or daughter about his involvement with James Steele and George Mason. He hoped they never found out.

Anna Louise said, "I can't believe people can be so mean."

Defensively, Lake said, "It's not a matter of bein' mean, honey. People just like the status quo. They don't like change. They see Randy Joe pitching for the Negro team as an indication of change."

"Well, if that's what he wants to do," Anna Louise said, "then I think it's his own business."

"I can't say I approve of Randy Joe pitching for the Negroes," Dorothy said, "but I tend to agree with Anna Louise."

Lake sighed. "I agree with her, too, but that's not the position I have to take in this town. If you wanna feel that way, fine...but I'd appreciate it if you wouldn't tell people that's how you feel."

Dorothy and Anna Louise accepted their responsibilities as banker's wife and daughter. They would abide by his wishes.

"I wonder," Anna Louise asked, "how Coach Marshall is taking all this?"

Marshall was not taking it too well. He was staring at a plate heaped high with food, lamenting what had happened to his wife Sheila. "Damn it, James Steele and George Mason have screwed everything up. What am I gonna do without Randy Joe?"

Sheila, the home economics teacher at the high school, moved some salad around on a plate. She knew her husband had been counting on Randy Joe to lead the Jason Bulldogs to a championship, which would do a lot to help her husband get a college coaching job. Vic had even thought that some college might take him with Randy Joe in a package deal.

"Vic, you can blame yourself for a lot of this. If you hadn't started meddling, hadn't tried to stop Randy Joe from pitching a game for the Negroes, maybe this wouldn't have happened."

She was right, but it wasn't something he wanted to hear. "I wish you wouldn't call them Negroes. They're niggers, pure and simple."

"I wish you wouldn't ask me to ridicule an entire race of people because of something that happened to you."

Vic Marshall had started to college in the East on a football scholarship, but had lost his starting position to a Negro. That's when he'd transferred to a Texas school, where he wouldn't have to worry about something like that. Marshall had grown up southern and prejudiced. He'd always contended the Negro who beat him out was given preferential treatment.

"Damn it, Sheila, what I was doin' I was doin' for Randy Joe. I was tryin' to protect'im from bein' taken in by those people."

She laughed, sarcastically. "I can't believe you said that, Vic. If anyone wants to use Randy Joe, it's you. You think he can get you out of this town."

Marshall was not a verbal match for his wife. "Randy Joe could be *our* ticket out of here. He's the perfect split-T quarterback and there's a half dozen big schools just waitin' to offer him a scholarship. Some big name coach is gonna offer me a job if I can talk Randy Joe into goin' to his school."

"What big name coach?"

"I don't know yet, but it's done all the time."

Sheila said, "The way I see it you've got a real problem, Vic. To get this big job you're talking about you need Randy Joe. And I'd say chances are good he's not even going to be in school here in the fall."

"Hell, that's what I'm tryin' to tell you."

"You don't have to tell me...I know it. But there's something else you ought to consider. Even if Randy Joe did go to school here in the fall, there's no assurance he'd go to college. It's my understanding he plans to skip college for now and just play baseball."

"Yeah, but we could talk him outta that."

"What do you mean we?" she asked.

"Well, you know he likes you."

Sheila wanted to tell her husband it might be the other way around. She felt a strong sexual attraction to Randy Joe. "Under the circumstances there's not much point in speculating on what we can or can't get Randy Joe to do. You've got your helpers to thank for that."

One of those helpers, George Mason, was having a pleasant dinner with his family. His wife Sarah and daughter Doris were talking about their trip to Europe. Mason was privately looking forward to the month. It would give him some peace and quiet.

Mason had received the first call from Aaron Berkley about the confrontation with R.M. Keegan. The lumber company superintendent had told Mason he was thinking about taking a vacation, leaving town, until Keegan was gone from Jason. Berkley had also wanted reassurance that what he'd done was God's will.

Doris interrupted his thoughts. "Well, daddy, you think y'all stopped Randy Joe from playin' for the niggers? Gary told me about it."

Mason hadn't counted on Steele telling his daughter about their conspiracy. "J.D., James and I were actin' on behalf of the town."

"I'm proud of you, daddy. I'm glad the Keegans are havin' to leave town...especially Randy Joe. I think it's gonna make things a lot easier for Anna Louise."

"What do you mean by that?" her mother asked.

"Oh, you know...Randy Joe's asked Anna Louise out a few times. I think she's gone with him because she felt sorry for'im. She doesn't need to be goin' with white trash like him."

"You're right, Doris," Sarah Mason agreed. "I don't know why Dorothy and J.D. allowed it. They're a lot more liberal than we are."

Mason laughed. "I'll bet that's the first time anyone ever called J.D. liberal."

"Have you noticed, daddy? The Lakes say *Negro* instead of *nigger*."

"Now that you mention it, I have noticed."

"You still haven't answered my question about whether Randy Joe's gonna play or not," Doris said.

"That's because I don't know the answer," he said.

In his frumpy cafe, Big Bill Perkins knew the answer to her question. Sources had told him Randy Joe was definitely going to pitch. There are some things, Big Bill mused, that the Lakes, Steeles and Masons can't do. Well, he'd show them. He'd call on some good ol' boys to take care of the problem.

EIGHTEEN

Randy Joe had trouble finding a place to park at his house. Several cars were parked around the house and people were milling around outside. He thought something was wrong, but when he cut off the Plymouth's engine he and Gretchen heard people laughing and talking. Milltown people were standing on the porch and in the yard eating and drinking.

He and Gretchen pushed their way through the packed house. The dining table was loaded down with food. He saw Weave and Jolene. Weave was working on a piece of fried chicken.

"What's going on?" Randy Joe asked.

"A little show of support for your dad and mom," Weave replied. "I think everybody in Milltown's either here or been here. Everybody brought food. Better get you somethin' to eat."

"Later," Randy Joe said. "Where's mom and dad?"

Jolene said, "Last time we saw your dad he was out in the back yard drinkin' a beer. Your mom's probably in the kitchen."

Randy Joe didn't know how he felt. What had happened to his father wasn't occasion for a party. But he realized neighbors and co-workers were reacting the only way they knew how. A warm glow of gratitude spread through him.

Before he could escape the crowd, Weave's dad pulled him aside. "You remember how I got on your case 'bout pitchin' for the niggers?"

"Yes sir, I do."

"I was wrong. You need to show them town bastards they

can't push Milltown folks around. You get out there and pitch the best game you ever pitched...for your daddy."

He hadn't gone far when Gretchen's dad, Max Turner, seconded Severage's words. Then Jolene's dad did the same.

Randy Joe found his father in the back yard drinking a beer, more or less surrounded by both Negroes and white men, all of whom were drinking beer. The Negroes were those who worked for his father at the mill. On seeing him the men all started offering words of encouragement about Sunday's game.

Wouldn't it be something, Randy Joe thought, if dad being fired united the Milltown whites and Negroes? Damned if it didn't look like it was happening.

He had forgotten why he'd been looking for his father. He guessed he'd just wanted to make sure he was okay. He looked more than okay.

En route back around the house, Randy Joe was pulled aside by Russ Petry and Lewis Alexander, two of his high school baseball teammates. The wiry Lewis said, "Damn, if this ain't somethin'. Two days ago my dad was cussin' you for pitchin' for the niggers and your dad for lettin' you. Now he's all for you pitchin' the game."

Randy Joe laughed. "I guess it's kind of a natural reaction for someone from Milltown. When one of us gets screwed by someone from town, then we all unite. Until then we fight among ourselves."

Back near the front porch Randy Joe ran into J.B. and Sarah Smith. As usual, their clothes looked fresh off the ironing board. "Randy Joe, I've been lookin' for you," Smith drawled. "I just want you to know that I had nothin' to do with you not bein' able to work."

"I already knew that, Mr. Smith."

"There's somethin' else, too. Sarah and I...well, we've been talkin'. If you wanna finish high school here at Jason, we'd be glad for you to live with us."

"We've always thought of you as one of our own kids," Sarah said.

No, I didn't know that, he thought. But he was moved. "I really appreciate the offer," he said, "but I've kinda lost interest in graduatin' from Jason High School."

"What about football?" Smith asked.

"It's not one of my priorities."

"Can't say as I blame you," Smith said. "But if you change your mind, our offer stands."

The party wasn't over until late and Randy Joe wasn't in the mood to go to school on Friday. He knew there would be a lot of whispering. He knew it wouldn't take much to set him off. He was like a bottle of nitro-glycerin on a bumpy road. One wrong word from Gary Steele and the tubby fart would think he'd been caught at ground zero.

Randy Joe had been warned by his dad to stay clear of trouble. So he worked at being cordial when Vic Marshall called him aside after algebra class and said, "Sorry about what happened to your dad. It's hard to figure why things like that happen."

He wanted to say, "It's not hard for me to figure, you sanctimonious sonofabitch." Instead, he said, "Yes sir, it is."

"This puts us on the spot for the upcomin' football season, You know the team was countin' on you."

Randy Joe shrugged. "Well...not much I can do about it."

"Maybe I can do something about it," the coach said.

"What do you mean?"

"I know your parents want what's best for you...and what's best for you is to stay here, play football and finish school. I been talkin' to Sheila and...well, we were talkin' and you know we don't have any kids and all, so we thought we'd talk to your folks about you stayin' with us this next school year."

Randy Joe wanted to laugh. Instead, he said, "That's very generous of you and Mrs. Marshall. But I'd need a job, too."

"I know...and that can be arranged, too. Big Bill told me he'd find somethin' for you to do."

"Coach, I appreciate the offer, but..."

"Before you say no, there's somethin' I want you to do for me."

"What's that?"

"This afternoon I'd like you to go by my house and let Mrs.

Marshall show you the room you'd be stayin' in if you stayed with us. I can't be there...got a meetin'."

"Coach, I..."

"No arguments, Randy Joe, will you do that for me?"

"Well, yeah...I guess so."

"It's settled then."

He had lunch in the school cafeteria with Weave and Jolene. The conversation turned to Weave's plans to join the Air Force. "What do you think about Weave goin' in the Air Force?" Jolene asked.

Randy Joe replied, "I don't wanna tell Weave what he should do."

Weave laughed. "Since when? You been tryin' to tell me what to do ever since I known you."

"It hasn't done a helluva lotta good. You never paid any attention. But you might be doin' the best thing. If I was gonna stay in Jason I'd probably be drafted right after gettin' my cap and gown. Gary Steele's daddy's on the draft board. If you hadn't noticed they fill their quota with Milltown boys before any town boys get drafted."

"Looks like somethin' could be done about that," Jolene said.

"Who's gonna do it?" Randy Joe asked. "There's nobody in Milltown with any clout. Guys like Gary's dad run the school board and draft board."

"Speakin' of one of your favorite people...you seen Gary today?" Weave asked.

Randy Joe grinned. "No...he must be keepin' a low profile. I usually see him in the hall."

"I imagine he's afraid you're gonna whip his ass," Weave said.

After lunch they went outside to mingle with other students under the big shade trees on the northeast side of the campus. Even there socio-economic levels at the school were defined. Town kids seemed to have jurisdiction over some trees, the Milltown kids over others. There were some poorer town students who associated with those from Milltown, but on the whole there was clear segregation.

Gretchen joined them under the shade of a big oak as they all tried to escape the brutal rays of the noonday sun. The humidity was   oppressive, but it would only get worse.

Randy Joe finally saw Gary Steele, but at a distance. Gary, in his new Buick convertible, with Doris Mason sitting beside him, drove past the tree-laden corner of the school grounds. "Want me to invite'em to join us?" Weave asked.

Randy Joe grinned. "Sure...why not?"

Patti Sue joined their quartet for a brief period of time. She didn't stay long, which, he figured, was because of Gretchen. The two girls were civil to each other, even faked liking each other, but there was too much competition between them for a real friendship. Later, after he'd left his friends and was heading back toward the school building, he ran into Anna Louise. He sensed she had been waiting for an opportunity to see him apart from his friends.

"Randy Joe, I just want you to know that I heard what happened and I'm so sorry. My mother and father feel badly about it, too."

"That's strange," he said, coldly.

"What do you mean?"

"Your father was one of the men responsible for gettin' my dad fired."

"That's not true."

"It is true. George Mason, James Steele and your dad. They had lunch with Aaron Berkley yesterday...hatched up the plot to threaten my dad...to tell him he'd lose his job if I pitched Sunday."

"You're wrong, my father wouldn't do something like that."

"Just tell'im he did me a favor. I always planned to rid myself of this town. He just hurried the process."

Vic Marshall's house was eight blocks east and one block north of the school. When he arrived Sheila Marshall had just pulled into the driveway in a year-old Chevrolet. It was maroon and white, the school colors. "Randy Joe...nice to see you," she said, smiling.

"Nice to see you, too, Mrs. Marshall." She looked very good to him. He'd always thought she was pretty. She had always stirred him.

"Well, come on in, Randy Joe. I understand Vic told you we'd be glad to have you live with us this coming school year."

"Yes, ma'am, he did." He followed her into the house, admiring her shapely legs and the way she walked. She was wearing a well-fitted green skirt and a silk soft-colored gold blouse that accentuated her full breasts.

The house was a nice, typical white frame with polished hardwood floors. To the right in the small entry hall was a miniature desk. Sheila Marshall put some books, a sheaf of papers and her purse on top of it and said, "How about something to drink?"

"Well, I'm in kind of a hurry."

"Oh, you can't be in that big of a hurry. How about a Coke?"

"A Coke will be fine."

"Just have a seat and I'll be right back."

She went on through the house to what he guessed was the kitchen. He seated himself in the living room on a patterned couch. The room was semi-dark, cool and quiet, the only noise the low hum of a window air-conditioner.

Randy Joe decided if the rest of the house was furnished anything like the living room he would be impressed. The furnishings, the drapes, the rug on the floor, the entire room provided the same beautiful and casual ambiance of Sheila Marshall. With the right fabrics and mahogany, she had made the room a warm and special place.

"Your Coke," she said, handing him a perspiring glass filled with ice and dark liquid. She had a duplicate glass in her other hand.

Randy Joe's heart ticked a little faster when Sheila sat down beside him. She could just as easily have sat down in the easy chair across from the couch. "I was sorry to hear about your dad losing his job," she said.

He knew she meant it. He had always thought she and her husband were different as night and day. He'd never understood why someone like her would marry a guy like Vic Marshall.

"Thanks," he said. "Maybe it's for the best."

"You don't believe that, Randy Joe."

"You're right...I don't guess I do."

"It must have been devastating to your father, losing a job for no good reason. He must be wondering if there's any justice in the world."

Randy Joe sipped some Coke. "Then you know why he was fired?"

"Anyone with an ounce of sense knows why he was fired."

He semi-laughed. "You sound bitter about it."

"I am bitter," she said. "I don't like to see people bulldozed by men like James Steele and George Mason. Or my husband."

Their eyes met and the exchange was one of understanding. "You didn't mention J.D. Lake," he said.

"He's a reluctant player," she said. "Maybe I shouldn't, but I feel a little sorry for him. He's got a position in the community to maintain...and he can't stand up to Steele and Mason. My husband's the same way. He can't stand up to them."

Puzzled, Randy Joe asked, "Why are you tellin' me this?"

"Because you already know most of it. Vic wants to believe you don't, but I know you do. You're an intelligent young man...a lot more intelligent and perceptive than the people who are trying to manipulate you. My husband is one of those trying to use you."

"How's that?"

"He thinks he can ride your coattails to a college coaching job."

Randy Joe laughed. "I don't know why he thinks he can do that."

"I happen to know there are at least six or seven major colleges that will offer you football scholarships," she said. "Vic...and some of those college coaches, too...think you have the kind of athletic ability to be an All-America quarterback. He'll try to sell you on going to a school that will offer him a job."

"I've already told Coach Marshall I was goin' right out of high school into pro baseball. Besides, if I don't play football this fall I don't think there'll be any college offers."

"That's why he wants you living with us," she said. "He thinks he can brainwash you into doing what he wants."

"I get the idea you don't want me here."

She leaned close. "That's not true. I'm very fond of you. I just want you to know what he's trying to do." Her lips were so sensuous. Without thinking he allowed his impulses to take control. He kissed her gently, then pulled back not knowing what to expect. There was surprise in her eyes, then a hunger he didn't anticipate. Suddenly, she was in his arms, her body straining against his. And their kisses were unquenchable fire.

"Coach Marshall?" he asked during a brief interlude when their lips parted.

"Not for at least an hour," she whispered. "I'm supposed to pick him up in an hour."

Randy Joe was overwhelmed by his possibilities with this woman, and passion stripped away the slightest reluctance. He wasn't sure what a mature woman expected, so he allowed animal instinct to take over. He removed her hose, garter belt and panties. She groaned in an ecstasy of anticipation.

Then her hands were fumbling with his belt, unzipping his pants, freeing his penis. Then he was on top of her, would have penetrated her, but she pushed him away and said, "No, not yet."

Suddenly she was on top of him, unbuttoning his shirt, pulling his pants down until they lay crumpled at the foot of the couch. Then she was kissing his chest, his navel and his penis. She took his penis in her mouth and began doing things he'd never before experienced. He'd never had oral sex and it was all he could do to keep from going. But he was bound and determined not to let that happen until he'd had all she had to offer.

He pulled her up, kissed her, then was on top of her. It took a few moments of effort to penetrate her. She was deliciously tight. Then he was moving inside her and she was responding, her beautiful legs wrapped around him.

Randy Joe wasn't sure how long it lasted, but was glad he'd practiced control with Gretchen. What was happening now shouldn't end too quickly. He'd had sex, but this woman was teaching him to make love.

They made love until she said it was time for her to pick up Coach Marshall. Randy Joe was halfway home before he realized she hadn't shown him his room.

NINETEEN

As Randy Joe came in sight of his house he saw not one, but two new Cadillacs in front of it. What the hell now? he thought. He knew one of the cars belonged to Simmy, but couldn't put an owner with the other. He opened the screen door, went inside and saw his folks sitting at the dining table with Simmy and another man. All had cups of coffee and his dad and mother seemed to be in a good mood.

"Come in here, Randy Joe," his father called out. "There's someone I want you to meet."

As he entered the room the stranger stood to his feet and extended a hand. He shook the man's hand while his father was saying, "This is Mr. Walz...he owns the lumber company."

Sam "Dutch" Walz. Randy Joe had never seen him before. In fact, most of the workers at the mill had never seen the man responsible for their paychecks. He lived in Lufkin, a good seventy miles away, and rarely came to Jason. "Glad to meet you, Mr. Walz."

"Likewise, Randy Joe," Walz said, smiling. "You and Simmy here...you kinda got some folks stirred up."

"Yes sir, but it wasn't intentional."

Walz looked to be in his sixties, over six feet, with massive, muscular shoulders. His very appearance spoke of aggressiveness and power, yet he had a mouth that looked as though it smiled often. His large, deep gray eyes showed compassion and understanding. "Intentional or not, you caused me to make a long drive on a Friday afternoon. Don't you realize I have better things to do?"

"I'm sure you do. So what are you doin' in our neck of the woods?"

"I came to talk your daddy into coming back to work for me."

Randy Joe glanced at his father, who was grinning like a Cheshire cat. It didn't take a genius to see Walz had been successful.

"You wanna cup of coffee, Randy Joe?" his mother asked.

"Yeah, mom...that would be great."

She went into the kitchen and R.M. Keegan said, "Mr. Walz here used to play some baseball."

Walz smiled. "I'm afraid I wasn't very good, but I tried my hand at catching. I've always loved baseball, though. I'm from Philadelphia, you know...and they had some good teams there when I was growing up."

"I'll say," Randy Joe agreed. "The Athletics won nine pennants from 1901 to 1931 and the Phillies won in 1915 and 1950. It's a shame the Phillies couldn't give the Yankees a better battle in the fifty World Series."

The recitation seemed to delight Walz. Randy Joe continued, "I guess you saw a lotta the great Connie Mack teams."

"Yes I did," the lumber magnate said. "In my opinion he was the greatest manager in the game."

Randy Joe doctored his coffee with sugar. "You might get some argument from a few people. Some people say the greatest was John McGraw. Others like Miller Huggins. Now they're puttin' a *great* label on Casey Stengel. Maybe it's deserved. The Yankees have won five pennants in row."

Walz asked, "Do you think he's going to make it six?"

"My pick in the American League this year is Cleveland," Randy Joe replied. "They got the best pitchin' staff of any team in baseball."

"And in the National League?"

"I think it's a tossup between the Giants and Dodgers."

It was as if he and Sam Walz were alone. Walz invited more participation when he said, "Simmy here tells me you're the best natural pitcher he's ever seen...that you throw a natural sinker."

Randy Joe laughed. "He may be exaggeratin' a bit."

"Ain't no exaggeratin' to it," Simmy said. "You come see'im Sunday, Mr. Walz, and you'll see fo' yo'self."

"I may just do that," Walz said.

"If Randy Joe's got a problem," R.M. Keegan said, "it's that he thinks the strike zone is high and inside. If it was he could be the greatest pitcher in baseball."

Walz laughed. "A little wild, huh?"

"A little wild may be an understatement," Keegan said.

Simmy smiled. "I call him pleasin' wild. Ain't nobody gonna dig in on 'im."

"Simmy...your dad, too, tells me you wanna play big league ball," Walz said.

"Yes sir, I do."

"Who you wanna play for?"

"Well, my favorite team's the Yankees. If I have a choice, that's who I'd like to play for."

"I gotta lot of friends up in Philadephia. What do you think about the Phillies?"

"They got Robin Roberts...one of my favorite pitchers. If he had some help the Phillies would have a shot at the pennant this year."

Walz laughed. "Why don't you go up there and give him some help after you graduate from high school?"

"I'd like to be able to help somebody."

His mother interrupted the baseball conversation. "I asked Mr. Walz and Simmy to stay for supper, but both of'em are afraid of my cookin'."

"Now that's not true, Mrs. Keegan," Walz said with a chuckle. "I just gotta get back to Lufkin pretty quick. My wife's expectin' me to take her out for supper."

"My wife's 'spectin' me, too," Simmy said.

Boy, mom's really in the swing of things, Randy Joe thought. What would folks think if they knew she had invited a Negro to supper? "You really think you might come to the game, Mr. Walz?" he asked.

"Yeah...I really think I might. I'd like to see if you're as good as Simmy says you are. And by the way, you got your job back, too. Sorry all this happened the way it did. I figure as a bonus you shouldn't have to work tomorrow. You still get paid."

R.M. Keegan intervened, "No, Mr. Walz, I'm not gonna have that. If Randy Joe's gonna get paid, he has to work for the money. That's the way we do things around here."

"Sorry," Walz said. "Guess I was bein' a bit presumptuous."

"No harm done," Keegan said, "it's just that this family doesn't take somethin' for nothin'."

When Walz and Simmy got ready to leave there were the usual formalities, the shaking of hands, the expressions of appreciation. Randy Joe and R.M. Keegan were standing on the porch as the two Cadillacs moved out. Then Randy Joe blurted out, "What happened here today?"

His dad laughed. "Let's get some coffee and I'll fill you in."

They joined his mother at the dining table. Then his dad said, "Never thought I'd owe my job to a colored man, but seems Simmy knows Mr. Walz pretty well. You might even say they're friends."

"Wonder how that happened?" Randy Joe asked.

"Well, Mr. Walz is a Yankee," his mother said. "Some of them think differently about Negroes than folks in these parts."

"Dad, what did Mr. Walz say about what happened...the way Aaron Berkley threatened you and all? Is he still gonna be superintendent of the mill?"

His mother laughed. "Aaron Berkley was here before you arrived."

His father grinned. "That's right. Mr. Walz made him come over here and apologize...told him if he didn't do it, or if he gave me any more problems, he'd find himself a new superintendent."

Randy Joe grunted. "I wish to hell Mr. Walz had fired his ass. How many people know what's happened?"

"I guess everybody by now," his father replied. "Mr. Walz had Aaron over here eatin' crow around two o'clock, then told'im to get in touch with all the foremen at the mill. You know how fast news travels around here. Everybody in town'll know by tonight."

Angrily, Randy Joe said, "There's some people I'd like to tell myself...Mr. Steele, Mr. Mason, Mr. Lake, Big Bill and Coach Marshall."

"Let it go, son," his father ordered.

"You know what's funny?"

"What?"

"A Negro man just kicked the three richest, most powerful men in Jason right on their collective asses. Who woulda ever believed somethin' like that could happen here?"

They were just finishing supper when there was a knock on the door. Gretchen's dad, Max Turner, entered before anyone responded. No one in Milltown kept their doors locked. It was obvious that Turner was upset. "R.M., I gotta see you...outside."

"What's wrong, Max?" Keegan asked.

"Let's go outside and I'll tell you."

The two men went out on the front porch, leaving everyone else at the supper table. Randy Joe could hear their muffled voices, but couldn't understand what they were saying. His father returned a few minutes later, alone, looking concerned about something.

"What's wrong, R.M.?" Bernice asked.

"Looks like trouble. Big Bill's got a few of his cronies together and they plan to put the fear of God into Simmy and the people in the Quarters. One of Max's crew got word to him about it."

"When's all this gonna happen?" Randy Joe asked.

"Tonight."

"Somebody's gotta do somethin'," Randy Joe said.

"Somebody is. Max and me are gettin' a few men together."

"I'll go."

"No you won't, son. I don't want you involved. We'll handle this."

Bernice was concerned. "Do you have to get involved, R.M.? Why don't you just call in the law?"

"The law's gonna be conveniently missing," he said. "You know there's no law for the Negroes here...not much for us. The law's for people like the Steeles, Masons and Lakes."

Randy Joe said, "I could help, dad. I'll get Weave and some of the guys and..."

"Stay out of it," Keegan said. "I've handled clowns like Big Bill before. He's not gonna be that much of a problem."

Randy Joe looked at his father and pictured Big Bill in his mind. In terms of size there was a tremendous discrepancy. His father was a dwarf compared to Big Bill. However, if his dad got riled he wouldn't want to be in Big Bill's shoes.

"I gotta go," Keegan said, "but this shouldn't take too long."

Randy Joe saw the worry in his mother's face. She knew her husband was absolutely fearless, which caused her great concern. After his dad left Randy Joe tried to reassure his mother and then walked down to Weave's house. He was surprised to find that Andrew Severage had gone with Max Turner and his dad. "Can you imagine that?" Weave asked. "My dad tryin' to protect the niggers?"

"No, I can't," Randy Joe admitted. "Or Gretchen's dad either for that matter."

"Hell, J.B. Smith's even with'em," Weave said.

"You're kiddin'?"

"No I'm not. Jolene's daddy's with'em, too...and Coach Rice."

Rice standing up for the Negro community didn't surprise Randy Joe. He was that kind of man, one who seemed perfectly fitted to fight for the underdog. He also knew Rice's participation could mean the end of his coaching career in Jason.

"Coach Rice has balls," Randy Joe said.

"I'm glad you didn't say brains," Weave said, laughing, "or I'd have to disagree with you." Weave then outlined what he had learned about the raiding party. "Dad says Big Bill and some guys from town are plannin' to burn down all the outhouses in the Quarters, maybe even a few houses, shoot up the place and scare the shit outta all the niggers. Then they're goin' out to Simmy's house and burn a big cross, maybe shoot up his place a little, too. What's this shit about burnin' a cross supposed to mean?"

Randy Joe shrugged his shoulders. "Hell, I don't know."

Weave grinned. "Shit, I thought you knew everything."

He returned Weave's grin. "If I don't know, it's probably not worth knowin'. How did your dad find out what Big Bill was plannin'?"

"Big Bill was braggin' about it and one of his nigger cooks

heard it. She got word to the Quarters and a couple of men there were gettin' their people together. One of'em told Max Turner."

"Big Bill wants to steamroller over a few Negroes."

"Maybe they'll steamroller over a few white men, too."

Randy Joe laughed. "Dad will put a few nicks in the steam-roller."

"What time's it supposed to happen?"

"Near as anybody can tell...around ten o'clock."

Randy Joe said, "I figure I know where Big Bill's gonna get stopped. I'm gonna see if Gretchen wants to watch a real live show."

TWENTY

Big Bill Perkins figured six good ol' boys could handle what he had in mind for the Quarters, plus scare the shit out of Simmy Weatherspoon. The two pickup trucks in which the six were riding carried four five-gallon cans of gasoline, enough to burn down every outdoor toilet in the Quarters, and to touch off the big cross they'd erect in Simmy's front yard. Hell, if there was gasoline left over Big Bill figured they might even burn down a few houses. Each man also had a shotgun, just in case the coloreds got brave.

Big Bill considered himself the champion Nigger Knocker in the county. He based his unofficial title on a game he and some friends often played at night after a few beers. They'd drive around looking for a colored man walking alongside the road, hopefully with his back to the vehicle. The object of the game was for the driver to come as close to the victim as possible without hitting him. The rider on the passenger side of the pickup would then pop the target on the back of the head with a stick, which would send him tumbling.

Nigger Knocking was one of Big Bill's favorite pastimes. His regret was that the game had become harder and harder to play. There were fewer and fewer targets. A Negro walking at night would hear a vehicle coming and move to the other side of a ditch. It was hard to find a colored person who wasn't aware of the game.

A lot of things were changing that Big Bill didn't like, but he considered the alleged nigger threat the worst change of all. He was pretty damn sure a Communist, maybe more than one, had been talking to the colored people in Jason. He'd asked some of them about it, but they'd all told him no, that as far as they knew they'd never talked to a Communist. That's what he expected them to say. They sure weren't going to tell him if they'd fallen under the spell of the Red Menace.

Big Bill figured the Communists had him on their list. After all, he was one of the most outspoken anti-Communists in the county. He hadn't read anything on Communism but had heard the Reds liked to stir up the colored people. That was enough to get him highly pissed off.

Big Bill had spent his entire life in Jason. Just past thirty, he'd never married and still lived with his parents. Failure to marry wasn't from lack of trying. He'd tried to develop a relationship with every eligible woman in Jason. He made trips to Beaumont for relief. The whores on Crockett Street were the only ones who took him seriously. For a price.

In high school Big Bill had played football, but at best was mediocre. Now he imagined he had been great. The cafe was inherited. It had belonged to his parents. He changed the name. Big Bill's Cafe had once been Perkins' Cafe.

Big Bill liked to believe the high school players looked up to him. He was most anxious for Randy Joe Keegan to hold him in great esteem. Randy Joe was a star and Big Bill wanted to be his pal. He couldn't understand Randy Joe being taken in by the coloreds. He figured the kid had been brainwashed. The Communists had done it to captured American soldiers in Korea.

Big Bill wasn't a religious man, but he figured anybody who knew anything about the Bible understood that the Scriptures didn't hold with whites and blacks mixing. He'd been taught that all his life.

Though Big Bill and his folks didn't live in the same style as the Lakes, Masons and Steeles, they didn't want for anything. He bought a new Cadillac every even year and a new GMC pickup every odd year. His fifty-four Caddy was yellow and his fifty-three pickup was green.

As he eased the pickup along the dirt road leading to the Quarters, Big Bill felt pretty good about what he was going to do. Jack Moon and Shelly Worley were in the cab with him. Following behind was Ben Thompson is his black fifty-one Ford pickup. Charley Alford and Jeff Ballard were riding with him.

Moon was a short, muscular,square-built man with a strong jaw and permanent five o'clock shadow. He was forty years old and owned a service station. Worley was thirty-eight years old and worked as a butcher for the town largest grocery store. He was almost six feet tall, stooped and thin.

Thompson was closer to Big Bill's age and size. He had heavy jowls and a belly to match. He worked construction jobs, usually as a pipeliner, but spent the better part of six months each year drinking coffee at Big Bill's Cafe. Alford, forty-six years old, was a meter reader for the city's electric company. He was slightly built, and seemed to have a permanent scowl on his tanned and weathered face. Ballard was the youngster of the group. Only twenty-two, he looked farm boy strong.

As Big Bill drove across the railroad spur he was suddenly forced to brake to a stop. "What the hell?" There in his headlights and the bright moonlight, standing in the middle of the road, was a group of men. The one standing in front was R.M. Keegan. The sight of him, his granite-like features, sent a chill down Big Bill's backbone.

Big Bill cut the truck's engine, but left the lights on. He opened the door and stepped out. His five conspirators fell in behind him and, without touching him, propelled him to the forefront. The cafe owner knew all six of the white men in front of him and the six colored men standing with them. "Hey,

R.M., what you guys doin' here?"

"I live here," Keegan said, coldly. "The question is what are you doing here, Big Bill?"

Big Bill laughed uneasily. "We're just ridin' around. Any law against that?"

"I don't guess there's much law against anything you do or wanna do," Keegan replied. "But the way I hear it you're here to harass some of the people livin' here."

"Now why would I wanna do somethin' like that, R.M.?"

"You're the only one who can answer that question," Keegan said.

Big Bill had always been a little afraid of the man. Keegan's eyes were those of a man who wouldn't be afraid to spit on the Devil. However, bolstered by the five men backing him up, Big Bill decided the men in front of him were no match for his little army. The coloreds, he figured, would run at the first sign of trouble.

He looked past Keegan to Coach Leon Rice and said, with sarcastic disdain, "Didn't know you lived over here, Leon."

"I don't," Rice said with equal disdain. "I was just over here visiting R.M. and we decided to take a walk."

"Looks to me like you're not particular who you walk with," Big Bill said. "And I'm not talkin' about these white fellas."

"It's a free country," Rice said. "I can walk with anybody I wanna walk with."

Communist thinking, Big Bill thought. Maybe Leon was a Communist. What better place for one to be than in the school? He'd damn sure mention his suspicions to George Mason and James Steele. They'd know what to do with a Commie.

"The way we heard it," Keegan said, "you came over here to do some burning. What's in the back of your pickup, Big Bill?"

"What's there ain't none of your business, R.M."

"What if I make it my business?"

"You don't wanna do that," Big Bill said with a touch of bravado. "I ain't gonna let you."

R.M. Keegan walked straight toward his pickup. Big Bill got in front of him and put his fists up in a defensive position. Keegan hit him flush on the nose with a hard right. Blood spurted and Big Bill staggered backwards. Before he could regroup Keegan was all over him, pounding his face with a flurry of lefts and rights. Big Bill tried to protect his face, but everything was going woozy. He tried to grab Keegan, but the man was too quick. He felt his knees buckle until they were on the ground. Then he was falling forward until his face ground into the dirt and gravel of the road.

But Keegan wasn't through with him. He was on top of him. Keegan had his hair in his hand and he was bouncing his face on the road like it was a basketball. Then everything went blank for Big Bill.

Leon Rice and J.B. Smith pulled Keegan off him. They had never seen a man so icily berserk. For a few moments there was almost complete silence, except for the chirping of crickets and the normal noises from the sawmill. Then Rice spoke. "You boys had better get Big Bill to a doctor. How did you boys see it? Looked like self-defense to me."

Big Bill's five colleagues glanced furtively at Keegan. Moon cleared his throat. "Yeah...right. Self-defense."

"The way I see it," Keegan said, "you boys made a little mistake tonight. I don't figure it's gonna happen again, do you?"

Big Bill's little army gave sheepish assurances it wouldn't. They carried their fallen comrade to his pickup.

J.B. Smith, all starched and ironed, said, "I don't think they'll be back. Do you, R.M.?"

"Not tonight," Keegan agreed. "But when Big Bill recovers...well, we'll see."

After all the men had left the road and disappeared, Weave uttered, "Damn, I can't believe what I just saw. Randy Joe, your ol' man is one bad sonofabitch."

Randy Joe laughed, joined by Gretchen and Jolene. They had been crouching in high weeds in a depression away from the road. "Now, aren't you glad I talked you into seein' it?"

Weave admitted he was glad he had attended the spectacle, but added, "The chiggers are about to eat me alive."

"We could go over to my house and have some lemonade," Gretchen suggested.

The idea didn't exactly tickle Weave's fancy. He wanted to

be alone with Jolene. Randy Joe said, "I'd like some lemonade. Weave...he wants to get Jolene in the bushes. And I figure Jolene wants him to get'er there."

Randy Joe went with Gretchen to her house while Weave and Jolene went to look for a dark place. Randy Joe had suggested they just lie in the ditch alongside the road, but they nixed his idea. Weave was already doing a lot of scratching.

Later, when Randy Joe and Gretchen were sitting in the porch swing drinking lemonade, she asked, "You get any chiggers?"

"Yeah," he admitted, "but I wasn't about to scratch in front of Weave. I want him to think I'm immune."

She laughed. "I'm gettin' some bites."

"Wish I was where some of the chiggers are," he whispered.

She whispered back, "You can be...anytime you want."

"I was a little worried about what might happen tonight. Hell, I'm still worried."

"About how Big Bill might retaliate?"

"Yeah. It's not over. It's gonna be a long time before it is."

"It will be...someday," she said. "I'm just glad you're here...that you're not gonna have to leave."

He smiled. "It's been a helluva day, hasn't it? A helluva week."

"I can't believe a ball game can be this important to so many people," she said.

"It's not the ball game. There's a whole lot more goin' on here than a ball game. It's like Coach Rice told me...there's change in the air. People feel it and they're scared. I don't know why. Mr. Lake's not gonna lose his job to a Negro. The change is probably gonna make Mr. Mason and Mr. Steele richer."

Gretchen said, "They just don't want their children and grandchildren having to contend with the nig...Negroes."

"They're like the Nazis...they want a perfect little society, where they can choose who's part of it and make their own rules."

"I think you wanna be part of their society, Randy Joe."

"That's where you're wrong. I just wanna get inside their circle, kick ass and make'em like it."

"And you think that's what money will do."

"Money and fame...damn right. Money's all they understand, but for someone like me it'll take the fame, too."

She sighed. "Which is where baseball comes in."

He laughed. "That's not the only reason I play baseball.
There's something about baseball I don't understand...somethin'
mystical and even supernatural. Playin' baseball makes me feel
like nothin' else I've ever experienced in life. It's love, honor,
religion...everything that's worthwhile in one package. I don't
pretend to understand...I only know how it makes me feel to
stand on the mound with a baseball in my hand and the game on
the line. It makes me feel like I'm up there in the clouds with
God. It makes me feel like I'm special, like there's really some
meanin' to life."

She said, "I've never heard you say anything like that
before."

"I don't guess I ever did."

"Whether you play baseball or not, you're special."

He smiled. "That's a prejudiced point of view."

She laughed. "Guilty as charged." Then on a more sober note
she said, "You haven't told me how you felt when your dad
attacked Big Bill tonight."

"Whew...I'm not sure I can. I know dad can explode, but I
was probably just as surprised as you were. I guess a lot's been
buildin' up inside him over the week. For a minute there, I
thought he might kill Big Bill...and that scared the hell out of
me."

"He mighta killed him," she said, "if Coach Rice and Mr.
Smith hadn't pulled him off."

"Yeah...I gotta remember to thank both of them."

"You can't."

"Why's that?"

"Because you weren't there to see it."

"Damn if you're not right. I wasn't thinkin'."

"That's a first."

He laughed. "Oh, no...it happens all the time."

"At least I know now where you got your temper."

"You knew anyway. But mom's got a bit of a temper, too.

You just don't see it as often as you see dad's. But when you do...look out."

"That's hard to believe," Gretchen said. "Your mother's such a sweet, gentle woman."

"That doesn't mean she doesn't have a temper. She's got a dandy."

They talked until about eleven o'clock, then Randy Joe left to get some sack time. When he got home he found his father, Jim Claxton, Max Turner and Andrew Severage sitting on the front porch drinking beer. He knew if he didn't ask a question or two his father's suspicions would be aroused.

"You guys get that situation with Big Bill straightened out?"

His father's companions laughed and R.M. Keegan said, "Yeah, I think it's all taken care of. I don't think there's gonna be any trouble...at least not for a while."

"What happened?"

Severage started to say something, but Keegan hushed him and replied, "Nothin' for you to worry about, son. Just remember to believe about a fourth of what you hear."

Randy Joe had expected just that kind of response from his father. He knew the man would never brag about beating up on Big Bill. It wasn't his nature. Others would tell the story for him and embellish it considerably.

He talked to the men briefly about the game on Sunday, then went in and went to bed. He didn't fall asleep immediately because Tommy Frank was snoring and his mind had suddenly turned to Sheila Marshall. She'd been in the back of his mind since the afternoon, but now she came to the forefront.

He wondered what she was doing, how she was feeling, whether she had enjoyed their lovemaking as much as he had. He thought she had, but he couldn't be sure. One thing the past week had taught him, as if he hadn't known already, was that it was hard to be sure of anything.

Then there was his dad's attack on Big Bill. He'd been very proud of his father, the way he'd stood up to Big Bill and his cronies. But what was going to happen next? The confrontation, the beating that Big Bill had taken, was sure to breed a simmering enmity between the two men. In fact, how would Big Bill react to him now?

There were a lot of unanswered questions, a lot of uncertainty on the horizon.

Finally, he fell into a restless, fitful sleep. It seemed he had been in bed only minutes when his father was shaking him, saying, "It's time to get up." He remembered that Sam Walz had been willing to pay him for a day's work without having to spend ten hours in the swamp. He wished, just once, that his father wasn't such a stickler for the old adage, "A day's work for a day's pay."

TWENTY-ONE

Conversation in the back of J.B. Smith's pickup truck while en route to the swamp was livelier than usual, all centering on R.M. Keegan's encounter the night before with Big Bill Perkins.

"Randy, I heared yo' daddy done beat dat white man within an inch o' his life," Sleepy Jones said."I heared Big Bill was knocked out so bad dat he ain't waked up yet."

Randy Joe lied, "Well, it's all news to me. I didn't know a thing about it until you guys told me."

"I done got it right from de hoss's mouth," Sleepy claimed. "I talked to one of de coloreds dat was wid'em."

Yank Johnson said, "Colored folks over in de Quarters sho' do 'preciate what yo' daddy done did. People was up late last night all over de Quarters talkin' 'bout it."

"Not me," Iron Man Davis said. "I done went to bed early. But I heared all 'bout it early dis mornin'. Yo' daddy sho' must be some powerful man to do Mr. Big Bill dat way."

Randy Joe laughed. "All I know is that when he whips my ass

I can't sit down for a week."

Morning in the swamp was pretty much like it had been the previous Saturday. Fighting off mosquitoes and snakes as well as heat and humidity. Iron Man, as always, worked as if the world was depending on him to fell and trim just one more tree.

Randy Joe kept up his normal banter with Iron Man, talking about snakes and alligators. He even dwelled on the possibility of a panther living in the swamp. That didn't sit too well with Iron Man, who had the mistaken idea that a mere bobcat would attack and eat a man.

"A bobcat will eat a black man," Randy Joe agreed, "but they'll shy away from a white man. I think they just like dark meat."

Iron Man looked up from some intense sawing and said, "Mr. Randy, dat don't make no sense."

"Hey, I agree with you," Randy Joe said, shrugging his shoulders. "But I'm not a bobcat. I'm not the one who devised the laws of nature."

"What you mean by dat?"

"All I'm sayin' is a higher being figured all this out. I got nothin' to do with it. If I had anything to say about it bobcats would treat Negroes just like they treat white people. But I'm not one to tamper with God's laws."

"You sayin' de Lawd say it okay fo' a bobcat to eat a black man?"

"I'm ain't sayin' anything. I don't want to get struck down by lightnin'. I'd be the last one around here to criticize the mysterious ways of the Lord. But you tell me, Iron Man, why will a bobcat eat a black man and not a white one?"

"I don't know if dat be de truth."

"It's in all the books. I'm just surprised you didn't know it."

"I ain't read no books lately," Iron Man said. "I ain't never read no book."

"Well, since you don't read books I figure you oughta trust your ol' partner here to tell you what's right."

"How ol' Iron Man gonna trust you? You is de craziest white boy I ever seed."

"Damn, Iron Man, you could hurt my feelins' sayin' stuff

like that," Randy Joe joked.

"I don't mean to hurt yo' feelins', but you does like to carry on wid bullshit all de time."

Randy Joe shook his head in dismay. "I'm not believin' what I'm hearin'. I can't believe you'd doubt what I say about bobcats."

"Bobcats is mean," Iron Man said. "Dey'll eat anybody."

Randy Joe sighed. "What can I say? I try to be a source of information and all I get is a lot of doubt. Maybe I oughta just quit tellin' you stuff."

Iron Man grinned and fired a squirt of snuff juice into the water. "Now don't you go doin' dat. What you think I is gonna talk to my wife 'bout when I git home?"

"Now that's encouraging," Randy Joe said. "I'm educatin' you and you're educatin' your wife."

Iron Man grinned again. "She de one who say you crazy."

Lunchtime conversation centered again on R.M. Keegan's encounter with Big Bill and on Sunday's game. Hank Jones said, "Tell me, Mr. Randy, is you as tough and mean as yo' daddy?"

"Course not, Hank. You know me...mild-mannered, hard to rile."

Hank laughed. "Sho' nuff. I done seed you out on de ball field 'nough to know dat you can be mean and scary."

Randy Joe feigned dismay. "I can't believe you'd say that, Hank."

"Ol' Hank, he ain't nobody's fool," Iron Man said. "You de spittin' image of yo' daddy."

Randy Joe laughed. "I may be the spittin' image, but don't expect me to fight Big Bill. He's too big a man for me to tangle with."

"I bet you give dat big man a run fo' his money," Hank said.

"Hopefully," Randy Joe said, "we'll never know."

"You ready fo' de game tomorrow?" Sleepy Jones asked.

"Yeah...ready as I'll ever be."

"I sho' gonna be watchin'," Sleepy said. "What 'bout you, Iron Man?"

The old logger grunted, "Yeah... Hank gonna pick me up."

Yank Johnson laughed. "Dis ain't like de white high school

now, Iron Man. Dis game gonna cost you a dollar or two."

"I gotta dollar or two," Iron Man said, indignantly.

"Ain't dat de truth," Hank responded. "De man's got de first dollar he ever made."

"Ain't so," Iron Man said, argumentatively.

Randy Joe laughed. "Hey, you guys get off my partner's case. We need him at the game. You guys may be the only ones there."

Sleepy gave his best look of dismay. "What you talkin' 'bout, Randy? Dey's gonna be mo' folks dan you ever seed in one place befo'. Ain't a colored man in the county what ain't gonna be dare."

Randy Joe laughed again. "Well, there oughta be at least one colored female. You're gonna bring a date, aren't you, Sleepy?"

The tall man grunted. "I ain't spendin' no money on no woman fo' no baseball game. Women don't know nothin' 'bout baseball."

"That's not true. I got some girlfriends comin' to the game who know a lot about baseball. And you don't wanna tell my mother she doesn't know anything about it."

Sleepy maintained, "Well, I don't know none knows anythin' 'bout it."

TWENTY-TWO

Sunday broke clear and humid, high blue sky with a scattering of white pillowy clouds. A good day for a baseball game. The day looked better than Randy Joe felt. He had a painful headache and a fever. The headache was not uncommon. He had them three and four times a week during certain seasons of the year. Aspirin didn't help.

He thought his mother's coffee might help, but it didn't. She insisted that he eat a big breakfast. It didn't help either. It only made him queasy.

He didn't tell her about the headache and fever. There was nothing she could do. She would only worry. So he sneaked a couple of aspirin, got a cold, wet cloth to put on his head, went back in the bedroom and laid down.

That's where Tommy Frank found him. "You sick?" he asked.

"Another headache, but don't tell mom or dad."

"You gonna feel like pitchin' today?"

"Sure...I always feel like pitchin'."

"Seems to me you just about always have a headache when you play baseball and football games."

"Seems that way to me, too."

Randy Joe put on his gray Longhorns uniform about ten forty-five, ate one of his mother's typical Sunday dinners of roast beef, mashed potatoes, gravy and English peas at eleven, then had his dad drive him to the park. Before leaving Jo Beth said, "I'm gonna be at the game with some of my girlfriends so don't do anything stupid."

He understood it was her way of wishing him luck. His entire family would be there, plus a lot of friends.

When he arrived at the ball park it was an unseasonable ninety-plus degrees and the temperature hadn't stopped climbing. He could already feel the heat and humidity sapping his strength.

The job of introducing him to the other players went to Muddy Tate, the team's shortstop and manager. Tate was an inch over six-feet tall, with stooped shoulders, a large upper body and thin legs. His calves and ankles looked fragile. He weighed a hundred and eighty pounds.

The introductions went rather quickly and Randy Joe hoped he would be able to retain the names and faces in his memory bank. The way his head was pounding, he wasn't sure he'd be able to do it. Being able to put names with faces was something he prided himself on.

There was Tater Green, the wiry first baseman. He didn't look like a first baseman, looked like he needed a few good meals. Second baseman Cut Brown was the opposite. He was stocky, around five-eight, one-seventy.

Then there was Buck Frazier, the catcher, who was six-feet, two hundred pounds. Frazier had a bit of a belly, but muscular arms and legs. His legs and thighs looked heavy.

The third baseman was Cooter Davis, five-ten, one-sixty. Davis had long legs and a short torso, like a frog. Center fielder Peewee Darthard was wide-bodied and quite muscular. He looked like a tough, scrappy ball player. Jackie Monk, the right fielder, was a lean hundred and seventy pounds, stood six-feet, two inches, was streamlined as a gazelle. Leftfielder Rooster Solomon was heavy, built along the lines of catcher Buck Frazier with two hundred pounds of muscle.

Tate next introduced him to the pitchers, who were as different as night and day. Gar Foster was a righthander who stood six-feet, four inches tall and weighed two hundred and forty pounds. In sharp contrast was slighty-built Pooh Wiley, a lefthander, who stood six-feet tall and weighed in at a hundred and sixty. The other pitcher was Skeeter Hodnett, five-nine, one-eighty-five, who looked like a block.

Tate read the "Is that all?" question in Randy Joe's eyes and answered. "Dat's it. Everybody on de team plays mo' dan one position. You wanna take battin' practice?"

"You bet," Randy Joe replied.

The Lake Charles Cajuns had arrived and were warming up on their side of the field. Even playing catch the Cajuns looked very confident, the way Randy Joe expected a professional team to look.

There was obvious surprise on the Lake Charles team when Randy Joe stepped up to take batting practice. They hadn't expected to see a white face on the Longhorns squad. Lake Charles manager Bill McKagen asked Muddy Tate, "Who the hell is that?"

Tate smiled. "He's jest a local boy what's playin' wid us today."

"Damn, Muddy, you didn't tell me you were gonna run a ringer in on us," McKagen said, smiling.

Muddy had never seen Randy Joe pitch. All he knew was what Simmy Weatherspoon had told him. He knew he had three pitchers wondering why one of them, not Randy Joe Keegan, wasn't pitching against Lake Charles. Muddy wondered himself, but Simmy was the boss.

In the Longhorns dugout Muddy asked Randy Joe, "How much time you need to warm up?"

"Fifteen...twenty minutes."

"Buck'll be over here to warm you up. He need to get de feel of you. You jest takes it easy 'til you ready to warm up."

Muddy hadn't been gone from the dugout long when big Gar Foster plopped himself down next to Randy Joe. His skin was a glistening black, aided by the sweat that seemed to be gushing from every pore of his body. He looked like a mountain of coal. "I'll be relievin' if you get in trouble," he said.

"I hope that's not necessary."

"Dey sho' 'nuff got some good hitters, now."

"You've pitched against them?" Randy Joe asked.

"Naw, I ain't never pitched 'gainst dem, but I done heard dey gonna win de league championship dis year. I done heard dey got de best hittin' and best pitchin' in dat league."

Randy Joe laughed. "Good...I like to pitch against the best.

I usually have trouble with a bad team, don't you?"

Gar gave him an uncertain look, a bit disbelieving. "Yeah, I like to pitch against de best. How old is you?"

"Sixteen...but I'll be seventeen next month."

"Lawd help, you jest sixteen years old and you gonna pitch 'gainst dese pros. I ain't believin' Simmy done got you out here fo' dis."

Randy Joe shrugged his shoulders. "I don't think age has much to do with it. How old are you, Gar?"

"Twenty-five."

"You must have a lotta games under your belt."

"Oh, yeah...I done been pitchin' fo' a long time. I been pitchin' up in de Negro American League."

"What brought you to Jason?"

"Since de major leagues started takin' Negro players de Negro league 'bout gone," Gar said, sadly. "Dey ain't but a few teams left. I is here hopin' one of dem big league scouts sees me and signs me up."

"I wouldn't think many big league scouts would come to Jason."

"Dis team goin' on tour," Foster said. "We gonna play all over de country."

"I thought Simmy's team played mostly in Texas and Louisiana."

"Not dis year. We gonna play all de way up into Canada."

Randy Joe said, "Maybe the right people will see you play."

"I hope so," Gar said. "I gotta make it in de next year or two or I ain't gonna make it."

Randy Joe knew Foster was disappointed that he wasn't going to start against Lake Charles. After all, if he showed well against the Cajuns the word would get to the right people. He wouldn't be able to play for Lake Charles, of course. Negroes weren't allowed to play for pro teams in some states. But he could be signed by the organization and assigned to another team. Randy Joe figured Gar might even enjoy seeing him knocked out of the game so he could come in.

The pain in Randy Joe's head had intensified by the time he started loosening up. He was aware of the noise of the crowd

settling in and the relentless sun. The temperature was ninety-
five.

The covered stands were now filled with black faces. There
were whites, too, but it was obvious segregation was in fashion.
The whites were herded together in one part of the stands. Most
of them were sitting on the uncovered bleachers along the third
base line, the area where the Negroes had sat and stood on
Tuesday night.

Gary Steele and Doris Mason came by where Randy Joe was
warming up, making sure he saw them. They wanted to make
sure that he saw Monte Roper and Anna Louise were with them.
Randy Joe gave them nothing more than a passing glance. The
heat and humidity had steamed the anger out of him. He felt a
confusing dullness, the result of the fever. He was surprised to
see Big Bill Perkins in the park, a bandage adorning his nose.

Over in the Lake Charles dugout pitching coach Don Boswell
was telling manager Bill McKagen and hitting coach Carlin
Sumner what he'd learned about Randy Joe Keegan. "The kid's
only sixteen years old...won't be seventeen until next month."

"What's he doing playing for a buncha niggers?" Sumner
asked.

McKagen laughed. "Better watch your tongue, Carlin. You
may not always be coaching in the South."

McKagen had arranged the game with the Longhorns because of a scheduling fluke that gave his team a Sunday off in
league competition. He didn't like days off early in the season.
Also, the men who ran the big club wanted him to keep a sharp
lookout for talent. They were especially interested in signing a
few Negroes.

"The kid ain't very big and he don't look very stout,"
Boswell said. "Course, you never know."

"I sure as hell know," Sumner said. "I don't know why
people think bein' a hotshot in high school means a kid can throw
in the pros. If we don't tee off on this kid we oughta pack it up."

McKagen wanted to believe Sumner, but there was something about the kid that bothered him.

Randy Joe wasn't thinking about the Cajuns. The pain in his
head was too intense for that, but his arm felt good. There was

a lot of pop on his fastball, even though he wasn't opening up. Buck Frazier caught him only a few minutes before getting a sponge to put inside his mitt.

Muddy Tate walked over to where Buck was taking Randy Joe's pitches and asked, "How he look, Buck?"

"He sho' throw a heavy ball. Gonna break a lot o' bats de way he throw."

It bothered Muddy that he'd been ordered to let the white boy pitch, but checking out the crowd he had to admit it would be the biggest he'd played before as a Longhorn. The reason was that there were almost as many whites as Negroes in the stands. The gate receipts would be good.

At the first sign of the white kid having trouble, Muddy figured on getting Gar Foster in the game. Gar could hum it. Then Muddy encountered Simmy Weatherspoon, who'd been down watching Randy Joe warm up. "He somethin', ain't he?" Simmy said.

"Yeah," Muddy replied. "Buck say he throw a real heavy ball."

Simmy said, "It usually take him a while to settle down. Jest be patient wid'im if he walk a few or hit a couple o' batters. Even if he put a few batters on base, dey ain't gonna do much wid'im."

So much for taking him out at the first sign of trouble, Muddy thought. He figured Simmy ought to let him do the managing, but held his tongue. Zeke Lott, who was with Simmy, said, "No matter how wild he get, Muddy, don't you be worried none. Dat boy'll pitch his way outta any trouble he get in."

Yankees scout Tommy McGuire and Pirates scout Slap Peterson went to the Lake Charles dugout to visit with Bill McKagen, who was a friend. They were friends with Don Boswell and Carlin Sumner, too.

"What the hell you guys doin' here?" McKagen asked, joking. "Hope you're not here to scout any of my boys."

"We're always lookin' at your boys," McGuire replied. "Came to see what they could do with the kid pitcher over there."

McKagen asked, "Whatta you guys know about that kid?"

"I know if I was gonna bat against him I wouldn't dig in," Peterson said. "He's wild as a March hare and throws bullets."

Sumner said, "Our boys ain't afraid of some kid pitcher. He can't throw as hard as some of the ones we've faced this year."

"Afraid he can, Carlin," McGuire said. "Slap and I saw'im pitch last Tuesday night. He threw a no-hitter and struck out twenty-two in a seven-innin' game."

"You're talkin' high school," Sumner said with disdain. "This ain't no high school ball club he's pitchin' against today."

"I know you're proud of your sticks," Peterson said, "but warn'em to be loose at the plate. This kid's capable of hurtin' somebody."

"What you're sayin' is," Boswell interjected, "we need to make'im pitch...not go up swingin'... and he'll give us the base on balls."

"No, Don, I ain't so sure o' that," McGuire said. "The kid's what I'd call pleasingly wild. He may walk a few, hit a few, but he seems to get it over when he needs to."

McKagen asked, "What else you know about him?"

"Eighteen wins and no losses this year," Peterson replied. "He's got the most natural sinker I've ever seen. Curveball's deadly, too."

Sumner grunted, "Damn, you guys sound like you're ready to put this kid in the Hall of Fame."

McGuire and Peterson laughed. Then McGuire said, "Not quite, but he's gotta shot at gettin' there."

McKagen grinned. "You two assholes come back and see us when you got better news."

When the two scouts had left Sumner said, "Those shitheads were just tryin' to psyche us out. You know they're both as full of shit as a Christmas turkey."

At two o'clock the Longhorns took the field to a standing ovation. Randy Joe took his warmup tosses, then catcher Buck Frazier fired the ball to second baseman Cut Brown. The ball was flipped around the horn, then back to Randy Joe.

"Play ball!" the umpire shouted.

The headache and fever had made Randy Joe feel weak, but standing on the mound he now felt ten-feet tall. Even with the temperature hovering at ninety-five degrees and the sun beating down he felt as cool as if he was standing in an icehouse.

TWENTY-THREE

Second baseman Johnny Silverman had seen a lot of fastballs in his day, but none like the one thrown to him by Randy Joe Keegan. The switch-hitter, batting lefthanded, thought the ball was coming right down the center of the plate. It didn't stay there and was already in the catcher's mitt by the time he managed a weak swing.

The New York native was a good contact hitter, but the ball had been a blur. Silverman's eyes flew wide-open at Randy Joe's next pitch, which looked like a white blur headed for his neck. He unceremoniously hit the ground, stirring up a storm of dust around the batter's box. Dirt stuck to his sweaty uniform.

The bastard's throwing at me, Silverman thought, angrily.

The infielder, twenty-three years old, wasn't afraid. He couldn't afford to be if he was going to make the majors. And Silverman was confident he was going to get to the big show within the next three years. He had three years of college ball under his belt and two years as a pro. No high school pitcher was going to make him look stupid.

He dug in again. But while he was bravely talking to himself about what he was going to do, his mind was telling him something altogether different. It was analyzing the speed of the two pitches he had seen. And his brain was telling him to be nervous and scared.

Randy Joe's next pitch also came inside. Silverman wanted it to be a ball, but knew it was a strike before the umpire's coarse cry. What's wrong with me? he thought. Batting average over three hundred, on-base percentage almost .450, and I feel like I've got a toothpick in my hands instead of a bat.

The next pitch was high and outside, but Silverman swung. He was ready to get away from the plate. Throwing his bat down and going back into the dugout he said to his teammates, "I'll get'em next time."

Indiana-born Buddy Garrick, the Cajuns shortstop, found Randy Joe's offerings equally unsettling. The righthanded hitter took a fastball inside that had him mumbling to himself, then bailed out of the bucket three times while swinging at curveballs.

Big and powerful right fielder Harry Wade, who hailed from Muskogee, Oklahoma, waved at a couple of fastballs and took two inside. Then Randy Joe fed him a hard sinker that sawed his bat in two. But the lefthand hitter had enough pop to flare the ball to left. It looked like a sure hit until Muddy Tate made a diving catch near the foul line.

Randy Joe's teammates hadn't known what to expect from their new white pitcher, but coming into the dugout after the third out they were laudatory and anxious to do some backslapping. Randy Joe wanted to hand out some accolades himself. "Damn nice catch, Muddy."

Muddy smiled. "Keeps pitchin' like dat. We'll make de catches."

Even the other Longhorns pitchers, Gar Foster, Pooh Wiley and Skeeter Hodnett, gave smiles and words of encouragement. Randy Joe appreciated it. He knew all of them wanted to be on the mound.

Muscular Peewee Darthard, a switch-hitter, was swinging from the right side against Cajuns lefthander Sherill Lawson. Lawson was twenty-three, a three-year pro and Mississippi native. He'd already picked up four wins on the year against no losses, and had a minuscule earned run average.

Lawson went into his windup, then came hard inside with a fastball to Peewee. Everyone understood it was a message, a warning for what Randy Joe had done to the Lake Charles hitters. On the next pitch Peewee, unintimidated, grounded a hard shot between second and first. Second baseman Johnny Silverman leaped for it but it got by and was handled by right fielder Harry Wade.

Righthand hitting Cut Brown worked Lawson for a two-ball, two-strike count. Peewee was moving on the next pitch, which Cut grounded to second. The only play was to first.

Runner in scoring position and Muddy Tate at the plate. The Longhorns shortstop found Lawson's first offering to his liking and jumped on it. Unfortunately, Muddy didn't catch the ball solidly on his bat. The ball squirted straight up into the bright sun. It was handled easily by Cajuns shortstop Buddy Garrick.

That brought switch-hitting Buck Frazier to the batter's box, swinging from the right side. Lawson worked the count to three balls and two strikes, then grooved one. Buck caught almost all of it. Left fielder Layton White went up against the wall to make the catch.

The Cajuns came off the field to the exhortation of hitting coach Carlin Sumner. "C'mon guys, let's tee off on this little punk."

In the stands Tommy McGuire turned to Slap Peterson and asked, "Want any action on this inning?"

"I'll bet you five he strikes out the side."

McGuire laughed. "Not a good bet for me, Slap. McKagen's got his free swingers up."

Peterson countered, "The kid might be wild this inning."

"Okay, you wanna bet me he strikes out three in a row?"

"Wild as he is? I'm not that stupid."

Batting cleanup for Lake Charles was third baseman Max Stradlin, a compact one hundred and ninety pound six-footer from Florida. The two-year pro was definitely on his way to the big show. He was a home run, RBI man who was tearing up the league. Randy Joe started the righthand hitter with one of his special curveballs that had Stradlin bailing out of the batter's box. He followed with a chin-high inside fastball that the slugger barely avoided.

Stradlin was not one to be intimidated by any pitcher, but he'd never seen a fastball like Randy Joe's. Nor had he ever seen such a tight, quick-breaking curveball. The latter had tied him in knots and he knew the fastball had been thrown to set him up for another curve. He was determined not to bail out on the next one, but what Stadlin guessed would be a curveball was a blazing fastball on the outside corner of the plate. He didn't have a prayer of catching up with it.

Confused by his guessing game the third baseman then chased a curveball in the dirt. It had not been a quality trip to the plate.

Catcher Frank Goff, a Tennessee native, was a three-year pro with power stats similar to those of Max Stradlin. A catcher who could hit, Goff was also a shoo-in to make it to the majors. A year at Lake Charles, another year or two of grooming at a higher level and the tall two-hundred-pounder would be with the big club.

Goff saw an inside fastball from Randy Joe, then three curveball strikes that had him grumbling to himself.

Luke Adler, the first baseman and Michigan native, received similar treatment from the young righthander. The only difference being that the two-year pro, a lefty, got nothing to swing at except hard sinkers.

After the Cajuns were back in the field, pitching coach Don Boswell said, "Skipper, we sure wanna tell the big club's head scout about this Keegan kid."

"Don't worry. I'll be on the horn the first thing tomorrow."

Hitting coach Carlin Sumner grunted, "It ain't over yet."

"Hell, we ain't givin' up, Carlin," Boswell said. "But the kid's got speed and movement on the ball like I ain't never seen before."

Sumner again showed disdain. "Big game for 'im...adrenalin pumping. I'm bettin' he runs outta steam pretty soon."

Left fielder Rooster Solomon nailed Lawson's first pitch, clanging it off the tin wall in left. Rooster, demonstrating that he could fly on the basepaths, went into second standing up.

Lawson worked the count full on third baseman Cooter Davis, who then smashed a liner that had base hit written all over it. Cajuns second baseman Johnny Silverman, diving, speared the ball and came up throwing, doubling Rooster off second. Silverman's great play proved critical. The Longhorns next hitter, right fielder Jackie Monk, laced a single to center. Rooster would have scored easily.

Tater Green hit a long fly to right to end the inning.

The first hitter for Lake Charles in the third, New Jersey-born left fielder Layton White, was as nervous as a bitch dog in heat when he stepped into the batter's box. The three-year pro was determined to stand his ground against heat from the mound. From the on-deck circle, he'd had trouble even seeing Randy Joe Keegan's fastball.

And that's what Randy Joe started him off with, a fastball across the inside part of the plate at close to a hundred miles-per-hour. The ball was already in Buck Frazier's mitt by the time White swung.

Two more fastballs and White was gone.

Switch-hitting George Parrish, center fielder and two-year pro out of Chicago, batting lefthanded, had better luck. Randy Joe had him down two strikes and no balls and came in with a hard sinker on the inside part of the plate. Parrish caught it on the handle, breaking the bat.

The ball rolled weakly to the mound.

That brought Sherill Lawson to the plate. The pitcher, a three-year pro out of Mississippi, was considered a good hitter. Randy Joe retired the lefthander on three fastballs.

In the stands Anna Louise Lake taunted Gary Steele. "Well, you were right about the pros beatin' up on Randy Joe."

"It's not over," Gary said. "He's been lucky so far."

Monte Roper, Anna Louise's date, said, "It's hot out there. He'll slow down after a while."

Anna Louise was angry at herself for accepting the date with Monte. She didn't like him. She realized she'd been coerced into the date by her friend Doris Mason. She was also angry at James Steele, George Mason and her own father for getting Randy Joe's dad fired.

"I don't think so," she said in response to Monte's statement. "I think Randy Joe just gets stronger...and I think he'll win the game."

"My god, Anna Louise," Doris said, "you sometimes act like you're for the trash over in Milltown."

"Randy Joe Keegan's not trash, Doris, and you know it."

Doris was used to shoving Anna Louise around with her acid

tongue. But Doris sensed that on this particular day her friend might push back. She and Gary exchanged looks.

Randy Joe was the first hitter up for the Longhorns in the bottom of the third. Lawson figured on teaching him a lesson. His first pitch came high and inside, sending his adversary sprawling. Randy Joe picked himself up and stepped back in the batter's box. Lawson didn't like his confident air so he sailed another pitch high and inside. Again Randy Joe picked himself up gingerly. Lawson's teammates liked it. He was giving the kid a taste of what pro ball was all about.

Carlin Sumner turned to Don Boswell in the Cajuns dugout, grinned and said, "Let's see how your prospect handles that...see if it don't shake'im up a bit."

"It's not a bad move," Boswell agreed.

Lawson went into his windup, launched himself forward and unleashed a fastball for the outside corner of the plate. Randy Joe's eyes picked up the rotation of the ball practically from the time it left Lawson's hand. His bat met it precisely and sent a screaming rocket back at the mound. Lawson pawed frantically at the baseball with his glove, but was too late. It slammed into his left knee and dropped him like a big oak dynamited at its roots. The ball, after ricocheting off the lefthander's knee, went rolling toward the Lake Charles dugout. Randy Joe was standing on first by the time it was retrieved. Lawson was writhing on the ground.

Randy Joe looked on with some sympathy while Lawson was helped off the field by pitching coach Don Boswell and another Cajuns player. First baseman Luke Adler grudgingly said, "Nice piece of hittin'."

"Just lucky," Randy Joe said. "Sorry about your pitcher."

"Breaks of the game," Adler said.

The new pitcher for Lake Charles was Garrett Clark, a six-foot, hundred and seventy-five pound righthander from South Carolina. He was a two-year pro, had a good curveball and a sneaky fastball. Occasionally he'd fool hitters with a changeup. He had a good one. He was McKagen's number one middle reliever.

A worried Don Boswell told the manager, "I think Lawson's

gonna be all right."

"He'd better be," McKagen said. "I hope that kid didn't knock us out of the championship."

Clark's first pitch to Peewee Darthard was rapped straight to the shortstop for an easy doubleplay. Then Cut Brown went down swinging.

As the Longhorns took the field Zeke Lott said to Simmy, "You realize dat Randy Joe done throwed ten straight no-hit innins'...countin' de no-hitter dat he throwed Tuesday night?"

Simmy, puffing proudly on his cigar, replied, "'Course, I know it. I done told you dat boy gonna be de best dey ever was. And look at dis crowd. We done filled up dis ball park fo' de first time."

When Big Bill Perkins approached Vic and Sheila Marshall in the stands his greeting was warmly received by the coach, coldly acknowledged by Sheila. Big Bill knew she had never liked him.

"The kid looks good, don't he?"

Marshall grinned. "No doubt about that."

"What happened to your nose?" Sheila asked. She, of course, already knew. Everyone in town did.

Big Bill chuckled. "A little misunderstandin'. The important thing is that Randy Joe will be on the football field this fall."

"Yeah," Marshall agreed, "that's the important thing. Right now I'm enjoyin' this game and I ain't really a baseball fan."

"I'm like you there," Big Bill said, "but it's a helluva game."

Johnny Silverman approached his second at bat against Randy Joe with renewed determination. He'd had time to psyche himself up, to put the blur of the kid's fastball out of his mind. Then Randy Joe let loose with a bullet that grazed the bill of Silverman's cap. It was all over for the second baseman. He went down on strikes, swinging weakly.

With Buddy Garrick, though, Randy Joe got a sinker close to the middle of the plate and the shortstop bounced out unassisted to Longhorns first baseman Tater Green. Cajuns right fielder Harry Wade also got a piece of the ball, grounding to second baseman Cut Brown, who tossed to Tater for the third out.

Even though it was a three-up, three-down inning, the fact

that two hitters had made contact with the ball seemed to fire up the Cajuns. "He's tirin'," said Carlin Sumner. "We're beginnin' to time 'im."

Cajuns reliever Garrett Clark also had things under control. He got Muddy Tate on a comebacker to the mound, put Buck Frazier down on strikes, and got Rooster Solomon to fly out to his right fielder.

Randy Joe lost the no-hitter in the fifth. Max Stadlin and Frank Goff got back-to-back singles. Goff's hit to right moved Stradlin to third. Randy Joe then walked Luke Adler on four straight pitches.

Muddy Tate, aware the heat was affecting Randy Joe, got Gar Foster up and throwing in the bullpen, then strolled to the mound. "You okay?"

"Yeah...just lost my concentration. I'll be fine."

"Gar...he warmin' in de bullpen. Don't hurt yo'self. It's plenty hot out here today. Say if I need to pull you."

Leftfielder Layton White was the hitter. Because Randy Joe had been wild to the previous batter, White had been told to take a couple of pitches. It was a good decision on McKagen's part. The young pitcher's first three offerings were high and inside.

Randy Joe's uniform was wet with sweat and caked with dust. The fever had whipped his initial flow of adrenalin and was torturing his brain. His head seemed ready to explode. Angrily, his mind fought to ward off the devils that were thwarting his concentration. But by sheer will he was somehow able to enter an almost euphoric state, refusing to submit to the pain.

Layton White saw only the blur of the baseball as it whistled across the plate and settled in Buck Frazier's mitt. He cocked his bat and waited for the next pitch, but it too passed him in ghost-like fashion. He managed a swing at the young pitcher's three-two offering, but much too late.

As George Parrish stepped into the batter's box Carlin Sumner asked, "You wanna pinch hit for Clark?"

"Too early for that," Bill McKagen replied. "I don't wanna use up my whole pitchin' staff in an exhibition game."

Randy Joe threw three quick strikes to Parrish and three more to Clark. The rally died a quick death. Still, the Lake

Charles players felt it was getting close to crunch time. They had, after all, managed two hits in the inning.

Don Boswell was even more impressed with the Longhorns pitcher. Putting his hand on his heart he said, "That oughta prove the kid's got it here. He's not gonna fold."

Carlin Sumner laughed. "Damn, Don, I'm beginnin' to believe you're pullin' for 'em. We'll rock him in the next few innings."

McKagen grinned. "You guys speculate all you want. I'll settle for a couple of runs."

While Randy Joe was pitching flamboyantly, Garrett Clark was working with quiet efficiency. In their half of the fifth the Longhorns went down in order: Cooter Davis on a pop to third, Jackie Monk on a strikeout, and Tater Green on a grounder to short.

In the stands lumber company owner Sam Walz said to his wife Thelma, "Critical inning...real critical inning."

"How's that, Sam?"

"Randy Joe seemed to weaken in that last inning...got the top of the order up this inning."

Whether Randy Joe made it through the sixth or not, Walz had seen enough to know that he was something special. The kid was a natural at sixteen. What could he be when he got the right training and some experience?

Johnny Silverman had already fanned twice and his confidence had gone from steel to spun glass. Randy Joe sensed it and didn't bother to pitch fine, just blew three right past him.

Buddy Garrick and Harry Wade got the same treatment.

Back in the stands Sam Walz exhaled and said, "That shows me something. That really shows me something."

Randy Joe led off the bottom of the sixth for the Longhorns. Garrett Clark knew he had to send the kid pitcher the same kind of message his predecessor had sent, just to let him know his hit off Lawson's knee hadn't intimidated anyone. So he brought one in high and tight, forcing Randy Joe back on the seat of his pants.

The young pitcher bounced up off the ground and got back in the batter's box without bothering to dust himself off. It wouldn't have done any good anyway. The dust clumped on his sweaty uniform.

Clark brought in a fastball away that caught the outside corner, evening the count. Then he busted another fastball inside so close that it blew the dust off a button on Randy Joe's uniform top. Clark couldn't believe it. The pitch didn't even make the kid move. He just stared back at him. Damn, talk about cool, Clark thought. Or maybe the kid's just crazy. Good hitters were all crazy because they weren't afraid of heat.

Clark got his next pitch a little too much over the plate. Randy Joe turned on it and hit a screaming line drive that barely eluded the glove of second baseman Johnny Silverman. The green tin wall in right stopped the ball about three hundred and sixty feet from home plate. So quickly did the ball rattle off the wall and into right fielder Harry Wade's glove that Randy Joe had to hustle to beat his throw to second.

Peewee Darthard sacrifice bunted Randy Joe to third, but Cut Brown hit one back to the mound for an easy out.Muddy Tate flied to center. After six complete innings there was no score.

TWENTY-FOUR

Nothing much surprised R.M. Keegan, but he was taken aback when Big Bill Perkins made his way through the stands to greet him. "That boy of yours, he's really somethin'," Big Bill said, grinning. Keegan agreed. Then Big Bill directed some words of praise about Randy Joe to Bernice and greeted Max and Lisa Turner like old friends. It was as if the past Friday night hadn't happened.

When Big Bill left Max Turner asked, "What was that all about?"

Keegan shrugged his shoulders. "I have no idea."

Cajuns third baseman Max Stradlin had singled in the fifth, the beneficiary of Randy Joe's fever and lapse in concentration. Leading off in the seventh the Lake Charles cleanup hitter dug in with a confidence that was shaken when a blazing fastball forced him away from the plate.

The pitch didn't anger the hitter. He had expected it. He was developing an appreciation for the competitiveness of the kid on the mound. The inside pitch was his way of saying he owned the plate. Well, Stradlin wasn't buying it. He was going to show Randy Joe Keegan that the plate belonged to him. So he dug in again, making sure the young pitcher saw that his spikes were firmly set.

Stradlin was sure Randy Joe got his message because the pitcher flashed a brief, defiant smile. Then he came with a pitch that made the hitter come out of his spikes while abandoning the batter's box. The curve broke right across the inside corner of the plate. He'd never seen such a curveball, not one with that kind of speed and break.

Again there was the ritual of Stradlin digging in. And, again, Randy Joe came with a duplicate curveball that caused the righthand hitter to bail out. Then there was a fastball on the outside corner that Stradlin could only watch for a called strike three.

Catcher Frank Goff, who had also singled in the fifth, received similar treatment. Goff worked the count to two balls and two strikes before striking out.

Lefthand hitting first baseman Luke Adler, who had walked in the fifth, got three smoking fastballs that had him mumbling. He complained to second baseman Johnny Silverman, "Who was it said he was wild...tired out? Ain't sure I saw those last three pitches."

Silverman, who like his other teammates was developing an appreciation for Randy Joe's speed and stamina, gestured toward the blazing sun. "Maybe it's the bad lighting."

Weave, sitting midway up in the stands with Jolene and

Gretchen, said, "Seventeen strikeouts in seven innings...nine in a row. That ain't bad against a buncha pros."

Buck Frazier led off the Longhorns half of the seventh with a double that rattled the left field wall. Then Rooster Solomon hit a hard grounder to short. Cajuns shortstop Buddy Garrick forced Buck to retreat back to second and threw to first for the out.

Cooter Davis worked the count full, then hit a grounder up the middle. Garrick fielded the ball behind second base but his throw to first was too late. Buck moved to third.

Jackie Monk then hit a smash to second that resulted in a Silverman to Garrick to Adler doubleplay to end the inning.

"Hear that?" James Steele asked George Mason.

"What?"

"I heard somebody say Randy Joe already has seventeen strikeouts...nine in a row," Steele replied. "I thought this was supposed to be a good pro team."

"They're in first place in their league," Mason said.

"What class ball is that?"

"Class B, I think."

"Must not be much of a league," Steele said.

They had come to the game out of curiosity and because of the events of the past week. Not to attend would be to admit defeat, something they were not willing to do. It was important that everyone knew they still ruled the town. Their wives had refused to come. So had J.D. Lake. They worried about Lake, that he didn't have the stuff for tough leadership.

In the Lake Charles dugout Bill McKagen told Don Boswell, "Get Ryan up and throwing. We'll pinch hit for Clark this inning." Tom Ryan was a hard-throwing righthanded reliever from Montana. The three-year pro didn't have much of a curveball, just relied on smoke.

"Who you want pinch hittin'?" Carlin Sumner asked.

"Who do you suggest?" McKagen asked.

"Jensen's been strokin' the ball pretty good."

"Then use 'im."

Mike Jensen, who would be hitting third in the top of the eighth, was a big lefthand hitter out of San Antonio, Texas. He was a two-year pro who had averaged thirty home runs a year.

Leading off in the eighth was left fielder Layton White, who for the third straight time struck out, a victim of Randy Joe's curveball. Switch-hitting center fielder George Parrish suffered a similar fate, though he saw nothing but fastballs. That brought Jensen to the plate and some murmurs out of the stands. He was quite a specimen, six-feet, four inches tall and two hundred and forty pounds. And there wasn't an ounce of fat on his body.

Jensen prided himself on swinging a much heavier stick than those used by his teammates. Jensen and his bat were intimidating. But the big lefthand hitter had never faced anyone with Randy Joe Keegan's kind of heat. He just couldn't get his big bat around on the white blurs coming out of the kid's hand. Jensen's bat waved late goodbyes to three fastballs.

"Twelve strikeouts in a row...twenty in eight innings," Carlin Sumner ranted to the Cajuns players. "I ain't believin' this. You assholes had better start poundin' this punk or I..."

"Take it easy," McKagen said. "This ain't a reflection on you."

"The hell it ain't...I'm the hittin' coach."

McKagen chuckled. "Hey, give the kid out there some credit. He's in the kind of rhythm where it would be hard for big leaguers to hit'em."

"Well, I could damn sure hit the little bastard," Sumner said.

"Take a shot then," McKagen challenged. "It's just an exhibition game. You can play."

Sumner knew then he'd let his mouth overload his ass. He was thirty-three, had spent ten years in the minors and portions of two years in the majors as a reserve before landing the coaching job. He was a student of hitting and had done well in the minors, but had choked against big league pitching. Now he was on the spot. He knew he had to bat against Randy Joe Keegan to back up his boast.

"Next time we need a pinch hitter I'll take a cut at 'im," Sumner said, hoping the time wouldn't come.

Longhorns first baseman Tater Green was first up in the bottom half of the eighth and grounded to short for the first out, which brought Randy Joe to the plate. New Cajuns pitcher Tom Ryan looked at his adversary and decided to adhere to teammate

Sherill Lawson's admonition. Lawson, still smarting from Randy Joe's line shot to his knee, had said, "Stick one in the little shithead's ear for me."

So Ryan's first hummer was a knockdown pitch. Again, Randy Joe came up off the ground with a kind of unconscious look. The Cajuns pitcher had only to look at the kid digging in to see that his best fastball hadn't fazed the hitter at all. Ryan studied his options. Lawson had tried to punch out the kid with a fastball and almost had his knee shattered. Clark had also served up a fastball to the young pitcher and the right field fence had been dented with the ball. He'd fool the kid with a changeup.

Ryan's changeup was what made his fastball so effective. And the one he threw Randy Joe was as good as he'd ever thrown. But damned if the kid didn't seem to know exactly what was coming.

Craaack!

The split-second Randy Joe's bat crushed the ball the big crowd seemed to simultaneously rise to its feet. Everyone knew the ball was going out of the park, including Cajuns center fielder George Parrish. Still, he started running back with his eyes glued to it, realizing he was fast running out of room. When he knew any additional momentum from his churning legs would run him right into the fence he leaped as high as he possibly could, his glove grabbing for the sky.

Parrish's gloved hand, extending over the fence, snatched the ball from its flight as his body dented the green tin wall. That he held the ball after crashing into the fence was a miracle.

The crowd's fever-pitched roar died a grinding death, replaced by scattered applause for what was, without doubt, the best defensive play of the day.

Ryan, who had been standing just in front of the mound watching the flight of the ball, heaved a sigh of relief. He was grateful to Parrish, but was also wondering how a kid like Randy Joe Keegan could hit the ball so far and hard. He didn't look like a power hitter. Nor did he look like he had the stamina to pitch like he was pitching.

Peewee Darthard worked a two-one count on Ryan, then poked a single to left. He died at first then second baseman Cut

Brown popped to third.

Lake Charles second baseman Johnny Silverman had struck out three straight times, but leading off the ninth he got his bat on a sinker and took it to left for a single. It stopped Randy Joe's string of strikeouts at twelve.

Buddy Garrick then laid down a nice sacrifice bunt that advanced Silverman to second. That brought Harry Wade to the plate. He worked the count to two-two, then rifled a single to center.

Silverman, one of the fastest Cajuns players, rounded third and steamed for home with what he was sure would be the first run of the game. But he hadn't counted on the strong arm of Peewee Darthard. From the corner of his eye Silverman saw the ball coming toward catcher Buck Frazier and knew it had him beaten. The only thing he could do was slide hard into the big catcher. No chance of winning that confrontation.

Wade took second on Peewee's throw to the plate.

In the Cajuns dugout Carlin Sumner paced back and forth saying, "He's runnin' outta gas...he's runnin' outta gas." There might have been some validity to what he was saying. Randy Joe didn't seem to be throwing as hard as he had been.

Longhorns shortstop/manager Muddy Tate felt it was time for another conference on the mound. He was joined by Buck and the other infielders. "You gettin' tired?" he asked Randy Joe.

"I'm fine," the pitcher assured him.

"What you think, Buck?" Muddy asked.

"He a little slower dis innin', but he still fast," the catcher replied. "My hand feel like it been kicked by a mule."

Randy Joe joked, "You worried about the two hits, Muddy? Hell, the crowd was goin' to sleep and I wanted to see if you guys were on your toes. That's the reason I let those guys hit the ball."

Cut Brown, Cooter Davis, Tater Green and Buck grinned, but Muddy didn't show much of a sense of humor. "You get tired...you let me know," he said. "We wanna win dis game."

"I wanna win it, too," Randy Joe said. "Just to make you happy, I'll strike the next guy out."

Muddy wasn't sure how he should react. The boy seemed to

be a little arrogant and something of a jokester. But he seemed
to back up anything he said.

Randy Joe was hot and tired. The fever still had him, but his
arm felt very loose and fluid. He was ready to kick into overdrive.

Cleanup hitter Max Stradlin was the victim of Randy Joe's
resolve to put the next batter down on strikes. The kid's curveball
again proved Stradlin's undoing.

In the Cajuns dugout manager Bill McKagen, seemingly
talking to himself but directing the question to pitching coach
Don Boswell, asked, "You ever see anything like this kid?"

"No," Boswell replied, "never have."

McKagen smiled. "You know, it's almost like he's teasin'
us...like he just lets us hit the ball once in a while, then shows us
he can shut the door in our faces anytime he likes—can get a
strikeout anytime he wants one."

"From what I've seen so far," Boswell said, "I don't think
he's ever intentionally let anybody hit the ball, but you're
right...he seems to be toyin' with us. He's got that killer instinct,
though. If he could get twenty-seven straight strikeouts, he'd do
it."

McKagen laughed. "Hell, he's got twenty-one now...but
who's countin'?"

Muddy Tate led off the bottom of the ninth for the Longhorns
and tattooed a Tom Ryan fastball for a single to right. Buck
Frazier followed with a ringing single to left, prompting Bill
McKagen to visit the mound. McKagen didn't want to use up his
pitching staff for an exhibition game, but Randy Joe Keegan had
made the game important. The manager realized the kid pitcher
had the Cajun players as riled up and committed to winning as
they'd have been in the World Series.

"Tom," the manager said, "if they're gonna beat you, make
'em beat your best stuff. Throw this guy low fast-balls...outside
corner." Then to the infielders gathered around the mound
McKagen said, "Boys, think doubleplay...that's what we need
now."

Longhorns left fielder Rooster Solomon might well have
been included in the conference. He hit Ryan's first pitch to
second for a four-six-three doubleplay. Muddy moved over to

third.

A Longhorns victory then rested with the bat of third baseman Cooter Davis. He flied to left to end the inning.

Randy Joe didn't get a strikeout in the tenth, but his sinker got him three easy ground balls. Even without the strikeouts Randy Joe felt he was in a groove, pitching better than he'd ever pitched in his life. The headache and fever were still with him, but he figured he could live with pain if his delivery was always so fluid. His pitching arm felt so wonderfully right that he really didn't want the game to end.

Jackie Monk was first up for the Longhorns in the bottom of the tenth. He hit a fly ball to right for the first out. First baseman Tater Green, next up, grounded to third for the second out. That brought Randy Joe to the plate.

The Cajuns pitchers had seen just about all of the high school kid they wanted to see. Tom Ryan figured if Randy Joe hit him again it wasn't going to be a good pitch. So, trying to keep the ball on the outside part of the plate he walked him on four pitches.

Peewee Darthard, who had two of the Longhorns ten hits, then grounded to second to end the inning.

On his way out to the mound for the eleventh inning Randy Joe saw George Parrish coming out of the Cajuns dugout swinging a bat. He walked over to the Lake Charles center fielder and said, "That was one helluva catch you made in the eighth."

"Thanks," Parrish said.

"Sorry things can't be better for you at the plate."

"I think they're about to get better."

"Not this trip," Randy Joe promised.

In the dugout Bill McKagen told Carlin Sumner, "Get a bat. You can pinch hit for Ryan."

Sumner wanted to beg off, but all his students were looking at him. He'd opened his mouth and now he was going to have to prove himself. Well, he thought, there were signs that the young pitcher was tiring. All three batters in the tenth had gotten wood on the ball.

George Parrish stepped to the plate determined to earn

Randy Joe's respect as a hitter. After all, the kid had just flat out told him he wasn't going to get a hit. The center fielder reminded himself that he had gotten wood on the ball in the third when he grounded back to the pitcher. He'd struck out in the fifth and eighth.

Parrish didn't know where the kid's stamina came from, but the fastball that shot from Randy Joe's hand for a called first strike was even more of an indistinct blur than what he had been throwing in the early innings. New beads of perspiration popped out on Parrish's forehead as his mind computed the speed of the young righthander's pitches. They might give a guy a chance in the majors if he had a little trouble hitting the curveball, Parrish thought, but if a man couldn't hit a fastball he was dead in the water. Nevertheless, it didn't take much baseball knowledge to see that this kid's fastball wasn't normal.

Randy Joe fed Parrish two more fastballs and he was history. Cajuns pitching coach Don Boswell shook his head in dismay.

That brought Carlin Sumner to the plate. There was considerable interest on the part of the Lake Charles players as they watched to see what their hitting instructor could do against the high school pitcher for whom he had such disdain. Those who had been facing Randy Joe's offerings the entire game hoped the young pitcher would throw the instructor the stuff he had been throwing them.

Sumner, fortunately, did swing from the left side. That, however, didn't keep Randy Joe from starting him off with a curveball that broke over the plate right at his fists. The instructor's mind told him it was the best curveball he'd ever seen.

He wasn't sure he even saw the next two fastballs. It was like he just sensed where they crossed the plate. He stepped out of the batter's box having never swung at a pitch. But he now knew what the Cajuns players had been seeing all day long.

"Bullets," a dismayed Sumner told McKagen. "Eleven innings and the bastard's still throwin' bullets."

He didn't get upset when Johnny Silverman struck out to end the inning. Damn, he thought, they were lucky everybody hadn't struck out.

TWENTY-FIVE

When Big Bill approached Simmy behind the Longhorns dugout the pulpwood contractor gave no indication he knew anything about the cafe owner's foiled plans of the past Friday night. Simmy subscribed to the teachings in the Biblical *Book of Ecclesiastes,* that there was a time and place for everything. "What you say, Big Bill?" he asked, smiling.

Big Bill grinned. "Helluva ball game, Simmy."

"It sho' is."

Zeke Lott, standing with Simmy, was not so kind as his friend. "What happened to yo' nose, Mr. Big Bill?" he asked. Zeke wanted to see what lie the cafe owner had concocted.

Big Bill smiled sheepishly and replied, "That's from stickin' it where it didn't belong. But enough about me...what about the job Randy Joe's doin' on these pros?"

Simmy said, "He sho' doin' a job all right."

"I done told you he de best pitcher I ever seed," Zeke added. "Maybe I give'im three dozen donuts for what he doin' in dis game."

"Well, he's a hoss in baseball, but he's an even bigger hoss in football," Big Bill said.

"De white boys gonna have a good football team dis year?" Simmy questioned, politely.

"With Randy Joe at quarterback they'll be good," Big Bill replied. "No problem with the defense, but he makes the offense go."

Zeke said, "De boy's good at anythin' he wanna do."

"Guess y'all was scared y'all was gonna lose'im," Simmy said, "what wid his daddy gettin' fired at de mill and all."

"Damn right we was scared," Big Bill agreed. "I'm just glad Mr. Walz came over here and took care of the problem."

"I'm glad, too. I may want'im pitchin' some mo' games fo' me."

Big Bill's eyes showed Simmy's statement didn't sit too well with him. But, then, Simmy hadn't intended for it to. He wanted the cafe owner to know that he hadn't been intimidated by anything that had happened over the past week.

Big Bill cleared his throat and said, "Well, I hope this is Randy Joe's last baseball game of the summer. I hope he'll get busy and start thinkin' about football. A lot's ridin' on'im this fall."

"Playin' baseball ain't gonna hurt de boy," Zeke said.

"It ain't a matter of it hurtin' him, just a matter of him gettin' mentally ready for football," Big Bill said. "Besides, Simmy, I hear your team's goin' on some big tour."

"Dat's right," Simmy said. "Dey's gonna be playin' all over de country. And we de only team around here dat play any baseball in de summer. So I don't guess you has anythin' to worry 'bout."

A pleased look came across what could be seen of Big Bill's face. Before leaving Simmy's and Zeke's company he said, "Now y'all come by the cafe, you hear. I'll buy you a cup of coffee."

When the cafe owner was out of earshot Zeke chuckled and said. "Dat would be de first cup o' coffee de man ever bought me."

Simmy grinned. "He ain't never bought me no coffee either."

Zeke asked, "What you think dat was all 'bout, anyway?"

Simmy shrugged his shoulders. "De man tryin' to cover his tracks. He tryin' to find out if we knowed what he was up to Friday night."

"He must think we stupid," Zeke said.

Simmy laughed. "He think ever'body wid a black face is stupid."

On the field Longhorns second baseman Cut Brown was

coming to the plate for the fifth time in the game. He hadn't been able to scratch out a hit and was frustrated.

The new pitcher for Lake Charles was Ed Warren, a six-foot, two-inch lefthander out of California. Warren had a major league fastball but little else. He was often wild. The three-year pro had been assigned to the Cajuns to work out his control problems under the tutelage of Don Boswell.

Warren's first pitch was a fastball on the inside part of the plate. Cut dropped a perfect bunt down the first base line, catching the first baseman playing deep and Warren falling to the third base side of the mound. It was a base hit all the way.

Muddy Tate, the next hitter up, played it by the book. He laid down the expected sacrifice bunt that moved Cut to second. That left it up to catcher Buck Frazier or Rooster Solomon to drive in the winning run.

Buck, a switch-hitter, had a double and single in his previous four trips to the plate, but both hits had come batting lefthanded. With a lefthander on the mound, he switched to the right side of the plate.

Warren was not afraid to pitch inside and did, brushing Buck back. He then did a decent job of working the outside corner of the plate. Buck, a free swinger, was not looking for a walk, so he took a couple of cuts at pitches outside the strike zone. With the count one and two he had to start guarding the plate. That's when Warren fed him a changeup. The pitch fooled Buck and he grounded to short. Cut couldn't advance.

That left everything up to Rooster, who had doubled in the second inning against Cajuns lefthanded starting pitcher Sherill Lawson. Warren, however, didn't make the same mistake his predecessor did. He kept the ball away from Rooster, who flied to center for the final out of the inning.

In the stands Vic Marshall told Sheila, "I see James Steele and George Mason over there. Think I'll go over and say hello." Sheila nodded. She didn't care what her husband did. Her mind was on the game and Randy Joe. She had some regrets about what had happened between them, but some good feelings, too.

Discovery would be devastating to them both. She wasn't worried about hurting Vic. He was incapable of real feelings anyway. But she had her parents to think about, especially her mother.

"You guys enjoying the game?" the grinning Marshall asked on his arrival at where Mason and Steele were sitting.

Steele grumbled, "Can't say as I am," removing the grin from the coach's face. "Randy Joe pitchin' this well for the niggers just creates more problems for us," Steele explained. "You see what's happenin' here?"

"What do you mean?" Marshall asked.

"We gotta nigger team that may beat a white team and we got white people pullin' for the niggers. That's not right, Vic...and you know it's not right."

"No...no it ain't right," the coach agreed. "But I think most of these white people here are just pullin' for Randy Joe, not for the nigger team."

Steele shook his head in disgust. "It's the same thing, Vic. The boy sold out to the niggers. His daddy, too."

Marshall said, "Well, when you put it that way..."

"What do you know about Leon Rice?" Mason asked.

The question, which came out of the blue, startled Marshall. He didn't like Rice, mostly because he put teaching ahead of coaching. "I don't know much about him," he said.

"Did you know he was with that bunch that beat up on Big Bill Friday night?" Steele asked.

"No...sure didn't."

"You ever see Rice talkin' with the niggers much?" Mason asked.

"He talks to Simmy some, but I think it's about arrangements for the high school team to use this field."

"Bad idea, the school gettin' hooked up with Simmy on usin' this field," Steele said.

Mason agreed. "At the time, James, it seemed innocent enough."

"That's the way it always begins," Steele said, "and then the Communists have you by the balls. Tell you what, Vic, we want you to keep a close eye on Mr. Rice. We think he may be a Commie."

"Sure, I'll keep an eye on him," Marshall said, happy to be

included in the conspiracy.

"George and me are gonna begin a thorough background check on the man," Steele said. "Anything you find out will be appreciated."

When Randy Joe went to the mound for the twelfth inning his legs felt a little weary, but his arm felt fine. With the intense heat he figured he'd dropped a few pounds but didn't think the weight loss was affecting him. He'd been drinking water, cautiously, in the dugout. The headache and fever were still with him.

Shortstop Buddy Garrick led off the inning for Lake Charles. He hadn't had much of a day at the plate. He had struck out twice, sacrificed and grounded unassisted to first. Randy Joe came with a fastball that brushed Garrick back from the plate. Then he threw a curveball that had the shortstop bailing out of the batter's box, but it missed the strike zone.

Two balls, no strikes.

The kid pitcher came back with another curveball that caught the inside corner, then fired a fastball that came in high on the batter.

Three balls, one strike.

Randy Joe came with the heater again. It caught a corner.

Full count.

Randy Joe knew Garrick would be expecting a fastball. That's why he opted for a curveball. The pitch he threw was a beauty, had the Cajuns shortstop falling out of the box, but it was too low. Garrick trotted down to first and Randy Joe paced around the mound, angry that he'd tried to be too fine with the hitter.

Recipient of his anger was right fielder Harry Wade, the number three batter in the Cajuns order. Considering the success of his teammates against Randy Joe, Wade was having a pretty good day. He had one of Lake Charles's four hits. He'd also flied out, grounded out and struck out. Anyway, he'd gotten his bat on the ball three times.

Randy Joe blew the lefthand hitter away with three fastballs.

Big Max Stradlin, cleanup hitter for the Cajuns, also had one of his team's four hits, but he'd struck out on three other trips to the plate. Randy Joe made the mistake of trying to blow him down again, the same way he'd nailed Wade. The Lake Charles third baseman worked the count to two-two, then lined a sharp single to right. Garrick, moving on the pitch, went to third standing up.

Runners at first and third, one out. For the first time in the game Randy Joe felt some doubt about his pitches having the proper zing. He tried to fight off the feeling as catcher Frank Goff came to the plate.

Initially, the young pitcher tried to be too fine with Goff, throwing him three straight balls. The catcher had one of his team's hits, had struck out twice and grounded out. With the three ball count he began to feel confident about his chances of getting on base.

Randy Joe reached back for something extra. He got a curveball strike on the inside corner of the plate, then another. With the count three-two, Goff popped the next curveball to Cooter Davis.

That brought Luke Adler to the plate. The first baseman hadn't touched Randy Joe for a hit, but had worked him for a base on balls in the fifth inning. He'd struck out twice and grounded out.

Randy Joe came at the lefthand hitter with some good sinkers, but with the count two and two got the next pitch a little too close to the center of the plate. Adler hit it solidly, but Longhorns center fielder Peewee Darthard flagged it down in right-center.

While the Cajuns were taking the field Nate Oliver cornered Simmy. The pulpwood contractor had tried to avoid the outspoken and wrinkled Nate and his friend Tate Moore all during the game, but knew it was only a matter of time before the two caught up with him.

"Dis a good game, Simmy," Nate said, "but it ain't right, dat white boy pitchin' fo' a colored team. De Bible say it ain't right."

"I keep tellin' you to show me where in de Bible it say dat, Nate," Simmy countered. "You ain't showed it to me yet."

Turning to Tate, Nate said, "You seed it...ain't you, Tate?"

Tate nodded that he had.

"De Lawd don't want coloreds mixin' wid no white folks,"

Nate said. "It ain't right and it ain't never gonna be right."

"Damn it, Nate," Zeke said, "you oughta take yo' bullshit over dere to Mr. Big Bill Perkins. Both of you thinks de same way, ceptin' he don't blame de Lawd fo' his craziness."

Simmy laughed. "Why don't I buy you fellas some popcorn and a Coke. Den you can go watch de rest o' de game."

"I wants an R.C.," Tate said.

"All right," Simmy agreed, taking a dollar bill from his pocket. "Y'all take dis money over to de concession stand and buy yo'selves some popcorn and cold drinks."

Cooter Davis was the first Longhorns hitter in the bottom of the twelfth. The third baseman had one of his team's eleven hits, had popped to the infield twice, then flied to left. Cajuns hurler Ed Warren fed the righthand hitter a steady diet of fastballs and he grounded to second on a two-two pitch.

Jackie Monk, next up in the inning, had one hit. In his other trips to the plate he'd struck out, hit into a doubleplay and flied to right. Warren didn't bother trying his curveball on the lefthand hitter. He kept throwing the fastball and Monk grounded out third to first.

Tater Green was hitless in four trips to the plate. Warren made it five, striking him out on good, hard fastballs.

As Randy Joe took the mound in the thirteenth inning he realized he was getting weaker. Still, his tiger's heart wouldn't let him quit. The teeth of some other beast gnawed on nerves frayed by tension, heat and fever, but he would not give in.

Cajuns left fielder Layton White, leading off in the inning, had struck out three times and grounded out second to first. He hadn't been a problem for the young righthander, but this time he worked the count full and walked on a curveball in the dirt.

Switch-hitting center fielder George Parrish, who had grounded out and then struck out three times in a row, also worked the count full. Then a blazing chest-high fastball almost took some buttons off his uniform shirt. Trotting to first Parrish breathed a sigh of relief that the ball had hit only his shirt.

There was excitement in the Lake Charles dugout as manager Bill McKagen called on pinch hitter Dooley Cox to take pitcher Ed Warren's place in the batter's box. Cox, a stocky six-footer out of Atlanta, Georgia, was a two-year pro who swung from the left side. Hitting coach Carlin Sumner, strangely quiet since his plate appearance in the eleventh inning, dared to say, "We got'em now."

Indeed, that seemed to be the case. Randy Joe walked Cox on four straight pitches, which prompted Muddy Tate, the other infielders and Buck Frazier to visit the mound again. Gar Foster was warm and Muddy really planned to make a pitching change. But the look in Randy Joe's eyes caused him to hesitate. Still, he felt compelled to say, "I think you done had enough. I think it's time to bring Gar in."

Randy Joe gave him a steely look and said, "Why? I'm gonna fan the next three guys."

Muddy got an eerie feeling just hearing Randy Joe say it. He figured the other players felt the same. So he said, "It's yo' ball game. You deserves it."

Second baseman Johnny Silverman, four strikeouts and a single for the day, stepped to the plate. He'd been caught up in the enthusiasm of the dugout. The kid pitcher had finally had it. The game was now theirs for the taking. That was before he caught fleeting glimpses of three fastballs on the inside part of the plate. Silverman trudged back to the dugout, mumbling.

Buddy Garrick, hitless for the day but with a base on balls in the twelfth, was a victim of Randy Joe's curveball. The shortstop just couldn't keep his feet in the batter's box as the baseball came spinning at him and then broke over the plate. Randy Joe needed just three pitches to get him.

Harry Wade, the lefthand hitting right fielder, was just as helpless at the plate as his two teammates. He fanned on three fastballs on the outside corner.

Don Boswell, the Lake Charles pitching coach, captured the consensus of the Cajuns dugout with one word. "Unbelievable."

If anyone was ever destined to be a closer it was Nolen Ellard, the Cajuns new pitcher in for the bottom half of the thirteenth. He was a muscular lefthander, six-feet, two inches tall, two hundred pounds, a three-year pro out of Muncie, Indiana. Ellard, who had a tendency to be wild, threw heat like no one else on the Lake Charles pitching staff.

The first batter he faced in the bottom of the thirteenth was Randy Joe Keegan. Boswell had warned him to keep the ball away from the slender kid, but Ellard, who had never been that coachable anyway, figured he had the situation well in hand. His plan was to flatten Randy Joe, then strike him out.

Sure enough, his first pitch sent Randy Joe falling out of the batter's box. That seemed to light up something in his opponent's eyes.

Ellard swore the next pitch was the fastest he'd ever thrown, but Randy Joe turned on it and drove it high and deep over the right field wall.

The fans in the stands went wild, dancing, hugging each other. Some whites were even hugging blacks, to the disgust of James Steele and George Mason.

"No movement on his ball," Randy Joe told Muddy Tate after he'd rounded the bases.

TWENTY-SIX

By the time Randy Joe stepped on home plate to give the Longhorns the victory he wanted to be submerged in cold water, to chase away the heat of the fever that was ravaging his mind. There had been some occasional chills, but it was the heat that really bothered him. It was like his head was in an oven and someone kept turning up the temperature dial.

As bad and numb as he felt there was satisfaction in the accolades he received from his new teammates. And from the opposition. Almost every player on the Cajuns ball club shook his hand and expressed grudging admiration. He even had to admit to himself he'd done better than expected. He'd given up no runs on just five hits in thirteen innings and had struck out twenty-eight.

"Where did you learn to hit like that?" Lake Charles batting coach Carlin Sumner asked him.

"I was just lucky. I'm really not a good hitter."

Sumner gave him an incredulous look.

Cajuns pitching coach Don Boswell said, "Take good care of that arm. You gotta valuable piece of merchandise there."

And Lake Charles manager Bill McKagen said, "Son, I'm gonna tell our chief scout about you, but I've seen all I need to see."

Buck Frazier told him, "Randy Joe, my catchin' hand look like a wad o' raw hamburger meat, but I catch you anytime."

Simmy found him and discreetly pressed some folded bills in his hand, which Randy Joe quickly stuck in the back pocket of his uniform pants. He didn't think anyone saw the transaction, but Simmy whispered as best he could above the noise, "Randy Joe, you worth every penny."

"You sho' is," Zeke agreed. "You come by de shop on Monday and you gonna get three dozen donuts."

Randy Joe grinned. "That gooda game, huh?"

Zeke laughed. "De best I ever seed."

Randy Joe caught a ride home with Gretchen and her folks. He apologized to Max and Lisa Turner for the smell of his uniform, which was soggy with sweat and caked-on dirt.

Turner laughed. "With the windows down and the wind blowing in, Gretchen's the only one who can smell you. You plannin' on takin' a bath before y'all go out tonight?"

"Thinkin' about it," Randy Joe replied, smiling. "But then again...maybe not. I can't impress Gretchen either way."

Gretchen laughed, made a fist and punched him in the stomach. His head was hurting so bad he didn't even feel it. He didn't want to go out, just wanted to soak in the tub, crawl out and hit the sheets. He couldn't do that, though, because Weave, Jolene and Gretchen were counting on an evening out. And he could think of a lot of things worse than getting it on with Gretchen.

The ride home seemed to last forever. While he was running the tub full of water he took the money out of his back pocket.

Two twenties and a ten. He took the two twenties to the kitchen where his mother was fixing supper and handed them to her.

"What's this for, Randy Joe?"

"For a rainy day," he replied. "You keep it, mom. That much money might burn a hole in my pocket."

"Well, some of the girls do need new shoes."

"I'd rather you bought yourself somethin' with it."

"Maybe I will," she said.

He knew she wouldn't.

By the time Randy Joe bathed and got dressed his mother had supper on the table. He wasn't hungry, but forced himself to eat a little. If his mother suspected he had one of his bad headaches she would make him call off the evening. So he just kept drinking ice water.

The nice thing about summertime, besides baseball, was girls in shorts, especially if a girl like Gretchen was wearing them. When he picked her up she was wearing white shorts that did an excellent job of showing off her beautifully tanned legs. The little white blouse she had on didn't detract from her firm bosom either.

They went to the drive-in movie. Gretchen knew something was wrong almost immediately after they parked. "My god, Randy Joe, your forehead feels like it's on fire. You're burnin' up with fever."

He downplayed her concern, but no more than thirty minutes later Weave was at the wheel of the Plymouth driving him home. R.M. and Bernice Keegan took their son to the only hospital in Jason. But Randy Joe didn't know it. He had passed out.

The fever raged and Randy Joe was out of his head for the better part of two days. The fever broke late on the second day and he fell into an almost comatose state. The doctor had difficulty determining what was wrong with him but finally came up with a diagnosis of bronchitis.

Late the third day Randy Joe became more aware of his surroundings, and by Thursday evening he was laughing and joking with visitors. Later that evening he attempted getting out of bed and learned he couldn't walk.

His mind knew fear when his legs buckled. The doctor told

him not to worry, that it was just a natural reaction. There had been fever, dehydration, weakness that came from just lying in bed and being fed through his veins.

He was better Friday morning, though still very weak. That's the morning Sheila Marshall came to see him. She had come a couple of other times. Once he was too out of it to know and the other time his room had been crowded with people. Coach Vic Marshall had been with her on the first visit, mostly to be seen, to make sure everyone knew he was doing his duty. This time Randy Joe and Sheila were alone.

She took his hand in hers and said, tenderly, "We were all worried about you."

He laughed. "If I'd been conscious I'd have been worried about me, too."

"The game, Randy Joe...it was just wonderful."

"To tell you the truth, I don't remember that much about it. I was in kind of a fog....the fever, I guess."

"People are saying they don't know how you managed to pitch that well as sick as you must have been."

He grunted, "Give me high marks for stupidity."

She leaned over and kissed him gently on the lips. Realizing what she had done, she momentarily lost her composure. "What are your plans for the summer, Randy Joe?"

"Work...same old stuff. As soon as I can get my strength back, which shouldn't take me more than two or three days, I'll be cuttin' cypress trees in the swamp with ol' Iron Man."

Sheila sort of semi-laughed. "Iron Man? That's an unusual name."

"Fits him like a glove. He's sixty years old...can do more work in a day than three guys my age." After saying it he wished he hadn't brought the age thing up.

But she handled it well. "Let's see, you're going to be seventeen next month. I'm not sure I should be fooling around with someone that old." Then she said, "I think you ought to be very careful, not go to work too soon."

"Can I ask you something, Sheila?"

"Of course."

"Why did you marry Coach Marshall? You two don't go

together."

"There are some questions that can't be answered. That's one of them. I ask myself that question over and over."

"Love...marriage, it's all pretty strange," he said. "I'm always askin' myself why certain people are together."

"Well, you date some of the prettiest girls at the high school. Can't you see yourself married to one of them someday?"

"No, not really. I'm not even sure why I dated some of 'em...Anna Louise for one."

Sheila laughed. "I can't understand that one either."

"Gretchen thinks it's because I'm tryin' to prove somethin'."

"Are you?"

He shrugged. "I don't know. It doesn't matter now anyway."

"Why's that?"

"With what Mr. Lake tried to do to my dad, I'm not sure I could keep a civil tongue around him."

"I think you're misreading J.D. Lake."

"How's that?"

"He was an unwilling participant," Sheila replied. "The real culprits were James Steele and George Mason...and my husband."

"Coach Marshall?"

"He's the one who started it all. Steele, Mason and Big Bill got caught up in it because they're all racists...just like Vic."

"Why's Coach Marshall so down on Negroes?"

"I probably shouldn't tell you this, but when he first started to college one beat him out of a position on the football team."

Randy Joe laughed. "I didn't know that."

"Since I told you, there's only three of us in town who know it. Of course, there's more to it than the Negro just beating him out. He was raised down here where hating colored people is popular."

Sheila stayed for another thirty minutes or so and they talked about all sorts of things. They avoided talking about their new relationship. But for some reason he found the danger of their newfound intimacy appealing.

Two surprise visitors on Friday afternoon were Simmy Weatherspoon and Zeke Lott. Zeke handed him a familiar-looking box and said, "I brought you dese donuts...figure de hospital food ain't all dat good."

Randy Joe laughed. "You figured right. I don't know what shit tastes like, but there's gotta be some similarity."

Simmy and Zeke laughed, then the baker said, "Now dey's still three dozen donuts down at de shop fo' dat game you pitched. Dis ain't one of dem dozen."

"He oughta be givin' you mo' dan three dozen donuts fo' dat game," Simmy said. "Everybody still talkin' 'bout it."

"I vaguely remember it," Randy Joe said, smiling.

"Dat manager fo' de Lake Charles team, he done told me he want yo' address," Simmy said. "I jest told'im to write to dis town and folks at de post office see to it dat you get de letter."

"How you feelin'?" Zeke asked.

"Fine...just a little weak. But a few days outta this place and I'll be good as new."

Simmy and Zeke exchanged glances, and Simmy said, "De Longhorns gonna be goin' on tour in two weeks."

"Yeah, I know," Randy Joe said. "Must be nice...playin' baseball all summer. Hope it's what I'm doing next year."

Simmy asked, "How you like to be playin' all dis summer?"

"Are you askin' me to go on tour with your team?"

"If it be okay wid yo' folks," the pulpwood contractor said. "De players on de team sho' would like it."

The prospect of playing baseball all summer excited Randy Joe, but then he sighed and said, "I can't. I gotta job. I gotta work and make some money this summer."

"How much you figure on makin'?" Simmy asked.

"At least five hundred dollars," he replied.

"I pay you dat to play fo' my team," Simmy said, "but you can't be tellin' nobody 'bout it. If de team do well, you liable to make a whole lot mo'."

Randy Joe started working on a way to broach the subject to his folks. About the prospect of more money he asked, "How's that?"

Simmy explained, "Dey's a big tournament up in Wichita in August. Win it and every player gonna get mo' dan seven hundred dollars."

Five hundred dollars for playing baseball all summer, plus

the possibility of seven hundred more. Randy Joe was hooked. It was a way to fulfill an obligation to his family and to do what he wanted to do.

"Tell me more about it," he said.

"De way de tournament work," Simmy said, "dey's sixteen teams and de owners o' de teams all put up a thousand dollars. De winner get ten thousand dollars and de owner get his thousand back. De team dat finish second... De owner jest get his thousand back. De other money go fo' de expenses o' de tournament...room and board fo' all players, payin' fo' de umpires, de baseballs and all dat other stuff."

Randy Joe said, "So it's a winner-take-all situation."

"Dat's what it is," Simmy agreed.

"I like it," Randy Joe said. "That's the way I like to play...winner take all...and the loser goes home with his tail tucked between his legs."

Zeke laughed. "I figure dat you like it."

"Win or lose, I'm gonna pay you five hundred dollars at de end o' de summer," Simmy said. "You can't say nuthin' 'bout it 'cause rest o' de team don't make dat kinda money. Dey gets to split up what's left o' de gate receipts from de tour... if dey's anythin' left."

"How does that work?" Randy Joe asked.

"Well, we usually get fo'ty percent of de gate when we on tour 'cause we de visitin' team," Simmy replied. "Outta dat we give ever' player two dollars a day meal money, plus pays fo' his room. We has to pay to operate de bus, fo' laundry, all dat kinda stuff. Sometimes we don't gets enough from a game to pay de expenses. You need to know dat, 'cause dey's times when de players don't get no two dollars a day meal money 'cause dey ain't any. Dey may be times when you has to sleep on de bus 'cause dey ain't 'nough money fo' de rooms. If we makes a profit on de tour, de players splits it. But you don't get to play ever' day and de gate receipts hardly ever come to two hundred dollars...and it cost somethin' fo' fo'teen men to travel 'cross de country."

Randy Joe said, "I feel kinda guilty...getting paid five hundred dollars when the others guys might not get nothin'."

"Ain't no reason fo' you to feel guilty," Simmy said. "You leavin' a job to play. All de other players got no jobs to leave."

"They can't find jobs?"

Simmy laughed. "Dey don't want no job. All dey wants to do is play baseball."

"I can't fault'em for that," Randy Joe said. "That's all I want to do, too."

TWENTY-SEVEN

Randy Joe's request did not draw an enthusiastic response from his parents, especially his mother. Bernice Keegan said pitching a home game for the Negro team was one thing. Traveling with them was something else.

By the time he talked to his folks on Friday night Simmy had already approached them with the proposition. He hadn't painted a rosy picture. He wanted all his cards on the table, no misunderstandings.

Sitting in Randy Joe's hospital room, R.M. Keegan said, "Part of me says it's okay and another part says no."

Randy Joe had never been one to pout when his parents denied a request. He had always tried to use reason and logic to influence their thinking. But this request defied logic and he knew it. So he simply appealed to them on the basis of, "I really wanna do this. It's important to me."

Bernice knew her son was mature for his years, but motherly instinct prevailed. "You won't eat right...won't get your rest."

R.M. Keegan couldn't help but smile. She was like an old hen. No matter how old her kids got, no matter how mature, she'd never want any of them to leave the nest. "Bernice, Randy Joe can take care of himself. I'm not sayin' I'm for this, but I believe the boy can handle himself. Hell, it's not gonna be long before he's drafted in the Army and then he'll have to."

"Well, R.M., there's no point in rushing it," she said, curtly.

"I'm not tryin' to...just lookin' at it from Randy Joe's point of view...thinking what I'd wanna do."

"There's no doubt about what you'd do," she said. "You'd go. Come hell or high water, you'd go. Of course," and she laughed, "Randy Joe's always been more responsible than you."

Keegan laughed. "It's hard to be responsible when it comes to baseball." Then on a more sober note he said, "There's not a day goes by but what I wonder, what if? If it hadn't been for the damned war."

Bernice was sympathetic, knew her husband's dream of being a major league ball player had been smashed at the Battle of the Bulge. "How long did Simmy say the team would be on tour?" she asked.

"Ten weeks," R.M. said, hopefully. "They'll be back before football practice starts."

"Well, he ain't even outta the hospital yet. He may still be too weak to do anything by the time Simmy's team leaves."

"The doctor's releasin' me Sunday," Randy Joe said, "and in a week I'll be good as new."

"You don't know that," Bernice said.

"Well, let's just take a wait and see attitude," R.M. suggested. "We don't have to decide anything tonight."

Earlier that day Leon Rice had visited Randy Joe. He'd told the baseball coach about the opportunity to go on tour with the Longhorns. Rice was less than enthusiastic, too.

"There are two things to consider," the coach said. "If you play for money you'll lose your high school and college eligibility. Then, too, you know how important your legs are to pitchin'. Pitchin' as weak as you are, you could do permanent damage to your arm. You proved to yourself what you had to prove. Why not leave it at that?"

"I'm not gonna pitch 'til I'm fully recovered."

Rice had given him a disbelieving look. "You forget...I know you, Randy Joe. When the competition begins you forget everything else."

Randy Joe knew he was right, but had said, "Hell, coach, aren't you just afraid my goin' on the tour will stir up some people again?"

"No," Rice had replied. "Outta sight, outta mind. When you're flaunting somethin' in the faces of people right here in town that's one thing. But if you're not around they're not gonna care. Is that the reason you wanna do this...to keep rubbin' the noses of certain people in the dirt?"

"No sir, I just wanna play baseball."

"If you take care of yourself, do things right, there'll be a lotta years of baseball ahead for you. I just want you to be sure you know what you're doing."

"Well," Randy Joe had said, "I guess I'm gettin' the cart before the horse anyway. I haven't talked to my folks about this yet."

A shocker came later in the day with a visit from Big Bill Perkins. The cafe owner looked sheepish and silly when he presented Randy Joe a box of candy. The bandage was gone from his nose and his face had mended somewhat.

"You doin' all right?" Big Bill had asked.

"Fine...still a little weak."

"Well, get your strength back...football season's comin' on."

Randy Joe had laughed. "Oh, yeah...I wanna get my strength back, football season or not."

"About the trouble between your dad and me, Randy Joe, I wanna put all that behind us."

"Well, I'd say that was between you and my dad."

"I know your dad ain't for the niggers either. It was the circumstances and all that caused our problem."

"I'm glad you know who my dad's for. Hell, most of the time I don't have a clue."

Big Bill had pondered a moment before asking, "What you know about Communism?"

"Enough. I'll probably have to spend part of my life fightin' the bastards."

"Well, there are Communists right here in Jason."

Randy Joe had laughed. "In Jason? You have any names?"

"Can't say, but they're the ones stirrin' the niggers up."

"First I heard they were bein' stirred up."

"It's been a quiet thing."

Randy Joe had chuckled. "Seems to be a contradiction there."

"Whata you mean?"

"If everything's so quiet, how do you know the Negroes are bein' stirred up."

Subtlety was lost on Big Bill. "Some of the niggers ain't even noticed it."

"Hate to think somebody was stirrin' me up and I hadn't noticed."

"Randy Joe, you don't think about niggers the way most of us do."

"I'm no Abraham Lincoln. I like some Negroes...dislike others. I like some white people...dislike others."

"The teachers up at school been teachin' you that kinda stuff?"

"No, I'm capable of decidin' that kinda stuff myself."

"Word is that Leon Rice is a Communist sympathizer."

Randy Joe laughed. "Next to my dad, Coach Rice is the most patriotic man I know. He teaches it...and practices it."

"People say he has a soft spot for niggers."

"Well, if Coach Rice has one, put me down for one, too."

Big Bill had said, "We need to know who's gonna be with us."

"Well, if the Communists attack Jason, I'm sure my dad and I will be on the front lines."

"What about to keep the niggers in line?"

"I ain't convinced they're outta line."

Big Bill had left a bit miffed. And of all his visitors, Randy Joe had not been happier to see one leave.

Anna Louise had visited shortly after Big Bill left. She'd been there a couple of other times, once when he was unaware that anyone was around and later when the room was crowded with other people.

"Glad you're almost back to normal," she had said, smiling.

"Normal for me would be considered crazy for most people."

She had teased, "There may be something to what you say.

At least, you wouldn't get any argument from some people."

"You know how much I care about some people."

"Randy Joe, that was a wonderful game you pitched last Sunday."

"You stayed until the end?"

"Yes...for every bit of it."

"As hot as it was? You're a glutton for punishment."

"I didn't pay much attention to the heat."

"I doubt your date and the other friends you were with enjoyed the game all that much."

She had smiled. "No, I don't guess they did. You're not one of Gary's or Monte's favorite people."

"Oh, does that mean I'm tight with Doris?"

"No, she's not one of your biggest fans either. But with all of them, I think it's just a matter of not really knowing you."

"And you do?"

Her face had colored a bit. "Not as well as I'd like to. And I do want to apologize, Randy Joe...for my father."

"It's not your place to apologize for him."

"No, I guess not."

"Well, I mighta been wrong about him anyway."

"What do you mean?"

"The way I understand it, he didn't wanna be involved in the deal with Aaron Berkley...the deal that got my dad fired."

"Maybe so, but he could've said something to Mr. Steele and Mr. Mason. He could've stood up like a man."

"This is a side of you I've never seen, Anna Louise. You're really peeved, aren't you?"

"Yes I am...and not just at my father. I'm upset with Mr. Steele and Mr. Mason. And Doris and Gary and..."

He had laughed. "Don't go recitin' the phone book to me."

"I just don't want what happened to destroy our friendship."

"It won't. I was upset with you because of your father, but I've had time to cool off."

"But not about everyone?"

"No," he had acknowledged. "There are still a few folks on my list. But some of them were on there before this ever happened."

"I can't blame you."

"Tell me, Anna Louise, are the Masons and Steeles paranoid about Communists?"

"Daddy said Mr. Mason and Mr. Steele are. Why?"

"Big Bill was here. He said there was word Coach Rice is a Communist sympathizer. I have a feelin' some people are tryin' to get rid of him...spreadin' the rumor."

"That's awful. Everyone knows it's ridiculous."

"Well, a rumor's never true until you get one person to believe it. I think some people are out to get Coach Rice because he sided with the Negroes the other night."

"Daddy hasn't said anything. He likes Coach Rice."

Anna Louise had promised she would let Randy Joe know if she heard anything further about the matter. She had also said her friendship with Doris had cooled and that she was not excited about the prospect of their European vacation together. "I'm not leaving until late in June. Maybe we can go out...do something before then."

"Maybe we can," he had said, though he didn't really mean it. More and more he was feeling he ought to make a greater commitment to Gretchen. She had always been there for him. She had come to the hospital daily. So had Patti Sue. But his attitude toward her had changed when she tried to stop him from pitching for the Longhorns. Patti Sue had apologized for allowing herself to be used by Coach Marshall, but for him the incident had poisoned their relationship.

Randy Joe and his parents reached an impasse on whether he would be playing baseball or cutting logs during the summer. He then told them about Big Bill's visit. "I really believe," he said, "that there are some people out to get Coach Rice."

"I'm not surprised," his dad said. "Leon's a little too progressive and a little too smart for the people around here. He's a good man who won't compromise what he believes in."

"I don't understand them tryin' to tie him to all this Communist stuff," Randy Joe said.

"Ignorance," R.M. Keegan responded. "Just plain ignorance. Too bad the politicians didn't let Patton whip the Russians at the end of the war. Then people couldn't use

Communism as an excuse for not solving their problems."

To Randy Joe's question about whether the Communists might be stirring up the Negroes, his dad said, "The only ones stirrin' up any coloreds here are people like Big Bill. Colored men I know just wanna make a livin' for their families and be left alone."

"I'm worried about Mr. Steele and Mr. Mason gettin' Coach Rice."

"There ain't much we can do," Keegan said. "They control the school board. They're not gonna listen to anybody from Milltown."

It just isn't fair, Randy Joe thought, that assholes like James Steele and George Mason have so much sway over a good man's life.

He slept fitfully. During the night he awoke with a plan he would set in motion as soon as he got out of the hospital.

Saturday morning brought pleasant news. He could go home after ten o'clock instead of waiting until Sunday. He was still weak, had difficulty walking from his room to his parents' car, but made the short trip as though it didn't bother him. He didn't want his mother to know how weak he was.

The noon meal was a big one, a kind of welcome-home feast. His mother's cooking, along with family support—and sarcasm on Jo Beth's part, tended to make him feel stronger. It just felt strange being home at noon on Saturday instead of working. He wondered how Iron Man and the guys were getting along without him.

Weave came by at mid-afternoon and Randy Joe said, "I was thinkin' about walkin' down to Big Bill's Cafe for a few minutes," Randy Joe said. "You wanna go with me?"

"Sure," Weave replied, "I could use a Coke and some fries."

"Didn't you eat dinner?"

"Course, but not enough to take me to supper."

Randy Joe explained to Weave that they were walking because he needed the exercise. It was only a mile to Big Bill's, but a tough one for Randy Joe because of the heat. On arrival they both ordered Cokes. Weave also ordered fries. Sure enough, just as Randy Joe had figured, Big Bill came over to the booth.

"Good to see you outta the hospital, Randy Joe."

"Good to be out."

"You feelin' okay?"

"Still a little weak, but gettin' stronger by the minute."

Big Bill grinned. "Good...ain't that long 'til football season."

"I'm looking forward to it...dependin'."

Big Bill frowned. "Depending on what?"

"You remember what we talked about in the hospital, the things some people are saying about Coach Rice?"

"Yeah...I remember."

"Well, if somethin' was to happen to Coach Rice...like him gettin' fired or somethin'...then I won't be playin' football. That's what I meant by depending."

Big Bill laughed uneasily. "You're not serious?"

"The hell I'm not," Randy Joe said, coldly.

TWENTY-EIGHT

When Big Bill told Vic Marshall what Randy had said, the football coach was more than a little upset. "The little bastard's tryin' to blackmail us," he grumbled.

Then Sheila Marshall asked, angrily, "Are you tryin' to get Leon Rice fired?"

"Uh...no, honey, nothin' like that."

"There's talk, Sheila," Big Bill said, "that Leon might be a Communist, takin' up for the niggers like he did."

"That's the most ridiculous thing I ever heard. I guess that makes Mr. Keegan a Communist, too."

"Well, Mr. Keegan was kind of a war hero...got lot o' medals and stuff. Could be he's just bein' misled."

Sheila emitted an uneasy laugh. "My god, Vic, this is crazy. You know Leon's no Communist."

Marshall shrugged his shoulders. "I never really known Leon all that well. He kinda keeps to himself, you know."

She gave them an incredulous look. "Well, hooray for Randy Joe. He at least has his head on straight."

"Didn't you hear what Big Bill said?" Marshall asked. "The little bastard's sayin' he ain't gonna play football if somethin' happens to Leon. Whose side you on anyway?"

"It's sure not on the side of stupidity," she replied. "Tell me, Big Bill, just who is it that's spreading these rumors about Leon? I don't suppose you're doing it, are you?"

"Not me. And they're not rumors...just questions about the man."

"I don't suppose James Steele and George Mason are asking these questions?"

Big Bill grunted before replaying, "Uhhh...they might be two that's askin'. But there's more than them."

"Well, gentlemen," she said, smiling, "I'd suggest you stop Mr. Steele and Mr. Mason in their tracks or you're not gonna have a very good football team this year."

Marshall said, "Randy Joe's bluffin'."

"You wanna take that chance?" she asked. "It seems to me he's not that interested in playing anyway."

She was right, which pissed Marshall all the more. He asked, "What are we supposed to do? James and George are on the school board."

Sheila shrugged her shoulders. "Don't ask me. They're supposedly your pals. I guess you're gonna have to go to them and beg."

Big Bill didn't like the way Sheila was talking to Marshall, but there was nothing he could say. He was just the messenger. She was the kind of woman who might kill the messenger.

"Sheila's makin' sense, Vic. We're gonna need some help on this so we need to talk to James and George. This is just a misunderstandin' that's been blown way out of proportion. I think we can get it cleared up."

"Funny," Sheila said, sarcastically, "but I somehow felt

Leon might become less of a Communist if making him a full-fledged one meant losing Randy Joe for the football team."

Marshall thundered, "That's enough, Sheila. It's enough the little bastard's got us over a barrel without you enjoyin' it."

"I'm not enjoying it. I think it's tragic when people try to destroy a fine man like Leon Rice. Randy Joe's just trying to do something...using the only weapon he's got."

Sheila knew her time to say something was in front of a witness. If they had been alone her husband might go into one of his blind rages and hit her.

"You're the coach," Big Bill said, "and it's your team. I just told you this so you'd know...so we can do whatever you think's best."

Marshall said, "Randy Joe knew you'd come tell me. The kid's a little too smart for his own good." He sighed and continued, "Well, I do need the little bastard. Wish I didn't but I do. I guess we'd better see James and George, make sure nothin' happens to Leon."

"You understand I don't give a damn for Leon?" Big Bill said. "I just don't wanna see the football season go down the drain."

"This is the season I've been waitin' for ever since I've been here," Marshall said. "We got it all this year, the defense and...with Randy Joe, the offense. Be a shame to spoil it all over somethin' stupid."

Sheila laughed. "Well, some truth finally crept into the conversation. You two don't give a damn about Leon, but you'll try to save him so you can save the football season."

Marshall didn't like his wife's sharp tongue, but she had summed it up. He would champion Leon to save the football season. Then, hopefully, he'd be able to latch onto a college team and get out of this hick town, away from guys like Big Bill, Steele and Mason. Someday he'd be a head coach at a major college, win a national championship and be able to tell everyone to kiss his ass. Such were Vic Marshall's dreams.

An hour later, in a back booth at Big Bill's Cafe, Marshall was begging James Steele to keep Leon Rice on the Jason High School payroll. And it wasn't going well.

"I can't believe this shit," Steele said. "I thought the four of us looked at things the same way...agreed on what was best for the town and this country. Now the little asshole threatens you and you wanna flush all your principles down the toilet."

"I agree with you on everything, James," Marshall crawfished, "but we're talkin' about a year at most. Then we can get rid of Leon."

"Ever think about how many minds he might poison in a year with his Communist garbage?" Steele asked.

"We can keep tabs on him," Marshall pleaded. "We can keep him under control at the school." He didn't know how he was going to keep tabs on Rice, or what controls he was talking about. It was hard to figure how to rein in a man who wasn't doing anything wrong.

"You gonna follow him over to Nigger Quarters, keep him from stirrin' the niggers up?" Steele asked, sarcastically.

"Now James, let's give some thought to what Vic's suggestin'," George Mason said. "If the football team does what he thinks it'll do, it'll be good for the town."

Steele shook his head in disgust. "I can't believe you can't win without the Keegan boy, Vic."

"Oh, he can win without him," Big Bill said, much to Marshall's chagrin, "but Randy Joe could be the difference between just a good season and the state championship."

"Makes sense," Mason agreed.

Steele said, "I can't believe you, George. You wanna go along with'em."

"Well, we hadn't made a definite decision on Rice anyway."

"Maybe you hadn't," Steele said. "I had."

Mason said, "I think you're right. But maybe a few months isn't gonna make that much difference."

Steele grunted, "When the niggers start takin' over you might change your tune. Besides, I don't like the fact that the Keegan punk is calling the shots."

"He isn't," Mason argued. "It might have taken us a year to get rid of Leon anyway. This way we use the kid and still do exactly what we wanna do. He hasn't saved Leon and when the time comes he'll know it."

The deviousness appealed to Steele—letting Randy Joe think he'd won, then pulling the plug on Rice. The more he thought about it the better he liked it.

Mason continued, "In the end we all get what we want. Vic gets the player he needs and we carefully gather all the ammunition we need to get rid of a Communist threat."

"I'd still like to see this town rid of the Keegans," Steele said.

Mason said, "We can work on that, too. We'll find a way around Sam Walz, or win him over to our side."

Steele flashed an insidious grin. "I expect Big Bill here would like to see R.M. Keegan out of town. I imagine every time he sees the man's face he thinks about gettin' his ass whipped."

Big Bill had never particularly liked James Steele, but at that moment he hated him. He didn't say anything, though, because Steele and Mason had the power and he never knew when he might need them.

The area where whites were served in Big Bill's establishment was L-shaped and the cafe owner's so-called private booth was at the little end of the L. It backed up against a wall. On the other side of the wall was the kitchen. This booth where the quartet met, where the cafe owner conducted all his clandestine meetings, was not as private as he thought. A small part of the wall was very thin when a portion of the second wall in the kitchen was removed. It was just a little section, not even apparent to the naked eye. Bertha Mae Davis had become expert at removing it.

Bertha Mae was two hundred and fifty pounds of cook, fifty-five years old, with legs that belonged on an elephant. And when it came to hearing what was going on, her ears were elephantine, too. Bertha Mae would remove the little section from the wall, press her ear up against the remaining wall and while the dishwasher kept watch, listen to all the plans made by Big Bill and his friends.

So she heard the conversation between James Steele, George Mason, Vic Marshall and her boss, whom she detested. And she'd do what she always did, which was call Simmy Weatherspoon. She wasn't sure how, or if, Simmy used all the information from her listening post at Big Bill's Cafe, but the pulpwood contractor was always generous. She always got a few dollars for her reports.

The thing Bertha Mae wondered most about was the word Communism that Big Bill and his friends were always using. She wondered what it meant.

TWENTY-NINE

It took Randy Joe the better part of a week to persuade his mother to let him go on tour with the Longhorns. When she finally relented it wasn't because she agreed it was the best thing for him to do.

"Mom, I'll make over twelve hundred dollars this summer," he said.

"There you go...counting your chickens before they hatch. The only way you're gonna get that other seven hundred dollars is if y'all win that tournament up in Kansas."

"We'll win."

Bernice couldn't help being amused by her son's enthusiasm, but there was concern, too. When it came to sports her son didn't know how to lose. He'd been on teams that had lost, of course, but he had never accepted defeat. "You can't pitch every game in the tournament, Randy Joe. You don't know how good the other Longhorns pitchers are."

"They're good," he assured. "The whole team is good."

"Maybe I need to remind you that the good team you're talkin' about didn't get you any runs against Lake Charles."

"Off day," he said.

"That's right...and they may have an off day in the tournament. Or the team may face a pitcher they can't hit. There's always that possibility, you know."

Bernice's caution couldn't stifle Randy Joe's enthusiasm. "Mom, you can go ahead and start spendin' that seven hundred dollars."

She smiled. "I'm not going to buy anything with it yet."

They were in the kitchen and Bernice was fixing supper. Randy Joe put his arm around her and said, "Mom, I love you...and someday I'm gonna buy you the prettiest house and furniture you can imagine."

It was hard for Bernice to keep her eyes dry. "Randy Joe, the only thing I want is for you to find your happiness. That's all I want for all you kids."

Randy Joe knew his mother was being her honest self, which made him all the more determined to give her the nice things she hadn't had all her life. His parents had done all the giving.

Simmy's invitation to Randy Joe had been much discussed in Jason and Milltown. J.B. Smith cornered him about the middle of the week to discuss it, the day before his mother agreed to let him go. Randy Joe was just walking by the Smiths' house late in the evening and J.B. invited him in for lemonade. "Your folks decided if they're gonna let you go with Simmy's team or not?"

"No sir...not yet. And I appreciate you keepin' my job open for me like you have."

Smith said, "A man who works like you do can always find a job. Seein' you pitch that game last Sunday...well, I ain't never seen anybody work that hard. I don't know how you held up so long in the heat."

Randy Joe had laughed. "I don't really consider pitchin' work. What Iron Man and the others do down in the swamp...that's work."

"You think a lot of Iron Man, don't you?"

"Yeah...Iron Man, Hank, Sleepy and Yank...I think a lot of all of'em. They're good men."

Smith had smiled. "They kind of defy that old sayin' about Negroes bein' lazy, don't they? You know, I wouldn't normally go to a Sunday baseball game. I went because of all that happened leadin' up to it...to show support for you and R.M."

"Yes sir...I know that."

Smith had sipped his lemonade, then asked, "You think any more about what I talked to you about?" For some time he had been exhorting Randy Joe to think about being a preacher, to seek the calling.

"Yes sir, I thought about it some...but not that much."

"I thought maybe your goin' to the hospital might be some sorta message to you."

Randy Joe hadn't wanted to offend Smith, and sure as hell didn't want to offend God. "As far as I know it wasn't," he said. "The message I got outta it was that if you do somethin' stupid, like pitch a game with a high fever, you have to suffer the consequences. I figure God gives us a brain and a free will and how we use both determines what happens to us."

Smith had laughed. "That's pretty good theology."

Randy Joe shrugged his shoulders. "I don't know about that...it's just the way I believe."

"For someone who doesn't go to church all that much, you gotta lotta religious sense. It's why I think the Lord has a use for you. It's why I have somethin' for you...to take on the baseball tour."

"My parents haven't told me I can go yet."

Smith, who had gotten up from the table and walked over to a sideboard, said, "They will...they will. You won't be workin' in the swamp this summer."

What Smith took from the sideboard and handed to him was a beautiful leather-bound Bible. "Sarah and I want you to have this to take on your trip," he said. "It's one we bought for Tommy, but we think you oughta have it.

Tommy was their eighteen-year-old son who had been killed in Korea. "I...I can't take this," Randy Joe said finally.

"Yes you can. We want you to have it...and I hope you'll read it on your trip."

"I just hope I get to go."

The next day, when his mother told him he could go, he had a fleeting thought that J.B. Smith might be psychic. But he quickly dismissed it.

When Randy Joe told Gretchen his good news she said, "I don't want you to go. But I know it's what you want. You're not gonna be happy unless you do it."

"I'll write."

"You'd better," she threatened, laughing.

"Anyway, time's running out so do you wanna go out?"

"When?"

"How about every night 'til I leave?"

"Sounds good to me. There's just one thing."

"What?"

"Let's not double-date with Jolene and Weave every single night."

He laughed. "I hadn't planned to."

He also hadn't planned to see Sheila Marshall before he left, but he called her on Friday morning and told her he was going on the tour. Of course he first asked for Coach Marshall, but was told he wasn't there. "He went on a fishing trip," Sheila said, "and won't be back until late Sunday night."

"Well, I really just wanted to talk to you," Randy Joe said. "About the trip."

"It'll be a great experience."

"Yeah...I'm lookin' forward to it."

"Are you still weak from the hospital?"

"I've been stronger, but in a few days I'll be okay."

"I'd like to see you before you leave."

"I'd like to see you, too."

"Are you doing anything now?"

"No."

"Then why don't you come over?"

He did and, they made love. If anything, he thought, it was better than the first time. He was more comfortable, more sure of himself.

Being with Sheila made Friday afternoon pass too quickly. When he got home to bathe and get ready for his date with Gretchen he was pretty well spent. He had only a couple of hours to regain his sexual strength. Gretchen, he knew, would be every bit as passionate as Sheila.

Later that night, parked on a dark country road after they'd made love, she said, "I hope you miss me when you're gone. I hope you miss me so much you can't stand it."

"I will," he said. "Sounds like you want me to be miserable."

"I do...because I'm gonna be miserable 'til you get back."

"No way," he teased. "You'll probably be out every night with one of the clowns around here."

"You know better," she said. "You know I go steady with you, even if you don't go steady with me."

"I'd call goin' out with you every night pretty steady."

She laughed. "Why don't you ask me to go steady then?"

"Hey, why do you have to ask somethin' if you're doing it?"

She laughed again. "You just can't say it, can you?"

"Maybe I'm just afraid of rejection."

"No, you think you might meet some sweet thing on your trip."

"This isn't a vacation, Gretchen, and there's not much you can do on two dollars a day meal money."

"Oh, I have every confidence you'll find a way."

"Well, I'm not gonna be looking."

"You've never had to look, Randy Joe."

"Why don't we go down to Big Bill's and get a hamburger and Coke. You just about sapped all my strength."

"You're just trying to change the subject."

"That's why I like you. You're a very smart girl."

THIRTY

Squirrel Simpson was traveling road secretary for the Longhorns. He was responsible for keeping the team's financial records, arranging sleeping accommodations and doling out meal money. Earlier in the year he had ridden a bus all over the country setting up the tour.

Squirrel was about sixty years old with white hair. His face was wrinkled and his eyes were dark and cold. He almost always needed a shave, and the need was obvious because the hairs that popped out on his face were as white as those on top of his head.

He was a surly, angry man who rarely had a kind word for anyone. A smile on Squirrel's lips was as rare as a summer snowstorm in Texas. He'd had his last humorous thought between the world wars.

Simmy had hired the wiry little man with the thin lips because he had, supposedly, held a similar position for a team in the almost-dead Negro American League. He was supposed to know what he was doing and had convinced Simmy he could get the team into the black. The team had been a financial drain on Simmy, which he wanted to change.

So Simmy was putting quite a bit of confidence in Squirrel, a man he hardly knew. They'd gotten along well until Simmy announced that Randy Joe was joining the team and sent Squirrel into a tirade against the young pitcher and whites in general.

"I done told everybody dis was gonna be an all-Negro team," Squirrel complained. "We don't need dis boy."

"You need to cool down some," Simmy said. "Randy Joe is different dan most white folks. And he's de best pitcher I ever seed. If we gonna win dat big tournament up in Wichita we gonna need'em."

It didn't take Squirrel long to read his boss, to understand that nothing he could say would change Simmy's mind. But that didn't mean he had to like the situation, or Randy Joe Keegan.

Randy Joe had no knowledge of Squirrel's animosity toward him. Nor did he know that before they left on tour the traveling secretary had done his best to turn the other players against him.

The team left Jason on Monday afternoon, traveling in an old school bus that had been painted white. Emblazoned across each side in orange was JASON LONGHORNS and the team emblem, a silhouette of a longhorn steer's head.

Driver of the bus was Grease Clifton, who could easily have passed for one of Randy Joe's logging buddies. Grease was fifty-five, but with none of Squirrel's worry wrinkles. He had a smooth, almost baby face punctuated by big lips and a set of teeth that looked like the grill on a fifty-four Buick. Grease liked to smile and his eyes always looked as though they reflected some mischievous thought. He wore blue bib overalls, a longsleeve checkered flannel shirt and highly polished brogans. There seemed to always be a smudge of grease on one of his shirt sleeves or overalls, the result of his constant work on the engine of the bus.

Squirrel always wore a suit. He had two that had seen better days, along with three worn white shirts and two wide ties. Grease had another pair of overalls and a flannel shirt.

There was plenty of room on the old bus for everyone to have his own seat. Randy Joe got one across from Cut Brown, the team's tough little second baseman. Grease put the bus in gear and headed east, toward Louisiana.

The Longhorns had a night game in Leesville against Fort Polk, a large Army facility that was the economic base for the town. Cut was less than thrilled about it and said, "Dem Army boys...dey ain't got no money. De gate gonna be awful small tonight."

Squirrel, sitting a couple of seats behind Grease, heard him and said, "Don't you be worryin' 'bout no gate, Mr. Cut Brown. I done negotiated a guaranteed fee fo' playin' dese Army boys."

Cut asked, "How much?"

"Dat's for me to know and fo' you to find out," Squirrel replied.

Cut leaned toward Randy Joe and whispered, "Probably a hundred dollars and de old man thinks he done cut a fat hog."

Randy Joe laughed and whispered, "Would that even pay expenses?"

"It's better than nothin'," Cut said. "But dis old man liable to get us on on de road and starve us to death. He don't eat. All he care 'bout is havin' a pack o' cigarettes in his pocket."

"Simmy won't let us starve, will he?"

"He done give Squirrel 'nough money to get us started. After dat, we on our own. Everythin' have to be paid outta de gate dat we get. And sometimes dat ain't much."

En route to Leesville Randy Joe got quite a bit of background on the squat-bodied Cut. He was a Mississippi native whose dad and mother still worked on a plantation. Early on Cut knew he didn't want to spend the rest of his life chopping and picking cotton, so had developed his baseball skills and joined a team in the Negro American League.

"Ever'body thinks it's wonderful dat de majors started takin' colored players," he said, "but dey forget dat fo' every one dat make it dey's a lot like me out here. When de team I was wid folded, dey was no place fo' me to go. So I guess in one way it was good fo' a player like Jackie Robinson, but not so good fo' players like me."

"You haven't given up gettin' to the big leagues, have you?"

"No, I ain't never gonna give up," Cut replied, "but de scouts lookin' fo' younger players. Dat's why all of us lies about our age."

"How old are you?"

"Twenty-seven. But if a scout axe you, I'm twenty-two."

Randy Joe laughed. "I'll remember."

Cut smiled, showing a nice set of pearly whites surrounded by his thick lips. "Now no scout's gonna be worried 'bout you bein' too old. You don't even look like you sixteen."

"I'll be seventeen this month."

Cut grinned. "Lawd, how I wish I was gonna be seventeen dis month. No use wishin', though. Dat's all behind me."

"What do you do in the off-season, Cut?"

"Whatever I can. I jest gets me a day job and waits fo' de baseball season to start up again."

"Maybe we'll get lucky and make a lotta money on this tour."

Cut laughed. "Dat show you ain't never done dis befo'. I be happy if we eats regular and has a place to sleep. Since you wid us I think we gotta chance to win dat tournament up in Kansas, but I heared you done went to de hospital after dat game against Lake Charles and ain't recovered yet."

"I'm not a hundred percent, but I'll pull my weight."

"You throw and hit like you did 'gainst Lake Charles and you gonna do mo' dan pull yo' weight."

"That's the only way I know how to throw," Randy Joe said.

"Well, if dat arm stay healthy you gonna be in de big leagues befo' you know it."

"I sorta gotta rubber arm, so I guess I'm lucky."

"Dey's lot o' people wid a rubber arm who can't do nothin' wid it," Cut said. "Even yo' changeup got somethin' on it."

"I don't know about that. My problem is gettin' the ball over the plate. I have some trouble doin' that."

"Maybe you tryin' to pitch too fine and dey ain't no need wid what you got."

"No, I don't try to pitch all that fine. Most of the time I'm just tryin' to get it over the plate."

"Well, don't matter none if dat fastball o' yours is right down de middle. Ain't many gonna hit it. I ain't never seed nobody throw de heat like you does. I oughta start callin' you White Heat."

Randy Joe laughed. "People tell me I oughta throw the fastball more, that I throw the curve too much."

"Well, ever'body got an opinion. All you gotta do is mix it up a little bit and ain't many gonna hit you."

The conversation with Cut lasted until someone invited him to sit in on a card game going on in the back of the bus. After Cut had left Randy Joe had time to reflect on all that he had said, including the fact that he had a wife and baby back in Mississippi. Even when he'd been in the Negro American League Cut had made only a hundred dollars a month, which had to make him drool at the possibility of the payoff for winning the Wichita tournament. Seven hundred dollars was more than he had ever made for a season of baseball.

Reflecting more on it, Randy Joe realized the chances of making the majors was slim for anyone, but even more so for someone with black skin. They couldn't all be Jackie Robinsons. Cut was a good second baseman, fielded well and swung a good stick. He might even be better than a half dozen or so of the second basemen currently on major league clubs, but just hadn't been in the right place at the right time, hadn't had the right people believe in him. Hell, all of life was like that. If a man was in the right place at the right time, wonderful. If not, life could be a real downer. Were a man's years on earth all a matter of luck, happenstance, knowing the right people? Or was there something more?

Randy Joe thought about the Bible J.B. Smith had given him, about pulling it out of his bag and reading it. His reverie was interrupted when Grease pulled the bus off the highway and yelled, "Piss stop."

Grease had stopped the bus in the middle of nowhere, just out in the boonies. Cut came by and said, "If you wanna piss or shit you better do it now. Ain't gonna be no stoppin' by no service station wid dis bunch o' coloreds."

Until then Randy Joe hadn't really thought about it, but Cut was right. Only a few service stations even had restrooms for *Colored Only*. All had restrooms for *White Only*. The law of the land dictated where a man dumped or pissed, so with his teammates he'd be making sojourns into a lot of wooded areas along various highways.

After they'd taken care of business and were back on the bus, Cut asked, "You play cards?"

"Depends," Randy Joe replied. "I play hearts and gin rummy."

Cut laughed. "You play wid dis bunch, you gotta play poker."

"I've played a little poker," Randy Joe said. "I'll watch a few hands. Shouldn't take long to learn how you guys play."

"What you has to watch fo' is cheatin'," Cut warned. "Dese guys loves to cheat."

So Randy Joe spent the rest of the bus ride to Leesville watching Cut, Buck Frazier, Tater Green and Rooster Solomon play cards. It was penny ante, but serious. A dollar was serious money when you only got two dollars a day meal money.

It was a little past mid-afternoon when Grease reached the outskirts of Leesville. Directed by Squirrel, he drove to the Negro section of town, an area of rundown shotgun houses with tin roofs. Squalor was prevalent, poverty rampant. It was a depressing sight to Randy Joe's eyes, but not much different than the Quarters in Jason.

Grease finally parked the bus in front of an unpainted wooden two-story building with a weathered sign that said Hotel. "Dis where we gonna be stayin' de night," Squirrel announced. "Muddy say who you be roomin' wid. I gonna give you yo' meal money now and it up to you whather you eats befo' or after de game. We leaves here 'bout six o'clock fo' de ball park."

As they started filing off the bus Squirrel reluctantly gave each of them two dollars. Muddy was waiting just the other side of him to make room assignments. "You wid Gar," he told Randy Joe.

The inside of the hotel looked no better than the outside. The lobby had wooden floors with ground-in dirt and a couple of ragged couches. What passed for a registration desk was an old wooden table with a hardback chair behind it. An effort had been made to put flowered wallpaper on the clapboard walls, but it was soiled and peeling. In a corner an army of ants hustled to and fro from behind a wall to a hole in the floor.

When Randy Joe walked in the desk clerk, who was also the manager and owner of the old building, got nervous. "He wid us," Muddy explained. "He on de team."

"I guess it be okay," the man said, reluctantly. "If he wanna stay here I don't guess de sheriff gonna say nothin' to me 'bout it."

Gar Foster and Randy Joe climbed the stairs to their room, which was number nine. The number had been scrawled on the door with a paint brush. The room was a lot like the lobby. It was small, had a single window, an open gas heater, one double bed and a dresser with a broken mirror. The window was open and the smell of garbage and outhouses filtered in. Randy Joe figured it was something he'd have to live with because it was too hot to shut the window. He eyed the double bed and wondered how much room he was going to have sleeping with the six-foot, four-inch, two hundred and forty pound Gar.

The big pitcher read his thoughts, grinned and said, "Don't worry none 'bout dat bed. Growin' up I hadda sleep wid my brothers. We slept fo' to a bed."

Randy Joe laughed. "Long as you are, where do you put your feet?"

"I jest hangs'em off de end."

Randy Joe had a thing about cleanliness. Just being in the room made him feel dirty. He figured he was going to have to do some serious adjusting because there would be a lot of hotels like this one during the tour. From what he could gather the place had twelve rooms, one bathroom and a single shower.

"You wanna eat befo' or after de game, roomie?" Gar asked.

Randy Joe shrugged. "Don't matter to me. You hungry?"

"Always is," Gar replied.

Randy Joe walked down the stairs of the hotel and out into the street where he was surrounded by black faces. He felt perfectly comfortable. He had always felt comfortable around Negroes and, of course, being in the company of big Gar Foster made him feel safe in this new environment. He figured they could handle just about any problem that might arise.

They walked down the steet until they came to a low-slung frame building with a Bar-B-Q sign. It looked as dingy as the hotel on the outside and had a screened window that ran the length of the front of the building. Smoke was billowing from a pipe on top of the roof and the unmistakable smell of barbecue filled their nostrils.

The inside of the place was dimly lit, filled with cigarette and kitchen smoke. The two kinds of smoke were mingling and hanging around the stained ceiling like low-flying clouds. It reminded Randy Joe of a foggy day on the Texas coast.

Gar's and Randy Joe's entrance caused a mumbling among the patrons, almost all males. Most were drinking beer and smoking cigarettes, which caused Randy Joe to wonder if Leesville was a dry area like Jason. If so, the beer was of a bootleg variety, which also caused him to wonder if the sheriff in Leesville controlled the flow of liquor as did his counterpart in Jason. Of course Louisiana was different, with parishes instead of counties and probably a whole lot different way of looking at drinking.

The inside of the barbecue place looked a lot cleaner than the outside. The wooden tabletops looked as though they were scrubbed often with harsh detergent, as did the floors. Gar found them a table in the back of the room and away from most of the patrons. A woman started toward them, then retreated and disappeared into the kitchen. Moments later she reappeared with a man wearing an apron smeared with barbecue sauce and God knows what else. He came to Gar's and Randy Joe's table and said, "Sorry, but we don't serve no white folks in here."

Randy Joe looked around, then said, "Who's white?"

Gar laughed. "Did you think dis boy was white? Well, he is white but he ain't. You done heared dat ol' story de whites tell 'bout a nigger in de woodpile. Well, dey was a white man in dis boy's daddy's woodpile. He white...but he black."

The man who had come out of the kitchen had a dubious look on his face, which for the most part was pleasant enough. He had full cheeks and a big mouth with large teeth, some of which had gold fillings. He was in the neighborhood of six-feet tall and was quite hefty. The apron couldn't hide the fact that he was developing a substantial innertube around the middle.

"Don't you go jivin' me now," he said.

"Man, I ain't jivin' you," Gar said, feigning hurt at such an assertion. "Dis boy jest like me. He a pitcher fo' de Jason Longhorns."

"You wid de Longhorns?" the barbecue man asked, obviously pleased to have such nobility in his place of business. "I sho' is lookin' foward to de game tonight."

"Well den," Gar said, "you knowin' yo' baseball and knowin' de Longhorns is an all-Negro team, what you gonna call dis boy since he a member of de team?"

The man laughed. "I guess he a Negro."

"Dat's de way we looks at it," Gar said.

"What you fellas want?" the barbecue man asked.

"How much yo' barbecue?" Gar asked.

"I bring you boys a big bait o' barbecue, all you can eat, fo' a dollar and a quarter a piece. Dat include a Coke, too."

"Look out now," Gar said. "Don't you come here talkin' 'bout bringin' me all de barbecue I can eat 'less you ready to back it up."

"I is ready," the man said.

"Den bring it on. Only I want a strawberry sodie pop wid mine. What you want, Randy Joe?"

"Just make mine the same."

When the barbecue man left their table, Gar said, "Dat's gonna happen a lot over here. Dey ain't used to no white folks comin' into no colored eatin' place."

"They got every right to keep whites out," Randy Joe said. "There's a Negro barbecue place in Jason that has a place in the back for whites. There's even a sign that says White Only."

Gar nodded. "Yeah...I know de place. I eats dare quite a bit."

"Where you from, Gar?"

"I's from right here in Lose'anna...not far from here."

"Been playin' semi-pro ball long?"

"Ever since I was twelve years old. I was big fo' my age."

"I can believe that. How old are you now?"

"Didn't I tell you dat?"

"Not that I remember."

"Twenty-five."

"You play up in the Negro America League like Cut did?"

"Naw...never did. Wanted to but never got de chance."

"Where have you played?"

"Well, fo' de past three years I been playin' fo' Simmy's team. Befo' dat I plays over here fo' different folks."

"So you never really played any pro ball?"

"Played 'gainst 'em, but never fo' 'em. But dat's what I wants to do. If de right people see me play I has a chance fo' de majors."

"I understand that dream," Randy Joe said. "It's just about all I ever think about."

"You gonna make it, You de fastest pitcher I ever seed. And I ain't never seed nobody throw de curveball no better dan you."

"Well...thanks, Gar," Randy Joe said, genuinely appreciative of the compliment. He'd never experienced anything but jealousy from the other pitchers on his high school team.

Gar grinned. "Maybe you better not be thankin' me, 'cause I'm gonna try to get you to help me wid my curveball."

"No problem there. I'll show you how I throw it, but I don't know what I do that's different from anyone else. A lot of stuff just comes kind of natural to me."

"You smoke?" Gar asked.

"No...never have."

"You better off. Ever'body else on de team smoke...always bummin' cigarettes. Dat's why I axed you...'cause I want a cigarette bad."

Gar left the table to bum a cigarette from one of the other

patrons, was successful, and ended up talking to the young girl who had started to wait on them. Randy Joe figured the girl was attractive enough, but didn't observe her all that closely. He didn't stare because he felt like a lot of eyes were giving him the once over.

The barbecue man came to the table and spread out pieces of butcher's paper to serve as plates. He put a good helping of barbecued ribs on each piece of butcher's paper along with several slices of white bread and some paper napkins. A bottle of hot sauce was already on the table.

"You ain't really no Negro, is you?" he asked.

"Does it matter?"

"Well, we ain't never had no white folks in here befo'."

"That's their loss," Randy Joe said. "They're just missin' out on some good barbecue."

The man smiled appreciatively. "Where you from?"

"Jason, Texas."

"And you really plays fo' de Longhorns?"

"Sure do."

"Well, I swear."

"You've seen 'em play?" Randy Joe asked.

"Sho' have...ever time dey comes over here. Don't know why I didn't recognize yo' partner right off. I seed ol' Gar pitch last year."

"Probably just the lighting," Randy Joe said, biting into a rib. "It's pretty hard to see in here."

Gar came back to the table and the waitress, who was now very friendly with him, brought their strawberry soda pops. She had a case of the giggles, obviously from something Gar had said to her earlier. "I jest told her we wouldn't mind sleepin' three to de bed 'stead o' two," he explained, smiling.

The barbecue was good. One helping filled Randy Joe, but Gar made the barbecue man make good on his all you can eat claim. While eating another big helping he told Randy Joe, "Better learn to eat heavy ever' chance you get, 'cause dey's gonna be some lean times."

"That's what Cut said."

"Ol' Cut know," Gar assured. "It get rough when you jest

playin' fo' part of de gate."

During the meal Randy Joe learned a lot more about Gar. He'd been born and raised at a little place called Sandy Hill, which was just south of Leesville. He was the sixth of thirteen children. His dad was a farmer and laborer, took whatever jobs he could find to help support his family. His mother had done pretty much the same, from working as a cook to taking in washing and ironing. Life had been no bed of roses for the Foster family.

"You see your folks much?" Randy Joe asked.

"I sees'em when I ain't playin' baseball. I goes back ever' year after de season."

"You work there?"

"Ain't much to do in Sandy Hill. I usually stays wid my brother in Alexandria. I works at de sawmill when dey needs somebody."

Randy Joe laughed. "Oh, so you work at a sawmill, too. Do you like it?"

"Can't say as I do. Sho' ain't as much fun as playin' baseball."

"Amen to that," Randy Joe agreed. "You ever worked on the green chain?"

"Sho' ain't and hopes I never has to. Worst job at de sawmill."

"Tell me 'bout it. I spent a summer workin' on the green chain."

"I never seed anybody but coloreds on de chain."

"I was the only white workin' there. My dad's one of those people who believes in a day's work for a day's pay and he figured I needed the experience."

"Yo' daddy sound like he a hard man. But my daddy de same way. He don't think nothin' 'bout no hard work."

"If I hadn't come on this tour I'd be workin' in the swamp, cutting cypress trees."

"Lawd help...down wid all dem water moccasins and all dat other nasty stuff what's in de swamp."

"I still prefer it to the green chain."

"I has to think 'bout dat. I sho' ain't likin' no swamp work."

After the meal and conversation Randy Joe was experiencing a growing appreciation for his roomie. Gar was eight years older, but he was still young at heart. He'd had a rough life, but wasn't crying about it. He was keeping his head up and doing his best.

Randy Joe knew what it was like to be poor. But compared to Gar, and probably the rest of his teammates, he had been a child of privilege. He figured no matter how poor his parents were, just being born white gave him a leg up on his colored teammates.

"Your folks livin'...so close to Leesville...they gonna be at the game tonight?" Randy Joe asked.

"Dey ain't got no car, so I don't 'spect so. My brother and sister livin' in town here. Dey might make it to de game."

"Hell, you must have brothers and sisters everywhere."

"Dey scattered all over. I even got one livin' up in Harlem, but I ain't never goin' back up in dat place."

"You were up there?"

"Oh, yeah...a couple years back. I ain't likin' what I saw."

"Bad, huh?"

"Bad ain't de half of it. Folks up in Harlem is crazy. I likes de South. Dey's a lot what needs changin', but it sho' better dan up North."

"To play in the majors you gotta go up North."

"Dat's true, but it be different fo' a ball player dan for a plain ol' colored."

By the time they left the barbecue place it was almost time to board the bus and head for the ball park. Their walk back to the hotel, however, was interrupted by a parish sheriff's car that pulled up and stopped in front of them. A wiry little man wearing a khaki uniform, cowboy hat and big gun got out of the car and confronted them.

"Excuse me, son," he said to Randy Joe, "but mind tellin' me what you're doin' down here?"

"Nothing. I'm just gettin' ready to ride the bus out to the ball park."

"You eat down here at that barbecue place?" the deputy asked.

"Yes sir, I did. Any law against it?"

The deputy had a weasel face, deepset brown eyes and bushy eyebrows. "Can't say as they's a law against it, son, but it just ain't done. We leave the niggers alone...they leave us alone. That's the way we do things here."

Gar was staying clear of the conversation. He knew it might get nasty if he opened his mouth. The man, a common reference by Negroes to anyone in law enforcement, didn't tolerate any lip from coloreds.

"Well, sir," Randy Joe said, "I'm not tryin' to cause any trouble. I'm just here to play baseball."

The deputy, whom Randy figured was in his late thirties, said, "You tellin' me you play for the nigger baseball team that's playin' here tonight?"

"Yes sir, I do."

"That's the damnedest thing I've ever heard," the deputy said. "You from up North, boy...one of them agitators?"

"No sir. I'm from Jason, Texas."

"Damn, son, that's worse. You're sellin' out your own people."

"I don't know what you mean. Like I said...I'm just here to play baseball."

The deputy grumbled something about the damned Army causing him all sorts of problems, then said, "Y'all leavin' tomorrow, ain't you?"

"Yes sir, we are."

"Well then, just don't be causin' any commotion down here and I'll forget about this."

"Excuse me, sir, but did someone complain about me causin' a commotion?" Randy Joe asked.

"If I didn't get a complaint I sure as hell wouldn't be down here," the deputy said. "Some of the niggers 'round here don't wantcha down here. This is their parta town and they don't want us in it."

The deputy wheeled on the heels of his cowboy boots, and got in his car. Gar said, "Damn if some nigger ain't called de man on you. I find out who I'm gonna whip his ass."

"It's not worth it, Gar. Let's just go play some baseball."

Several players had seen their brush with the law and questioned them about it on the bus. After Gar explained the situation Squirrel grumbled to Muddy Tate, "I done told you dat white boy gonna be nothin' but trouble."

One of the nice complements to the Fort Polk ball park was a field house with showers. They were able to dress at the park and would be able to shower after the game without lining up to use the lone one at the hotel. After he was dressed in his number fifty-two uniform, Muddy came by and said, "Simmy done told me 'bout you bein' in de hospital. He say you need to get yo' strength back. So you jest does yo' runnin' and stuff and you let me know when you able to pitch."

"I'm almost a hundred percent," Randy Joe said, lying to himself as much as to Muddy.

"Ain't no rush. De important thing is dat you be ready fo' de tournament in Wichita."

So Randy Joe went out on the field and started trying to run sprints in the outfield, but he really couldn't. His legs just wouldn't respond the way he wanted. He covered it up as best he could, did a little jogging, but had to acknowledge that he was far from recovered.

In batting practice he took his cuts and hit the ball pretty well, then played a little pepper. He figured on warming up during the game, getting one of the other pitchers to catch him.

Gar was the scheduled starter against Fort Polk and Randy Joe visited him while he was warming up with catcher Buck Frazier. "How you feelin'?" he asked.

"Real strong," Gar said, firing a fastball into Buck's mitt. "Ain't throwed in a while...need to get some o' de edge off."

Randy Joe watched his roomie for a while and wondered how he would fare against the Army boys. Gar's fastball was average but his curveball broke too far out in front of the plate, where it was easy for a hitter to pick up on it. The one thing he did seem to have was good control.

There was a pretty good crowd for the game. Most dressed in civilian clothes were Negroes and Randy Joe noted something else. There was segregation among the soldiers. The white soldiers were in one section of the stands, the colored ones in another. It was not the way he'd pictured things being in the military. It wasn't the way he'd told his friend Weave it would be.

The Fort Polk team was integrated. They had a squad of twenty-five players. Randy Joe counted five Negroes and two of them were starters. He figured another one or two might be pitchers.

The Longhorns jumped on the first Fort Polk pitcher quickly, scoring three runs in the first inning. Polk came back and scored two off Gar in their half of the inning. Then the fireworks slowed down. By the fifth inning Polk was leading four to three. It rocked on that way until the seventh when the Army team added another run.

Muddy got lefthander Skeeter Hodnett warming in the bullpen, but Gar managed to get out of the inning without further damage. In the dugout to start the eighth Muddy told Skeeter, "We get somethin' goin' I'm gonna pinch hit fo' Gar and you go in to pitch."

Randy Joe wondered who was going to do the pinch hitting. Other than Skeeter there was Pooh Wiley and him. He asked Cut, who said, "Pooh a better hitter dan Gar."

The Longhorns got a mini-rally started in the eighth. With two down Jackie Monk singled and Tater Green walked, which made Gar the scheduled hitter. Muddy, who'd turned his normal third base coaching duties over to Cooter Davis, walked up to Randy Joe and asked, "You wanna pinch hit?"

"Sure," Randy Joe replied. He went to the bat rack and pulled out his favorite stick. He'd been paying close attention to the Fort Polk pitcher, a big fireballing righthander, and had confidence he could hit him, given the chance. He knew his only problem would be running the bases on what were still weak and unwieldy wheels.

There was a chorus of boos as he stepped to the plate and he couldn't determine whether they came from the white or black section of the stands. He suspected both.

The big pitcher didn't see anything imposing about Randy Joe, certainly nothing to fear. But just to be on the safe side he burned one inside that forced him back from the plate. The pitch didn't run any tremors down Randy Joe's spine, even though a teammate had mentioned the righthander was a highly regarded prospect under contract to the Cleveland Indians. He was fulfilling his military obligation in the Army's special services branch and, when discharged, would join a Cleveland farm club. Randy Joe wasn't impressed with the fastball the guy had thrown him.

He watched the next pitch, another fastball, nip the outside corner of the plate. Not much movement on the ball, he noted. Just heat with no hop.

The count went to two-two on nothing but fastballs and Randy Joe knew why. He'd seen the guy's curveball and it was mediocre at best. The Polk pitcher had to know it, had to know with men on base he had to come with his best pitch. So there was no doubt in Randy Joe's mind that he was going to see a fastball.

And see one he did, an almost perfect pitch, low and heading for the inside corner. It was not a hitter's pitch, but Randy Joe knew he couldn't chance an umpire's call on one so close. He caught the ball squarely on the barrel of the bat with his best Ted Williams swing. It carried right down the right field line and just inside the foul pole, barely clearing the fence at the three hundred and thirty foot sign.

The Polk pitcher stood off the mound looking downcast and angry as Randy Joe trotted around the bases to be greeted at home plate by his jubilant teammates. Gar was most happy because he stood to lose the game if the Longhorns hadn't rallied. With Randy Joe's home run making the score six to five, he might be the winner.

He was. Skeeter, the blocky five-foot, nine-inch lefthander, retired six Polk hitters in a row. It was a good way to start the tour.

After they'd showered, changed and were en route back to the hotel, Gar was singing the praises of his roomie. But there was at least one person on the bus who wasn't pleased with the way things had turned out. The three-run homer didn't make Squirrel a Randy Joe Keegan fan. If anything, it made him hate the white boy more.

It was late when they reached the hotel. Randy Joe was ready to hit the sack, which he did, but Gar mysteriously disappeared. Randy Joe was almost asleep when Gar came in. He didn't turn on the only light in the place, an exposed bulb on the ceiling, but there was enough light coming in from the curtainless window so that it was easy to see.

"Is you 'wake, Randy Joe?"

"Yeah...I'm awake."

"You wanna do yo' roomie a favor?"

"Sure, Gar, what is it?"

"You wanna go fo' a little walk or somethin'?"

"A walk?"

Then in the semi-darkness he saw the girl. She was the one from the barbecue place. Randy Joe recognized her when she giggled. "No problem, Gar," he said, getting up and putting on his clothes. He went down to the lobby where the hotel manager was reading the newspaper and smoking a cigar. They talked a bit and then the manager pulled out a checker board.

They played a half dozen or so games. Then Gar and the girl came down the stairs and Randy Joe went to bed.

THIRTY-ONE

Squirrel Simpson had poured out a cauldron of bitterness toward Randy Joe Keegan in conversations with Longhorns manager and shortstop Muddy Tate. He'd pushed Muddy to complain to Simmy about taking the white pitcher on the tour, but the manager hadn't talked to the club owner about it. Muddy didn't want to antagonize Squirrel because he was handling the finances. He didn't want to anger Simmy either. Simmy owned the team and if it wasn't for him there would be no tour.

So Muddy was caught in the middle.

He didn't have anything against Randy Joe Keegan, but wasn't about to champion some white boy, either. All he knew was that, if the game against Lake Charles was an example, the white kid could throw a baseball better than anyone he'd ever seen. But, like Squirrel, he figured the team would do all right without him.

Squirrel and everyone on the team knew the white boy was supposedly weak from a hospital stay, but he sure hadn't seemed that way when he hit the home run against Fort Polk. Muddy admitted only to himself that Squirrel had agitated him into sending Randy Joe to the plate as a pinch hitter. He'd planned to use Pooh, but Squirrel had kept saying, "Why don't you use dat white boy and see what he's made of?"

Muddy knew Squirrel had counted on Randy Joe failing in the clutch, lessening his importance to the team and reinforcing the other players doubts about having a white boy with them. Squirrel had been doing a lot of negative talking about Randy Joe, trying to get all the players to accept his way of thinking. Muddy figured it was Squirrel who had called the sheriff's office in Leesville about a white boy making trouble in the colored section of town. He had confronted him about it, but Squirrel had denied making the call.

So Muddy had a dilemma. He had the man in charge of the money causing dissension on the team and a white boy behind the problem. The problem was further complicated by the fact that this white boy might be the difference in winning or losing the big tournament up in Kansas. The Longhorns had played in the tournament for three straight years but had never won it. The reason, Muddy knew, was a lack of standout pitching. Pooh, Gar and Skeeter were good pitchers, but Randy Joe Keegan might just be in a class all by himself. Muddy knew Simmy thought so, and he respected Simmy as a judge of baseball talent.

Muddy held himself somewhat aloof from the rest of the team. He was older, thirty-three, and knew his dream of being a major leaguer was nothing more than that. He figured he could still play baseball, could still contribute, but knew the scouts

would pass on him because of age. Like everyone on the team he
claimed to be younger than his actual years, but the scouts were
wise to such lying. Muddy had been around too long. They'd
seen him for years.

He had been born and raised in Longview, Texas. His dad
had worked in the East Texas oil fields as a laborer, but hadn't
been paid like his white counterparts. Still, he'd made more than
most of the Negroes in the area. That had proved good and bad.

When Muddy and his half dozen brothers and sisters were
younger it had been good because they had a little more than the
average black family in the area. But then his dad had gotten the
wanderlust, started chasing whores and disappeared out of their
lives. They'd dropped below the average then. His mother was
forced to take a job with a white family and they all had to work
to eke out an existence. Muddy had been forced to quit school in
the eighth grade.

After his father left there hadn't been much to smile about.
His dad had, before he left, bought him a baseball glove, ball and
bat. And it may well have been his father's love of baseball that
had caused Muddy to develop a love for the sport at an early age.
When he was fourteen he was playing on a men's team.

There weren't that many Negro teams in the area in 1935, but
enough so that Muddy could play a double-header every Sunday. Back then he hadn't dared think that a colored man might
someday play in the major leagues.

Six years later he was in the Army doing menial tasks during
World War II. He never went overseas to do any fighting, just
spent the wartime years cleaning latrines and working as a cook's
helper. When he got out of the Army in 1945 he was twenty-four,
a man with no skills and a desire to play baseball.

Muddy considered going North to find work and better
opportunities to play ball, but wasn't able to break away from
East Texas and his mother. So he worked at whatever he could
around Longview for the next five years, playing baseball every
Sunday during the season.

Then in 1950 he heard about the colored pulpwood contractor in Jason who owned a team. He caught a bus to Jason, visited
with Simmy, and ended up going to work for him. He cut and

hauled pulpwood during the off-season.

Muddy didn't consider Simmy that much of a colored man. He didn't act like any colored man he had ever known. He walked around in the white world like he owned it.

A lot was going through Muddy's mind as the wheels of the old white bus whined along on the asphalt leading to Alexandria, Louisiana. It was a typically hot, humid day for the area and most of the windows on the bus were down. Some players dozed and others smoked and played cards. Squirrel sat in the seat behind Grease, watching the road ahead and talking to the bus driver.

Muddy was sitting near the front of the bus, too, but decided to get up and go back to where Randy Joe was sitting. The white pitcher was stifling a yawn as he approached.

"Mind if I talk to you a bit?" Muddy asked.

Randy Joe smiled. "Glad for the company."

Muddy sat. "You kinda pulled us outta a tough spot last night."

Randy Joe shrugged his shoulders. "Just lucky."

"Ain't no luck when a man hit a ball like dat. You play any place 'sides pitcher?"

"Played some shortstop in high school."

The response didn't please Muddy, who was very jealous of his position. "You play any place else?"

"Any place except catcher. Gettin' behind the plate scares the hell outta me."

"De reason I axe," Muddy said, "is dat we might use you some place else if somebody get hurt or somethin'."

"I'll do the best I can wherever you put me."

"You hit pretty good in high school?"

Randy Joe again shrugged his shoulders. "I hit over four hundred, but that's high school. The pitchin' wasn't as good as what you guys are used to facing."

"Hittin' fo' hundred in battin' practice awful good."

"Well, I don't consider myself that much of a hitter. I'm not sure I can hit good pitchin' consistently."

"Dat pitcher wid Lake Charles was plenty good."

"I imagine we'll run into some better ones, don't you?"

"Maybe," Muddy agreed. "How you feelin'?"

"I'll throw when you need me."

"You jest keeps up yo' runnin' and throwin' easy," Muddy said. "We don't wanna rush things."

Muddy went back to his seat near the front of the bus and lit up a cigarette. A few minutes later Squirrel joined him and bummed one. "What you talkin' to dat white boy 'bout?" he asked.

"Jest findin' out what positions he plays."

Squirrel grumbled, "You starts lettin' dat boy has his way and dis team gonna fall apart."

"Why you say dat?"

"'Cause dis supposed to be an all-Negro team and dey ain't no place on it fo' no white boy. He gonna cause us nothin' but trouble."

"Simmy done put'em on de team and dat's dat," Muddy said.

"Simmy done fo'get he a black man," Squirrel said, angrily.

"He tell me he gonna put together de best Negro baseball team dey ever was, den up and put dis white boy on de team."

"Why you gettin' so upset 'bout it?" Muddy asked.

"'Cause out here settin' up dese games I done told ever'body dat we has an all-colored team. De people I done talked to gonna be upset wid me."

"Dey's gotta be mo' to it dan dat, Squirrel. What you got 'gainst white folks anyway?"

"Did de white man ever do anythin' fo' you?"

"Some has and some hasn't," Muddy replied. "I ain't got no quarrel wid white folks."

"Well, I does," Squirrel said. "De white man done kept us coloreds down...kicked us ever' time he get de chance."

"All white folks ain't like dat, Squirrel."

"Down here in de South dey is. Dey don't want us goin' to de same schools, de same churches, or sitttin' in de same eatin' places wid'em."

"I figure most coloreds don't wanna go to school wid de white folks," Muddy said, "and I sho' don't wanna go to no church wid'em. As fo' de eatin' places, I jest as soon goes to de colored places."

"See what you done sayin'," Squirrel said. "If you think

coloreds oughta be wid coloreds, den dis oughta be an all-colored team. When we beats some o' dese white teams on de tour, I want dem to be beat by an all-colored team. I want'em to know dat de colored ball players is jest as good as dey is."

"We gonna be beatin' dese teams wid coloreds," Muddy said.

Squirrel shook his head in resignation. "You see what happen last night, Muddy? We playin' dat Army team dat have mostly white boys on it and we beats'em. But it ain't no all-colored team dat do it. Dem Fort Polk boys sayin' today dat if it ain't fo' dat white boy we'da beat dem niggers. Dey ain't sayin' a colored team done beat'em. Dey givin' de credit to de white boy."

From the time Muddy had first met Squirrel, he realized he wouldn't be able to hold his own in an argument with the old man. Squirrel's logic was warped, but he could beat a man down with it. He just kept coming and coming, like a good pitcher who threw a lot of heat.

Still, he wondered what had caused Squirrel to have such hatred for white people. Over the years Muddy had liked some whites, disliked others, which pretty much summed up the way he felt about people of his own race.

Gar had lost what little money he had in a poker game in the back of the bus, so he made his way up front to sit and talk with Randy Joe. He grinned and asked, "You has a girlfriend back in Jason?"

Randy Joe grinned. "Yeah...a couple. Maybe three or four."

"Hope you don't mind dat I axed you to leave de bed fo' a while last night."

"Naw...I didn't mind."

Gar smiled, showing a perfect set of teeth, and said, "When I gits a chance at some poontang I jest naturally takes it. You knows what I mean?"

"Yeah, I know what you mean."

"Where you learn to hit like you does, Randy Joe?"

"I don't hit that well. I just been lucky."

"I ain't knowed you dat long, but you fulla shit."

Randy Joe laughed. "Why do you say that?"

"'Cause bein' a pitcher I done seed how you covers de plate wid a bat. Ain't nothin' lucky 'bout dat. Anyway, you done get me de win last night and I 'preciates it."

"Now, Roomie, I might not always be that lucky. What then?"

Gar grinned. "I'll take my chances wid you at de plate. Wish I could hit. I seed Muddy done been talkin' wid you. What he want?"

"He just wanted to know if I played any positions beside pitcher."

"What you tell'em?"

"I told him I played some shortstop."

Gar laughed. "Lawd amercy...Muddy don't wanna be hearin' dat. He ain't wantin' nobody on dis team playin' shortstop 'sides him."

"Well, I came along to pitch, not to take someone's position."

Alexandria was a much bigger town than Leesville. The Red River ran through it, separating it from another town called Pineville. Near the downtown area there were a lot of big two-story homes backed up to the river, homes that belonged to another era.

The area with the beautiful homes along the river was not the team's destination. Grease herded the bus into a section of town similar to the one they had left in Leesville. It was rundown, dilapidated, an afterthought of good architecture built with scrap lumber and tin.

Grease parked the bus in front of a hotel that looked to be a carbon copy of the one where they had stayed in Leesville. Randy's Joe's nose was again filled with offensive pungent smells that spoke of neglect and disease.

Squirrel reluctantly handed out the day's meal money and then Randy Joe and Gar climbed the stairs to their room. Randy Joe couldn't believe the room. It so closely resembled the one they'd had in Leesville Grease could've lost his way and returned them to their previous night's lodgings.

They hadn't eaten since yesterday afternoon and that, plus the cigarette smoke on the bus, had caused Randy Joe to have the beginnings of a headache. He was used to three good meals a day, so when Gar suggested they go eat he was more than ready. Buck Frazier, the big catcher, decided to go with them.

Gar, who knew his way around Alexandria, led them to a dingy little cafe with a plate glass window in dire need of cleaning. "Dey has de best chili in town," Gar promised.

The patrons in the place stared at Randy Joe, but not with the same hostility as in Leesville. No one said whites didn't eat there.

"Dey's lotsa white Negroes over here in Alexandria," Gar said. "Well, dey's almost. Dey's a mixture of French and Negro."

Buck laughed. "Ain't no mixture in you and me, Gar. We as black as de ace o' spades."

Gar said, "I has white and Indian blood in me."

Buck laughed. "I ain't never met no colored down here in de South what don't claim he's part white and Indian."

Randy Joe could see Buck hit a nerve with Gar, who argued, "Ain't jest no claim wid me. It's de truth."

They were sitting at a sturdy, scrubbed table in chairs that were as hard as any Randy Joe had ever sat on. A tired looking waitress, one Gar wasn't interested in, came over and took their order. They all ordered chili and water.

"Where you from, Buck?" Randy Joe asked.

Born and raised up in St. Louis."

"You a Cardinals fan?"

"Seed'em play a few times when I was a kid."

"How'd you end up here...with us?"

"Played in de Negro American League fo' a while and den somebody told me 'bout dis colored man in Texas what's tryin' to put together de best Negro team dey ever was. So I get in touch wid Simmy, he come see me play, den tell me I kin come on down and play fo' him."

"Family still up in St. Louis?" Randy Joe asked.

"Yeah...my mama still there. Don't know where my daddy is. He kinda roam all over."

"Brothers and sisters?"

"I gots fo' brothers and five sisters scattered 'round."

"Where are you in the family?" Randy Joe asked. "You the oldest, youngest...what?"

"De fourth. You sho' axe a lot o' questions.

Gar laughed. "Don't he? I ain't knowed Randy Joe no time and he know mo' 'bout me dan jest 'bout anybody else."

Randy Joe grinned. "You don't mind a few questions, do you?"

"Naw, I ain't mindin'," Buck said, laughing. "Be fo you axe, I'm twenty-five years old. If a scout axes, I'm twenty-two."

"Does it really make that much difference?"

"It sho' do," Buck replied. "Dey want young ball players. You get over twenty-five and dey don't want you."

Gar agreed. "Buck here, he hit over thirty home runs a year fo' the last few years, but if dey think he too old it ain't gonna make no difference. Jest like I been winnin' mo' dan twenty games a year fo' de Longhorns, but it don't matter none if dey think you is too old."

"How many games the Longhorns play a year?" Randy Joe asked.

Gar looked at Buck for confirmation, then said, "We play seventy-five...eighty. We wanna play mo', but it's hard to git teams to play us."

"You been playin' about half as many games as a major league team," Randy Joe said. "Not bad for a team with just twelve players. Anybody ever get injured?"

"Sho'," Buck replied, "but on dis team you has to play hurt. We don't have no substitutes. Course I likes it dat way 'cause I likes to play ever'day."

The waitress brought their chili and both Gar and Buck asked for a lot of extra crackers and a bottle of catsup. They doctored the chili liberally with the catsup, Gar explaining, "It make a bowl o' chili go a long way. De crackers and water fill you up, too."

"I don't know about this one meal a day stuff," Randy Joe said.

Buck laughed. "It sho' better dan no meal a day and we gonna have some o' dem days, too."

"Looks like we oughta take in enough to get two dollars a

day eatin' money," Randy Joe said.

"It look dat way," Buck agreed, "but at some o' de games 'gainst colored teams all dey does is pass de hat. Some folks jest don't have nothin' to give. It a lot better when we playin' de white teams."

"Well, there oughta be some way to spread the money out so there won't be days without meal money," Randy Joe said.

Gar agreed. "De players don't have nothin' to say 'bout no money. Mr. Squirrel Simpson...he de man dat handle de money and he ain't gonna tell us nothin'.' "

"Squirrel...he sho' don't like you," Buck told Randy Joe.

"Why's that?"

"Dat ol' bastard," Gar replied. "He a crazy ol' man."

"You jest be careful," Buck warned, "'cause Muddy pay too much 'tention to Squirrel."

Buck's revelation that Squirrel didn't like him bothered Randy Joe. He hadn't really said much to Squirrel except hello. The only players he'd learned much about were Cut, Gar and Buck. But the tour had just started and he hoped to become better acquainted with, and friends with, all his teammates.

The game that night was against a Negro team on a field that had none of the manicured look of the Fort Polk baseball diamond. The outfield was rough and uneven, with clumps of grass that might send a ball in any direction. The infield grass was almost as bad and the shaved part of the diamond was cracked with clods of dirt everywhere. Fielding a ball here was made even harder because the field's lights weren't much more illuminating than the street lights in Jason.

The Alexandria team was no match for the Longhorns. The final score was sixteen to four and it could have been much worse. Lefthander Pooh Wiley pitched the entire game and might have had a shutout if it weren't for his own carelessness and a couple of errors caused by the grounds. It was hard for Pooh to maintain his concentration against a team of undisciplined free swingers.

Randy Joe did some running and threw some with Gar, but didn't get into the game. He wasn't all that disappointed. The five pitchers the Alexandria team used didn't even have good batting practice stuff. Such pitchers usually caused him more trouble than good ones.

Buck, however, seemed to relish the offerings of the opposition's hurlers. He tattooed three pitches that went for home runs. In all, the Longhorns hit seven roundtrippers. Randy Joe figured his teammates might have scored more runs, but after they saw the game was going to be a laugher they all started trying to hit the long ball.

The stands at the ball park were not the greatest, but they were filled. Randy Joe estimated the crowd at five hundred, but Gar told him the promoter would probably call it closer to a hundred. "Den when he take out his expenses," Gar said, "we be lucky to git outta here wid twenty or thirty dollars."

"That's not very smart business," Randy Joe opined.

"It don't has to be smart," Gar said, "but it's what you has to put up wid if you wants to play baseball."

The team spent the remainder of the week playing in Louisiana and Mississippi, in places like Vicksburg, Jackson, Baton Rouge and Lafayette. The games were all against Negro teams, all on less than adequate fields. The gate receipts were less than adequate, too. Just a couple of days out of Alexandria there was no money for rooms, so the team slept on the bus. That meant no showers because the teams they played didn't have field houses. The players took on a ripe, gamey smell. Gar was especially upset by it.

"I sweat so much," he told Randy Joe, "dat I likes to take three showers a day if I gits de chance."

Randy Joe's passion for cleanliness had taken a severe beating. He thought if he ever got in a shower again he might never get out. The only positive thing was that the Longhorns were undefeated, but in his opinion they hadn't played a serious opponent. The players were fattening their batting averages on batting practice pitchers. Gar, Pooh and Skeeter had great pitching stats, but they had faced hitters of questionable ability. As for Randy Joe, he couldn't argue with Muddy's decision not to use him because he really hadn't been needed.

He was feeling a lot better, but still wasn't a hundred percent. He kept telling himself he was, but knew deep down it wasn't true. His legs ached, were still very weak.

Squirrel was becoming more and more difficult. He was openly antagonistic toward Randy Joe and intolerant of questions from the other players. The others were openly bitter to Squirrel for arranging a tour that was making them miserable financially.

Finally, when they were en route from Louisiana to Beaumont, Texas, Randy Joe went to Muddy and asked, "You have anything against creeks?"

"What you mean?"

"I mean...I've got soap. We could at least stop at a creek and wash up. Hell, if we can find what passes for a swimmin' hole we can get in it and take a bath."

"Well, I don't know," Muddy said.

Squirrel grunted, "Ain't right dat a ball club have to stop and take a bath in a creek."

Cut said, "Shut up, old man. Ain't right dat we ain't got money fo' no hotel either. You nickel-and-diming us to death. Muddy, I like Randy Joe's idea."

"De creek have to be shallow fo' me," Gar said. "I don't know how to swim."

Gar's problem was one shared by about half the team, but Randy Joe assured his teammates they could find some shallows. Muddy gave in to the suggestion and Randy Joe sat up closer to the front of the bus, near Grease, to pick out a likely creek. He located one, plus an old and weedy dirt road leading off the highway and up the stream. Grease guided the old bus up the road until they were soon out of sight of the highway. He stopped at a place that had obviously been used by campers and fishermen.

Randy Joe checked the creek. There was a perfect hole for what they had in mind, three- to five-feet deep with shallow gravel ripples at both ends. "Great place," he shouted, coming out of his clothes. Moments later he was in the water with a bar of soap and his teammates were quickly joining him. Even Grease came out of his overalls and got in the cool water. Only a sullen Squirrel, still in his old suit, remained on the bank.

"Damn," Randy Joe said as they passed the soap around,

"am I the only one who's been circumcised?"

"What you talkin' 'bout?" Buck asked.

"Never mind," Randy Joe said, laughing.

Having the cool creek water carry their sweat and body dirt downstream seemed to rejuvenate the entire team. They also washed their uniforms in the creek, which while not on par with using a washing machine was better than nothing.

"Dis a nice place," Cut said. "I ain't mindin' if we could stay here fo' a while."

"Some white man come down here and catches you in dis creek and you be singin' a different tune," Squirrel warned, still miffed that Muddy had gone along with Randy Joe's suggestion.

"A runnin' creek is public domain, belongs to ever'body," Randy Joe said. "Now, the land belongs to somebody, but it's not posted. My guess is it belongs to the state or a timber company."

Squirrel's animosity bothered Randy Joe, but there was nothing he could do about it. However, stopping at the creek had given Randy Joe an idea, which he planned to discuss with his teammates.

When Grease brought the bus into the outskirts of Beaumont there was no attempt to find a hotel for the night. He drove straight to the ball park. It was a considerable improvement over the fields they'd played on in Louisiana and Mississippi, with the exception of the one at Fort Polk. This was a city-owned ball park, well manicured. It had nice stands, but no dressing rooms so they dressed on the bus.

"How you feel?" Muddy asked Randy Joe.

"Fine."

"Is you ready to pitch?"

"I'm ready."

The Beaumont team was all-white, a semi-pro outfit that was considered a power along the Gulf Coast. It was made up of former pros, college and high school stars. It was a well-financed outfit, had a good following, so the gate promised to be decent.

When warming up Randy Joe realized he didn't have his normal stuff, but he thought it was probably good enough. His legs were still weak, though, and he figured that was going to put more of a strain on his arm. He also thought part of his weakness might be the result of not having eaten all day. Squirrel had told the team there wasn't enough for meal money, though everyone suspected he was lying.

Some of the Longhorns players chewed on grass in an attempt to quell their hunger and kidded about turning into cows. They were trying to turn a serious situation into a funny one.

As game time approached the crowd continued to grow, which was probably more cause for enthusiasm among the Longhorns players than the Beaumont team. The prospect of a good gate, a chance to eat again, provided tremendous incentive.

The Beaumont pitcher was, Randy Joe guessed, about thirty years old. He had a decent fastball and curve, but his greatest asset was control. He seemed to be able to put his pitches exactly where the catcher wanted them. In the top of the first the Longhorns hit the ball, but right at Beaumont infielders and outfielders. The pitcher was keeping them from getting the fat part of their bats on the ball.

As Randy Joe took the mound for the Longhorns there were boos, catcalls and some racist comments from the stands. He'd always enjoyed being booed by an opponent's fans, but some of this crowd's derision went way beyond the bounds of decency. It was one thing for people like Gary Steele to call him *nigger lover* behind his back, quite another for fans to do so openly.

After his warmup pitches, after Buck had pegged the ball to second, the catcher came out and said, "Don't pay no 'tention to what dey's sayin'. We all used to it."

Buck's statement made Randy Joe realize that nothing said to or about him was going to be worse than what had been said to or about his teammates. In fact, he was ashamed to admit that he'd voiced a lot of comments about Negroes that were just as bad as the flak he was now receiving. But for the moment his composure was shaky. His first pitch to the Beaumont leadoff hitter sailed high and inside, acknowledged by a chorus of boos from the stands. He followed that pitch with three others that didn't find the strike zone.

He couldn't get a pitch over the plate to the next hitter either, which prompted Muddy to visit the mound with Buck and the other infielders. "Yo' arm botherin' you?" Muddy asked.

"Naw...it's just a lack of work," Randy Joe said.

"Git it over," Muddy said. "We gonna give you plenty o' support."

Randy Joe believed that. Even though the competition hadn't been great, he'd seen his teammates make some phenomenal catches during the tour. They could go get the ball. The problem, he felt, was that he was a strikeout pitcher who, because of his weak legs, didn't have the old velocity that made hitters look silly. Okay, he thought, I need to remember what my dad said and start using my head.

The curveball Randy Joe threw to the number three hitter in the Beaumont batting order was not the greatest, but it had good location. The guy got wood on the ball but it was just a nice little grounder to Muddy, who with the aid of Cut and Tater turned a double play.

Runner on third and the cleanup hitter in the batter's box. Randy Joe threw the big lefthand swinger a mediocre fastball and he turned on it, driving it deep to right. Jackie Monk, with his gazelle-like speed, ran back as far as the fence would let him go, leaped and caught the ball as he slammed against the green tin.

Rough inning but no score.

That's the way the game progressed early, from inning to inning. Randy Joe was averaging a strikeout an inning, but didn't have the kind of stuff he had exhibited when pitching against Lake Charles. It was obvious that whatever illness beset him after that game had taken its toll. The Beaumont team was hitting the ball hard and only some great infield and outfield play kept them from scoring.

In the fourth inning the Longhorns picked up a couple of runs. But in the bottom half of the fourth Randy Joe was tagged for a home run. It stunned him momentarily because he had never before given up a home run. Fortunately, no one was on base so the Longhorns still held a precarious one-run lead.

In the sixth the Longhorns loaded the bases with one out and Randy Joe came to the plate. In two previous appearances he'd struck out and fouled out. This time he caught a fastball solidly and drove it to deep right center. It bounded off the top of the wall and all three Longhorns runners scored. But Randy Joe kept falling down in his attempt to reach first base. His legs just wouldn't carry him, so with a relay throw from the outfield the Beaumont second baseman threw him out at first.

As he walked gingerly back to the dugout and sat down, Muddy came over from the third base coaching box and said, "You want me to bring in Skeeter?"

"Let me see what I can do this next inning," Randy Joe replied, "but tell'em to get ready."

Randy Joe's problem in running to first base wasn't lost on the manager of the Beaumont team. The first hitter up in the top of the seventh dropped a bunt down the third base line. Randy Joe fell down trying to field it.

Muddy had seen enough, knew that his pitcher's wheels weren't functioning properly. He went to the mound, took the ball from Randy Joe, and brought Skeeter into the game. Randy Joe had finished every game he'd ever started, so being lifted didn't set well with him. He didn't say anything, though, because he knew Muddy's decision was best for the team. It was just hard for him to admit that he was out of gas.

Sitting over in the dugout with Gar, Pooh, Grease and Squirrel, Randy Joe watched Skeeter do a good job of stopping Beaumont over the final three innings. Skeeter gave up a couple of runs, but the three Randy Joe had knocked in sealed a five to three win.

The victory went to Randy Joe, but there was a hollow feeling to it. Giving up the home run bothered him. Having to leave the game bothered him. He was beginning to have some doubts as to when he'd get his strong legs back. Until he did he wouldn't have the hop on his fastball that made it a great pitch.

It was eleven o'clock before the game was finally over and the Longhorns players were feeling the gnawing pangs of hunger. They boarded the bus and were told by Squirrel that they'd be driving straight on through to Waco, which was some three hundred miles northwest.

"What 'bout our meal money?" Gar asked.

"You gonna git yo' meal money," Squirrel replied. "Jest hold yo' hosses. Don't matter none, no way. Ain't no place open dat we can eat."

"I can go in some place," Randy Joe volunteered, "and get us somethin' to go."

Squirrel wasn't thrilled with Randy Joe's suggestion, but his teammates were. After Squirrel reluctantly gave them their meal money, they gave it to Randy Joe to use when the opportunity presented itself. The opportunity turned out to be a truck stop cafe that was open all night. While Grease got the bus gassed up, Randy Joe went inside the cafe and ordered twenty-six hamburgers and thirteen coffees to go. Squirrel wouldn't let Randy Joe order for him, claiming he wasn't hungry. Some of the players suspected he was the only one who hadn't missed a meal or a day of buying a pack of cigarettes. They figured he'd hoarded some money for himself.

The cafe was pretty well empty, except for a half dozen or so truckers. Some were eating, others just having coffee. One of them, sitting on a stool near Randy Joe, asked, "You with that busload o' niggers out there?"

Randy Joe grinned and replied, "Yep...sure am."

"Baseball team, huh?"

"Sure is."

"Hell, I heard of'em," the man said. "I haul through Jason once in a while, heared tell o' that nigger baseball team they got there. But I didn't know no white boy played on it."

"This is the first year I've played," Randy Joe said.

"Travelin' with'em...do they treat you all right?"

"Well, yeah...no problems."

The questioner wore a greasy straw cowboy hat, a western shirt that didn't hide his paunch, jeans and worn cowboy boots. He grinned, further exposing his jowls, and said, "I always thought niggers smelled bad until I had to be around 'em in the Army. 'Course the Army made 'em keep themselves pretty clean. Now that I haul a lot of cows, though, I don't think anything stinks. What position you play?"

"I'm a pitcher."

"Figures," he said. "Thinkin' position...and niggers can't think."

The man was making Randy Joe angry, but he held his peace.

He wasn't afraid of the guy, just afraid that any disturbance he might cause would create even greater problems for his team-mates. When he had the hamburgers and coffee and was ready to leave, he told the trucker, "You know, you don't have to be a black man to have a black heart."

When he walked out the door the guy was still pondering his statement.

THIRTY-TWO

Pooh Wiley was from Waco, which meant a bed and a good meal at his mama's house. They arrived in Waco in the wee hours of the morning. The players continued sleeping so Grease just drove the bus to the ball park and killed the engine.

On the way to Waco Randy Joe had gotten to know Pooh a lot better. He was already impressed with the lefthander's poise on the mound, plus his curveball. Pooh's curveball was far superior to Gar's or Skeeter's. But neither Pooh nor Skeeter had a fastball comparable to Gar's.

Pooh, like Muddy, was another who knew what it was like to be abandoned by a father. Neither he nor any of his brothers and sisters had any idea as to their father's whereabouts. All the twenty-one year old pitcher knew was that his daddy had left when he was five years old, leaving his mother the task of supporting the children. She'd done that with a variety of jobs, the steadiest of which was in the kitchen of a cafeteria at Baylor University.

Pooh had dreamed of attending Baylor, playing football and baseball for the Bears. Getting older he had realized the futility of that dream. Baylor did not accept black students.

After graduating from Moore High School, which made him one of the more educated on the Longhorns team, Pooh had pursued his dream of playing major league baseball. He'd initially tried to catch on with the Memphis Red Sox in the Negro American League, but the team was already loaded with good pitchers. So Pooh had played wherever he could, which had included playing for a semi-pro outfit in his hometown. They played the Longhorns and Pooh pitched so well that Simmy had recruited him.

The team the Longhorns were scheduled to play in Waco was the Negro outfit Pooh had played for. They were a pretty talented bunch, Pooh said, and in two to four games with the Longhorns each year always gave Simmy's team some tough games.

Randy Joe wasn't sure how his teammates felt after a night of riding and sleeping on the bus, but he felt like hammered dung. The hamburgers from the truck stop cafe had staved off the hunger momentarily, but he would have given anything for a cup of his mother's good coffee. He also wanted a bath, a shower, or just another creek in which to wash off the dirt and sweat of the previous night's game

Even in the early morning it was stifling hot, the sun beating down with gleeful intensity. The bus was no place to escape from the heat. There was some shade made by the tall fence surrounding the baseball stadium and its stands, but colonies of ants were enjoying it.

Katy Park was a nice baseball facility and had been home for a class B professional team. Looking through the gate Randy Joe could see it was superior to any ball field where he had previously played, the premiere diamond thus far on the tour

"Place 'round here to getta cup a coffee?" Randy Joe asked Gar.

"Dey's some places," the big pitcher said, "but Pooh gonna be back after a while. He gonna show us where to go."

"Pooh...he seems to be a nice guy."

"He okay," Gar said. "His oldest brother...he a mean'un."

"His oldest brother lives here?"

"He in prison now...killed a man."

It was mid-morning when Pooh returned to join his team-mates. He looked fresh, clean, and like he'd had a decent meal. He was, however, more than willing to take Gar and Randy Joe to a place where they could get some coffee. Pooh was glad to be in his native Waco, anxious to show off the town to his friends.

They walked to the place Pooh had in mind, which was about ten blocks from the baseball stadium. It was a ramshackle frame building that had seen better days. There were two old metal signs nailed to an outside wall, one advertising Lucky Strike cigarettes and the other advertising RC Cola. The signs were rusty on the edges and peeling.

The place looked like a tavern inside, but without the benefit of beer and other liquor. The only woman in the place was fatter than a prize hog at the fair. When she moved every part of her body shook. Men were sitting at various tables in pairs or threes, all smoking and drinking coffee. A few were eating breakfast.

They got a table and ordered coffee. Pooh offered them a cigarette from a fresh pack. Randy Joe said no but Gar took one and joined Pooh in lighting up. Once smoke was billowing around their table it looked pretty much like all the others, except for Randy Joe. His presence had caused a bit of a hush and a lot of staring.

Feeling it necessary to explain, Pooh said, "Dey ain't used to no white folks bein' in here."

Randy Joe shrugged his shoulders. "I understand." But he was thinking, at least I'm allowed to come in here. Pooh and Gar can't go in a white cafe. Since being on the tour Randy Joe had given a lot of thought to the fact that a white man could walk into a black eating establishment without any particular fear of reprisal, but it didn't work both ways. If Pooh or Gar went into a white cafe with him chances were pretty good they'd all be thrown out, even arrested. He'd always been aware of the double standard without giving much thought to it, but now it was coming home to him in a special way.

"Great lookin' ball park," Randy Joe said to Pooh. "You play there often?"

"Quite a few times," Pooh replied. "It de best park I ever

played in. You knows it's a pro park."

"Yeah," Randy Joe said, "which means it has dressin' rooms and showers. I can hardly wait to get in there and take a shower."

Pooh grinned. "Dey be openin' it up fo' us 'bout fo' o'clock."

"You think we'll get our meal money before then?" Randy Joe asked.

Gar laughed. "Not if ol' Squirrel kin help it. He gonna hold on to de money as long as he can."

Pooh frowned. "Dat ol' fool. He gonna git hisself killed if he ain't careful. He done holdin' back money on us."

"You know, there's no reason for us not to eat well," Randy Joe said. "With a little plannin' we could have good meals every day. And to tell you the truth, I don't know if I can get my strength back eatin' the way we are now."

Talking about eating well had gotten the attention of his teammates. Gar said, "You talk 'bout eatin' good. What you has in mind? Ain't nobody gonna eat all dat well on two dollars a day, 'specially when we don't always gits de two dollars."

"If we pooled our money, bought groceries and cooked, we could eat well," Randy Joe said.

Gar laughed. "Cooked? Who gonna do de cookin'?"

"I will," Randy Joe replied. "Hell, I can cook anything."

"Where you gonna do all dis cookin'?" Pooh asked.

"You remember that creek where we stopped yesterday?"

"Sho' do," Gar replied.

"Well, there's places like that everywhere. I can cook almost anything over a campfire. All we need are a few pots, pans and dishes. Hell, we can get the stuff we need at an Army surplus store. With what we spend on hotels...when we get to stay in one...we can buy cots and blankets. We can eat better chow than we can get in any cafe."

Pooh looked dubious. "You willin' to cook fo' dis bunch?"

"Sure...why not?"

"What kind o' stuff you gonna be fixin'?" Gar asked.

"When was the last time you had a good steak?"

"Lawd, I don't remember de last time."

"Well, a year or two ago we had a surplus of beef in Texas and t-bone steak was sellin' for nineteen cents a pound. I know damn well I can put a one pound steak on your plate for a dollar or less."

"De man's right 'bout dat," Pooh agreed. "Dey ain't no doubt dat you can eat cheaper at home dan in a cafe."

"Tell you somethin' else we can do," Randy Joe said. "If we camp by a creek, river or lake, I can probably catch us a mess of fish to eat."

"You done talkin' my language now," Gar said. "Ain't nobody like fish mo' dan me. But you done know who gonna be 'gainst dis?"

"Mr. Squirrel Simpson," Pooh said. "And he liable to make Muddy 'gainst it. Muddy think he have to listen to Squirrel."

"Well, we've gotta get ever'body to agree or it's not gonna work," Randy Joe said. "Everybody's gonna have to chip in their meal money...and we gotta get Squirrel to give us the hotel money for the cots and blankets. Hot as it is, I don't guess we really need blankets...but we get up north the nights might be cooler."

They discussed Randy Joe's idea for a good while. The young pitcher told Gar and Pooh he thought it might be better if they talked up the proposal with the other players. "I don't really know everybody yet," he said, "and I sure don't know how to read Muddy."

"Muddy all right," Gar said. "He jest always scared somebody out to get his job. Ain't nobody want it but him, havin' to work fo' Simmy like he do."

"You act like you're not that fond of Simmy," Randy Joe said.

"Simmy okay," Gar said. "He jest different dan most of us. Ain't no black man know Simmy dat well."

Their second cup of coffee was interrupted when a heavyset man with a scar on his cheek came and towered over their table. He was backed up by another man of lesser size. "White boy...I jest wanna know what you is doin' in here," the big man said.

Randy Joe looked up at the man, whom he guessed to be in his thirties. He had a big thick nose with flared nostrils, heavy lips and mean eyes shot through with red veins. He was muscular with a big, angry voice.

"I'm havin' coffee with my friends." There was no quaver in his voice, no fear. The man was a heavyweight, but Randy Joe had fought people just as big. He had never backed down to anyone.

"Dey's white places you kin go to git yo' coffee," the man said. "You ain't got no business bein' in dis place."

Randy Joe said, matter-of-factly, "I came here because I wanna drink coffee with my friends."

"Lookie here now," Pooh said, "we ain't lookin' fo' no trouble."

The big man grunted, "Well now, Pooh, you bringin' dis white boy in here...it sho' seem like that just what you lookin' fo'."

By now some of the other patrons were gathering around to get a closer view of the confrontation. This seemed to encourage the agitator, who said, "I ain't never whupped me a white boy's ass befo'."

Randy Joe stood to his feet. "You still haven't, asshole. And if you plan to, I hope you brought your supper 'cause it's gonna take you all day."

The fact that the slightly built kid seemed more than ready to fight startled the big man. He was momentarily at a loss for words, but having instigated the confrontation he was now duty-bound to continue. Then Gar stood, all six-feet, four inches and two hundred and forty pounds, and said, "When you git through wid him, you has to whip my ass, too."

The big man snarled, "I ain't afraid o' no big nigger like you."

"Dat's good," Gar said. "If you ain't 'fraid, maybe it be mo' of a fair fight."

The scar-faced man gave Gar a hard look, but turned his attention to Randy Joe. He made a menacing move toward the young pitcher but never anticipated what happened. One of Randy Joe's fists caught him in his soft belly and, when he grunted and bent forward, the other fist caught him flush on the jaw. His eyes glazed, he staggered and fell to his knees, and then his face became a punching bag for a combination of rights and lefts from the kid he had tried to intimidate. Blood spurted from his nose and mouth and he tried to fight back, but Randy Joe's surprise attack left him stunned and, ultimately, unconscious on the dirty wooden floor.

The big man's companion pulled a knife and Gar hollered, "Oh, no you don't," and crashed a chair over the man's head. The knife wielder's head slam-dunked the floor and he was out like a light.

Pooh, watching to see that trouble didn't come from another direction, said, "You had all de coffee you want?"

Randy Joe laughed, uneasily. "I have."

"Me, too," Gar said.

They paid the bill and left, the two bullies still lying on the floor and the other customers murmuring about what had taken place. Outside Pooh said, "Dat may not be de end of it. I done run into dat man befo' and he a mean one."

Gar laughed. "He sho' don't look mean now. I sho' didn't know you could use yo' fists like dat, roomie."

Randy Joe grinned. "It's a matter of when you use'em. My dad always told me if it looked like there was gonna be a fight to always get in the first lick. Makes a difference...most of the time."

Pooh joined Gar in laughing, then said, "Looks to me like you got in all de punches, not jest de first one."

"I appreciate you takin' care of the guy with the knife, Gar. I'm not sure I coulda handled him.

Back at the bus Gar and Pooh started talking to the other players about Randy Joe's cooking and camping idea. Some of the players were worried about turning over their meal money. "What 'bout cigarettes?" Cooter Davis asked. "We turn all de money over, we ain't gonna has enough fo' cigarettes."

"You better worry mo' 'bout eatin' dan cigarettes," Gar told the thin third baseman. "Wid dat ol' man handlin' de money, we liable to be eatin' grass all de way to Canada."

Squirrel had disappeared. It was something Squirrel had been doing on all their stops. "Tell you what I think," Peewee Darthard said. "I think dat ol' man usin' some o' our money on whores and whiskey."

"Now you don't know dat to be no fact," Rooster Solomon

said.

"I ain't sayin' it a fact," Peewee said.

"Well, we needs to do somethin'," right fielder Jackie Monk said. "Maybe Randy Joe gotta good idea here. We kin at least tries it."

"I think we oughta save enough back from de meal money fo' a pack o' cigarettes a day," Cooter said.

"I ain't sayin' we can't do dat," Gar said. "If Randy Joe kin do what he says, din maybe dey's gonna be some meal money left over."

"Sho' be nice to eats ever'day," Rooster said.

"We goes 'long wid Randy Joe, maybe we eats two...three times a day," Pooh said.

So the team, with the exception of Randy Joe, took the idea to Muddy, who generally kept to himself. While the team, including Grease, was gathered around he puffed on a cigarette and pondered the situation. The suggestion made some sense, especially if it meant the ball club would eat on lean days when the gate was small or nonexistent. But he wasn't ready to commit. He'd have to talk to Squirrel. Simmy had put him in charge of the money. It would first be necessary to sell Squirrel on the idea.

"You tell Squirrel dat it be Randy Joe's idea and he ain't gonna be fo' it," Skeeter said.

Muddy countered, "Maybe I tell'im it be my idea. I thought 'bout it befo' anyway."

"When he see Randy Joe doin' all de buyin' and cookin' he gonna know," Rooster said. "'Course my idea is dat we beat de shit outta de ol' man, take what money he got dat belong to us and leave'im here."

Muddy frowned. "Simmy done hired'im. We stuck wid'im."

"So what you gonna do?" Jackie Monk asked.

"When de time right," Muddy said, "I'll talk wid Squirrel. We got dis game where de gate gonna be okay. Den we has to play in Dallas and I don't knows what to 'spect."

Squirrel showed up after two o'clock and with his normal reluctance gave the players their meal money. It caused Pooh to say, "I hate to take de money 'cause he act like it comin' outta his own pocket."

Pooh showed Gar, Buck and Randy Joe a good barbecue place where they ate their fill. Then they went to the stadium to get ready. Randy Joe and Gar took a shower before dressing for the game.

"Wish we had dis shower on de bus," Gar said.

It was still three and a half hours until game time, so Randy Joe sat down in the dressing room and wrote a letter to his folks and to Gretchen. Gar sat across from him, his back to the wall, and asked, "You mind writin' a letter fo' me?"

"No...not at all. Who you wanna write?"

"I wanna write my mama. I ain't never wrote her no letter."

"What you wanna tell her?"

"Jest tells her dat I is okay and dat I be home after de season."

So Randy Joe wrote the letter, what Gar had suggested plus other things that had happened on the trip. After he'd read the letter to Gar, the big pitcher said, "Kin you writes somethin' else on dat paper?"

"Sure...anything you want."

"Tell her dat I has me a white friend...and tell her all about yo'self."

Later, when they were jogging across the outfield grass, Gar said, "Dat sho' is a fine lookin' book you has in yo' suitcase...it look like leather."

"Yeah, the cover is. It's a Bible a neighbor gave me before goin' on this trip."

"You read de Bible much?"

"Some. Probably not enough."

"I can't hardly reads nothin'. Didn't go dat far in school... didn't learn dat much 'bout readin'."

Randy Joe didn't know what to say, but figured he ought to respond in some way. "I love to read...read all the time."

"How hard it be fo' you to teach me to read?"

"Well...I don't know. I've never taught anyone before."

"You be willin' to teach me?"

"I can try. We'll need to get the right book, though."

"I want you to teach me to read de Bible."

"Well...it might be harder than most books. Some of the

language is different."

"What you mean?"

"There's a lot of words like *thee* and *thou* in the Bible...words we don't use nowadays."

"Dat don't matter none," Gar said. "It sho' would make my mama proud to known I done read de Bible."

The game turned out to be one of those best forgotten. Pooh, pitching before family and friends, started overthrowing the ball from the first inning on. He didn't stay within himself, was wild and walked a number of hitters. To compensate for his wildness he grooved a few, which were hit over or against the outfield wall. When it was finally time to turn out the lights the Longhorns had lost their first game on the tour by a score of nine to six.

No one felt worse than Pooh after the game. He knew the trap he'd fallen into, but it was one of those cases where only hindsight provides all the answers. Skeeter relieved Pooh, but by the time he entered the game the damage had been done. The only positive thing was that there was a big crowd that had to pay to get in the gate. All the players felt the team's take had to have been pretty good.

After they'd showered and were heading toward the bus, Randy Joe and Gar were confronted by the big man from the cafe. This time he had a half dozen more men backing his play. And a knife in his hand.

His friends also started brandishing knives or razors, backing Randy Joe and Gar up against a wall of the stadium. Randy Joe had a pocket knife, but it was like a safety pin compared to the weapons they were facing. The big man he had beaten to the floor in the cafe was uttering all sorts of expletives. He was planning to carve Randy Joe like a butcher cuts a steer.

Randy Joe and Gar were posed to go down fighting. They had nothing to fend off the aggressors except the small bags holding their uniforms, gloves and baseball shoes. Randy Joe unzipped his bag, took out his baseball shoes and dropped the bag, all the time watching the big man. Gar followed suit. Baseball shoes were no match for knives and straight razors, but the metal cleats could do some damage.

When it looked as though all hell was going to break loose,

bloodcurdling screams stopped everyone in their tracks. The knife and razor wielders looked up to see eleven men swinging baseball bats racing toward them. Randy Joe took advantage of the distraction and slammed the knife hand of the big man with a baseball shoe. He yelled, dropped the knife, turned tail and ran, his followers at his heels.

Randy Joe picked up the fallen knife, grinned at Gar and said, "Be a good knife to clean catfish with." To his bat toting teammates who were now gathered around he said, "Thanks, guys."

The near-fight had everyone's adrenalin pumping. It was what everyone wanted to talk about, including Squirrel. "I done told you dat white boy be nothin' but trouble," he told Muddy.

Muddy didn't want to argue with the old man, but was feeling pretty good himself, relishing the way the team had responded to the trouble, all looking out for each other. Muddy wanted to believe if he'd been in Randy Joe's or Gar's shoes the team would have come to his rescue. "'Case you didn't see, Gar was in trouble, too," he said.

Squirrel grunted, "Dat's 'cause Gar hangin' 'round too much wid dat white boy. He keep on and he liable to git hisself killed."

Cut overheard Squirrel and said, "Randy Joe ain't never done nothin' to you, ol' man. He ain't never said nothin' bad 'bout you and he know you talkin' shit 'bout him. He one of de team jest like me and you might as well git use to it."

"He jest like all dem white folks," Squirrel countered. "He done treatin' you equal now, but when he git away from here we jest be 'nother bunch o' niggers to him."

Cut argued, "Randy Joe...he ain't dat way. You has a hard on fo' all white folks and dey ain't all de same, jest like all colored folks ain't de same."

"You jest mark my word," Squirrel cautioned.

"What I wanna mark," Cut said, "is how much money we done took in tonight."

Squirrel grumbled, "Dat's fo' me to know."

"I think it somethin' fo' all of us to knows," Cut said, angrily. "We de ones playin' de games. De folks is comin' to see us play, not to see you hand out de meal money."

Squirrel puffed up. "Simmy done put me in charge o' de money."

"I ain't arguin' dat," Cut said. "But I think we need to know where we stands. I ain't likin' it when I has to go hungry all day. Randy Joe...he gotta plan where we never has to go hungry."

"What you talkin' 'bout?" Squirrel asked, angrily.

Muddy intervened and briefly outlined Randy Joe's plan, seeing that everything said was further antagonizing Squirrel. The road secretary kept trying to interrupt Muddy, but Cut stifled him several times with, "Hush, and let de man talk."

When Muddy had finished Squirrel said, "Dis ain't no campin' trip we on. What you talkin' 'bout ain't no way fo' no pro' team to be travelin', less you wants to end up in jail."

"Well, sleepin' on de bus and eatin' grass ain't no way fo' a professional team to travel either," Cut argued.

Squirrel smoked his cigarette and looked straight ahead.

THIRTY-THREE

When it was common knowledge Randy Joe had left Jason on tour with Simmy's team, James Steele called George Mason and suggested they meet with J.D. Lake. Mason suggested that Coach Vic Marshall also meet with them. The meeting site was the First State Bank after the close of the business day.

Steele had a lot on his mind. "You reckon the Keegan boy is getting paid to play for Simmy's team?" he asked.

"I'm sure he ain't," Marshall replied, defensively.

Steele surpressed a devious chuckle. "I knew that's what you'd say, Vic. You're so damned scared you can't win without the kid that you'll say anything."

"What's this all about, James?" Lake wanted to know.

"Simple little problem," Steele replied. "If the kid's gettin' paid he loses his amateur status...can't play high school ball."

"You like that possibility, don't you?" Lake said, sarcastically.

Steele replied, "Well, if you think I don't give a damn if the little shit plays high school ball or not, you're right. But I'm here to solve a problem, not create one."

"What do you mean?" Lake asked, suspiciously.

"If people in other towns find out we gotta pro playin' for us, then we're gonna end up havin' to forfeit all the games we win anyway. Do we wanna take that chance?"

"I'm willin'," Marshall replied.

Steele laughed. "You don't have a vote, Vic."

"Why doesn't he?" Lake asked.

"Because, J.D., he's not one of us."

"Well, maybe I'm not one of *us* either," the banker said, "because I think Vic has a right to voice an opinion."

Steele grunted, "I don't know what's gotten into you lately, J.D., but I sure as hell don't like it."

"You don't have to, James."

Mason, playing the role of the peacemaker, said, "Now hold on here, fellas. James has brought up somethin' we have to deal with, so let's do it without gettin' peeved at each other. We're all on the same side here. We all want to do what's best for the town."

Lake frowned. "Maybe I'm tired of all this sides business. It gets a little old."

Steele gave a disgusted look and Mason said, patronizingly, "I know what you're sayin', J.D., and I sympathize. But we still gotta obligation here. James is already committed to lettin' Randy Joe play football here next season, but if the boy's takin' money we gotta problem if somebody from another school finds out about it."

"Vic, what's the rule on that anyway?" Lake asked.

"If he takes money he's ineligible for everything," the coach said, reluctantly. "They can't pay for his hotel room, meals or anything."

"Here's what I agreed to," Steele said. "I agreed not to interfere with the Keegan kid playin' football, which is a courtesy to Vic and George. They seem to think the team can't win without him. But I'll be damned if he plays baseball for the high school team. After the football season I want Leon Rice fired and I want Randy Joe Keegan ineligible to play baseball."

Lake said, "Now wait a minute...we haven't established that he's actually playing for money."

Steele laughed. "Get your head outta your ass, J.D. The boy's out there on the road with the niggers. You think his folks are payin' for his room and board?"

Lake knew the Keegans couldn't afford that, but hated Steele's gloating. He desperately wanted the lawyer to be wrong, but knew in his heart he was right. "So why did you want this meeting, James...just to tell us you hold Randy Joe Keegan's future in your hand?"

"No...no, J.D., nothin' like that," Steele replied, grinning. "My intentions are honorable. I just think you oughta talk to Simmy, make sure he's gonna disclaim makin' payments of any kind to the Keegan boy. Otherwise, we might have a problem gettin' him through the football season. You're gonna have to talk to Randy Joe's folks...make'em understand he paid all his own expenses on the trip."

Lake knew Steele had him over a barrel and was enjoying it. The banker wanted Randy Joe to play football, not for his sake but for the town's. He knew Vic Marshall was right, that the team wasn't strong enough to win without Randy Joe at quarterback. "I'll talk to Simmy," he said, "but I think Vic should talk to Randy Joe's folks."

"Just a minute," Marshall said. "I really don't know his folks."

"Then you ought to get to know them," Lake countered, coldly. "They're nice people."

Mason laughed and said, "J.D.'s right, Vic...that chore should belong to you. The rest of us here are probably about as welcome at the Keegans house as dog shit in the middle of the floor."

Steele joined Mason in laughing and said, "Now, George,

people over in Milltown might like dog shit in the middle of the floor."

Lake felt he was caught in a vise. It seemed that everything he did was wrong. The more he tried to escape the devious plots of James Steele and George Mason the more entwined he became. If Randy Joe was ineligible to play high school sports, then he was ineligible. There shouldn't even be a question about it. But he kept telling himself that this little mistake of playing for Simmy's team shouldn't jeopardize Randy Joe's opportunity to play a last year of football. He had trouble selling himself, though, because he was going to allow Mason and Steele to make Randy Joe ineligible for baseball. And he was going to allow a fine man like Leon Rice to be fired.

Lake's dilemma was no more troubling than Marshall's. The coach left the meeting sick to his stomach. If Steele or Mason blew the whistle on Randy Joe, making him ineligible for baseball, then he'd be ineligible for college football, too. That meant Marshall would lose his ride into the college coaching ranks. And no matter when the proper authorities found out about Randy Joe's professional debut with the Longhorns, they'd take away all the games Jason won. Every game would have to be forfeited. If Jason won a state championship it would be given to the team they'd beaten. Marshall's coaching career would be over.

With heavy heart he went after the meeting to drink coffee with Big Bill Perkins, a man he could confide in. Big Bill, sitting in his favorite booth, listened intently to all Marshall had to say before responding. "Somehow, we gotta stop James and George. They're gonna screw up everything."

Marshall shook his head in resignation. "I agree, but how?"

"Shame they couldn't be in an automobile accident, ain't it?"

"You better be careful talkin' like that."

"I'm dead serious. I can even fix it." Big Bill liked for people to think he had special connections with hit men out of Beaumont. In truth, he knew a couple of local bootleggers and that was about it.

Warily, Marshall said, "I don't wanna have anything to do with somethin' like that."

"You wouldn't be involved in any way," the cafe owner said, really getting into the swing of things. He didn't know his big cook was listening to everything being said, and was about to die laughing.

"Well, let me try to reason with them first," the coach said. "I think I can talk to George, but James...that's another matter."

In the meantime, J.D. Lake had called Simmy and said, "I have to talk to you."

"What you wanna talk 'bout?"

"I'd rather not say over the telephone. We need to meet."

"You want me to come up to yo' office?"

"Yes...that would be fine. How long will it be?"

"In 'bout thirty minutes."

Before Simmy was able to leave his house, though, he got a call from Bertha Mae Davis, Big Bill's cook. She gave him some very interesting information. He made a mental note to give Bertha five dollars the next time he saw her.

About thirty minutes later Simmy parked his Cadillac in front of the bank. J.D. Lake unlocked the front door and let him in. It was quiet inside. Simmy, who had done a lot of after hours business with Lake, chewed on his cigar and listened to the banker's tale of woe. Concluding, Lake said, "So, Simmy, you see our problem. Are you willing to help us?"

The pulpwood contractor pondered a few moments, then said, "Now, Mr. J.D., you know dat when I axed Randy Joe to pitch fo' my team I wasn't thinkin' 'bout it messin' him up fo' no school ball."

"I know that, Simmy."

"As fo' whather he's bein' paid, dat's fo' Randy Joe to say. Course dey's a way I wouldn't be payin' him."

"What do you mean?"

"Let's jest say dat some folks here in town what wants him to play football gives him five hundred dollars in an envelope. He don't know where it come from, but it sho' don't come from me. Den, supposin' dese same folks give me 'nother five hundred dollars. Dat'd mean I wasn't out nothin' fo' de boy's room and board, so he didn't get nothin' from me. Now de problem is, if de team win a tournament up in Kansas, Randy

Joe due 'nother seven hundred dollars or so."

Lake couldn't help but laugh. "You old bandit. This is the same thing as blackmail."

Simmy laughed. "Ever wonder why dey don't call it whitemail?"

Lake said, chuckling. "I like it. The only problem...or I should say problems...are James Steele and George Mason."

"Dey's only problems if you wants'em to be," Simmy said.

"What do you mean?"

"Mr. Steele and Mr. Mason...dey has some secrets dat folks in dis town don't know 'bout."

Intrigued, Lake asked, "What are you talking about?"

"Well, you know dat Mr. James and Mr. George make it plain dey don't like colored folks, but dey has a fondness fo' colored whores. Dat's why dey goes to Beaumont ever' once in a while."

"You're joking?"

"No I ain't. De man what owns de whore house dey goes to...he a good friend o' mine."

"Well, nobody's going to believe that."

"Dey'd believes pictures, wouldn't dey?"

"I'm not going to get into something like that," Lake said. "I just couldn't."

"You don't has to," Simmy said. "I see to it dat Big Bill git de pictures. He gonna love dat...somethin' to hold over Mr. James and Mr. George. And when dey see'em, dey gonna be willin' to give all de money you need fo' Randy Joe...and me."

Lake wanted to show elation but he couldn't do it openly. He just wished he could be present when Big Bill showed Steele and Mason the pictures.

THIRTY-FOUR

In Dallas the team stayed in a rundown hotel on Hall Street, just off Central Expressway. The street in front of the hotel was a walkway for whores, which excited all the players. They started hitting on Squirrel to give them their meal money early so they could do some negotiating. The old man reluctantly gave it to them and then disappeared, as was his custom.

Gar found a whore to his liking and engaged her in conversation. Randy Joe watched his roomie's rising excitement from a distance. Gar's gesturing reminded him of an evangelist in a tent revival.

Finally, Gar returned to where Randy Joe was standing, disgust written all over his face. "Who dat woman think she is? She want two dollars. Ain't no woman worth no two dollars."

Randy Joe laughed. "Maybe she'll put it on sale before we leave."

Gar grinned. "She might jest do dat, 'cause ain't none o' dese players gonna pay no two dollars."

However, a little later, when they were eating barbecue in a cafe across the street from the hotel, Cut came and joined them. "You know dat woman you was talkin' wid?" he told Gar. "I seed her wid Squirrel."

"Damn," Gar said, angrily. "You shittin' me, Cut."

"No, I ain't," Cut said. "De ol' man...he wid dat woman."

"Den you know damn well he messin' wid our money."

Cut shook his head in agreement. "I done told you...he holdin' out on us, makin' us sleep on de bus and not even gittin' our meal money some o' de time."

Randy Joe felt compelled to defend Squirrel. "Maybe he's

been savin' his money. We can't be sure what he's spendin' belongs to the team."

His teammates gave him a looks of dismay. Cut said, "You sho' don't need to be takin' up fo' Squirrel...bad as he talk 'bout you. How he gonna save any money? He smoke two, three packs o' cigarettes a day."

"I'm just sayin' that we shouldn't jump to conclusions," Randy Joe said. "You know...innocent until proven guilty."

Gar laughed. "Dat's a rule fo' white folks. Colored folks...dey guilty 'til dey proved innocent. Dat's de way de law treat us."

"Then you shouldn't treat each other that way."

"You one strange white boy, Randy Joe," Cut said. "Ain't you never heard dat ol' sayin' 'bout a nigger will lie and a nigger will steal?"

"I heard it," Randy Joe replied. "I heard a lotta old sayings I don't believe."

Gar sighed. "Dat sho' was a fine lookin' whore. Maybe I oughta give her all my meal money."

Randy Joe laughed. "You're pitchin' tonight. You probably need some fuel in your belly more than you need a whore."

Gar grinned. "Bein' wid a woman like dat jest make me stronger."

"Bullshit," Cut said. "You spend de afternoon wid her and you be draggin' yo' black ass out to de mound."

Randy Joe comforted Gar. "Well, Roomie, we'll be spendin' the night here. After the game...well, maybe she has a after midnight rate."

"You ever git any poontang from a colored girl?" Gar asked.

"No...sure haven't."

"Does you want to?"

"I have a girlfriend at home."

"So does I," Gar said, "but dis gonna be a long summer."

Cut chuckled and said, "Don't white folks say dat a white man can change his luck by gittin' it from a colored gal?"

Randy Joe smiled. "I heard that. My luck's been pretty good so I don't need a change."

"Well, I ain't leavin' dis town widout gittin' some," Gar said.

Randy Joe said, "I've been meaning to ask...where'd you get

the name Gar? Is that your real name?"

"Sho' is," the big pitcher replied, grinning. "De way I hears it, jest befo' I was born my daddy catch dis big alligator gar outta de river. When he show dat gar off, people say dat sho' is a fine lookin' gar. Den when I was born my daddy think I was fine lookin' and he remember what people say 'bout dat gar. He say to my mama, why don't we name dis boy Gar? Well, she ain't got no special name picked out so dat's what dey names me."

Randy Joe laughed. "Helluva story...whether it's true or not. You ever eat any gar meat?"

Gar feigned dismay. "What you mean has I ever eat any gar meat? Dat's some o' de best meat dey is. Ain't you never had none?"

"Can't say as I have. Always thought they were fulla bones."

"You knows dey's a fish gar and an alligator gar?"

"Sure, I've caught both," Randy Joe said. "The fish gar doesn't get as big as an alligator gar and has a longer nose. Hell, I've seen alligator gars that weighed over two hundred pounds."

"Hmmm...dat'd be a lotta fine eatin'," Gar said. "But my daddy...he think the fish gar de best eatin'."

"When I caught'em I always just threw'em out on the bank," Randy Joe said. "You eat'em, Cut?"

"I likes any kinda fish," the second baseman said.

"Gar, how the hell does your mama fix gar?" Randy Joe asked.

"De way most people does in Lose'anna. First you skin de gar, den you boil de meat fo' a long time. After de gar done boiled so it comin' 'part she mash it up wid boiled taters and onions and fries it."

"So she makes fish balls?"

"Yeah...dat's what she does."

Randy Joe said, "So much for Gar's name, Cut, what about yours?"

"My name John. I git de name Cut when I first start playin' baseball...de way I cut 'round de bases."

"I'm the only one without an unusual name or a nickname."

"I done told you we callin' you White Heat," Cut said.

"Why don't you just call me Heat?" Randy Joe suggested.

"Well, dat can be de short part of it," Cut said, "but all de guys like White Heat."

The game that night was against a pretty good Negro club from the south part of Dallas. They came out swinging against Gar and scored four runs early. The Longhorns battled back to tie, but in the sixth the Dallas team broke through for two more runs. That's the way the game ended, the second straight loss for the Longhorns.

When they got back to the hotel Gar disappeared, leaving Randy Joe to his own devices. He would have just gone on to bed, but Grease found a checkerboard and challenged him.

"How long you been driving the bus?" Randy Joe asked.

"Ever since Simmy have a team," Grease replied. "Long years 'go I play a lot o' baseball my own self. Simmy and me...we play on some o' de same teams. I loves de game."

"What do you do when you're not driving the bus?"

"I drive a pulpwood truck for Simmy."

"You have a family?"

"I has a wife. De kids...dey all growed up."

"So you've known Simmy a long time?"

"Oh, yeah...we goes way back. We goes back befo' Simmy done make all his money."

"Simmy make all his money from pulpwood?"

Grease grinned. "Now dat's a good question. Ain't nobody know. Least, ain't no colored I knows dat knows."

"Somebody has to know somethin'...at least suspect somethin'."

Grease laughed. "Now I ain't sayin' it's true, but dey's talk dat Simmy own a whore house down in Beaumont. Dey's mo' talk dat he de real owner o' most o' de colored clubs in Jason County. I ain't sayin' dat's true and I ain't sayin' it ain't. But de man got lots o' stuff goin' 'sides pulpwood."

"I'd heard talk about the clubs," Randy Joe said, "but I didn't know about the whore house."

"Like I say," Grease said, "I ain't sayin' dat it's true, but Simmy...he got some partners and I don't think dey colored."

"Well, he'd have to have somethin' goin' with the sheriff to operate the clubs."

"Ain't no doubt 'bout dat."

Randy Joe learned Grease had been born in Jason County right at the turn of the century. His folks had migrated to Texas from Virginia in hope of owning their own farm. That dream had died and his daddy had ended up working for a sawmill. That was really the story of all the men in the Clifton family, working at sawmills or in the log woods.

As a young man Grease's fancy had turned to baseball, but he'd never dared dream of playing in the major leagues. In his youth he'd never known anyone who even thought a black man would ever play with a team like the Brooklyn Dodgers or Cleveland Indians.

"Course when de Dodgers brought Jackie Robinson up to de big leagues my playin' days was over," he told Randy Joe. "Now all dese colored boys wanna play wid a team like de Dodgers. But back when Simmy and me was playin' we jest wanted to play any place we could."

Grease said he'd been a catcher and a decent hitter. He said Simmy was the best pitcher he'd ever caught.

"How long have you known Squirrel?" Randy Joe asked.

"I ain't knowed Squirrel all dat long, jest since Simmy hired him to be de travelin' secretary of de team."

"Don't understand why he doesn't like me. He's never even talked to me."

"Squirrel...he a strange one. I don't know dat he like anybody. He jest likes to sit and smoke and look mean."

"That pretty well sums him up," Randy Joe said, laughing.

Grease grinned. "You don't has to worry none 'bout Squirrel. De players all likes you and dat's all dat counts."

The next day the team pulled out of Dallas and headed to Wichita Falls, Texas. En route, Gar asked Randy Joe to pull the Bible out of his bag so they could begin his reading lessons. Randy Joe turned to The Gospel According to John and Gar asked, "Why ain't we startin' at de first?"

"Well, if it's all right with you I thought we'd skip around a bit, read a few passages and then go back to the first."

"Dat's fine wid me," Gar said.

So Randy Joe started the big pitcher off with the first two

verses of the first chapter. *"In the beginning was the Word, and the Word was with God, and the Word was God."*

"What do it mean?" Gar asked.

Randy Joe laughed. "Hey, I'm just teachin' you to read. I'm not gonna attempt to explain the Bible. I'm no theologian."

"You not a what?"

"I knew I shouldn't have used that word," Randy Joe said, "because I'm not sure about it myself. But I think a good way to define theologian is someone who studies God."

Gar responded, "Den my mama must be one of dem 'cause she study 'bout God all de time."

Randy Joe started to offer a better explanation, but decided Gar's mama was probably just as good a theologian as anyone else. "As for that scripture, Gar, I think it means Jesus is the word of God and that He was with God from the beginning of time. That's kinda how I remember it was explained to me in Sunday School."

Randy Joe was the first to admit he didn't know what he was doing when it came to teaching reading, but he had Gar read the two verses over and over. He figured repetition had to be beneficial.

Finally, Gar said, "I got dem two, Randy Joe...let's go on to somethin' else."

So Randy Joe turned to the third chapter and sixteenth verse. *"For God so loved the world that He gave His only begotten Son, that whosoever believeth in Him should not perish but have everlasting life."* It was a verse J.D. Smith quoted a lot.

It soon became apparent to Randy Joe that Gar had a photographic memory. The reading lesson was going a lot better than he had anticipated. Gar also seemed to comprehend the meaning of the verses.

Damn, I think he comprehends them a lot better than I do, Randy Joe thought. If the guy had been given a decent break, there's no telling what he could have done.

The reading lessons attracted the interest of Tater Green and Jackie Monk, both of whom came and looked over their shoulders and listened to what transpired. Tater even asked, "You teach me to read, too, Randy Joe?"

"I can try. That's all I'm doin' here with Gar. Hell, if Gar keeps this up, he'll be able to teach you better than I can."

Gar beamed at the compliment and continued working on the words with a hunger Randy Joe had never seen in any of his white classmates. If Weave had been this eager he wouldn't consider himself such a dumbass.

The reading lesson made the hundred and fifty mile trip from Dallas to Wichita Falls pass quickly. "Who we gonna be playing here?" Randy Joe asked.

"We playin' some team from de Air Force base," Tater said. "Dey supposed to be pretty good."

They were.

Skeeter got banged around pretty well in the first couple of innings. By the time the dust had cleared the Longhorns were down six to nothing. In the dugout Skeeter said, "I jest ain't got it tonight."

"Tell Muddy," Randy Joe suggested.

"We ain't got nobody else," the pitcher said. "Pooh and Gar...dey jest pitched games."

"Tell him I'll go in," Randy Joe said.

Skeeter grinned. "Ain't much glory when you losin' like dis. Jest long relief wid nothin' but de end of the game to hopes fo'."

"It don't matter," Randy Joe said. "Your wing's tired."

"You sho' you wanna go in?" Skeeter asked. "I mean...you ain't got yo' strength back yet."

"I feel pretty good. Tell Muddy."

After Skeeter had talked to the manager, Muddy came over and said to Randy Joe, "You sho' you up to pitchin'? I was gonna axe you to go a few innings tomorrow night."

"I'm fine," Randy Joe assured. "Skeeter's arm's hurtin', but he doesn't wanna say nothin'. He stays out there and he could hurt it permanent."

"Jest don't goes hurtin' yo' arm," Muddy warned.

Randy Joe felt a little stronger than he had in Beaumont. His fastball had some pop to it. He still wasn't his old self, but he was better than anything the Wichita Falls team had ever seen. In seven innings he struck out fourteen, hit three, walked three, gave up two bloop singles and didn't allow any runs. In the meantime, the Longhorns rallied for an eight to six victory. Randy Joe knocked in three of the runs with an opposite field double.

It was a bus filled with jubilant players that pulled out of Wichita Falls and headed for Lawton, Oklahoma, just a short distance north and across the Red River. They'd eaten earlier and figured Squirrel had arranged for hotel rooms in Lawton. All the laughter turned to anger and frustration when the traveling secretary said they were short on money and would have to sleep on the bus.

A few, including Gar, were so mad they were ready to check the traveling secretary's pockets. But Randy Joe tried to bring a little levity to the situation. "Hey, guys, hold on a minute...this is watermelon country."

The statement took Gar and the others by surprise. "What you talkin' 'bout, Randy Joe?"

"I'm talkin' watermelons...the biggest, juiciest watermelons you ever put your mouth on."

"De fact dey here ain't doin' us no good," Gar said.

"That's where you're wrong," Randy Joe said. "I may be the best watermelon bandit in the world."

"You talkin' 'bout stealin' watermelons?" Cut asked.

"I never thought of it that way," said Randy Joe. "They got so many watermelons up here that they just rot in the fields."

Cut laughed. "Trouble is...you let a colored man steal one o' dem rottin' watermelons and he goin' to jail."

"I'll get the watermelons, Cut," Randy Joe said. "Don't be a pussy. Nobody's gonna catch us."

"Well, I sho' would like some watermelon," Gar said. "Been a long time since I had watermelon. But Muddy...he gonna be 'gainst stoppin' de bus to steal watermelons."

Randy Joe laughed. "Tomorrow's my birthday...and a man oughta get to do what he wants on his birthday. I wanna treat you guys to some watermelon...if you can clear it with Muddy."

Gar grinned. "You right...a man gonna be seventeen oughta git to do what he wants to do."

So Gar and Cut went up to the front of the bus to present the watermelon caper to Muddy, who at first vigorously shook his head no. But Gar and Cut got considerable support from other members of the team and Muddy was soon wavering. He was remembering the team spirit outside the stadium in Waco, when they'd all rushed to the aid of Randy Joe and Gar. Squirrel wanted to protest, but the mood of the team was against him so he decided to keep his mouth shut.

Muddy finally gave in. "Y'all does whatever you wants to, but I ain't bein' no part of it."

Randy Joe came to the front of the bus to help keep an eye out. "Now I don't know exactly where a watermelon patch is," he admitted, "but one shouldn't be hard to find."

When they were on the Oklahoma side of the Red River Randy Joe had Grease cut the lights on the bus and drive down a side road off the main highway. It was a farming area and he was pretty sure it wouldn't take long to find a field full of watermelons. Sure enough, Grease hadn't driven far until Randy Joe spotted a field. It was after midnight and they could see the big watermelons glistening in the full moon. They had discovered the mother lode.

Randy Joe had Grease find a place and turn the bus around so it would be headed back toward the highway. There were no houses around. They couldn't see a light in any direction.

"Okay," Randy Joe said, "you guys sit tight and I'll go out there and get us some watermelons. They're big ones. I can't carry more than one at a time."

He crossed a ditch, straddled the fence and went into the field. He picked up the biggest melon he could find and carried it back to the bus. He was going for another when Gar said, "Ain't nothin' to dis. Ain't nobody 'round. Let's help out ol' Randy Joe."

Gar and three other players crossed the fence with Randy Joe. They handed melons to players on the other side who carried them to the bus. "That's enough," Randy Joe said. "Let's get outta here."

"Can't has too many watermelons," Gar said, picking up another.

This field belonged to Henry MacDonald, a farmer who had been having considerable trouble keeping teenagers from stealing his watermelons. About the time Gar was insisting on a second load of melons, MacDonald had arrived at the field with his double-barrel twelve-gauge shotgun loaded with birdshot. He'd walked to the field without the aid of a light, hoping to catch the teenagers in the act.

My god, MacDonald thought, there's a whole busload of them. The farmer, who had a little sight problem anyway, couldn't tell the color of the bus and couldn't make out the writing on it. So he just raised the shotgun and fired at the thieves in the field.

At the first roar from the shotgun Randy Joe and the other players in the field fell to the ground. Those on the other side of the fence raced back to and got on the bus. Grease stomped the accelerator and headed it back toward the highway.

"Is everybody okay?" Randy Joe semi-whispered.

Gar, Tater, Cut and Buck all replied that they were fine.

"We gotta to get outta here," Randy Joe said. "When I count to three, everybody jump up and head for the fence."

He made the count and they jumped up and ran. There was the roar of two more shots. Randy Joe leaped the fence and Gar fell over it. Once they were on the other side and running toward the highway, Randy Joe asked, "Anybody hit?"

"I is," Gar replied.

They found the bus waiting about a quarter mile away, its engine running and Grease ready to accelerate at a split-second's notice. Randy Joe told him to head back to the highway, then back across the river to the Texas side. All the while Squirrel kept mumbling, "I knowed dese watermelons gonna be nothin' but trouble."

"Hush yo' mouth, Squirrel," Cut ordered. "Ain't no trouble comin' dat I sees."

It took very little time to reach the Texas side of the river. Once there Randy Joe had Grease pull the bus off an old side road that led up the river bank. It led to a crude campground, which is where Grease killed the engine.

There had been a lot of excitement and loud talking among the players during their escape, but once they were stopped the laughter started when Gar asked, "Who want some o' dis watermelon?"

"How many we git?" Cut asked.

"Twenty-eight," Buck replied.

"Den we got two days worth," Gar said, laughing.

"Gar, you oughta see de back o' yo' shirt," Tater said. "It's all tore up."

"I feels somethin' but it don't hurt none," the big pitcher said.

Randy Joe checked Gar's back and saw that his roomie had caught a load of birdshot. A lot of the shot was sticking to the skin or just under it. "I guess the man just picked out the biggest target," Randy Joe said. "We can get all that shot out with tweezers and bathe your back in alcohol. You'll be okay."

"You can do dat later, roomie. Right now I want some o' dat watermelon."

Muddy had felt considerable fear at the prospect of being caught stealing a white man's melons. But he couldn't help but notice that the incident had brought the team even closer together. They seemed to be losing some of their fear about treading on a white man's turf. He knew Randy Joe was responsible for that.

The watermelon feast turned the team into a boisterous bunch, all reliving the excitement of having been shot at. Randy Joe cut one of the melons and took half of it to Squirrel. "I don't want any," Squirrel said. But a few minutes later Randy Joe saw that he was eating the melon.

After Gar had eaten his fill of watermelon, Randy Joe used tweezers to pick the pellets from his back. Then he bathed it in alcohol. Gar acted like the process didn't bother him, but Randy Joe figured his back was going to be sore for a few days.

Sleep was difficult because of the early morning excitement and heat, but they finally got in a few hours.

THIRTY-FIVE

After the watermelon raid and a few hours sleep the bus was drenched by the morning sun and its unbearable rays. Sweat streamed down the back of Randy Joe's neck and his entire body felt the stiffness that comes from sleeping in cramped quarters.

He went down to the river and found just the right sand bar. Soon, along with his teammates, he was frolicking in the water. They passed around a bar of soap and bathed. Because the running river water was cool they hesitated to leave it.

Finally, Gar said, "Let's git our eatin' money from Squirrel and go on to town."

It seemed like a good idea. The only problem was that Squirrel said, "What you want eatin' money fo'? You got all dese watermelons."

"De watermelon is good," Gar replied, "but I want some meat."

"Well, dey ain't no eatin' money," Squirrel said, sarcastically. "Y'all done spent it all."

The players were already on the verge of rebellion about the way Squirrel was acting, but the road secretary's sarcastic tone really set off Gar, Cut and Buck. They grabbed Squirrel and dragged him off the bus. Muddy made a feeble attempt to stop them, even pleaded with them, but the trio said they'd taken all they were going to take.

From up the river where he was checking things out Randy Joe saw his three teammates, followed by the others, carrying Squirrel down to the water's edge. He started running back but couldn't get there before they had thrown him in the river.

The water wasn't over Squirrel's head, but the old man

started sputtering and flailing about. Randy Joe was afraid he was going to drown so he went in the water after him. "Let de lyin' old bastard drown," Cut hollered. "He done stole from me fo' de last time."

By then, however, Randy Joe had Squirrel and was dragging him to safety. Squirrel was wearing one of his old suits and the cigarettes in his shirt pocket were soaked. "Don't be worried none 'bout dat ol' fart," Gar told Randy Joe. "We was jest baptizin' him a little."

While Randy Joe and Grease were seeing to Squirrel, Buck turned to Muddy and said, "We done had 'nough o' dis ol' man tryin' to starve us to death. Either we know what de money situation is all de time or we gonna make Grease drive dis bus back to Jason."

The rest of the players grumbled their approval and Muddy said, "Ain't no excuse fo' de way Squirrel been actin'."

"I say we take de money Squirrel got in his pocket, buys him a bus ticket back to Jason and go de rest o' de way on our own," Gar said. "Randy Joe got de right idea 'bout how to spend de money."

"He sho' do," Tater agreed. "I think we eats mo' regular his way."

Muddy saw the handwriting on the wall. He didn't know how Simmy would react when he heard about the rebellion, but Simmy wasn't having to deal with it. So, flanked by members of the team Muddy approached Squirrel, who was sitting on the ground still coughing. "Squirrel, de team don't like de way you been handlin' de money. Dey want me to handle it from now on. We gonna put you on de bus back to Jason."

Squirrel muttered a few expletives, then said, "You ain't gettin' shit from me. Simmy gonna hear 'bout dis, too."

Gar and Cut grabbed the old man up and started searching him. "Ain't gittin' shit, huh?" Gar said, taking a roll of bills from one of Squirrel's pockets. Cut also took a money belt from Squirrel's waist.

"We oughta kill dis ol' sumbitch, tellin' us dey ain't no meal money," Buck said. "We oughta make 'em walk back to Jason."

"You guys hold on," Randy Joe said. "I don't think Squirrel

was tryin' to steal anything. He was probably just tryin' to keep some money back for when we were really up against it."

Squirrel hollered at Randy Joe, "You de problem. Ain't fo' you dis wouldn't be happenin'."

"Now you ready to quit takin' up fo' de ol' bastard?" Gar asked.

Randy Joe sighed and walked up toward the bus while Muddy and the others dealt with Squirrel. Grease told Squirrel, "You de craziest ol' man I ever seed. Dat boy de last chance fo' a friend you got on dis trip."

Squirrel grumbled, "I ain't needin' no white boy fo' no friend."

"Den you a bigger fool dan I thought you was," Grease said.

Later, after he'd dried out some, Squirrel came back to the bus and approached Muddy. "I need to talk to you," he said, gruffly.

"Den goes ahead and talk," Muddy said. "Dey ain't no secrets wid dis bunch no mo'."

Squirrel looked as sheepish as his craggy old face would allow. "I don't wanna leave. I wanna stay wid de team."

Cut laughed. "What fo'? You ain't carryin' de money...what you gonna do?"

"I set up dis tour," Squirrel replied. "Dey's all kind o' ways dat I can help."

Gar said, "He don't wanna go back and face Simmy...tell de man what he done done. He jest be extra weight. He jest cost us mo' money."

"Wait a minute," Randy Joe interjected. "Like Squirrel said, he did set up the tour. He knows the kinda deals he made with these people and you might want 'em to set somethin' up for next year, too. Besides, one more mouth to feed's not gonna make that much difference."

The players began mumbling among themselves. With Squirrel's attitude toward Randy Joe they had difficulty understanding why their teammate cared what happened to him. But if Randy Joe wanted to give the old man another chance they figured they ought to be willing to go along.

Muddy said, "Well, Squirrel, dey's been lots o' hard feelin's goin' 'round since de day we starts on dis tour...feelin's dat hurt de ball club. If you gonna stay wid us, you has to be part o' de team."

"You right," Squirrel agreed. "I ain't been actin' right, but dat all gonna change."

Buck, Gar and Cut were dubious. Buck said. "How we know he ain't gonna act de same way'."

"We don't," Randy Joe said, "but if that's the case it doesn't matter where he catches the bus home. Maybe I'm wrong, but I think Squirrel wants to stay on the tour because he loves baseball and just wants to be around it. I think we can all understand that."

Squirrel said, "Randy Joe's right. I does love baseball. I wanna to be part o' dis team, de best colored team dey ever was."

Gar laughed. "You mean de best two-color team dey ever was."

Squirrel grinned, the first time any of the players had ever seen the corners of his mouth turn upward. "Yeah...dat's what I mean."

That afternoon, while the other players were finding places to eat in Lawton, Randy Joe, accompanied by Squirrel, had Grease drive him to an Army surplus store. He bought fourteen military mess kits, cast iron pots and skillets, and fourteen folding canvas cots. He then went to a grocery and fishing tackle store where he picked up other necessary supplies.

Grease then drove the bus north and they found a camping spot on East Cache Creek. It's where they would camp after the game. "Long as we're here we might as well put out a few set poles," Randy Joe said. He'd bought a roll of staging, which was heavy-duty line, plus hooks and sinkers. He cut the staging into proper lengths, then with Grease's and Squirrel's help added hooks and sinkers.

"I used to fish a lot," Squirrel said, "but I kinda got 'way from it. But I likes to fish fo' perch."

"I got some hooks and line for bream and bass, too," Randy Joe said, "and a folding shovel from that Army surplus store. We don't have time now, but in the morning why don't we dig us some worms and catch us some bream?"

Squirrel seemed pleased at the suggestion and nodded

agreement. Grease said, "I wanna git in on some o' dat perch fishin'."

Randy Joe used the knife from the Waco fight to cut and trim a dozen fishing poles. Then he and his companions, carrying the poles, went up the creek looking for good holes. When they found a good stretch of water they tied one of the rigged lines to a pole, put a piece of beef liver on the hook, then stuck the pole in the bank so the bait was in the water at the proper depth. The size of the hole dictated how many set poles they used in it.

When Squirrel had put the last pole in place Randy Joe said, "That oughta do it. We oughta get a few catfish. We'll run the hooks after the game, then again early in the morning.

The game that night in Lawton was against a team from Fort Sill, the big Army base located there. Even though Randy Joe had pitched seven innings the night before, he insisted he was strong enough to start against the Lawton team. He told Muddy, "It's my birthday and I want somethin' to remember it by."

Randy Joe went the entire nine innings, striking out eighteen, hitting four, walking two and giving up two hits. The Longhorns walked away with a six to one victory.

The ball park where they played was nice, with dressing rooms and showers. The team was already in a jubilant mood and being able to shower made it better. Randy Joe told Muddy, "I've got five dollars that I brought from home and I saw a Dairy Freeze just north of here on our way outta town. If you get Grease stop the bus, I'll buy everybody an ice cream cone."

"Bein' it's yo' birthday," Muddy said, "we oughta to be buyin' you de ice cream."

"Naw...this is somethin' I wanna do."

The Dairy Freeze was about to close when Grease stopped the bus in front of it. The owner was there, though, and willing to accept a few extra dollars for fourteen cones of his soft, swirling ice cream. Randy Joe was the last one served and was standing just outside the door of the bus when the Chevrolet pickup pulled up.

The three guys who got out of the vehicle were white, strong-looking and in their mid-twenties. Randy Joe didn't pay any particular attention to them because he was more interested in getting on the bus with his teammates. But the trio came toward Randy Joe in triangle formation, the leader a heavyweight. "Hey, just a minute there," he said.

Randy Joe turned to face them. "Yeah?"

"Saw you pitch tonight," the leader said. "You're pretty good."

"Thanks."

"Can't understand you playin' for this bunch o' niggers, though."

"What niggers?"

The leader was momentarily stymied by Randy Joe's response. He recovered and said, "Unless you're blind, boy, I'm talkin' about the ones you're about to get on the bus with."

"Oh, you mean these colored guys," Randy Joe said, feigning surprise.

The leader muttered, angrily, "You're a little bit of a smartass, ain't you?"

Gar and Buck had exited the bus and were standing behind Randy Joe. The rest of the players were also ready to empty out to his defense.

"No, I ain't a little bit of a smartass, I'm a whole lotta smartass."

"Well, we just want you to know we don't like niggers in this town," the leader said. "Be best if you boys get on your bus, get outta here and don't come back."

Randy Joe laughed. "You boys are pretty brave...runnin' us outta town when we're leavin' anyway."

The leader snarled, "Well, I guess there's still time for me to whip your ass, you nigger lovin' little bastard."

When he said it the man stuck his face forward toward Randy Joe, which was just too much temptation. He stuck his ice cream cone right on the guy's nose, shocking the leader and his two friends. Before his adversary could recover Randy Joe's fist had followed the ice cream cone, smashing the bully's nose and causing blood to spurt and mix with the ice cream and portions of the cone that had been implanted by the blow.

The leader's two friends were stunned by the suddenness of Randy Joe's attack, but any thoughts of aiding their comrade were squashed by Gar and Buck, whose menacing moves toward them resulted in a retreat toward the pickup. In the meantime, Randy Joe's staccato-like blows to his adversary's face sent the guy reeling backward until he was sitting on his butt, but that didn't keep Randy Joe from nailing him with one last blow that left him prone on the blacktop.

He then got on the bus with Gar and Buck, Grease put it in gear and they took off. "Squirrel right 'bout some things," Gar said, laughing. "You trouble waitin' to happen."

"Yo' hand all right?" Muddy asked. "You gonna mess 'round and break yo' hand doin' dat kind o' stuff."

Randy Joe laughed. "My hand's fine. I hope we don't have any more trouble like that."

Buck grinned and said, "Things lookin' up fo' us. We done had ice cream and got a bus load o' watermelons."

"When we get our camp set up, we'll cook hamburgers," Randy Joe said. "That is...if anybody's hungry."

"Dis bunch always hungry," Cut said.

When the camp was set up, and before Randy Joe and Grease could begin cooking the hamburgers, Tater and Cooter came from the back of the bus carrying a big chocolate cake. Peewee said, "De guys all got together and paid dis colored woman in Lawton to bake you dis birthday cake. Sorry ain't no candles on it."

Randy Joe was choked up by the thoughtfulness of his teammates, but joked, "What makes you think I like chocolate cake?"

"You wid us, ain't you?" Gar said.

Randy Joe cut the cake and served all the players and Grease. He noticed Squirrel sitting away from the group, like he didn't belong. He cut an especially big piece of cake and took it to him. "You like cake, don't you?"

Squirrel smiled. "Sho' do."

After they'd eaten the cake Randy Joe and Grease cooked the hamburgers, which tasted especially good in the night air. It was hot and sultry, but the sky was lit like a Christmas tree by the moon and stars. The sound of the running creek added a special feeling of peacefulness to the setting.

"When we gonna go git us some mo' watermelons?" Gar asked.

Cut laughed. "When you wanna git shot 'gain?"

Gar smiled. "Ain't de worst thing ever happen to me."

Randy Joe got a flashlight and said he needed to go check and bait the set poles. Grease and Squirrel volunteered to go with him. They had four catfish on. Squirrel and Grease landed the fish, all of which were in the two- to four-pound range. "We bait all the hooks up good, we oughta have more than that in the mornin'," Grease said.

When they got back to the camp just about everyone was stretched out on a cot. Randy Joe's cot was next to Gar's and the big pitcher was still awake, staring up at the stars. "Dey's a lot of 'em, ain't dey?"

"And stars beyond the stars," Randy Joe said. "The universe is endless."

"God sho' made it big."

"Yeah...He sure did."

"How many fish you catch?"

"Four. There'll be more on by morning."

"You know, dis ain't a bad way to live."

"No, it's really not. How's your back?"

"Little sore, but it sho' was worth it."

The team awoke the next morning to the smell of bacon, eggs and coffee. Grease had even made biscuits in a Dutch oven covered with coals. After breakfast Randy Joe, Grease and Squirrel went to check the set hooks and take them up while the rest of the players continued to relax and drink coffee.

"Ain't bad, is it?" Buck said to Muddy. "Dis de first time I really been full since we been on dis trip."

Muddy laughed. "Dis ain't de first time dis been thought of. Problem was we thoughta buncha colored men might get in trouble doin' it. I don't mind helpin' wid de cookin', though."

Buck laughed. "If we gonna eat good...I sho' ain't mindin'."

Six more catfish had fallen victim to the set poles. After Randy Joe, Grease and Squirrel brought them back to camp they dug some worms and went bream fishing for a couple of hours. Then Randy Joe and Muddy cleaned and cooked the fish. They served them with fried potatoes and hush puppies.

The team's next game was only a short distance away, at Chickasha, Oklahoma. After a dip in the East Cache Creek the team boarded the bus and Grease headed it north. They had to find their night's camping spot before playing the game.

Over the next few weeks the team played games almost nightly while traveling across Oklahoma, Kansas, Nebraska, South Dakota, North Dakota and into Saskatchewan, Canada. Most of the time they camped out and to some extent lived off the land. Each day they became more of a team, depending on each other. They became like a well-trained Army unit on bivouac, each knowing and doing a job without complaint.

While on the road Randy Joe kept giving a willing Gar both reading and writing lessons. He couldn't believe the progress Gar was making, how anxious he was to learn. Both Tater Green and Jackie Monk got involved in the reading lessons and were also doing well.

Their only textbook was the Bible, which Randy Joe had thought was about as tough a reader as any they could find. His pupils, however, seemed to discount the difficulty of their textbook. They absorbed it with a voracious appetite.

Everyone on the team had difficulty reading, but some were initially unwilling to admit it. However, when they saw a big, strong man like Gar willing to start from ground zero, attitudes changed. Before long everyone was involved in one way or another, all spending much of their free time practicing reading and writing. They even got in spirited discussions about what certain scriptures meant, something Randy Joe would not participate in.

Squirrel's attitude toward Randy Joe seemed to have completely changed. They talked together a lot and Squirrel was always anxious to go fishing with him. In fact, several of the team got heavily into the fishing. When Gar learned some of the disciples were fishermen he got into it in a big way.

The players didn't totally ignore the towns. When opportunity presented itself they drank beer and chased whores. Failure to do so would be an insult to every living baseball player who was worth anything, and to the memory of the dead ones.

However, the important thing was that they were building up quite a nestegg. With the money they were going to win at the Wichita tournament Randy Joe figured all his teammates, including Grease and Squirrel, would go home with as much money as he would make over the summer. That made him feel pretty good.

They lost a few games, but very few. Randy Joe kept getting stronger, more and more impossible to hit. The strange thing, Muddy thought, was that the slightly built kid was also the purest hitter on the team. He was consistent and had a knack for getting the big hit, but he always downplayed his batting prowess.

They were in Canada, just a day before the schedule called for them to head south for Wichita, when Squirrel died. He was sitting in his usual seat on the bus, wearing one of the same old faded suits, when his heart just quit on him. It was Muddy who first noticed that the lighted cigarette that usually dangled from Squirrel's lips had fallen into his lap and had burned a hole in his trousers. When he tried to shake Squirrel awake he discovered the old man was dead.

"What we gonna do?" Cut asked.

Muddy shook his head in resignation. "I don't know."

"Call Simmy," Randy Joe suggested. "Ask what he wants us to do."

"You mind goin' through his stuff?" Muddy asked Randy Joe. "You was gittin' to know'im better dan anybody else."

Randy Joe's search of Squirrel's small bag and his suit pockets revealed no clues regarding family. There were a few faded pictures of Squirrel with a woman, whom Randy Joe believed was his wife. He'd told him his wife had died ten years earlier. He'd also told him about a daughter who lived in Little Rock, Arkansas. Randy Joe figured Simmy might know the daughter's address.

Since he wanted to, Muddy told Randy Joe to go ahead and make the call to Simmy, which he did that evening. It was the only time they could be reasonably sure that Simmy would be home.

"So ol' Squirrel died," Simmy said, sadly. "Well, he been sick fo' some time. Least ways, dat's what I heard."

"Do you know his daughter?" Randy Joe asked.

"You mean de one dat live in Little Rock?"

"That's the only one he ever told me about."

"Yeah...I knows her. She a hard one."

"Well, I guess she's the one who oughta decide what to do with the body, don't you?"

"Can't tell 'bout dat girl. I'll call and git somebody to git in touch wid her. No tellin' what man she stayin' wid now."

"When you want me to call you back?"

"Call me back 'bout de middle o' de day tomorrow. I might know somethin' by den."

The team played a game that evening and stayed in a hotel that night. Squirrel's body remained on the bus. Fortunately, the Canadian nights were cool.

"We need to git an early start tomorrow," Grease said. "Never can tell when dis ol' bus gonna take a notion to break down." It had broken down several times on the trip, but Grease was something of a magician with a wrench and pair of pliers.

"How we gonna leave early when we don't know what to do wid Squirrel?" Gar asked.

"We're just gonna to have to take him with us," Randy Joe replied. "Squirrel would feel better if he was in the United States."

"De ol' man stink befo' he die," Buck said. "Now dat he's dead, how long it gonna be befo' he start stinkin' worse?"

"I don't know," Randy Joe said, "but we really have no choice. Grease says we need to get on down the road. We sure don't wanna miss the tournament in Wichita. The only real problem I see is gettin' Squirrel's body by the customs people at the border. If they stop us we're gonna have all kinds of questions to answer."

"You talkin' 'bout real trouble now," Muddy said. "If dey catches us maybe we say dat he jest died, dat we didn't know."

"Won't work," Randy Joe said. "They'll know he's been dead for a while."

Muddy asked, "Den what we gonna do?"

"Let's just get rollin' and we'll think of something."

It was almost noon when they arrived at the border. Randy

Joe was sitting next to Muddy on one of the front seats. Gar was sitting next to Squirrel, whose head was tilted forward like he was asleep. The customs agent who came on board the bus was a young guy, one whom Randy Joe figured was anxious to go to lunch. He counted heads and they presented him with the papers they'd filled out when they'd crossed the border.

When he looked curiously at Squirrel, Randy Joe whispered to him, "The old guy's really sick. We're gonna take'em to a doctor in Minot. Wake 'em up and he's liable to puke all over you."

The customs agent looked at Squirrel with cautious eyes, then said, "He looks sick, looks like he's turnin'..."

"Yeah, I know," Randy Joe said. "Like he's turnin' white."

As soon as they pulled away from the customs station Gar jumped up from the seat next to Squirrel and moved toward the back of the bus. He grumbled, "I ain't likin' sittin' next to no dead man."

His teammates couldn't help but laugh, though they felt uneasy about it. The laughter was more relief than anything else.

At a pay phone in Minot, North Dakota, Randy Joe once again called Simmy. "You get in touch with Squirrel's daughter?" he asked.

"Sho' did, but you ain't gonna like what she say."

"What do you mean?"

"She say she ain't got no place to put de ol' man."

"Hell, what does she mean by that? He's her daddy."

"Dis girl jest don't care. She de same as a whore, only she don't charges fo' it. She got half a dozen kids and ain't got no money to bury Squirrel."

"What are we supposed to do?"

"I guess you jest buries him up dare. If you needs some money, I'll send it."

"No, Squirrel's got some money comin'. We got plenty of money."

"How you do dat?" Simmy asked, bewildered.

"Muddy will tell you about it when he sees you," Randy Joe replied.

Back on the bus Muddy said, "Well?"

"We gotta problem," Randy Joe said. "Squirrel's daughter doesn't want the body."

"Damn, what we gonna do?" Cut asked.

"Simmy said for us to have him buried up here. It don't seem right, though, burying him this far north."

"I don't see dat we gotta choice," Buck said. "We jest need to drop him off wid de undertaker and git on down de road."

"I hate to leave him up here to be buried with strangers," Randy Joe said. "I mean...there at the end he was part of this team. Squirrel changed a lot after y'all baptized him in the river."

"Well, he 'came yo' friend mo' dan anybody else's," Muddy said. "What you wanna do wid him?"

"I don't know," Randy Joe said. "I know he was lookin' foward to the tournament in Kansas. More than anything else, he wanted to see us play in that tournament."

"No doubt 'bout it," Grease said, "de man love his baseball."

"Well, what you wanna do, Randy Joe?" Buck asked.

"Let's take him to Kansas. We'll think of somethin' by then."

"Dat's crazy," Cut said. "Ridin' on dis bus wid him stinkin'...it's gonna make us all sick."

"I got an idea about that, too," Randy Joe said. "Muddy, if you'll give us Squirrel's share of the money, Grease and me will go get Squirrel a casket. We'll let you guys out at a cafe so you can be eatin' while we're doin' it."

Muddy chuckled. "I don't know what crazy thing you has in mind, Randy Joe, but you and Grease can take Squirrel's money and do whatever you think is best fo' de ol' man."

So Grease drove to a funeral home and went in with Randy Joe to negotiate for a casket. They left Squirrel sitting in his usual seat on the bus.

After the funeral director, a tall, somber-looking man with Ichabod Crane features had showed them around and given his spiel, Randy Joe said, "You don't understand. We want a plain, vanilla casket."

"Well, I think I've showed you just about everything I have," the man said, looking peevish. "I don't have anything cheaper than what I've shown you."

"What I'm looking for," Randy Joe said, "is one of those caskets like they use in western movies. You know, just a plain wooden box."

"Well, there is a man here in town who builds those for paupers and such," the undertaker responded, haughtily. "I can give you his address."

Following the directions given them, Grease and Randy Joe found the casket builder and the simple box that they wanted. Getting Squirrel in it was no easy task. Rigor mortis had set in and they had trouble getting his body straightened out. Finally, they wrapped the body tightly with a sheet and tied it up with rope. "I think that'll hold him down," Randy Joe said.

They put the casket on top of the bus, covered Squirrel's body with ice, covered the casket with a tarpaulin and tied it down. "We'll have to put ice on him every once in a while," Randy Joe said, "but the tarp will keep everybody from knowin' what we got up there."

When they picked up the team at the cafe Gar said, "Dis is spooky. I ain't gonna sleep on dis bus wid dat ol' man ridin' on top o' me."

"He really wasn't that old," Randy Joe said. "He was only sixty."

"He look a lot older," Gar said.

En route to Kansas there were a lot of jokes and laughter about what they were carrying on top of the bus. None of the players lost any sleep over it. Gar, when he wasn't reading the Bible and practicing his writing, slept like he didn't have a care in the world.

Grease would stop the bus periodically and Randy Joe would buy ice. Then they'd find a private place and ice Squirrel down. Water from the melted ice would leak through the cracks in the casket and onto the top of the bus. They drove straight through to Wichita, stopping only for gas and at streams to clean up and do a little cooking. Players started talking to Squirrel's casket as if he could understand them..

They pulled into Wichita right on schedule, the day before the big tournament. There was no camping prior to these games. The promoter had made arrangements with the local university to provide dormitory rooms. The school cafeteria was open to serve all their meals.

The Longhorns were put in a dormitory separate from the other teams. They were assigned cafeteria tables in a corner of the dining hall that made them seem less important than the other players. "John Brown will be turnin' over in his grave," Randy Joe said.

His teammates didn't say anything.

During the tour he'd learned a lot about the Longhorns players and maybe more about himself. He was warmed by their hunger and thirst for knowledge, saddened that they had been deprived of opportunity because of skin color. Gar was reading the Bible like he'd been reading it all of his life. Some of the others had improved their reading skills tenfold. It made Randy Joe realize what any person, given the opportunity, could do.

While they were eating supper Gar asked, "You decide yet what you gonna do wid Squirrel? We can't jest leave him on top o' de bus while we here."

"I've given a lot of thought to it," Randy Joe said, "and figure we oughta bury Squirrel tonight."

"We ain't got no place to bury him," Buck said, "'less we buries him out in a field someplace."

"I gotta place in mind," Randy Joe said. "But we're gonna have to work fast. Grease and me...we've already scouted the place out."

"When we gonna do dis buryin'?" Cut asked.

"It's gonna have to be after midnight."

Randy Joe had planned on soliciting the aid of just two other players and Grease to bury Squirrel, but the entire team insisted on participating. "If one gonna git caught, den all of us oughta git caught," Gar said.

Grease drove the bus to the baseball stadium, which stood quiet and solemn, a silhouette against the darkened prairie sky. The stadium's field lights were off, but a couple of bulbs were burning in the entry leading to the stands.

They quickly took the casket off the top of the bus and hustled it inside the ball park. It was necessary to climb a fence and push the coffin over the top of it. They placed it at the base of the backstop behind home plate.

Randy Joe and Cut got tools and wheelbarrows from the groundskeeper's shed. They wheeled the tools to home plate and the players took turns digging the grave. With four manning shovels it didn't take long.

When they were ready to lower the casket into the ground, Gar stopped them. "Now wait jest a minute. We need to say some words over dis man."

"Good idea, Gar," Randy Joe said. "You say'em."

"Now I figured on you bein' de one to do de talkin'," Gar said.

"You can do it as well as I can...probably better."

Gar pondered, then began, "Lawd, maybe dey ain't much to dis ol' man, but we sho' 'preciate it if You takes over now and looks after him. We done brought him from Canada...all iced down in de best suit he has. We figure he gonna like it here 'cause he love baseball. We figure You likes de game, too, so You done understand why we puts him here.

"De ol' man cause us some grief early on, but he straighten up after we done throwed him in de river. I don't know if he was ever baptized or not, but if he ain't we 'preciate it if You counts de time we throw him in de river as his baptizin'.

"Well, dey ain't much mo' dat I can say, 'cept ain't nobody want dis ol' man 'ceptin' You. De way I understands it, You willin' to take ever'body dat nobody else wants. Well, he Yo's now and dat's all I has to say."

Randy Joe had heard a few funeral sermons, but never one that matched Gar's. He nodded his appreciation and they lowered the coffin into the ground, then quickly covered it, stomped and smoothed out the area. The excess dirt was carried off in the wheelbarrows. Then the wheelbarrows and tools were put back in the groundskeeper's shack.

"Nice job," Randy Joe told his teammates when they were on the bus. "If somebody notices a little disturbance with the ground there, they're just gonna smooth it out. They're not gonna dig six feet down."

"Thing I likes 'bout it," Grease said, "is dat ol' Squirrel gonna have de best seat in de house. Ain't nobody 'ceptin' de players and de umpires gonna be closer to de game dan he is."

They'd buried Squirrel behind home plate, behind and to the right of where the umpire crouched to call balls and strikes. Cooter had put a new pack of cigarettes in the casket and said, "You know how dat ol' man like to smoke."

No one talked on the ride back. They were feeling the pain of losing one of their own. They had joked about Squirrel's body riding in the casket on top of the bus. But it was different now. They were all feeling a bit of their own mortality.

When they got back to the dorm most of the players went to their rooms to rest. They were scheduled to play the following afternoon, which was Tuesday. There would be no room for mistakes. The tournament fielded sixteen teams. They had to win three straight to get to the championship bracket.

Randy Joe stayed in the dorm room briefly, then went outside to survey the endless Kansas sky, to wonder about his place in the universe. It was his way of giving thanks for being alive. He felt restless, but more sad and weary. It was hard to believe Squirrel's daughter hadn't wanted her father's body.

Maybe it had all worked out for the best, he thought. As long as any of the thirteen people who'd buried Squirrel were alive, he'd always be remembered. None of them would forget carrying him across country on top of the bus, or the unique place where they'd buried him.

Randy Joe was standing there looking at the sky when Gar came out and joined him. Gar stood there with him a few minutes, then said, "You a good friend. I ain't gonna forget what you did fo' me."

"Hell, I haven't done anything for you, Gar."

"You done somethin' fo' ever'body on dis team and dey all knows it. We all wants to do somethin' fo' you, but we don't know what to do."

Randy Joe laughed, uneasily. "Let's all just play good ball."

THIRTY-SIX

Letters from Randy Joe had made the summer a bit more tolerable for Gretchen, but the letters weren't like seeing him in person. She missed him a lot, as she often told Jolene and Weave. The couple included her in many of their summer activities.

Some of his letters were hard for her to interpret. She expressed that to Weave and Jolene.

"Randy Joe's been my best friend for as long as I can remember," Weave said, "and there's still a lot about him I don't understand. He's changin'. All the time he's changin'."

"What do you mean?" Gretchen asked.

"See him two or three times during the day and it's like you're talkin' to two or three different people. He'll be real cocky and sure of himself one minute, real humble and unsure the next. His moods are about as predictable as Texas weather."

Gretchen asked, "How do you think he's gonna act after goin' on this trip with all those...colored men?"

Weave laughed. "You can say nigger in front of Jolene and me."

Jolene laughed, too. "Sure can. It's hard not to say it."

"I'm just tryin' to watch it because Randy Joe doesn't like for me to say it," Gretchen said.

"After spendin' so much time with'em he's liable to come back sayin' it more than Big Bill does," Weave said.

"You don't believe that," Gretchen said.

Weave sighed. "You're right...I don't. I don't think we've seen the end of the trouble here, either. Gary Steele's dad is out to get Randy Joe...and he's not gonna rest 'til he does."

Weave, of course, hadn't seen the pictures Simmy gave to

Big Bill Perkins. Simmy had Bertha Mae Davis put the envelope holding the pictures on top of the candy and gum display case near Big Bill's cash register. When the cafe owner opened the envelope and looked at its contents he was like a little boy who'd gotten everything he wanted for Christmas. He immediately called Vic Marshall.

"You gotta get over here, Vic...now."

"What's the problem?" the football coach asked.

"No problem," Big Bill said, laughing. "We just got an answer to our prayers."

The pictures made Big Bill forget the war against Communism he was waging with James Steele and George Mason. They had treated him like shit. Now he had them by the balls.

Big Bill hustled Marshall to his private booth and had a waitress bring coffee. Then he showed the coach one of the pictures. "Ain't that the shits," he said. "The way the mighty Mr. Steele talks about niggers. Then he beds down with nigger women."

Marshall's mouth was agape. It stayed that way as Big Bill showed him picture after picture of Steele and Mason having various sexual relations with black women. There were twenty pictures. When he'd seen them all the shocked coach asked, "Where'd these pictures come from?"

Arrogantly, Big Bill replied, "I told you...I have contacts. I could've had Mason and Steele taken out, but I figured what the hell. This way's as good as any to bring'em into line."

Bertha Mae, her ear glued to the wall, had to fight off uproarious laughter. Tears of joy rolled down her cheeks.

"I can't believe these pictures are real," Marshall said.

"Oh, they're real all right," Big Bill assured. "See...on the back of the pictures here...written in pencil. It's the name of the whorehouse down in Beaumont. Remember...a couple of times when we needed to see'em they told us they had business in Beaumont. I remember George tellin' me him and James went to Beaumont once a week to take care of business. I'll bet their wives don't know what kinda business they been takin' care of."

Marshall asked, "What are you gonna do with the pictures."

Big Bill laughed. "First thing...I'm gonna have some fun, let

James and George see'em. I want'em to know I got'em."

"What then?"

"Well, I don't think you have to worry about James givin' you any more trouble about Randy Joe. If he does, or if anything goes wrong to keep Randy Joe from playin', then his old lady is gonna see some of these pictures. Hell, I might even give one to his preacher, too...might even have some of 'em framed and put up on the wall here."

"I can't have anything to do with this," Marshall said, soberly.

Big Big laughed. "Hell, I ain't askin' you to have anything to do with it. I wanna handle this myself."

A little later that day J.D. Lake got a call from Simmy. "Big Bill has de pictures. Maybe you wanna call 'em like we talked 'bout."

"I'll do that," Lake said, smiling. "Maybe I'll just go by his place for coffee. I don't have much to do. My wife and daughter are in Europe."

Lake couldn't wait to see Big Bill. He was anxious to implement the plan that he and Simmy had worked out. He called first. "Something important I have to talk to you about," he told Big Bill. Then he drove down to the cafe. Big Bill led the banker to his private booth and had a waitress bring coffee. He liked Lake. The banker always treated him as an equal.

"What can I do for you, J.D.?"

"We've got a problem," Lake said, concern written all over his face. "We've got to make sure that Randy Joe Keegan doesn't get any money, including expenses, for playing for the Jason Longhorns."

"Yeah...Vic told me we had to be careful about lettin' anybody find out about that."

"We've got to do more than that," Lake said. "We've got to reimburse Simmy for Randy Joe's expenses and what he's paying him. That way, if Simmy's called in to give some sort of testimony he can say that Randy Joe didn't receive a dime from him or the ball club."

"What kinda money we talkin' about here?" Big Bill asked.

"Roughly eighteen hundred dollars. Now I'm willing to put

up part of it, but I don't think I can get much help from James or George. And we've got to keep this very quiet. It would really be better if just one or two people put up all the money."

Big Bill mused, "About eighteen hundred, huh? Why don't we just make it an even two thousand?"

"That's fine with me, but where are we going to get the rest?"

"J.D.," Big Bill said, pompously, "just leave that up to me. And there's no need for you to put up any money. I'll have the two thousand for you, in cash, in a couple of days."

Lake said, "I hate to put a burden like this on you."

"It's absolutely no problem, J.D., no problem whatsoever."

When Lake left and got in his car he laughed out loud. He wondered if Mason and Steele would withdraw the money from his bank.

Big Bill called George Mason first. Mason was an asshole, but Steele was worse. "You need to get your partner and come on down to the cafe."

"What's the problem?" Mason asked.

"It has to do with the school...the football team."

"We've taken care of that problem."

"Afraid not," Big Bill said. "Nothin's settled yet."

"Well, if somethin' needs settlin' James and I will handle it. You don't need to be involved."

"I wanna be involved." He then made mention of a certain establishment in Beaumont. There was total silence on the other end of the phone. He continued with, "We need to meet 'cause it looks like some of our most influential citizens frequent the place."

Mason said, icily, "What do you want, Big Bill?"

"I want you and Steele down here in the next thirty minutes or you're not gonna like the consequences."

Mason laughed. "A threat, Big Bill? You can't threaten us. I hope you're not implyin' we're among those influential citizens who frequent that place in Beaumont you mentioned."

"What if I said I had proof?"

"I'd say you were lyin'."

Big Bill laughed. "You wanna take that chance? If you come down here I'll show you the proof."

There was a pause on the other end of the line. "I'll just call your bluff and come down there," Mason said, "but I'm not gonna bother James with this. And pulling this kinda thing...you've buried yourself in this town, Big Bill."

Thirty minutes later Mason's arrogance had waned. He called Steele and had him get down to the cafe right away.

"Where'd you get these?" Steele asked, angrily.

Big Bill grinned and replied, "I've got friends who sort of specialize in this sort of thing. I thought you knew that, James."

"Well, I'd suggest you tell your friends they're askin' for real trouble," Steele said. "I'm not the kind of man who takes this kind of shit sitting down."

"James, the kinda people I'm talkin' about will squash you like a mosquito," Big Bill said. "You don't wanna threaten 'em."

"Maybe we'd better listen to what he says," Mason interjected, fearfully. "We don't want any trouble."

"What do these people want?" Steele asked.

"They don't want anything," Big Bill replied. "It's what I want."

Steele grumbled, "And what's that?"

"I want you to back off Randy Joe...completely. I know you agreed to let him play football, but then you plan to expose his so-called professional experience with Simmy's team so he can't play baseball. When you do that every football game Jason wins this year will be forfeited."

Steele quasi-laughed. "What difference does it make? As long as you know you've won, you've won."

"It makes a helluva lot of difference," Big Bill said. "It'll hurt the school and it'll hurt Vic."

"I can't believe you're kissin' the Keegan boy's ass after what his daddy did to you," Steele said.

Big Bill's face reddened. "I ain't kissin' nobody's ass, James. When it comes to the welfare of the school I just don't hold grudges. You shouldn't, either."

"So you're tellin' me that I gotta forget what the Keegan boy's done or some of these pictures will start showin' up?"

"That's right?"

"That's blackmail."

"No it's not, since I ain't askin' anything for myself. Hell, years from now you'll be thankin' me."

"Don't hold your breath," Steele said.

"No reason we can't keep on bein' friends," Big Bill said, facetiously.

Steele grumbled, "We're not friends...never will be."

Big Bill's voice hardened. "That's what I figured you'd say, James. Well, I don't give a rat's ass about bein' your friend. All I can say is that if anybody messes up things for Randy Joe or Vic Marshall these pictures are gonna see the light of day."

"Now wait a minute," Mason said. "That doesn't seem hardly fair. Somebody else could expose Randy Joe."

Big Bill laughed. "Fair? Since when have you and James been concerned with what's fair?"

"You may have a few pictures, Big Bill, but we don't have to take any bullshit from you," Steele said.

"The hell you don't," the cafe owner said. "You're not gonna bully me, James...not anymore. If I tell you to eat a yard of my shit, you'll do it."

Steele challenged, "It'll be a cold day in hell before..."

Mason intervened. "Let's all settle down here. Obviously, Big Bill, you've got somethin' that James and I don't want to become public knowledge. What can we do to get the negatives?"

Big Bill replied, "Gettin' the negatives...that's a few years down the road. You boys are just gonna have to trust me."

"How the hell can we trust you?" Steele asked.

Big Bill laughed. "You can't."

Steele and Mason exchanged glances, then Mason asked, "What about Leon Rice? We still gonna get to fire him after the football season?"

"I imagine Randy Joe will want him coaching baseball for his last year."

Steele vented his frustration with a stream of expletives. "I thought you were on our side in the battle against Communism."

"Oh, I'm against Communism all right," Big Bill said, "but y'all been quick to call somebody a Communist if it suits your purpose."

"Damn," Steele said, "You and Vic wanted Rice's head, too."

Big Bill laughed. "So I've changed my mind. And these pictures got me to thinkin' that you boys aren't as down on niggers as you claim to be. Of course, it looks as though you don't mind goin' down on a nigger woman. Wonder what your preacher would think about that, George? Reckon he'd say *amen*...the way you're always doin'?"

Mason turned whiter and Steele said, "I've listened to enough of this bullshit."

Big Bill laughed again, infuriating Steele even more. "James, your kid's been mouthin' off about Randy Joe bein' a nigger lover. Maybe he'd like to see a picture of a *real* nigger lover."

Steele's face flushed and Big Bill continued, "If I was you, James, I'd have my kid keep his mouth shut. Of course, he'd never open his mouth in front of Randy Joe because he's got a yellow streak a mile wide. But I just want you to know that if Gary screws up he's gonna get some pictures of his daddy and daddy's friends."

The lawyer wanted to fight back, but he knew Big Bill had him. "Look," he said with frustration, "George and I are agreed that we're not gonna do anything to jeopardize the Keegan boy's elgibility for any sport, including baseball. We'll keep our mouths shut, but we gotta know when we can get the pictures and negatives."

Big Bill grinned. "You're lookin' at five or six years down the road...when Randy Joe Keegan's out of college and there's nothin' you can do to hurt his career."

"You're a bastard," Steele said.

"Yeah, I know," Big Bill agreed, smiling. "Oh, by the way, we need to raise two thousand dollars to pay Simmy for Randy Joe's salary and expenses. That way, if Simmy's ever questioned he can say he never spent a dime on the boy. I figure a thousand from each of you boys will do it. Bring it to me in cash."

Steele said, angrily. "That's blackmail."

Big Bill shrugged his shoulders. "The money's not for me."

"We'll have the money for you tomorrow," Mason promised.

Outside the cafe Steele said, "You need to be tougher, George."

"Tougher? That man could ruin us."

Steele grunted, "That sonofabitch...we come up with the right amount of money and we can buy him. He'll do whatever we want."

Mason shook his head. "If it had to do with somethin' besides high school sports...maybe. You know Big Bill thinks he's a sports legend in this town. I don't think we can buy him because he enjoys the power he has over us more than he wants money."

"Maybe you're right," Steele said. "I'm gonna be lookin' for those negatives. When I find 'em, I may kill that bastard."

"Fine," Mason agreed, "but in the meantime you need to kill Gary's big mouth. And you need to go down to the bank and pick up a thousand in cash. I'm gonna do it now. Do you wanna go with me?"

"Might as well," Steele grumbled.

Vic Marshall, in the meantime, dreaded his visit to the home of R.M. and Bernice Keegan. He accepted that J.D. Lake was right in saying he should be the one who talked to them. The coach made his visit after the mill whistle had sounded and Keegan was off work. Marshall found the Keegans enjoyable and ended up having supper with them.

After the coach had explained that receiving money for playing ball would make Randy Joe ineligible for high school sports, Keegan said, "Well, I'm not gonna lie about it. We just ain't gonna say anything."

Marshall said, "I can't ask for any more than that. I don't know what financial arrangements Randy Joe has with Simmy, but Simmy's not gonna be payin' him a dime...not even his expenses on the trip. Whatever Simmy promised is comin' from other sources. That way Simmy won't be lyin' when he says he didn't pay Randy Joe anything."

"I never been one to break rules," Keegan said, "and I doubt Randy Joe gave much thought to breakin' rules when he went on this tour. I always did think it was a shame, though, that they took Jim Thorpe's medals away because he was ignorant of the rules."

Marshall agreed that it was a shame. Then Keegan continued, "James Steele and George Mason will keep quiet about this?"

Marshall replied, "They're not gonna say a word."

Gretchen had been talking to her parents for some time about the possibility of going to the big tournament in Wichita. "We never go anywhere," she complained.

Max Turner laughed. "Wichita's still not goin' anywhere."

After they'd talked it over, though, Max and Lisa decided to talk to R.M. and Bernice Keegan about making the trip. Max loved baseball and lived the games through Randy Joe.

"Well, I can't take off a week...you know that," R.M. said. "Sure, I'd like to go but I just don't see any way."

"I'm not talkin' about a week," Max said. "I'm talkin' about a couple of days. We can leave early on a Friday mornin' and be there for the championship game on Sunday."

The Turners had invited the Keegans over for lemonade after supper and they were sitting on the front porch. Bernice sipped her lemonade, laughed and said, "Aren't you counting your chickens, Max. What if the Longhorns aren't in the championship game?"

Max grinned. "With Randy Joe playin' for'em, I'm willin' to take the chance they'll be there. We can go in my car. And we're not gonna be the only ones from Jason there."

"Who else is going?" Bernice asked. "Besides Simmy, I mean?"

"Big Bill, Coach Marshall and his wife," Max answered. "They're all goin' up together."

Lisa shook her head in dismay. "Strange about Big Bill, isn't it? You'd think he wouldn't wanna have anything to do with any of the Keegans, but it seems just the opposite."

Max laughed. "Funny how a good ass-kickin' will get a man goin' in the right direction.

When Max and Lisa told their daughter they would, indeed, be going to Wichita, Gretchen was one happy girl.

THIRTY-SEVEN

The Longhorns played the second scheduled game on Tuesday. In the first game of the day a team from Ponca City, Oklahoma ousted one from Salina, Kansas. The opponent for the Longhorns was the Islanders, a team out of Grand Island, Nebraska.

Randy Joe had pretty much regained all his strength and was throwing the ball with the kind of velocity he had exhibited in his first start for the Longhorns. Counting that first victory he had, in both starting and relieving roles, compiled a record of fourteen wins and no losses for Simmy's team. As important as his pitching, however, was his bat. He was stroking the ball at a four hundred plus clip and had contributed several key pinch hits that enabled the Longhorns to win games.

Muddy figured that just as important as Randy Joe's arm and bat was the intangible way he had contributed to making them a real team, one where personal goals took a back seat to the unified effort of winning. Having a white boy on an otherwise all black team had caused problems from the beginning, but Randy Joe had earned the respect of his teammates and they'd rallied around him.

Muddy thought Randy Joe had something in common with Jackie Robinson, and that Simmy had some ulterior motive for putting the white boy on the team.

Grand Island was one of the strongest teams in the tournament. Promoter Basil McMurrey had paired teams in such a way as to almost ensure that the favorite, the Wichita Tornadoes, would end up in the championship game. McMurrey, a rotund law school dropout in his late forties who chewed his cigars instead of lighting them, was smart enough to know that a local team was going to draw a better crowd.

So Wichita's march to the championship game was to be through some of the lesser competition. On the other hand, McMurrey didn't want the Longhorns in the championship game. His attitude was that he "didn't want the niggers in the tournament anyway." If they reached the championship game, it would be through the stiffest competition the tournament offered.

Grand Island was certainly that, a solid team comprised of a number of ex-pros and former college stars in their late twenties and early thirties. The Islanders were known for good hitting, strong pitching and excellent defense. McMurrey believed Grand Island was the team most likely to reach the championship game against, he hoped, Wichita.

What the promoter hadn't counted on was the new white pitcher for the Longhorns. The kid didn't look all that strong, but there was something about him that bothered McMurrey. When he was warming up before the game there was a calmness about him that made the promoter nervous. And there was that name that his teammates kept calling him.

White Heat.

When the Grand Island players saw Randy Joe Keegan on the mound they didn't like what they saw. Or didn't see. The velocity of his fastball made it a blur. His curveball broke so late and sharply that no righthand hitter could hold his ground in the batter's box.

What made him more dangerous, and his pitches seem even faster, was that he was wild. When he let loose the ball he didn't seem to know where it was going. Digging in was not recommended.

Among those watching the game were the manager and players from the Wichita Tornadoes. They came to scout the Grand Island team, but when the dust had cleared the Longhorns walked off the field with a two-to-nothing victory. Randy Joe Keegan had struck out twenty, hit four batters and walked six. He'd given up only an infield single.

The next day the Wichita Tornadoes easily polished off a team from Columbia, Missouri by a score of sixteen to three.

That brought a smile to promoter Basil McMurrey's face. Things were going just as he planned. The smile turned to a frown, though, when he thought about the Jason Longhorns. Well, now they had to get by Ponca City, Oklahoma, a team that was on par with Grand Island. The white pitcher, the one called *White Heat*, was used up. Ponca City would send the niggers packing.

Ponca City had advanced by beating Salina, Kansas on Thursday. Gar was the starting pitcher and got roughed up a bit in the first three innings. The Longhorns were trailing four to nothing and Ponca City loaded the bases in the fourth. Muddy had Skeeter relieve the big guy, but the Oklahoma team jumped all over the lefthander. Before Skeeter could get them out the Longhorns were trailing nine to nothing and it looked like the Jason team would be making an early exit.

"Let me pitch," Randy Joe told Muddy. "Skeeter told me his arm's hurtin'."

"Pooh can pitch de rest o' de game," Muddy said. "Ain't no use you hurtin' yo' arm fo' nothin'."

Randy Joe laughed, something that didn't escape his downcast teammates. "Pooh's got to pitch tomorrow."

The way he said it, the team trailing nine to nothing, got the juices of the other players flowing. "Dat's right," Buck agreed. "Pooh...he gotta pitch tomorrow. We a long way from losin' dis game."

Suddenly, the spirit was back. Then Randy Joe added to it with, "You know where ol' Squirrel's buried. Grab you a handful of that dirt when you go up to the plate and let's bury these guys."

Cooter Davis did as Randy Joe directed and promptly cracked a single. Jackie Monk followed suit and did the same. The Ponca City pitcher, who'd been sailing along, walked Tater Green. That brought Randy Joe to the plate.

The pitcher looked at the white kid and wasn't impressed. So he grooved one. Randy Joe took it over the center field fence.

In the sixth the Longhorns, rubbing the handles of their bats with dirt from Squirrel's grave, got two more runs to cut the Ponca City lead to three. And when the Jason team was on the field Randy Joe was throwing lightning. He had that *pleasing* bit of wildness that set the hitters up perfectly.

In the ninth the Longhorns loaded the bases again. This time it was Buck Frazier who hit a towering home run that gave Simmy's team a 10 to 9 victory.

Randy Joe had pitched five hitless innings, struck out ten, hit two and walked three. The game almost caused promoter Basil McMurrey to go into cardiac arrest. The niggers, he thought, only had to get by one other team to get to the championship game. What if a bunch of niggers won his tournament? It could ruin all he'd worked for over the years.

McMurrey made a tidy sum from the annual tournament which more than compensated for the time and effort he put into it. None of the other teams even had a Negro. The Longhorns were the only team in the tournament that was exclusively colored, with the exception of the kid pitcher. The niggers just didn't belong, McMurrey thought, wishing he hadn't taken Simmy's entry fee.

Simmy, accompanied by Zeke Lott, had arrived in Wichita for the Longhorns first game. He had shaken his head in amazement at the way Randy Joe had handcuffed Grand Island in the first game, then he had been been shocked and delighted by the way the team pulled its second game out of the fire. But what amazed him even more was the amount of money the team had accumulated. Muddy gave credit for the financial windfall to Randy Joe, the camping out and cooking.

"You done kept us from bein' outta dis tournament," Simmy told the young pitcher.

Randy Joe grinned and replied, "Not me. It's the magic dirt on ol' Squirrel's grave that did it. It's gonna take us all the way."

Simmy and Zeke laughed. Then the baker said, "Ain't no way I kin give you 'nough donuts fo' de two games you done pitched. I don't make dat many in a day."

"How yo' arm feel?" Simmy asked.

"Fine."

"I don't want you hurtin' it none," he said. "You done pitched fo'teen innins'."

"I got a feeling," Randy Joe said, "that Pooh's gonna pitch

a great game tomorrow."

The Longhorns adversary for the afternoon game on Friday was out of Iowa, the Sioux City Indians. Promoter Basil McMurrey had his fingers crossed that Sioux City would be able to derail the Longhorns. Going into the tournament he'd figured the four strongest teams were Wichita, Sioux City, Ponca City and Grand Island. The Longhorns had already knocked two of the four out of the running, but the white kid with the blazing fastball had to be tired. He'd pitched fourteen pressure-packed innings and there was no way he was going to pitch on Friday. They had to be saving him, hoping he'd have something left if they happened to win and played on Saturday.

One person who had paid close attention to the Longhorns first two games was Dobie Cox, manager of the Wichita Tornadoes. Cox was six feet tall and in his late forties. He had a thick moustache, the same color as his mane of gray hair. His face was tan, lined and wrinkled by days in the sun. He'd been a terror in the minors, a power hitting outfielder, but for some reason had never been able to hit in the majors. Major league curveballs damn near gave him ulcers. He'd been given a brief shot, a cup of coffee with Cincinnati.

In the two games he'd watched the Longhorns play, Cox became fascinated with Randy Joe Keegan. During all his years in baseball he'd never seen a pitcher with such velocity. He'd also never seen a pitcher with such a late, fast breaking curveball. Dobie Cox felt an almost mystical fear where Randy Joe Keegan was concerned.

Had he been a religious man, after seeing what the young pitcher did to the Grand Island team, he would have prayed that his team didn't have to face him. Since he wasn't, he just hoped it wouldn't happen. With Randy Joe having pitched the game on Tuesday, Cox figured the only way he would pitch again would be if the Longhorns made it to the championship contest.

Like promoter McMurrey, Cox's fears subsided when the Ponca City Chiefs took a nine to nothing lead over the Longhorns. And like McMurrey those fears again surfaced when the colored team rallied for a 10 to 9 win.

Cox knew talent. He knew the Longhorns were a talented

bunch, free swingers who could tattoo a baseball. But he also sensed that Randy Joe Keegan provided a certain spark that ignited his teammates.

Seeing Randy Joe come into a game that was seemingly lost, seeing him pitch with the confidence that he was closing in on a victory, sent chills up and down Cox's spine. It wasn't something that could be taught. That was something that, he hated to say it, was God-given.

In the late innings of the game between the Longhorns and Ponca City, Cox looked for signs of weakness from Randy Joe. Did his fastball have a little less pop? Did his curveball hang a little?

He wasn't able to pick up any sign of weakening. If anything, as with the Tuesday game, the longer he pitched the stronger he seemed to get. But after the game Cox thought, he pitched nine innings on Tuesday and five today. There's no way he's going to pitch tomorrow. Sioux City is a powerhouse. No way this team of niggers can beat them.

Why then, he'd asked himself, would I rather my team face Sioux City than the kid pitcher? He knew the answer to the question. His team could beat Sioux City, but he wasn't sure they could beat the Longhorns with Randy Joe Keegan pitching.

Randy Joe's parents and the Turners arrived during pregame warmups. Seeing them in the stands shocked him. He hadn't anticipated their coming. Simmy hadn't said anything about it. Maybe he hadn't known, Randy Joe thought. Or, maybe he'd wanted it to be a surprise.

Randy Joe signaled and his parents and the Turners came down from the stands to the low fence that surrounded the playing field. He hugged his mother and shook hands with everyone else. He wanted to kiss Gretchen, but didn't.

Briefly, he filled them in on the Longhorns' first two games of the tournament. "We have some guys who can hit and field the ball," he said. "This team...Sioux City...is one of the strongest in the tournament."

"Who's pitchin'?" his father asked.

"A kid named Pooh Wiley. He's from Waco...has a good curveball and great control."

R.M. Keegan grinned. "Your control gotten any better?"

Randy Joe laughed. "It depends on who you ask."

A little later Randy Joe was further shocked to look up in the stands and see Big Bill Perkins, Vic and Sheila Marshall waving at him. Seeing Sheila triggered some feelings in him that he didn't quite understand. He was, of course, glad to see her, and uncomfortable to see her husband there with Big Bill.

It was one of those days for Pooh. His curveball started hanging and he was rocked for four runs in the first inning. Gar warmed up in the bullpen and, in the second when Pooh got tagged for two straight hits, Muddy brought the big righthander into the game.

Randy Joe wasn't sure what the problem was with the pitching of his teammates, unless it was just a case of tired arms. He knew they were all good hurlers, had seen them prove it time and again on the tour. But Gar didn't fare any better than Pooh. Skeeter, who'd had problems the previous day, was next to try to throw up a barricade at home plate.

He couldn't.

By the time Sioux City finished their half of the third inning the Chiefs were ahead thirteen to zip.

It was a blowout.

The Longhorns, who had been victims of racial innuendos, snickers, comments and derision for the entire week, were now really catching hell from the fans who considered the game a test between black evil and white supremacy. His teammates claimed they were used to it, that it didn't bother them, but Randy Joe knew that wasn't entirely true.

Without Muddy instructing him to do so, Randy Joe had warmed up while Skeeter was getting pounded. He was ready to pitch. He wanted to pitch. He wanted to shove a baseball down the throats of those fans who were so deliriously happy with the way the game was going, those whose vocal chords were loaded with boos, catcalls and jeers for his teammates. He wanted to show them there was no quit in the Longhorns.

When the final Sioux City out was recorded in the third, when his teammates came in the dugout, Randy Joe joked, "Damn, you guys sure like to make it tough...spotting them that many runs. We're gonna use up all the dirt on ol' Squirrel's grave."

Muddy knew what Randy Joe was trying to do, but saw the team was too downcast and beaten to respond. The manager didn't know anything about psychology, but even if they were beaten he wanted to make a game of it. He wanted to leave the ball park with his head held high.

"Pooh de leadoff man dis inning," Muddy said. "Does you want to go in, Randy Joe?"

"Damn right," the young pitcher replied. "It's time we showed these clowns a little Texas-style nigger baseball."

None of the players had ever heard Randy Joe use the word *nigger*. At first there was just quiet in the dugout, then Buck started laughing and the others joined in. "You show'em, Randy Joe...a little nigger baseball wid a pinch o' *White Heat,*" the big catcher said.

Suddenly the dugout was alive and the players were chanting "Nigger ball...nigger ball."

The chant from the dugout was heard by all the fans, especially the racists who had been deriding The Longhorns. It shocked them and weakened their ridicule.

Randy Joe laughed. "I'll get the first one. Y'all can decide who gets the next one."

Their teammate's intent was obvious to all the players. Randy Joe was thinking long ball. First he rubbed up the handle of his bat with some dirt from the top of Squirrel's grave. Then, just before stepping into the batter's box, he incited the crowd with a Babe Ruth move. He pointed to the right field fence.

The Sioux City pitcher grinned at Randy Joe's hotdogging. He'd been warned about the thin, white kid who played for the Longhorns. He'd even seen him hit the grand slam against Ponca City. There was no way the kid was going to do it against him. He had good stuff and good control. Keegan wasn't even going to see a pitch that he could pull.

The Chiefs hurler got his first pitch right where he wanted it, knee high and on the outside corner. He couldn't believe it when Randy Joe got wood on the ball. It didn't go over the right field fence as the hitter had promised, but it did clear the left field wall,   an opposite field homer on what most would have considered a perfect pitch.

As Randy Joe rounded the bases the Longhorns players were hooting and hollering as if they were ahead in the game, not trailing thirteen to one. In the stands Zeke turned to Simmy and said, "Well, dat's some consolation. We at least got a run."

"We gonna git some mo', too," Simmy promised. "We may not win dis game, but befo' it's over dey gonna know dey was in a ball game."

Simmy's prophecy seemed to have some merit as the Longhorns struck for two more runs in the inning. The Sioux City manager told his pitcher, "Don't worry...just throw strikes. We'll get you some more runs."

Wichita Tornadoes manager Dobie Cox had started to leave the stands after Sioux City had seemingly buried the Longhorns in the third inning. But then he heard all the noise in the Jason dugout and saw Randy Joe coming to the plate. Even after Randy Joe hit the home run Cox thought, the kid can't be coming in to pitch again. His curiosity made him return to his seat.

The velocity on Randy Joe's fastball was something to behold, though the Chiefs players didn't seem to be able to see it all that well. It was just a white blur in the sweltering Kansas sunshine. And the Longhorn players kept calling out, "White Heat...White Heat."

The Sioux City manager used six pitchers in trying to stop the Longhorns attack, but when the final Chiefs player struck out swinging the Jason team had a sixteen to thirteen victory. The crowd, most of whom were rooting for Sioux City, was stunned.

In the six innings he worked Randy Joe had struck out thirteen, hit two, walked two and allowed two hits. He'd also ripped a three run double, a single, and scored three runs.

Dobie Cox was stunned, too. If his team got by McCook, Nebraska later that evening, which it was almost sure to do, they'd be facing the Jason Longhorns in the championship game. Surely, he thought, the kid's not going to pitch tomorrow. He's pitched twenty innings in the last four days. And if he does pitch, what's he going to have left?

The question was running through Muddy's mind, too. He

wondered what he was going to do for pitching against what was considered the best team in the tournament. It was a foregone conclusion that Wichita would dispose of McCook and appear in the championship game.

In the midst of the jubilation over the victory against Sioux City, Muddy called his pitchers together to discuss how they'd handle the championship game. Randy Joe spoke up, "I'm scheduled and I'm ready."

"Ain't yo' arm tired?" the manager asked.

The young pitcher laughed and lied, "Naw...I was taking it easy this afternoon."

Muddy shook his head in dismay, "Well, if you want to start, you got de right. But all you pitchers better be ready tomorrow. Dis is what we been playin' fo'. Dis mean a lot mo' money in yo' pockets."

Randy Joe looked at his fellow pitchers and joked, "What are you guys going to spend all that money on."

Gar grinned, "Less you ain't noticed, Randy Joe, when we doin' all dat campin' out dey wasn't no women 'round. I ain't complainin', mind you, 'cause de eatin' was good and we done already got some money to take home fo' a change. But I figures on spendin' some o' dat extra money on gittin' me some poontang."

Randy Joe laughed. "You've got a one-track mind, Gar."

"Maybe," Gar said, grinning, "but it be on de right track."

After the meeting with Muddy, Randy Joe talked briefly with Big Bill Perkins, Vic Marshall and Sheila. He would have preferred to talk only to Sheila, but knew that was impossible.

"That was some game," Big Bill said, beaming. "I'm not much of a baseball fan, but that one had me on the edge of my seat."

Randy Joe wanted to ask, "What in the hell are you doing here?" Instead, he said, "I'm a little surprised to see y'all here."

Marshall laughed. "I'm a little surprised to be here myself. If you wanna blame someone, though, blame Sheila. Big Bill and I were talkin' about you the other day and Sheila said, 'Why don't we just all go up there and watch Randy Joe play?' So here we are."

Randy Joe and Sheila exchanged glances. "Hey, I'm glad to see you. Nice to have someone from home here," he said.

"I see your folks and the Turners came up," Sheila said. "How long have they been here?"

"They must have arrived about the same time you did...just before the game started."

"Randy Joe, your dad and I had a good talk not long ago," Marshall interjected. "I'm sure he'll fill you in on it." Then the coach smiled and continued, "You're not gonna have much free time before football practice starts. I imagine you've really missed goin' fishin' this summer, so you'd better catch up next week."

"To tell the truth, I've done more fishin' this summer than if I'd stayed in Jason."

Marshall showed surprise. "You have?"

"Yeah...when I have more time I'll tell you about it."

Sheila questioned, "Pitchin' like you did today, I don't imagine you'll be pitchin' tomorrow?"

"I'm startin' tomorrow," he replied. "I don't know how long I can go, but I'll give it my best."

Big Bill's toothpick wiggled in the corner of his mouth. "Well, you don't have anything to worry about, Randy Joe. We've taken care of everything."

Randy Joe wanted to ask, "What did I have to worry about?" He chose, however. not to say anything.

Later, in his parents' motel room, his dad explained about the coach's visit, how things were being handled to keep him from being declared ineligible. Randy Joe had known what he risked in going on tour with the Longhorns, but he liked living on the edge. He wasn't sure why, but he liked putting people in situations where they had to make hard decisions.

He had supper with his parents and the Turners in a little cafe in downtown Wichita. He would rather have eaten with his teammates at the school cafeteria, but figured he also needed to spend a little time with his folks and Gretchen.

After supper they drove out to the stadium to watch the Wichita Tornadoes play the McCook Red Sox. Randy Joe didn't care who won the game and wasn't really very interested in watching it. All week he'd been hearing about what a power-house Wichita was, but he hadn't bothered to watch any of the games in which the Tornadoes were playing. There had been other things to do, like rest on a comfortable bed.

Now, with a chance to more or less scout the opposition for the championship game, he watched the Wichita and McCook hitters with only cursory interest. He was tired, so weary that he could have laid down in the stands with the crowd roaring and gone right to sleep. The August heat had taken its toll, sapped much of his strength and taken away at least ten of his normal hundred and sixty pounds.

After watching a little of the game he asked Gretchen if she wanted to go for a walk. She did. They were both anxious to get away from the eyes and ears of their parents.

When they were far enough away from the stadium's crowd and noise, he kissed her gently, then more passionately.

"I've missed you," she said.

"I've missed you, too."

"Has it been all you thought it would be...the trip, I mean?"

"It's been more," he said. "I've learned a lot...made a lot of new friends. Now it's all come down to this one game tomorrow. A lot of scouts have been here this week and I guess most of 'em have seen me pitch by now, but tomorrow's the big test. Tomorrow they see how I handle the pressure."

"Are you nervous?"

He laughed. "Honestly?"

She reciprocated the laughter. "Of course. If you can't be honest with me, who can you be honest with?"

"I'm too tired to be nervous, Gretch. I'm so damned tired I may have to crawl out to the mound."

THIRTY-EIGHT

August 14, 1954

After his shaky first inning of pitching, one in which he had hit a batter and walked two, Randy Joe refused to accept the fact that his arm was tired. With the bases loaded he'd gotten the adrenalin flowing enough to strike out the side, but it had taken a lot out of him.

No matter what, he had to hang in there. The team was counting on him and if he just pitched decently they'd have a chance to win.

"Damn it, Buck," he joked at his catcher, "if you can't hit that clown on the mound, we're gonna make you catch without a cup."

Buck laughed and feigned holding his crotch. "When you done talkin', Mr. Randy Joe Keegan, put yo' money where yo' mouth is. Five dollars says I gits mo' hits dan you does."

"Hold it, Buck...that's not a fair bet. You might get more at bats than I do. You're hitting fourth, I'm hitting ninth. So if you get an extra time at bat we take your last at bat off. It still might not be fair because that pitcher might walk me every time I come up. I think he's afraid of me."

Buck and the other players chuckled. Then the catcher asked, "It a bet or ain't it?"

"It's a bet," Randy Joe replied.

The clown Randy Joe referred to was Mark McDonald, ace of the Wichita Tornadoes pitching staff. He was six-four and weighed two-twenty. A senior at the local university, he was a lefthander with control and a blazing fastball.

Buck, hitting righthanded, took one of the big lefthander's pitches deep to center. It rattled off the wall and the catcher went into second standing up. Rooster Solomon laid a bunt down the third base line and was thrown out. Buck took third.

McDonald bore down and struck out Cooter Davis. Then Jackie Monk grounded out short to first.

Water and the brief rest in the dugout did wonders for Randy Joe's morale. He had time to give himself a good talking to, so was hyped up to face Tornadoes second baseman Reggie Rivers.

Rivers was a barrel-chested man, muscular and hairy, with a lot of hair on his face. He had the eager look of a killer leaving the scene of the crime. A switch hitter, Rivers sprayed the ball to all fields. He was twenty-six years old and had spent a couple of years in the minors before having to return to construction work and semi-pro ball.

Rivers had watched Randy Joe pitch in all three of the Longhorns tournament wins. During that short period of time he had developed a real hatred for the young pitcher. Much of it was personal frustration at his own failure to make it in pro ball. He saw in Randy Joe someone who had a great baseball future ahead of him and it angered him. A virulent racist, Rivers also detested the young righthander for pitching for a *nigger team*.

The second baseman, batting lefthanded, had carefully laid his plans. All he needed was the right pitch.

With the count one and one, Rivers got the pitch he wanted. He laid a bunt down the first base line. As Randy Joe was fielding the ball, Rivers ran out of the base line and slammed into him, burying a knee in his ribs. As they both fell to the ground Randy Joe put the tag on the second baseman, but it was obvious to everyone that he was hurt.

While Randy Joe's teammates rushed to his aid, Rivers got up smirking and looked down at the fallen pitcher. His look didn't escape Randy Joe, who through teeth clinched in pain uttered, "It's gonna take more than that, asshole."

Rivers frowned and was tempted to kick or punch his downed adversary, but there were too many black faces around him. And they all looked angry. "Ain't no sense in dat kinda stuff," Cut said while Rivers was walking back to the Wichita dugout. "Is you okay, Randy Joe?"

He wasn't but grinned. "How would you like to be that sonofabitch the next time he comes up to the plate?" He asked, loud enough for Rivers to hear.

Cooter said, also loud enough for Rivers to hear, "Jest don't hit him in de head, Randy Joe. You might kill'em."

The home plate umpire came out and asked Muddy, "Your man gonna be able to pitch?"

Randy Joe was struggling to his feet and Muddy, concerned, asked the same question. "Hell yes, I'm able to pitch," Randy Joe said, angrily. "They haven't seen pitchin' yet. The bastard just knocked the breath out of me."

He figured it was worse than that, of course. His ribs felt like they were on fire. But he'd be damned if he'd let a shithead like Rivers make him leave the game.

Wichita's pepperpot shortstop Ed Beasley was the eighth hitter in the lineup. He would be a senior at the University of Kansas in September and had dreams of a major league career. He was five-nine, one-seventy and was hitting over three hundred. He was a line drive type hitter, usually made contact, had a good eye for the strike zone and frequently walked.

Beasley might have had a chance if he hadn't followed Rivers in the lineup. Randy Joe was so steamed that he reached back for something extra and gutted three fastballs that had the shortstop swishing air and talking to himself.

Pitcher Mark McDonald was the next batter. He got the same treatment as Beasley.

In the top of the third Tater Green was the leadoff man for the Longhorns. Randy Joe, who was on deck, figured that for any other team the first baseman wouldn't be hitting eighth. Tater didn't have much power, but could spray the ball to all fields.

While teaching Tater to read Randy Joe had formed a strong affection for the wiry, almost emaciated man. He'd also learned a lot about him, including the fact that Longhorns pitcher Skeeter Hodnett was his cousin and that both had been raised by their maternal grandmother in Zwolle, Louisiana.

Tater, twenty-eight, was a year older than Skeeter. Both shared the dream of playing baseball in the majors, but the possibilities of playing for any team besides the Longhorns were slipping away with the passing years.

Tornadoes pitcher Mark McDonald didn't waste a lot of time with Tater. His southpaw slants to the lefthand hitter sent the first baseman back for a seat on the pines.

McDonald had been warned by his manager, Dobie Cox, about Randy Joe Keegan. The warning did not go unheeded because the lefthander had also seen Randy Joe hit. The slender pitcher didn't look like a hitter, especially one with power, but looks could be deceiving.

McDonald had great confidence in his pitches and thought he could get Randy Joe out, but he first had an obligation to his teammates to send the Longhorns pitcher a message. After all, in the first inning Randy Joe had knocked Lucky Winters cap right off his head.

So McDonald sailed a fastball right in under Randy Joe's chin. But his adversary didn't even flinch. The big lefthander couldn't believe it. Anybody else would have bailed out of the batter's box, but the Keegan kid just stood there and watched the ball all the way into the catcher's mitt.

Randy Joe's failure to even acknowledge that the ball was close bothered McDonald. But something else bothered him, too. Keegan was a switch hitter. He was swinging from the left side. Did that mean the kid didn't respect his curveball? Had his opponent seen him pitch the Tornadoes opening game against Columbia, Missouri?

McDonald was playing mind games with himself. The truth was that, while Randy Joe was a righthanded pitcher, he was a natural lefthanded hitter. He often hit righthanded against a lefthanded pitcher, but overall felt more comfortable swinging from the left side. The decision to hit lefthanded on occasion was because of his collision with Reggie Rivers. The pain to his ribs wasn't as bad swinging from the left side.

McDonald, misreading the situation, was angered by what he thought was an affront to his pitching. So this time he came inside with a fastball that made Randy Joe hit the dirt. Catcher

Joe Bartosh, grinning behind his mask, asked, "How you like that, Keegan?"

Picking himself up out of the dirt, Randy Joe replied, "His fastball doesn't have much movement on it."

Bartosh signaled for a curveball, which he knew was what McDonald wanted to throw. They had Randy Joe perfectly set up for the pitch. McDonald prided himself on having a good curveball, and he did, but when he threw his best hook to Randy Joe the Longhorns pitcher didn't seem a bit awed. His feet didn't get nervous. He didn't bail out of the batter's box. He simply followed the rotation of the ball and got the fat part of his Ted Williams bat on it.

The ball exploded like a cannon shot, right back at McDonald. He couldn't get his glove up in time. If the ball had been a little more to the left it would have taken his head off. As it was the line shot fell in front of center fielder Cal Oliver and bounced into his glove so quickly that he could have thrown Randy Joe out at first if he'd had the arm strength.

Shaken by the rocket that almost took his head off, McDonald looked in for the sign from Bartosh. The hitter was center fielder Peewee Darthard. Peewee hailed from Tupelo, Mississippi, was the sixth of thirteen children, and the only thing the twenty-five year old was scared of was not being called to supper on time.

McDonald felt the need to establish some sort of intimidation factor so he went into the stretch, checked Randy Joe at first, then let loose a blazing fastball high and tight. Peewee didn't even blink.

Randy Joe didn't get a sign to steal, but he figured McDonald's next pitch was going to be a curveball. It was. The split second the Tornadoes pitcher released it Randy Joe was off and running.

The down and away curve was a tough pitch to handle, but Bartosh came up with it beautifully and fired a perfect peg to Reggie Rivers at second. Rivers took the ball right off the bag, turned and saw gleaming spikes coming right toward his chest. The second baseman went flying backward and the ball went flying toward the shortstop.

Rivers, flat on his back, was trying to get his breath. His teammates on the field rushed toward the collision and both dugouts emptied. The crowd was going crazy because everyone knew why Randy Joe had stolen the base.

It had been payback time.

Thanks to the umpires and Tornadoes manager Dobie Cox no punches were exchanged, but the players were milling about in threatening fashion and it was obvious there was a storm brewing. In manpower the Tornadoes had about a two to one advantage over the Longhorns. But Randy Joe's teammates weren't intimidated. If they had to, they were ready to fight.

Rivers finally got his breath back and play resumed. He glared menacingly at Randy Joe and said, "It ain't over."

Randy Joe laughed. "It sure as hell ain't. Remember that the next time you come to the plate."

The Longhorns weren't able to take advantage of Randy Joe's stolen base. Peewee lined to left and Cut Brown popped to the first baseman.

THIRTY-NINE

When Reggie Rivers took the cheap shot at Randy Joe in the second inning there had been a ripple of concern among only a few people in the stands, those from Jason and the major league scouts. Bernice Keegan had the typical mother's concern, one shared by Lisa Turner. R.M. Keegan and Max Turner were dominated by a passion for retaliation. Gretchen's reaction was fear, plus a combination of what the Keegans and her parents felt.

Big Bill and Vic Marshall were fearful that the injury might keep Randy Joe from playing football. Marshall's fear was even more pronounced because he now had everything back in place.

He was counting on riding Randy Joe's passing arm to a state championship and a college coaching job. Sheila's concern was different, but just as pronounced and much more sincere.

Simmy's and Zeke's concern was a lot like that of the Longhorns players. It wasn't simply a case of liking and wanting to protect the young pitcher, but also one of knowing how important he was to the championship game. If he was hurting, though, Simmy was willing to forfeit the chance for victory. He, as much as anyone there, wanted Randy Joe Keegan in the majors. He'd wanted him to have the experience with his team over the summer and he wanted him to carry that experience right into the major leagues. Randy Joe Keegan, Simmy believed, was more important than any one game.

The scouts, of course, just didn't want a great talent like Randy Joe injured by some bush league play. They took special note of Reggie Rivers, not that he had a prayer of ever getting back into pro ball. It was one thing to play hard, quite another to play dirty.

Yankees scout Tommy McGuire said to Pirates scout Slap Peterson, "Too bad all these other asshole scouts are here. I was hopin' I wouldn't have anyone but you to compete with for the Keegan kid."

McGuire and Peterson had covered every game of the tournament.

"I didn't think you wanted him," Peterson said. "Seems like you told me he might not be strong enough to hold up for a full professional season."

"Damn it, Slap, it was you who said that three months ago."

"It wasn't me," Peterson countered, laughing. "From the first I've said the kid would look good in a Pirates uniform."

McGuire grinned. "Well, your boss better get his checkbook out, because I've got a bonus figure in mind and he's not gonna to like it."

"What are y'all willing to pay?" Peterson asked.

"You gotta be kiddin'," McGuire replied, still grinning. "We're friends, Slap, but this is business. I'll just tell you that you don't have a prayer of signin' that boy. If our money don't get him the old Yankee pinstripes will...or a trip to Yankee

Stadium."

Peterson laughed. "I hate to bust your bubble, Tommy, but we're gonna give you a real run for your money on this kid. I hear the Phillies are, too. I hear that one of his favorite players is Robin Roberts, so that gives them a leg up."

"Strange, ain't it," McGuire said, soberly. "I don't guess there's a scout here, including me, who's not interested in Mark McDonald...big, strong, great fastball. You put him up alongside Randy Joe Keegan and there's no comparison physically. McDonald's got great potential, possibly enough talent to be a great major league pitcher. So, Slap, tell me why I'm more interested in the Keegan kid? Why do I think he's a winner and still have some questions about McDonald?"

Peterson shook his head in quasi-bewilderment. "There's something intangible about the Keegan kid. He's the most natural pitcher I've ever seen, but I ain't sure why. He probably don't weigh more than a hundred fifty pounds now, but I think he's stronger than McDonald. My god, look what he's done. He's already pitched twenty-two innings this week, won all three games for the Longhorns. He ain't given up a run yet."

"I don't mind tellin' you, that concerns me," McGuire said. "This year he won eighteen and lost none in high school and he has seventeen wins and no losses for the Longhorns. That's thirty-five wins and no losses in a period of six months. He's done some relief work, too. That's a lot of strain on the kid's arm. He has to be tired.

"You'd think that," Peterson agreed, "but it sure doesn't look like he's lost anything on the velocity of his fastball."

"Maybe not," McGuire said, "but Wichita's a good team and this is a pressure game. It should tell us a lot about McDonald. I've already made up my mind on Keegan."

FORTY

Cal Winters was first up for Wichita in the bottom of the third. In the bottom of the first Winters and Randy Joe had exchanged angry words after a fastball had unintentionally hit the bill of the right fielder's cap. After Randy Joe had showed concern, Winters had threatened, "You do that again, you little sonofabitch, and I'll take your head off."

It wasn't something Randy Joe could ignore.

The muscular, tough-talking right fielder dug in. He was twenty-seven, had bounced around in the minors for five years before being released. That had been three years earlier. Each year since he'd tried to catch on with a pro team, but without success. So he'd ended up with a truck driving job and with the Tornadoes.

Tobacco-chewing and angry about his lot in life, Winters was as tough as they came on a baseball field. He wasn't in any mood to take shit from a kid pitcher that had people oohing and awing.

Randy Joe's control wasn't good enough to hit the bill of Winters' cap again, but he did his damnedest. The inside fastball had Winters falling back on his butt and almost choking on his tobacco.

He got the message.

The problem with Winters was that he wasn't just mean and tough, he was also a little bit stupid. He thought he was bullet-proof. So on the next pitch, which was a blur of a fastball on the inside corner, the right fielder swung and turned loose of his bat. Randy Joe fell to the ground to keep it from taking his head off. The crowd roared approval.

Winters was grinning as the batboy returned his stick to him. Moments later he wasn't grinning. He was writhing in pain in the dust around home plate, trying to shake off the effects of a fastball that had caught him in the area of a kidney.

The umpire came out and gave Randy Joe a warning, but the only response he got was a cold stare. When the shaken Winters was on his feet and moving toward first base Randy Joe walked toward him and said, softly, "I can dodge any bat you throw, asshole. Do you want to take a chance on dodging my fastball?"

Winters started to make a menacing move toward the young pitcher, but hesitated when he saw no fear in Randy Joe's eyes. The little sonofabitch is crazy, he thought. So he trotted on to first, trying to shake off the pain where the baseball had hit him. He figured there was an inprint of the seams on his rock hard body.

The right fielder loved the adulation of the crowd and his tough guy image. He'd already made plans on how to further incite the crowd if he got on base.

Center fielder Cal Oliver was the number two hitter, a carbon copy of Winters in build. Oliver, however, possessed none of Winters' propensity for meanness. He was a nice guy, a good hit and run man, who had lived in Wichita all his life and had played for the local college. He was a solid player, but not one who attracted a lot of attention. He had walked in his first plate appearance.

Randy Joe heard Winters holler down to Cut, "Better get outta the way, nig...I'm coming down."

Randy Joe put his shoe against the rubber and went into the stretch as Winters moved off first. The base runner was getting a good lead. The young pitcher fired to first, the hard throw in just the right line to hit Winters' diving body if Tater happened to miss it. Tater didn't, but he put a hard slap tag on Winters that Randy Joe appreciated.

Winters, ruled safe by the umpire, climbed angrily to his feet and again took a lead, but a little shorter than the previous one. Randy Joe went into his stretch, looked at first, then fired a fastball toward home plate. He sensed, more than saw, that Winters was running on the pitch. He knew the base runner was dead meat because Buck had a rifle arm and Winters hadn't gotten a good jump.

Sure enough, Oliver swung and missed and Buck's peg to second was right on target. Though Oliver was a lefthand hitter Cut was covering the bag because the infield was playing him to hit to the opposite field. Muddy didn't figure any of the Wichita hitters could turn on Randy Joe's fastball.

Cut took Buck's throw right off the top of the bag and moved his glove into position to tag the charging base runner. Dead duck that he was, Winters took the opportunity to rake his spikes down Cut's left leg. The second baseman's pants ripped and the blood flowed, but he held the ball.

Winters trotted off the field to tremendous applause and Cut lay on the field in pain, his leg torn and bleeding. The umpires came out, but no doctor. Gar brought the team's first aid kit and he and Randy Joe bandaged Cut's leg.

"You able to play?" Muddy asked his second baseman.

Cut grinned through the pain. "Sho' is...long as Randy Joe don't lets'im hit de ball too far to either side o' me."

Randy Joe smiled and said, "You've got it, Cut."

Cal Oliver became a quick *K,* striking out on two more fastballs that had popped into Buck's mitt by the time the hitter got his bat over the plate. That brought first baseman Jack Jordan to the plate. He'd also walked in his first appearance.

Jordan was a stylish glove man around the bag and a good hitter. Just twenty-two and a Notre Dame graduate, the first baseman had been assigned to Wichita by the company he went to work for after getting his degree. In college he hadn't been considered professional caliber, but he was a late bloomer. He was hitting .350 for the Tornadoes, had decent power, usually made contact and could be counted on in the clutch. Major league scouts were taking a renewed interest in him.

If Randy Joe had known all this he might have been impressed. Since he didn't he struck Jordan out on three blazing fastballs.

In Jason's half of the fourth Muddy bounced out short to first, then Buck nailed an inside fastball for solid single to left. That brought left fielder Rooster Solomon to the plate.

Randy Joe couldn't understand why the man had been named Rooster, especially considering his muscular two hundred pound frame. Cut said it was because the San Antonio native strutted around like a banty rooster. He batted fifth in the order because he was a power hitter, but he always looked a little awkward at the plate and in the outfield. Again, looks could be deceiving. Rooster was the second fastest man on the team, next to Jackie Monk.

McDonald tried to jam him with a fastball and the left fielder did an inside out on him. He took the ball to right for a single and Buck chugged all the way to third. With the Longhorns mounting their most serious threat, chain-smoking Cooter Davis came to the plate.

The third baseman was the team's resident comedian. Slender and frog-like, Cooter didn't look like he could wield much of a stick, but he was a quality hitter. Cooter had grown up in Texarkana, on the Arkansas side, and had spent a couple of seasons in the Negro American League. He could read a pitcher better than he could read a book.

Cooter read McDonald pretty well and hit a rocket off him that should have been a base hit. Tornadoes shortstop Ed Beasley made a fantastic catch and turned it into a doubleplay.

Randy Joe had hoped for a little more rest, but he convinced himself that his arm and legs were not tired. He geared up to face the powerful fourth, fifth and sixth hitters in Wichita's lineup. Figuring economy was the best way to save himself, Randy Joe struck the trio out on nine pitches, all fastballs. He just threw for the middle of the plate and let the hop on his fastball do the rest.

Tommy McGuire shook his head in dismay and said, "Unbelievable. He has ten strikeouts in four innings and his arm oughta to be ready to fall off. He's got no business pitchin' today."

Slap Peterson laughed. "According to my figures he has fifty-three strikeouts in the twenty-four tournament innings he's pitched. And he's given up just three hits and no runs."

"Yeah...McDonald's been impressive, but nothing compared with that. This kid's in a class all by himself."

In the Wichita dugout manager Dobie Cox was thinking the

same thing. He looked for signs of weariness in Randy Joe, but couldn't find any. He's tired, Cox thought, but he won't even admit it to himself.

The Tornadoes manager loved great pitching, especially pitchers who would suck it up and never give in to a hitter. Randy Joe Keegan was that kind of pitcher and Cox had nothing but respect for him. He had nothing but disdain for the action of his own player, Reggie Rivers, who'd tried to hurt the young pitcher by banging into his ribs.

Cox, obviously, couldn't be open about it, but was eagerly anticipating how Randy Joe would pitch to Rivers in the bottom of the fifth. He figured the second baseman would be approaching the plate with fear and trepidation. He couldn't blame him. Whatever happened to Rivers was no more than he deserved. The Wichita manager had built up a healthy dose of respect for Randy Joe Keegan and his teammates. Never figured I'd respect a bunch of niggers, Cox thought, but these guys know how to play the game.

Jackie Monk was the first hitter for the Longhorns in the top of the fifth. Randy Joe had really grown to appreciate the right fielder when he'd gotten involved in the reading lessons with Gar. The tall, angular Jackie was like a speeding bullet on the basepaths and in the outfield. He took certain hits away from opponents with regularity and needed only the slightest hesitation from an infielder to beat out a normally routine grounder.

Born and raised a little south of Little Rock, Arkansas, Jackie was the oldest of ten kids born to sharecropper parents. He'd left home at sixteen to pursue a different life and dream, but it had been hard sledding all the way. He was now twenty-four and took whatever work he could find, wherever he could find it, between baseball seasons.

Dobie Cox had seen Jackie play enough to realize the danger his speed represented, what it could mean if he got on base. He had his infielders edge in a little, which opened some holes. But the Wichita manager knew that when he compensated for the hitter's speed he had to give up something.

Sure enough, Jackie chopped one of McDonald's pitches down the third base line, which would have been a hit if Lewis

Murphy hadn't been playing a little in front of the bag. Tater Green then came to the plate and tapped out second to first.

That brought Randy Joe to the batter's box and Cox didn't have any idea as to how McDonald should pitch to him. The kid, obviously, was seeing the ball about as well as any hitter could. Cox figured the best thing for McDonald to do was throw it toward the plate and just hope Randy Joe hit it to one of his infielders or outfielders.

McDonald was still smarting with indignation that his pitching opponent had chosen to bat lefthanded against him. At the same time he was thinking about the third inning when Randy Joe's rocket up the middle almost curled his toes. The big lefthanded pitcher knew what he had to do, knew that he had to drive the hitter back from the plate to keep the respect of his teammates.

So he came hard inside, a fastball that forced his pitching opponent to fall backward and sprawl in the dirt. What shocked McDonald was that Randy Joe came up off the dirt grinning and exchanging banter with his teammates in the dugout. It was not the reaction McDonald expected. It bothered Tornadoes catcher Joe Bartosh, too.

Bartosh growled, "Better be ready to duck again."

Randy Joe laughed. "If I walk I'm just gonna make you look bad. I'm gonna steal second and third."

"Just try it," the catcher warned.

"I will," Randy Joe guaranteed. "And by the way, Joe, I threw three right down the gut for you. Are you gonna just keep striking out or are you gonna hit somethin'?"

Bartosh's inability to hit Randy Joe's fastball, the fear that the young pitcher's speed had instilled in him, angered the big catcher. He called time and went to the mound to confer with McDonald.

"What's up?" the big lefthander asked.

"I want you to hit this sonofabitch."

The conference on the mound brought Dobie Cox out of the dugout to join his pitcher and catcher. "Anything wrong, Mark?"

"Naw... Joe just wants me to nail the little sonofabitch."

"Yeah," Cox said. "Well, Joe, you said yourself this kid's a little crazy. You hit him and you're playin' right into his hands.

The top of their order's comin' up, you know. Besides, you hit him and he's liable to come after you when you're at bat. You wanna take the chance of being able to get out of the way of his fastball?"

Bartosh lied, "I ain't afraid of him."

Cox shrugged his shoulders. "All right...you guys do what you want. Just remember there's no score in this game and one run might win it."

The manager returned to the dugout and McDonald said, "He's right. One run could win this game. Let's not put anybody on base if we don't have to. If somebody gets on, let's make'im hit his way on."

Bartosh was glad the pitcher made the suggestion. He didn't want to be the one to back down. "Okay, but strike the little bastard out."

McDonald didn't need the admonition. In all the games he'd ever pitched, he'd never wanted a strikeout more. Keegan, he thought, hit my curveball last time. I'll see if he can catch up to my fastball.

The big lefthander let loose with his best hard one, a pitch that tailed inside. Randy Joe turned on the pitch and drove a screaming liner to right. The ball ricocheted off the right field wall and Lucky Winters chased it down. By the time he got it back to the infield Randy Joe was standing on second.

Peewee Darthard came to the plate for the Longhorns and Randy Joe took his lead off second. McDonald's first pitch to the center fielder was an inside fastball. The next was a low curveball that Peewee tried to take downtown.

The split-second McDonald started toward the plate with the second pitch Randy Joe was sprinting toward third. Bartosh came up with the ball and fired to third, but too late to nail the runner who executed a perfect headfirst slide. Randy Joe got up grinning and signaled to Bartosh while the crowd booed.

Randy Joe's steal of third proved fruitless, however, when Peewee flied to center for the third out.

As Reggie Rivers got ready to face Randy Joe in the bottom of the fifth the rumbling among the crowd began to steadily crescendo. This was a knowledgeable baseball gathering and they remembered how Rivers had taken the cheap shot at Randy Joe in the second inning. They were also beginning to appreciate the competitiveness of the Longhorns pitcher, the fact that he couldn't be intimidated.

Rivers had exhibited a lot of phony bravado in front of his teammates in the dugout, but he was as nervous as a cat on a hot tin roof when he stepped to the plate. He'd never faced a pitcher with the velocity of a Randy Joe Keegan, or one who had made it so clear that he was in control.

As the second baseman set himself gingerly in the batter's box he was taken aback by the smile on Randy Joe's face. He had expected a scowl. Why was the crazy kid smiling? he asked himself.

Randy Joe's first pitch was behind Rivers' head, which had him diving across the plate instead of away from it. The second baseman could hear the crowd roaring, the boos that ricocheted around the stadium. He took consolation in the fact that they were for him, that the crowd was against the slender young pitcher on the mound.

But then Rivers had to step to the plate again. This time Randy Joe came with a fastball in the strike zone that tied the hitter up. He couldn't even swing. The pitch in the strike zone, however, provided Rivers with some relief. Maybe, he thought, the kid's going to try to strike me out. Maybe the pitch behind the head was going to be the extent of his retaliation.

Randy Joe's third pitch was another fastball that Rivers looked at for a strike. The second baseman was gaining confidence now. He was ready to swing at the next pitch. The problem was that he couldn't swing at the next pitch. It came hard and inside and chased him until it smashed against his ribs.

Allegedly tough Reggie Rivers went down in a heap, pain burning in his side like he'd been stamped with a branding iron. His teammates came to his aid, but there was no thought of rushing the mound and exacting some sort of frontier justice against Randy Joe Keegan. Rivers, his teammates knew, had set himself up for exactly what had happened.

Wichita manager Dobie Cox figured River's ribs were in no worse shape than Randy Joe's. Rivers, however, complaining of the intense pain, wanted to come out of the ball game. Cox guessed, rightfully, that it was because he didn't want to bat again.

Autry Hill went in to run for Rivers and to take over for him at second. Rivers' wife would be taking him to the hospital to have his ribs taped.

Shortstop Ed Beasley had watched the drama unfolding from the on-deck circle. It didn't make him anxious to step into the batter's box, but he was the kind of solid player who always did his best. Unlike Rivers, he played the game hard and clean.

Randy Joe threw Beasley nothing but heat. With the count one and two the shortstop hit a grounder to his counterpart. Cut took the toss from Muddy while crossing the second base bag and relayed to first for the doubleplay.

Randy Joe had been afraid Cut couldn't make the pivot at second after getting spiked in the leg, but hobbled as he was, the gutsy second baseman made the play flawlessly. Cut was one tough cookie, Randy Joe decided, the kind of guy anyone would be proud to have as a teammate.

Pitcher Mark McDonald was the next hitter for the Tornadoes. Randy Joe struck him out on three straight fastballs.

FORTY-ONE

Randy Joe was beat when he went into the Longhorns' dugout after the final out in the fifth inning. His uniform was soaked with sweat, dust still sticking to it from his slide in the first half of the inning. He got a cup of water and melted onto the bench.

"You okay?" Gar asked, sitting down beside him.

"Hot," Randy Joe admitted. "I bet I've lost ten or so pounds."

"You don't has it to lose, either," Gar said. "Now wid me ten pounds don't mean all dat much."

Skeeter and Pooh also came over and sat close to Randy Joe. "Now don't you go hurtin' yo' arm," Skeeter admonished. "My arm's hurtin' some, but I'm ready to throw. Jest don't go hurtin' yo'self 'cause dey's a lot o' games in yo' future."

"Dat's right," Pooh agreed. "Ain't none of us here wants you to mess yo'self up on our account. All us pitchers ready to throw."

"I know," Randy Joe said. "You guys have all pitched more than I did on the tour. You carried the team. I still have a little left."

"What you mean 'bout us pitchin' mo' dan you?" Gar asked. "You been carryin' de load, 'specially in dis tournament."

Randy Joe sipped water and replied, "Don't worry, Gar, I'm not gonna hurt my arm. I feel real loose and the heat helps. Hell, I feel so loose I can't even tell I've got an arm."

Cut led off the inning by banging a single to left, but limped noticeably in running to first. Muddy then came up and rapped a single to right. Because of the bad leg Cut stopped at second. Normally, he would have been able to make it to third on a hit to right.

That brought the ever dangerous Buck Frazier to the plate. Before leaving the on-deck circle he hollered over at Randy Joe, "You wanna make a bet on RBIs, too?"

Randy Joe laughed. "Five dollars...same rules."

Buck worked the count on McDonald to two and two, then hit a bullet that seemed destined for center field. New Tornadoes second baseman Autry Hill made a diving stab of the liner and flipped to Beasley on the second base bag. Cut tried to get back but was a dead duck.

Rooster Solomon came to the plate and promptly lined a single to left. Rooster and Muddy died on base when Cooter hit a long drive to center that was hauled in by Cal Oliver.

The Longhorns were tagging McDonald's pitches, three hits in the inning, but had fallen victim to a great defensive play. The Jason team had eight hits in six innings, but to McDonald's credit he hadn't walked a single batter and had made good pitches at the right time.

Randy Joe, on the other hand, had walked two and hit three. But in five innings of pitching he hadn't given up a hit.

Lucky Winters, the guy who'd spiked Cut, was first up for the Tornadoes in the sixth. Cut came up and told Randy Joe, "Put dat man on first fo' me, okay? I wants him to try to steal again."

It wasn't good baseball and Randy Joe knew it. If Muddy had known what Cut had asked him to do he'd have been pissed. But Randy Joe figured Cut deserved a chance to get even with Winters. So he walked the right fielder on four straight pitches. He did whiz them in close enough to make Winters nervous, which didn't take much since he'd hit him on both his previous trips to the plate.

As Winters was trotting toward first Randy Joe went toward him and asked, "You got balls enough to try to steal second again?"

It was like throwing down the gauntlet. Winters' manhood was being challenged and he had to respond. Cut was also motioning to Winters to come on down to second.

The crowd loved it. The game was a tense pitcher's battle, but the individual battles added spice to it.

Randy Joe didn't throw a pitchout. With his fastball and Buck's arm it wasn't necessary. He went into the stretch, checked the runner at first, then buzzed one under Cal Oliver's chin. Buck did the rest.

Winters was off and running with the pitch, his intent to carve up Cut's other leg. The little second baseman took Buck's throw just on the first base side of the bag, deftly avoided the hard, spikes up slide by Winters and tagged him in the face.

Blood spurted from Winter's nose and the Tornadoes dugout emptied to aid their fallen comrade, who was lying on the ground in a semi-conscious state. Battle lines were drawn and Longhorns and Tornadoes players milled around in an angry mood. Thanks to the umpires and Wichita manager Dobie Cox no blows were thrown.

With a towel and some ice Winters was able to stop his nose from bleeding. He was helped off the field by a couple of his teammates, but Randy Joe knew the Wichita right fielder wasn't through for the day. Winters was going to keep on playing. He could appreciate a guy like that. All the Longhorns players could.

Cal Oliver grounded to third and Cooter threw him out easily. Then Jack Jordan popped to third for the final out of the inning.

After six completed innings the Tornadoes still didn't have a hit, but the sixth was the first inning in which Randy Joe hadn't recorded a strikeout. There was optimism in the Wichita dugout that he was finally running out of gas.

In the Longhorns half of the seventh Cooter ripped a solid single to left. Then Jackie Monk beat out a slow roller to third. Runners on first and second, nobody out, and Tater Green at the plate. The Longhorns first baseman dropped a perfect sacrifice bunt down the first base line that moved the runners to second and third.

That brought Randy Joe Keegan to the plate and an uneasy murmuring among the crowd. Then Dobie Cox did something he'd never done in his managing career. He ordered the Longhorns pitcher, the number nine hitter, walked to load the bases. Normally in such a situation he would have counted on his pitcher to strike out the opposing pitcher. But he wasn't sure anyone could strike Keegan out and he needed to set up the possible doubleplay. He guessed McDonald would be more comfortable trying to make a right pitch to Jason leadoff hitter Peewee Darthard than to Randy Joe.

Cox's move proved to be the right one. Peewee hit a line shot that was speared by third baseman Lewis Murphy. He wasn't able to turn the doubleplay, but the runners had to hold. Then Cut Brown flied to left to end the threat.

In the Wichita half of the inning there was more evidence that Randy Joe was running out of gas, though the hitters still couldn't turn on his fastball. Power hitting Greg Braddock and Lewis Murphy flied to right. In between Joe Bartosh stuck out, but Cox knew the young pitcher had his catcher so buffaloed that he would have gone down on strikes if Randy Joe had just been throwing him batting practice pitches.

"What do you think?" Slap Peterson asked Tommy McGuire.

"Think he's runnin' outta gas?"

"Maybe," McGuire replied, "but he's still got a no-hitter. I know damn well McDonald's runnin' on empty."

Dobie Cox felt the same way. He just wanted to get one more inning out of his starter, then pinch hit for him in the bottom of the inning. But the Longhorns made his decision a little scary.

McDonald got Muddy Tate on a tall fly to left and Buck on a called third strike that the big catcher argued. But then Rooster got his third single of the day and Cooter followed with his second hit. Jackie Monk then came through with a drag bunt single down the first base line that loaded the bases.

Longhorns first baseman Tater Green, who hadn't had any luck in the hitting department all day, lined hard to the shortstop.

"Can you believe it?" McGuire asked Peterson. "McDonald gives up thirteen hits in eight innings but no runs."

Peterson said, "Says a lot for control. He didn't walk anybody."

"His luck may have outweighed his control today. But I'd say we're gettin' to the critical stage for the Keegan kid."

Peterson agreed. "I don't think he can hold'em much longer."

None of the Longhorns had mentioned to Randy Joe that he had a no-hitter going, hoping not to jinx him. Some of the more verbose fans, though, were doing everything in their power to put the hex on him.

As he trudged out to the mound for the eighth inning he wasn't really concerned about *no-hitting* the Tornadoes. All he wanted to do was survive, to hold Wichita until his team could score a run. And to keep the Tornadoes from getting one. All day, he thought, his team had been so close to victory. But McDonald and the Tornadoes defense kept snatching it away. They were playing one helluva game.

Feeling the end was near, that his team would surely get a run in the ninth, Randy Joe sucked it up and called on some inner strength. Leadoff man for the Tornadoes in the bottom of the eighth was Autry Hill, who'd taken Reggie Rivers spot. Hill was a great fielder but had never frightened anyone with his hitting prowess. He was twenty-five and in his college days had been a journeyman player at Kansas State. With the Tornadoes he had proven himself to be an outstanding utility man.

Going to his curveball, Randy Joe struck Hill out. That brought Ed Beasley to the plate. The shortstop had been a strikeout victim twice and had hit into a doubleplay. Mixing in a couple of fastballs with his hook, Randy Joe put a *K* beside Beasley's name for a third time.

That brought second string catcher Williard Bryant to the batter's box, pinch hitting for McDonald. Bryant was a big ol' boy with a big swing, but his bat speed didn't match up to Randy Joe's velocity. He went down on strikes.

In the stands Tommy McGuire laughed. "Just when I think he's had it the kid strikes out the side."

Slap Peterson grinned. "That's fifteen strikeouts and...can I say it...no hits."

The new hurler for Wichita was Doyle Settle, a five-foot, nine inch righthander built like a fireplug. The wide-bodied pitcher looked more like a football player, but had the reputation of being able to bring it. His curve wasn't much, but he had a big league fastball. Settle was twenty-three and a wheat farmer.

Settle made the mistake of starting Randy Joe off with a fastball, which the young pitcher crushed. The ball chased center fielder Cal Oliver all the way to the wall. It ricocheted off the top of the fence and went bounding toward left field, Oliver in pursuit.

Randy Joe chugged around first base and then motored around second. As he reached third Muddy was still windmilling his arm so he headed for home. Oliver had finally gotten the ball to the cutoff man, shortstop Ed Beasley, who relayed the ball toward catcher Joe Bartosh.

As Randy Joe kicked it into overdrive coming down the third base line he saw that Bartosh was blocking the plate. He also sensed the ball was en route to the big catcher's mitt. He knew a collision was inevitable, knew it was his only chance to reach the plate. The ball reached Bartosh's mitt at the same split-second Randy Joe smashed into the catcher.

They went tumbling, the dust flying. The crowd was roaring and Randy Joe looked up to see the umpire's unmistakable signal. He was out. Bartosh had held the ball.

Randy Joe was first up off the ground. He reached down a hand to help the big catcher to his feet. Bartosh didn't immediately take the extended hand, but then Randy Joe grinned and said, "Helluva play."

Bartosh took his hand, grinned and said, "Thanks. Helluva hit."

FORTY-TWO

When Randy Joe took the mound to pitch the bottom half of the ninth the mood of the crowd had changed. At least half of the stadium's capacity crowd was now rooting for the slender kid to get his no-hitter. There had never been a no-hitter thrown in the tournament and some of the people were ready to see some history.

A person who wasn't interested in seeing such history or a Longhorns victory was tournament promoter Basil McMurrey. He wanted the game to end. He wanted Wichita to win. He made that clear in no uncertain terms when talking to plate umpire Morris Mead following the top half of the ninth. After Randy Joe had been thrown out at the plate, Peewee Darthard had popped to second and Cut Brown had flied to right.

Mead was not a bad umpire, but he was a homer. There was no doubt about where his sympathies lay and he called the game accordingly. He wasn't overt about it, just gave any real close call to Wichita.

In the championship game, however, with Randy Joe pitching, he hadn't been able to give the home team much. The kid was just too damn good. The play at the plate had been close and the Keegan kid might have gotten a foot on it before being tagged by Bartosh, but in Mead's eyes a tie always went to the home team.

Now McMurrey, who not only ran the tournament but was in charge of semi-pro league games throughout the baseball season, was telling him it was time to put the screws to Randy Joe Keegan and the Longhorns. And the money McMurrey paid him for umpiring was substantial over the course of a season.

Mead's fulltime job was that of a postal worker and he had no love for colored people. However, from his position behind the catcher he'd grown to love watching Randy Joe Keegan pitch. He'd never before seen such velocity on a ball, nor a breaking ball quite like the one the kid threw. In his mind Mead had already envisioned Randy Joe going a long way in baseball. In the years to come, when Randy Joe was famous, Mead was looking forward to telling people that he'd once called balls and strikes when Keegan was pitching.

Now McMurrey was telling him to make the difference in the game, to be responsible for its outcome. It was being left up to him to take the no- hitter away from the kid and the game away from the Longhorns. Mead knew that Wichita manager Dobie Cox or his team found out what McMurrey had asked of him to do, they'd be pissed. Cox was a straight arrow.

Mead's battle with his conscience didn't last all that long. The money was more important than fairness. After all, life wasn't fair.

The crowd noise was hovering at a low rumble when Lucky Winters stepped to the plate to lead off in the bottom of the ninth. The right fielder's nose was swollen so that his eyes were slits in his face. Ordinarily, Randy Joe, who had a strange sense of humor anyway, might have found Winters' appearance funny. But for the moment he was too weary to see him as anything other than another obstacle to be overcome. There wouldn't be any cuteness on his part in this inning. Again, he just wanted to survive it, to give his teammates a chance to score in the tenth.

Randy Joe's memory bank told him that in Winter's three trips to the plate he'd hit him twice, walked him once. That wasn't going to happen this inning. If Winters got on base it would be because he hit his way on.

The young righthander's first pitch was a blazing fastball that ripped through the strike zone.

"Ball one."

Randy Joe couldn't believe the call. Neither could Buck. Nor could the crowd, its murmurs of disbelief falling to a low roar. Winters just thanked his lucky stars for the gift. He knew it was a strike, but also a pitch that he couldn't handle.

Randy Joe figured the ump had just missed one. It wasn't the first time and it sure wouldn't be the last. In fact, he thought up until that pitch the guy had called a good game.

The young pitcher came again with the heat, making a sonic boom through the strike zone.

"Ball two!"

Again, a portion of the crowd showed its displeasure while others expressed jubilation. Winters looked at the umpire a bit dismayed and Buck called time and walked to the mound. The catcher could see Randy Joe was steaming so he tried to calm him. "Jest take it easy. We both know de pitches was strikes."

"Us knowin' it ain't helping things," Randy Joe said, angrily. "If the guy wants to call a ball I might as well throw one. Don't raise your mitt on this one, Buck."

The big catcher grinned and said, "You know how hard it is fo' me to catch de high pitch."

This time Randy Joe reached down for something extra on his fastball and prayed for the control to put it where he wanted. The ball exploded out of his hand like a bullet in flight, nothing but a blur in the bright Kansas sunshine. The pitch was so fast that Mead could hardly see it. But he had confidence it would be stopped by the catcher.

It wasn't.

The ball hit Mead's mask with what seemed like the force of a cannon ball, sending the umpire reeling backward. Suddenly, something inside his head was spinning and he could feel the ground supporting his back. When he looked up he saw faces surrounding him and heard the noise of a crowd. It was like he'd been hit by Rocky Marciano.

He saw the Keegan kid standing above him, heard him ask

with false concern, "You okay, ump?"

Of course I'm not okay, he thought. You could have killed me.

Wichita manager Dobie Cox was also standing above him and saying to the other umpires, "He's had his bell rung. One of you other guys will have to call balls and strikes."

Mead, protesting, got to his feet and said he was all right, but his colleagues wouldn't listen. The problem, he quickly surmised, was that none of the other three were hometown umpires. McMurrey would not be able to influence them and the game might not end the way the promoter wanted.

The other umpires, after getting assurances that he was all right, sent Mead to handle the third base umpiring chores. His head clear now, Mead was relatively sure that Randy Joe Keegan had sent him a message. Thinking that might be the case, he shuddered and gave thanks that he was going to third. Maybe McMurrey wouldn't blame him if the game didn't go the way he wanted.

With three balls and no strikes, Lucky Winters was definitely going to make Randy Joe throw a couple of strikes before even thinking about swinging. The young pitcher obliged, two whistling fastballs about which there was no doubt.

Winters got ready for another fastball but Randy Joe crossed him up. It was a changeup that had the right fielder swinging before the ball reached the plate.

The crowd became increasingly excited as Cal Oliver stepped to the plate. He had struck out once, walked and grounded out. Oliver was a good contact hitter. Randy Joe started him off with a curveball strike, then hit the outside corner with a tailing fastball. Oliver didn't bite on another fastball just off the corner. Then the young pitcher came in with a hard slider on the lefthand hitter's wrists that Oliver couldn't handle.

The official scorer put another *K* beside Oliver's name and the crowd noise intensified. It was up to Jack Jordan, third man in Wichita's batting lineup and another quality hitter. In his previous at bats Jordan had struck out once, walked and grounded out. Jordan fouled off a couple of curveballs that nipped at the outside corner. Then Randy Joe exploded a fastball on the inside corner that the first baseman could only watch.

The crowd, some reluctantly, stood to its feet and gave Randy Joe Keegan an ovation as he left the mound. In nine innings he'd given up no hits, struck out eighteen, hit three and walked three. In twenty-nine innings of tournament pitching he'd given up just three hits, no runs, and had struck out sixty-one.

Wichita manager Dobie Cox and his team were among those who openly applauded Randy Joe's effort. In all the years of the tournament, no pitcher had ever been so dominant.

In the stands Tommy McGuire said under his breath, "Take him out now...take him out."

It was an opinion shared by Bernice Keegan. "Randy Joe's tired. He doesn't need to go out there again."

"I agree," Randy Joe's dad said, "but you know he's not comin' out of the game until he wins it or loses it. They'd have to drag him off the mound."

Gretchen said, "I can't stand that he might lose this game. What would that do to him?"

"I don't know," Keegan said. "I honestly don't know. He's not a good loser."

"Will you two be quiet?" Max Turner said, laughing. "Randy Joe's not gonna lose this game. Simmy's team ain't gonna lose. Hell, they've got Wichita right where they want'em."

In the Longhorns dugout, amid congratulations from his teammates, Randy Joe said, "It's not a no-hitter until the game's over. We need to score a run and I need to get 'em out one more time."

Maybe it was a matter of pressing. Whatever the reason, Muddy, Buck and Rooster couldn't get anything started against Tornadoes pitcher Doyle Settle. A popout, groundout and flyout put the Longhorns back in the field for the bottom of the tenth.

Greg Braddock was first up for Wichita in the tenth. Though he'd struck the big left fielder out twice, Randy Joe knew he was a hitter. He also knew his fastball was losing some of its velocity and hop. That meant more dependence on the curveball.

Randy Joe got two curveball strikes on Braddock, then tried to sneak a fastball past him. The big left fielder got some wood on the ball and dumped a single to right.

There was almost a unified sigh of relief from the crowd. The no-hit effort had finally ended. People began to rise to their feet in staggered groups to applaud his effort. He doffed his cap, but his primary concern was the the next hitter, Joe Bartosh.

The big Wichita catcher had struck out three straight times, but this time he dumped a perfect bunt down the third base line. Randy Joe threw him out but Braddock chugged into second.

Wichita third baseman Lewis Murphy had struck out a couple of times, then flied to right. He was a power hitter, but also capable of just making contact. Murphy was determined. He wasn't planning to go for the downs, just wanted a single.

Randy Joe worked on Murphy with curveballs away. He got a couple of strikes on the big third baseman, then Murphy got the end of his bat on a pitch. The ball eluded Cut's leap and felt softly in front of right fielder Jackie Monk, who was charging it with his world class speed.

Braddock rounded third and headed for home and Jackie unleashed a strike to Buck. A collision was assured. Braddock barreled into Buck and they went down in a rolling pile of arms and legs. Buck came up grinning, grasping the baseball firmly in his hand. Braddock was out.

Tornadoes second baseman Autry Hill then tapped a roller to Cut. He tossed to Tater to end the inning.

In the top of the eleventh Cooter Davis singled to center, Jackie Monk lined out to short and Tater Green popped to second. That brought Randy Joe to the plate. Wichita pitcher Doyle Settle was thinking about almost giving up an inside the park home run to his pitching opponent in the ninth. Whether or not that had anything to do with his inability to get the ball over the plate he didn't know. But for whatever reason he walked Randy Joe on four straight pitches.

Trying to get something going, Muddy had Cooter and Randy Joe execute a double steal. It was successful, but Peewee then flied out to end the inning.

Randy Joe wasn't sure he could make it through the eleventh. He was no longer battling just the heat, dehydration and the pain in his ribs but a severe headache as well. He remembered the way he'd felt when he pitched his first game for the Longhorns, the thirteen-inning game. He hoped this one didn't send him to the hospital.

Randy Joe also wasn't sure how many times he could reach down for something extra, but he told himself that he could do it at least one more time. Wichita shortstop Ed Beasley was the victim of the young pitcher's renewed determination. Randy Joe got a curveball strike on the hitter, then stamped him out with two fastballs whose velocity was reminiscent of what he had in the first inning.

Beasley went back to the dugout talking to himself and manager Dobie Cox shook his head in amazement. He had thought Randy Joe was on the ropes, that the kid had lost his zip. What do I know? he thought.

Reserve outfielder Bill Knight was sent to the plate to pinch hit for pitcher Doyle Settle. In three innings of pitching Settle had done a decent job, allowing no runs and two hits. But he wasn't much of a hitter and Cox needed someone on base.

Knight was six-three, a hundred and eighty pounds. He was a lefthand streak hitter. On this day he would begin no streak. Three times Randy Joe came at him with the heater and Knight went meekly back to the dugout. "Damnedest fastball I've ever seen," he muttered.

Lucky Winters, who'd struck out in his last plate appearance, got the same fastball treatment as Knight. The right fielder, like a lot of others in the Wichita dugout, had thought Randy Joe was fading. But Winters was ready to testify that the fastballs from Randy Joe he saw in the eleventh inning were like those he'd seen in the first.

Slap Peterson said to Tommy McGuire, "Just when you think he's had it he has an inning like that."

"Yeah, but he can't have any more left in him."

Lou Comer, another hard throwing righthander. was Wichita's new pitcher. He was an inch short of six-feet, weighed a hundred and ninety pounds, and relied on his fastball. He also had a pretty good curve and changeup. He'd watched the Longhorns hitters enough to know that his best bet was the curveball or changeup.

Using his curveball and change almost exclusively, his

fastball as a waste pitch, Comer got Cut to fly to center and Muddy to line to second. Then he hung a curve and Buck rattled the left field fence. He went into second standing. Comer got a couple of strikes on Rooster, then completely baffled him with a change to register his first *K*.

Simmy and Zeke were worried about Randy Joe's arm. The team owner didn't want to be responsible for the kid hurting himself. He went down to the Longhorns dugout and discussed his concern with Muddy, who was plenty worried about it himself.

"He's done pitched thirty innings in fo' days," Simmy said. "Ask him if he want you to take'im out."

Muddy said, "I been askin' him ever' innin'. He says he ain't comin' out 'til we wins."

Simmy could understand and appreciate the tenacity of the young pitcher. He liked to think he was the same way when he was young and pitching on sandlot fields at every opportunity. He also knew there were times when you didn't force an issue. This was one of those times. So he and Zeke went back to their seats.

In the twelveth Randy Joe felt groggy. He was seeing spots before his eyes. He hated the headache, the feeling that his body was disintegrating. He called on all the reserve strength he could muster.

Center fielder Cal Oliver saw a good fastball and dandy curve before grounding out second to first on a change. First baseman Jack Jordan looked at two sinking fastballs on the outside corner before grounding out third to first on a breaking ball.

That brought Greg Braddock to the plate. In the tenth Braddock had broken up Randy Joe's no-hitter with a single, had gone to second on a sacrifice, then been cut down at the plate trying to score on a single to right. Randy Joe knew Braddock had renewed confidence and would try to establish that the plate belonged to him.

He came inside with a fastball that drove the big righthand hitter back, then dazzled him with some curveballs. He went down swinging.

"Dis sho' reminds me o' dat first game you pitched fo' us," Cooter said in the dugout.

Randy Joe, who looked and felt like death warmed over, sipped some water from a cup, smiled, and said, "I hope it ends the same way. This is the thirteenth inning and we beat'em in the thirteenth. Aren't you up first, Cooter?"

"Sho' is."

"Well, damn it, grab a handful of dirt off ol' Squirrel's grave and get a hit."

Cooter obliged, rifling a single to center for his fourth hit of the game. Jackie Monk bunted and almost beat it out. His sacrifice moved Cooter to second. Tater then grounded out second to first, moving Cooter to third.

That brought Randy Joe to the plate with the opportunity to drive in the go ahead run. Those who'd seen the game against Lake Charles were having flashbacks to what Randy Joe had done then, but Tornadoes manager Dobie Cox wouldn't let it happen in Wichita. Again, going against the book, he ordered his pitcher to walk the hitter.

Then, with runners at first and third, Peewee Darthard hit a long drive to center that Cal Oliver chased down and caught at the wall for the third out.

In the bottom of the thirteenth Wichita's Joe Bartosh found a pitch to his liking and drove it off the wall in right center for a double. It was the catcher's first hit of the game and it came off a good curveball. Randy Joe acknowledged Bartosh's accomplishment with a silent salute that the big catcher understood. At first he had detested the young pitcher, but as the game had progressed Bartosh's appreciation for Randy Joe's ability had increased. He was glad to be on the same field with the kid and his teammates. They all knew how to play the game.

Lewis Murphy, who had poked a single to right in his previous plate appearance that had almost scored Greg Braddock, now stood in the batter's box with a chance to stroke the hit that would win the game. The third baseman liked the position he was in and liked his chances. He'd had a lot of game winning hits in his baseball career. He'd never, however, faced a pitcher with more bulldog tenacity than Randy Joe

Keegan. The kid kept sucking it up and reaching for something extra.

He did it again, much to the chagrin of all those in the Tornadoes dugout. Randy Joe set Murphy up with three blazing fastballs, then for a third strike had him swinging weakly at a hard-breaking curve.

Autry Hill and Ed Beasley also fell victim to Randy Joe's sudden burst of energy, both striking out. But as Randy Joe once more walked back to the Longhorns dugout he wasn't sure just how long he could keep the adrenalin flowing. There had to be an end to it. He just wished there would be an end to his headache, which was making him feel dizzier by the moment.

In the top of the fourteenth Cut Brown punched a single to center, but was out on the front end of a doubleplay when Muddy hit a hard grounder to short. Buck and Rooster then hit back to back singles off Comer, which brought Cooter to the plate. The third baseman had four consecutive hits, but the Wichita pitcher reached for a little extra himself and struck Cooter out.

"Unbelievable," Max Turner said. "The Longhorns have twenty hits and no runs. Those Wichita pitchers just don't give up any bases on balls and they get the doubleplay when they need it."

R.M. Keegan grinned. "I hope Randy Joe's takin' notes...about the bases on balls I mean. Here he's given up just three hits, struck out twenty-five and the game's even. It's hard to understand baseball. I guess the unpredictability is what makes it a great game."

"I don't know about all baseball games, but this is one damn great game," Turner agreed.

"Look at Randy Joe," Bernice said, her interest different than theirs. "He looks like he's going to pass out. He's sick."

Concerned, Gretchen asked, "Do you really think so, Mrs. Keegan?"

Randy Joe's dad laughed, but not with his usual good humor. "He's tired, Bernice...that's all. Hell, he oughta be tired. In five days he's pitched thirty-three innings."

Randy Joe was tired, but figured he'd have no trouble disposing of reserve catcher Lou Page who was pinch hitting for pitcher Lou Comer. Wichita, he guessed, had a good bench and bullpen. They kept parading out pinch hitters and new pitchers.

For some reason Randy Joe went wild in the fourteenth. He walked the pinch hitter on four pitches. Lucky Winters worked the count to three and one before hitting a grounder to third. Cooter scooped the ball and fired to Cut at second to get the lead runner. It was hit too slowly to get the doupleplay.

Sensing Randy Joe was having difficulty with his control, Dobie Cox told his next hitter, Cal Oliver, to exercise a little patience. Then with runners at second and first, one out and the big sticks coming up, the crowd sensed the game was all but over. Dobie Cox didn't feel the same way. He had discovered how tough the kid on the mound could be with the game on the line.

But then Randy Joe walked first baseman Jack Jordan, bringing cleanup hitter Greg Braddock to the plate. There had been an identical bases-loaded situation in the first inning and the young pitcher had struck out the big power hitter. Could it happen again?

Muddy called time and went to the mound to confer with Randy Joe. He was joined by Buck and the other infielders. "You done fo'?" the manager asked.

Randy Joe smiled, weakly. "To tell the truth, Muddy, I've been done for since the ninth inning...when I was thrown out tryin' to stretch that triple into a home run. But if you're askin' me if I'm ready to give up the answer is no. I wanna pitch to this guy. I think I can get him out. But if you guys want someone else to pitch, I understand."

They all exchanged glances and Cut summed it up for all of them. "You done brought us dis far, Randy Joe, and far as I'm concerned you kin takes us de rest o' de way. Jest make dat big man hit it to me."

Randy Joe worked the count to two and two on Braddock and then threw him a down and away curveball. It was a great pitch, but somehow the big leftfielder got his bat on it. The ball was a scorcher up the middle that had base hit written all over it.

Hobbled as he was, Cut made a diving stop of the ball and flipped to Muddy at second. The shortstops's throw to first got

Braddock by a half step to complete the doubleplay.

New pitcher for the Tornadoes was a stylish righthander named Wayne Meachum, a junior from Louisiana State University. Meachum had a good curveball, great control and a uniform that didn't have a bit of sweat or dirt on it. He acted like a guy who sweated only on command.

Jackie Monk and Tater Green were quickly victimized by Meachum's curveball, both striking out. That brought Randy Joe to the plate and forced a decision by Wichita manager Dobie Cox. In Randy Joe's two previous at bats, with runners on base, Cox had ordered his pitcher to walk him. With no one on base the Tornadoes manager wanted Meachum pitch to his mound opponent.

Meachum, cocky and sure of himself, got a curveball on the inside corner. Randy Joe turned on it and drove it over the right field wall.

"Foul ball!" the ump hollered.

But not by much.

Meachum viewed the hitter with a little more concern. He'd wanted the curve on the outside corner. The pitch had just gotten away from him. This time the Wichita pitcher got the ball where he wanted it and the hitter still got good wood on it, driving it to the opposite field and right down the line.

It was going, going...

"Foul ball!" third base umpire Morris Mead signaled.

The partisan crowd roared its approval, causing the home plate umpire to consider overruling Mead on the call. It was close, but he was pretty sure the ball was fair. The Longhorns players showed their disgust with the call. Dobie Cox also thought the ball was fair.

Tournament promoter Basil McMurrey made a mental note that Morris Mead was a man to be trusted, if the money was right.

After hitting the ball Randy Joe had started running hard for first, so from his angle he couldn't be sure about the low liner being fair or foul. He just knew he didn't have the energy to argue the call. His head had been hurting so much that he hadn't been paying much attention to his aching ribs. The two home run cuts brought them back to his attention. The pain in his side was intense.

Meachum was a smart young man. He considered the fact that Randy Joe had hit two good curveballs over the fence, one of which was an almost perfect pitch. He pitched carefully enough to walk his mound opponent, then got Peewee Darthard on strikes.

"The Meachum kid looks pretty good," Tommy McGuire said.

"Yeah," Slap Peterson agreed, "but I hear he wants to go to law school. He'll be too old to learn after all that schooling."

In the bottom of the fifteenth Joe Bartosh, Lewis Murphy and Autry Hill were the scheduled hitters for the Tornadoes. Bartosh went to the plate wanting to be patient, thinking Randy Joe might exhibit the same wildness he had in the previous inning.

Randy Joe's side was on fire, the pain in his head intense. Suck it up, he told himself. Don't be a damn sissy. His angry discussion with himself seemed to have put juice in his arm. Bartosh looked at some fastballs and curves he couldn't believe. After a brief appearance with a bat in his hand he sat back down in the dugout with another *K* beside his name.

Murphy and Hill fared no better, both going down on strikes.

In the top half of the sixteenth Meachum set the Longhorns down in order. Cut grounded out short to first, Muddy struck out and Buck flied to center.

In the Tornadoes half of the inning shortstop Ed Beasley grounded out to his counterpart, Meachum struck out and Lucky Winters popped to third. Normally, Wichita manager Dobie Cox would have pinch hit for Meachum, but he liked the way he was pitching and wanted to keep him in the game. He figured on winning or losing the game with the righthander.

Meachum seemed more than up to the task. In the top of the seventeenth Rooster Solomon struck out, Cooter Davis grounded out short to first and Jackie Monk grounded out second to first.

Cal Oliver was first up for the Tornadoes in their half of the seventeenth. He hit a grounder down the third base line that the normally sure handed Cooter misplayed. It was the first error of the game, somewhat surprising for a game of such intensity.

First baseman Jack Jordan did what everyone in the stadium

expected. He laid down a sacrifice bunt that moved Oliver to second. That brought big Greg Braddock back to the plate.

Randy Joe worked away from the big left fielder, getting two strikes with curveballs on the corner. Then he busted a fastball inside that Braddock got only the handle of his bat on. The ball looked like a looping foul over third, but it hit close to the line and umpire Morris Mead called it a fair ball.

Rooster, charging hard from deep left field, reached the ball quickly enough to keep Oliver from going beyond third. Randy Joe, irate over the call, charged Morris and had to be restrained by Muddy and Cooter. Even the jubilant Tornadoes players felt uncomfortable about the umpire's call.

Finally, after a battle of words, an angry Randy Joe Keegan was back on the mound, filled with resolve to nail the next two Wichita hitters and leave the runners stranded on base.

He got catcher Joe Bartosh on strikes, then ran the count to two and two on third baseman Lewis Murphy. The game ended on an anticlimactic note when Murphy dropped a dying quail single to right.

EPILOGUE

Disappointment can't be measured in tears or the lack of them, nor can an instance of heartbreak or despair be totally forgotten with the passing of time. And for the committed athlete there are no moral victories, no comfort in those trite words, *"It's not whether you win or lose, but how you play the game."*

For Randy Joe Keegan the loss in Wichita overshadowed his other pitching victories of that summer.

During the summer he had gained considerable insight into what it was like to be a black man in America. This new awareness, the friendships he developed with the other Longhorns players, would shape his attitude about race for years to come.

However, when one is seventeen and harboring a dream of major league greatness, no newly acquired perception, no enhancement of learning and clear-sightedness about the human condition can compensate for losing. For Randy Joe Keegan everything was secondary to winning.

It was, perhaps, the anticlimactic way in which the tournament championship game had slipped away that tormented him most. The accolades of his teammates, the stated respect of the victors regarding his ability, none of it meant anything to him.

There was no consolation in losing, even if people were saying it was the greatest pitching performance they had ever witnessed.

In sixteen and two-third innings of the championship game Randy Joe Keegan had given up one unearned run, allowed five hits, one of which was disputed and very questionable, and had struck out thirty.

In five days, two starts and two relief appearances, he had pitched a total of thirty-six and two-third innings, allowed just eight hits, struck out seventy-three and allowed only the one unearned run that spelled defeat for the Longhorns.

Randy Joe had himself wanted the seven hundred-plus dollars each Longhorns player would have received for winning the tournament championship, but he wanted the money even more for his teammates. He somehow knew he would never again pitch a game for this team. He also knew that most of the men he had grown to love and respect over the summer would, season after season, be riding a rickety old bus in the hopes of making a hundred dollars a month playing baseball, that the chance any of them would ever make the majors was slim. He wanted them to have the money and a winning memory of their summer together.

His Longhorns teammates loved the game, Randy Joe knew, as much as he did. They were willing to give their all to the game and didn't expect anything in return. It was enough just to play, to smell the freshly-mowed grass of a playing field and feel leather rubbed smooth with oil and spit. It was enough to rub one's fingers on the seams and skin of a new baseball, to hear the crack of the bat or to feel the tingle in one's hands as wood crashed against horsehide. It was enough to be pounded unmercifully by the summer sun, to have your sweaty uniform caked with dust, to strain for the extra base, all the time knowing that the race was lost.

It was enough.

Gretchen couldn't understand why Randy Joe didn't ride back to Jason from Wichita with her, why he chose to ride in the old bus instead of in her father's car. The Keegans and her parents tried to explain it to her, but she wasn't able to comprehend. She wasn't sure the four adults could either.

The long bus ride home meant more than just an opportunity to say farewell to his teammates. It was a period of healing for all of them, a time of reflection on what might have been. Randy Joe vowed to himself he would never lose contact with these men who had meant so much to him. It was, of course, a vow that he would break.

Gar Foster, whom he'd taught to read, would try to keep in touch with him over the years, but eventually their correspondence would end. Gar would play semi-pro baseball for another ten years, pursuing the elusive dream, traveling the back roads of the South and playing on fields better suited to cows. That summer of 1954, however, affected his life more than that of any of the other Longhorns players. He is now a minister, pastor of a Baptist church near Leesville, Louisiana.

After five more years of baseball, lefthanded pitcher Skeeter Hodnett returned to his native Zwolle, Louisiana and went to work for a lumber company as a common laborer. He has four children and thirteen grandchildren.

Pooh Wiley signed a contract with the Pittsburgh Pirates in nineteen fifty-five. He bounced around in the minors for a few years and had a brief stint with the Cleveland Indians. He's now a pitching coach in the Baltimore Orioles minor league system.

Catcher Buck Frazier played on various semi-pro teams until he was forty and his legs gave out. He returned to his native Missouri and worked as a dishwasher for a restaurant. He disappeared in nineteen seventy-nine and has not been seen or heard from since.

Tater Green returned to Zwolle, Louisiana at the same time as his cousin Skeeter. He, too, worked for a lumber company there. He has six children and nineteen grandchildren.

Second baseman Cut Brown continued playing for semi-pro Negro teams into his thirties, returning each year to his native Mississippi. He was murdered in the late sixties.

Shortstop Muddy Tate managed the Jason Longhorns until the team was disbanded in the sixties. He was killed in the early seventies when he lost control of the pulpwood truck he was driving. Grease Clifton, who was with him, was also killed.

Third baseman Cooter Davis played baseball a few more years and then returned to his hometown of Texarkana, Arkansas. He did construction work for many years, but is now unable to work because of inoperable lung cancer.

Jackie Monk played baseball until1957, then returned to Little Rock, married and went to work for a hospital. He continues to work for the hospital, has three children and seven grandchildren.

Peewee Darthard spent four more seasons after 1954 trying to land a pro contract, then returned to Tupelo, Mississippi and worked as a farm hand. He now owns a shotgun house on a small piece of land and continues to farm for a big landowner.

In the winter of1955 left fielder Rooster Solomon was killed in a bar fight in San Antonio.

Simmy Weatherspoon continued to field a Negro team into the sixties and was a leader in school desegregation during the same period. Integration of the Jason schools occurred in the late sixties and Simmy was elected to the school board. He died in 1975.

With some financial help from Simmy, Zeke Lott opened his own bakery in the late sixties. He died in 1977.

Squirrel Simpson remains buried in Wichita, but the ground above him is no longer a baseball field. It is now a shopping center.

Randy Joe Keegan played football for Jason High School in 1954 and took the team to within one point of the state championship. The Bulldogs won another bi-district baseball crown in 1955.

At his mother's urging he put his pro baseball career on hold after high school graduation and accepted a scholarship to the University of Oklahoma. Vic Marshall became an assistant coach for the Sooners.

In the 1957 football season Oklahoma won the Big Seven championship and had a nine and one record, the only blot a 7-0 loss to Notre Dame. The Sooners started 1958 with a 48-21 Orange Bowl victory over Duke.

In 1958 the team won another Big Seven title and again had a nine and one record. The loss was to Texas, 15-14. The Sooners started '59 with a 21-6 victory over Syracuse in the Orange Bowl.

Randy Joe signed a pro contract with the Yankees in 1959 and was assigned to one of New York's Class A farm clubs. That same year Big Bill Perkins was mysteriously killed in a fire. Investigators suspected arson and murder, but no one was ever arrested and charged with the crime.

This was the year that Gretchen Turner got married. She married an Air Force sergeant whom she met when visiting Weave and Jolene. Weave and Jolene got married a year after he graduated high school. After getting his diploma he had gone immediately into the Air Force, which was his home for thirty years. He and Jolene have two children and five grandchildren.

Gretchen, now divorced, lives in San Antonio. She has two children and three grandchildren.

Gary Steele, whose hatred of Randy Joe only intensified over the years, is now a United States Congressman. He married Doris Mason. Their fathers, James Steele and George Mason, still exercise control over much of what goes on in Jason.

Anna Louise Lake attended Southern Methodist University in Dallas where she met the man she eventually married. They live in Bethleham, Pennsylvania. Her father, J.D. Lake, died in 1980, but her mother still resides in Jason.

Patti Sue Trainor got married in 1960. Her husband is an executive in Dallas and she teaches school in suburban Plano.

Following her mother's death in 1965 Sheila Marshall divorced Vic and now lives alone in Beaumont, Texas, where she teaches school. She and Vic never had children. Sheila and Randy Joe had a rather erratic relationship while he was at the University of Oklahoma, but even that ended when he went off to play pro ball.

Vic Marshall remarried in 67 and is now an athletic director at an NCAA Division II college in Louisiana.

Randy Joe's professional career was shortlived and he never made much money at it. He had begun to have arm problems in '58 while in college. After two seasons in the Yankees farm system the pain in his shoulder and elbow was so intense he called it quits.

In 1961 he joined the Marine Corps. He was a major when he went to Vietnam in 1966. In the spring of '67 he was at Khe Sanh when a battalion of the Third Marines was called on to fight off a regimental-size attack by the North Vietnamese. There Randy Joe Keegan made the ultimate sacrifice for his country. There the dreams of all that might have been finally ended.

A final letter to his parents spoke of those shattered dreams.

Dear Mother and Dad:

It seems I've never really been able to accomplish all I set out to do. More than anything I wanted to be a major league baseball player, to pitch for the Yankees in the World Series. And, of course, I didn't just want to pitch, I wanted to win.

It's spring now and the memories of playing baseball intensify at this time of year. I must have a pretty good imagination because where I am now it takes a lot to be thinking about baseball. But I dream about it a lot. I dream about playing with the black kids on that old field over in the Quarters, about having to drag Weave over there.

God, how I miss it.

I don't know how many times over the years I've dreamed about that game I pitched for the Longhorns in Wichita, always wanting the pitch back that I threw to the guy who hit the single in the seventeenth. Maybe we just weren't meant to win. Where I am now, I keep wondering if I'm not in the same situation.

I'm not trying to depress you with this letter. I dream about the good times, too. It just seems that the failures overshadow the good times. I just keep wondering why certain things happen the way they do. I can't forget the one point loss in the high school football championship game, or the losses to Notre Dame and Texas that kept Oklahoma from having perfect seasons and maybe national championships.

And yes, I agree with you that not marrying Gretchen might have been my biggest loss. But hopefully she's happy, which is what counts.

Most of all, though, I can't forget the things I wanted to do for you. I know you don't expect anything from me, but that doesn't keep me from wanting to give you a home and a new car. I guess I was counting too much on pro baseball to enable me to provide you those things. It's a little harder to do on a Marine's salary.

I know it's not something you want to talk about, but I have put a little away and there's my GI insurance. If something happens to me there's probably enough to buy you a home there in Jason. It may not be what I'd have bought you if I'd won a couple of World Series games for the Yankees, but it'll be something to remember me by.

You gave me so much, a good mind and every opportunity you possibly could. I wish I could give you as much.

Love,
Randy Joe

The letter came to R.M. and Bernice Keegan a week after the telegram that informed them their son had been killed in action. With the money Randy Joe left them, plus his GI insurance, the Keegans bought a small home on the outskirts of Jason.

It fulfilled a promise Randy Joe had made to his mother in 1954.

F   Risenhoover, C. C.
RISENHOOVER
          White heat

91-77072

                              1659

$20.00

DATE		